# Praise for *Secrets of a Shoe Addict*

"What happens to three parent chaperones during a student trip makes it hard for their transgressions to stay in Sin City. How they recover, while learning what a good pair of heels can do for your psyche, is entertaining and fun."  —*The Charlotte Observer*

"Harbison's witty, fast-paced follow-up to last year's *Shoe Addicts Anonymous* chronicles the foibles of four women brought together by—in this case—not shoes but debt. . . . Zingy and funny."
—*Publishers Weekly*

"This is an engaging story filled with humor, angst, and down-to-earth problems that any of us could face. . . . How they solve these problems, how they developed from them, and the conclusion make for great reading."  —*Affaire de Coeur*

# Praise for *Shoe Addicts Anonymous*

"Kick off your Keds (unless you're driving) and meet a motley group of D.C. women who bond over designer shoes. It's chick lit with heart and sole."  —*People* magazine

"I would happily recommend *Shoe Addicts Anonymous* to anyone who loves shoes . . . or to smart, funny, realistic women."
—Jennifer Weiner, author of *In Her Shoes* and *The Guy Not Taken*

# Secrets of a Shoe Addict

Also by Beth Harbison

*Shoe Addicts Anonymous*

# Secrets of a
# Shoe
# Addict

## Beth Harbison

ST. MARTIN'S GRIFFIN
New York

SECRETS OF A SHOE ADDICT. Copyright © 2008 by Beth Harbison. All rights reserved. Printed in the United States of America. For information, address St. Martin's Press, 175 Fifth Avenue, New York, N.Y. 10010.

www.stmartins.com

The Library of Congress has catalogued the hardcover edition as follows:

Harbison, Elizabeth M.
    Secrets of a shoe addict / Beth Harbison.—1st ed.
        p.   cm.
    ISBN-13: 978-0-312-34826-7
    ISBN-10: 0-312-34826-6
        1. Female friendship—Fiction.   2.   Shoes—Fiction.
3. Chick lit.   I. Title.
    PS3558.A564S43 2008
    813'.54—dc22

                                            2008010612

    ISBN-13: 978-0-312-34827-4 (pbk.)
    ISBN-10: 0-312-34827-4 (pbk.)

    First St. Martin's Griffin Edition: June 2009

        10  9  8  7  6  5  4  3  2  1

*To the man who is honestly the love of my life,*
*and the best friend and husband a girl could have,*
*John Harbison.*

*And to my children, Paige and Jack Harbison,*
*who make me so proud.*

✳

# Acknowledgments

I'm lucky to have so many friends who fill my life with fun and made the writing of this book so much more fun: Steffi and Harry Alexander, Connie Atkins, Janie Aylor, Jim Aylor, Sherry Bindeman, Dana Carmel, Andy and Sue Conversano, Mimi Elias, Connie and Rusty Gernhofer, Scott Hicks, Elaine McShulskis, Amy Sears, Jacquelyn Taylor, and Steve Troha.

Particular acknowledgment is due Donnie Sears, whose stories never fail to amuse . . . since they didn't actually happen to me.

And to Greg Cunliffe, who is always here even though he's gone. Greg, I wish you could tell the Mrs. Gelsinon Story just one more time.

Huge thanks to Jennifer Rae Heffernan, from the Bowling Green Book Club in Ohio, for reading the manuscript so I could correct mistakes before the rest of the world saw them.

Finally, thanks to the brains of this operation: Jen Enderlin, Annelise Robey, and Meg Ruley.

✳

# Secrets of a
# Shoe
# Addict

✳

# Chapter 1

Loreen Murphy hadn't meant to hire a male prostitute in Las Vegas. It was all just a big, stupid, *expensive* misunderstanding.

The night had started out pretty normal. There was no visibly strange alignment of stars, no static electricity in the air, nothing to warn anyone that things were about to turn so weird.

She, along with other parents—mostly mothers—of the Tuckerman Elementary School band members from Travilah, Maryland, was in Las Vegas, where the kids were competing in a National Battle of the School Bands. Loreen, as the PTA treasurer, had been instrumental in working out a deal with the airline and several Las Vegas hotels so that parents and siblings could attend the contest.

And everything had gone fine, right up until they tucked in the little third place–winning musicians and handed their trust over to a hotel babysitter who looked a little like Joan Crawford but was able to produce identification to prove she was employed by the hotel.

So, confident that their kids would be fine, Loreen and her fellow PTA officers—Abbey Walsh (vice president of the PTA and wife of the local Methodist minister) and Tiffany Dreyer (president of the PTA)—went down to the casino and spent a little time playing the nickel slots and sipping free margaritas from the hotel bar.

For Loreen, life began to veer off course with the idea of taking a break after an hour of slot machines and free drinks to get up and move around so she didn't get slot machine elbow or whatever you'd call a repetitive-motion injury from playing the one-armed bandit for too long.

Besides, she'd allocated twenty-five dollars to gambling, and according to the slip the high-tech machine had just spit out at her, she had only ten dollars left. When that money was gone, she'd decided, the evening was over for her.

"Are you sure you don't want to come look around with me?" she asked Tiffany, Loreen's friend since both their kids had eaten a container of paste in Mrs. Kelpy's first-grade classroom and thrown it up in the cafeteria line half an hour later.

"No way." Tiffany kept her baby blues fastened on the machine in front of her. "I've invested almost two hours in this machine. It's going to hit the jackpot. I can just *feel* it."

"This is how gambling addiction starts, you know."

Tiffany nodded and lifted her drink to the one Loreen was taking with her to the bar. "I think alcoholism starts this way, too."

"Touché."

Loreen made her way through the crowd—hundreds of people

she'd never know. The feeling of freedom was exhilarating. Jacob was safely with the sitter upstairs, and Loreen, who was a month away from her final divorce decree, was a "bachelorette on the loose" for the first time in eleven years.

Robert, her soon-to-be ex, thought she was a control freak who focused too much on her child and not enough on her life. Well, she was going to change that tonight.

The lobby of the Gilded Palace was crowded with people, marble columns, and large potted palm trees. There was Muzak playing through some distant speakers, adding just enough vague ambience to make it feel like this was someone else's life and she was free to do whatever she pleased with it.

*That's* when the trouble started.

When Rod—that turned out to be his name, or at least the name he gave—first sat down and started talking to her, her first thought was that it must be on a dare from one of his drunk friends, who were undoubtedly hiding behind one of the gold Corinthian columns or enormous potted palms somewhere.

But if he had drunk friends with him, they were hiding for a really long time. And besides, Loreen wasn't unattractive enough to make a dare like that funny to a bunch of assholes. She was just . . . she looked like a mom.

Not a MILF, just a mom.

Her dark hair had lost some of the luster of youth and was cut in a sort of hopelessly plain brown variation of Prince Valiant. No matter where she went to get it styled, and no matter what pictures she took with her, she always seemed to leave with the same schlumpy mom look.

And the stylists' advice that "You have a different face. I can't make you look like TV actress *X*, movie star *Y*, fill-in-the-blank, but this is the same basic haircut. . . ."

In other words, *You're never gonna be that hot, honey. Give it up.*

It was true, too. Loreen was also suffering a little from post-childbirth spread. Nine years post-childbirth. Her butt was considerably wider than it had been the last time she'd been single. Her high-waisted jeans kept everything sucked in pretty well—someone trying to identify her across the room wouldn't call her "that fat woman over there"—but she wasn't exactly what you'd call buff either. And there *was* a telltale balloon of flesh below the waistband that she just couldn't seem to get rid of. At least not without a steady diet of carrots, celery, and Pilates.

But Rod looked at her as if she had just stepped off the cover of the *Sports Illustrated* swimsuit edition.

Upon reflection, that in itself probably should have made her more suspicious.

"Margarita, huh?" He nodded at her glass and smiled. The way his mouth curved, showing white-white teeth, made him look like a real-life movie star. "Pretty lady like you deserves something more special than that."

It was such a lame line and she knew it, but she got a kick out of it anyway. "Well—" She swallowed a burp and hoped he didn't notice. "—they put a Grand Marnier floater on top."

"Ah. So it's got a touch of class, like you." He smiled again. "I'm Rod, by the way."

"Loreen Murphy." Not only was it nuts to give her last name to a total stranger, but she held out her hand like a total dork. "Nice to meet you."

He lifted her hand to his lips and kissed the back of it, keeping eye contact all along, just like Leonardo DiCaprio did with Kate Winslet in *Titanic*. "Where are you from, Loreen?"

"Is it that obvious I'm not from here?"

He laughed. "You look way too happy to be from here."

"I'm from Maryland."

"And what do you do in Maryland?"

"I'm a Realtor." And a PTA treasurer, and a mom, and a soon-to-be ex-wife, and a whole lot of other easy-to-pigeonhole labels.

He looked impressed. "Keep your own hours and cream the top off every deal made. Good gig."

She shrugged. "It's feast or famine."

"What about tonight? Is it feast or famine tonight?"

"Feast." She smiled. It really was. This letting-go stuff was pretty good. Maybe Robert had been right. A little bit, anyway. "Tonight, it's all feast."

Rod chuckled charmingly and gave an approving nod. "Are you looking for company tonight, Loreen?"

For a crazy moment she was ten years younger, one impending divorce lighter, and free to be a flirt. It felt *awesome*. She took another sip of her drink. "Well, I don't know. Are you offering?"

"As a matter of fact, Loreen, yes. I am."

She could not *believe* this gorgeous hunk of man was coming on to her! This *never* happened at home!

*Take that, Robert.*

Just last week Jacob had told Loreen that Robert had a girlfriend who came over for dinner.

So, with that little piece of icky news in mind, what the hell? Rod was a gift from God as far as she was concerned. As for why he would be interested in her—well, why not? No, she wasn't a supermodel, but she wasn't a dog either. In her day, plenty of guys had come on to her. It hadn't happened for a while now, but maybe this was the first time she'd been relaxed enough—and anonymous enough—to put out an *available* vibe.

"Sounds good to me," she said with a laugh. Females all around them were looking on with clear envy, and Loreen liked it. "So you can tell all these other women you are *taken*."

A nod. "Consider it done."

She'd worried he wouldn't get the joke and would think she was seriously jealous already, so she was glad for his response. "Well, I'm honored."

Robert had moved on. So would she.

Even if it was for only a few minutes.

"The honor is mine." Rod lifted a perfect brow over one pale blue eye. Actually, his brows were so perfect that she concluded he had to wax them, which was a little troubling. But then again, one look at his whip of a smile and it didn't matter anymore. "Do you like champagne, Loreen?"

"Depends what you mean by champagne. I've never had the good stuff." It was true. Her experience was limited to the sort that tasted like melted Popsicles and could be used to sweeten coffee. But tonight she'd had enough tequila to lubricate her confidence and fuel her awkward flirting. "Does it come with the deal, Mr. Rod?"

"Of course, if you like. The menu is always à la carte." He signaled the bartender with one breezy motion and said to him, "Piper." Then he turned back to Loreen. "So you're a fine champagne virgin. And I get to break you in."

She smiled. In fact, she damn near trilled. "Be gentle with me."

"Whatever you like." He smiled, and the bartender set two tall phallic flutes on the bar and poured bubbling gold liquid in.

"Thank you, Piper," Loreen said to him.

Rod chuckled again. "You"—he clinked his glass to hers—"are adorable."

"So are you!" she gushed, a little too enthusiastically. Then, in a misplaced effort to regain the cool dignity she was going for, she said, "For someone so young, I mean." Oh, that was dumb. Really clumsy. And it didn't seem like she was going to be able to stop herself anytime soon. "How old are you anyway?"

He looked at her very seriously. "About the same age as you, I'd guess. I'm twenty-four."

"Smooth, Rod. That was really smooth."

He looked at her guilelessly. "What do you mean?"

"I'm *not* twenty-four," she said, downing the rest of her champagne. "And you know it."

"Twenty-three?" he guessed, then furrowed his brow in mock consternation. "Younger? Tell me I didn't just buy a drink for an underage Lolita."

"You're good. You're really good." Loreen smiled and took a sip of the champagne. It was sort of blah as wine went. Like unsweetened ginger ale. But, hey, if this was the drink for celebrations, she'd go for it, because *this* was a celebration. "This is great."

He gave a nod and looked deeply into her eyes. "So what are we going to do next? Or should I ask *when?*"

It would have been the perfect opportunity to say something sophisticated and witty, but apparently Myrna Loy wasn't available for channeling right then. "I—I'm . . . not sure."

"Obviously we could use some privacy."

*Mmmm.* His voice could melt butter.

As a matter of fact, his voice—or maybe his long-lashed baby blues or perhaps that shiny mop of dark hair that her fingers were just *itching* to run through—*was* melting something deep in Loreen's long-chilly nether regions.

And he wanted to be *alone* with her!

This was a night she'd *never* forget.

"Privacy would be nice," she said, then giggled as the champagne bubbles actually tickled her nose, just like all the bimbos in old movies said it did.

"I have a room upstairs unless . . . you'd prefer your room?"

She pictured meeting the babysitter and all the kids at the door and laughed. "Let's go to your room."

"Of course." He held a hand out and helped her off her stool. "Send the bottle up, please," he said to the bartender.

"You and Piper seem to know each other."

He looked puzzled for a second, then smiled. "There you go again. Yeah, Roger and I have worked here for a long time."

"Ah." She hadn't realized Rod worked there, but she'd already said so many dumb things that she didn't want to add to it by asking what he did, just in case it was somehow obvious. "How long have you worked here?"

"The hotel or the town?"

"Um . . . I . . ." She didn't really care either way. "The hotel."

"Oh, about a year and a half now."

Only a twenty-four-year-old could think that was a long time. "You like it?"

"It allows me to meet beautiful women like *you*. How could I not love it?"

She could have gotten stuck on that plural—beautiful *women*—but since this wasn't a real relationship in any sense of the word, she let it slide and just took the compliment. "You're quite the flatterer."

"No, I mean it." He stopped her and looked her in the eye. "Sincerely."

She felt the heat climb into her cheeks. "Thanks."

He pushed the elevator button, and they glided upward to a suite on the top floor. One entire wall consisted of windows that overlooked the aurora borealis–like glow of the Las Vegas strip. It was enchanting.

Loreen was standing in front of the window, looking for the big guitar they always showed in movies, when Rod came up behind her and put his arms around her. "Like it?"

"I love it. I could look at this view every night for the rest of my life." As soon as she said the words, Loreen had the horrible feeling that maybe this handsome stranger was a serial killer who was about to murder her, and, though he would be the only one to know, her final words would echo ironically through time.

There was a knock at the door, and Rod went to get it, murmured some things, and came back into the room with an ice bucket, a bottle, and two champagne flutes.

As he poured the champagne, Loreen noticed the label: PIPER-HEIDSIECK. Oh, shit. Rod hadn't been calling the *bartender* Piper; he'd been asking for the champagne.

But then, like an idiot, she'd proceeded to call the guy "Piper" and, worse, feel really clever doing so.

Fortunately, Rod seemed to think she was joking, and even said she was adorable. So . . . she'd go with that.

"That was nice of Piper to send up some more Piper," she said, knowing it was pathetic, but at the same time at a complete loss about what else to say.

Rod moved over to Loreen and smoothly took the glass from her hand and set it on the end table by the sofa. "I can't wait any longer to do this," he said, then lowered his mouth down onto hers.

He didn't give her time to work up some nervousness. He just went for it.

Never—*never*—had she been kissed like this. Everything in her tingled, from her head right down her spine and into the center of her being. Rod undressed her slowly, so slowly that even the fabric running across her skin felt like a caress.

He was an expert at touching a woman, pushing buttons she didn't even know she had, bringing her to the crest of ecstasy over and over again, then backing away just long enough to make her nearly scream with need.

By the time he finally got down to business, she wanted it more than she'd ever wanted anything in her life.

She couldn't say how long it lasted. Maybe an hour, maybe five, but the time Loreen spent with Rod was so intense that his abrupt withdrawal at the end of it came as a shock.

"Oh, shit."

It wasn't exactly the romantic conclusion she was expecting. "What's wrong?"

"The fucking rubber broke."

"What?"

"I said the *fucking—rubber—broke.*" Suddenly Rod sounded like a seven-year-old who'd struck out at bat.

So much for ol' Rico Suave.

But Loreen's first reaction was one of relief. The *"Oh, shit"* wasn't because he'd just realized what he'd done, with whom, and regretted it. "The rubber broke?" she echoed, trying to get a grasp on what he was *actually* saying.

"Yeah." He threw up his hands. "Fuck."

She swallowed the urge to say, *I believe we just did,* and instead asked, "Are you sure?"

He nodded. "I've done this enough to know when there's a problem, and *this* is a problem."

A moment of heavy silence dropped between them.

"Have you been tested?" Loreen asked, her former relief replaced rapidly by panic as she realized the implications. She'd just had sex with a stranger and the condom had broken, spilling all kinds of potential diseases and bacteria right into her most vulnerable parts. Short of slashing open her wrist and rubbing it on a petri dish, she couldn't do something more bacterially dangerous.

"I'm tested every month," Rod said. "What about you?"

"I haven't had sex in about a year."

He nodded like that was unsurprising. "Yeah. But have you been tested?"

That *yeah* was insulting. "My doctor did that test," she said, "along with every other medical test, last year when I couldn't shake the flu. It was negative."

His shoulders lowered slightly with relief.

She waited a moment, then, when he didn't volunteer the information, prompted him with "And *your* tests?"

He waved the question away like it was silly. "Negative on all counts. We have a really good doctor here who checks us out really thoroughly."

"Heck of a medical plan you have."

"It's the law." He shrugged. "What about pregnancy? Are you on anything?"

For the past year? On the remote chance that she'd have sex with someone without taking the time to plan? Not likely. Good thing she couldn't have more kids. "After my son was born, I had my tubes tied," she lied. It was easier than explaining that she just wasn't able to get pregnant, that a couple of years of trying with Robert had proved that beyond a doubt, and that it made her hang on to her only son's childhood like it was a life raft in the ocean.

"Good thing." Rod gave a dry laugh. "I'm sure the last thing you need is a pregnancy."

"Right," she agreed, because she was polite. But . . . what did he mean by that? The last thing *she* needed? Even though it was true, what was it about his words that sounded distinctly detached? No, they didn't know each other, and no, she *definitely* wasn't going to get pregnant from this, but still. . . . What a dick.

Nah, she was probably reading way too much into this. She'd had a weird night—a one-night stand! The first time in her life! That was so unlike her. And she was still out even though it was— she looked for the green glow of the digital clock by the bedside— 11:36 P.M.

Good Lord, she had to leave. Everyone was probably wondering where she'd disappeared to.

"I've got to run," she said, meaning it literally. She threw back the sheets and started running around the darkened room, collecting her clothes.

"Are you sure? I'm still available for a few hours. And I had a great time with you," Rod said, and back was the mellow, sexy tone that had drawn her to him in the first place. Then he grabbed her wrist, pulled her to him, and kissed her deeply. If it weren't for the time, she would have fallen right back into bed with him.

"I did, too," she said, wishing she could come up with something more clever—more *memorable*—than mere agreement.

"Maybe next time, then." He ran his hands down her back, sending tingles along the trail of his touch.

"I don't come here often," she said to him as she pulled back. She had to get dressed and leave, no matter how great his hands felt on her.

"Well, if you do," Rod said, pulling up his jeans and turning to her with the button tantalizingly undone, "you know where you can find me."

She nodded and gave a laugh. "At the bar downstairs?" She was joking.

He nodded. He was not joking. "Unless I'm already working."

"Oh." Okay, so he hung out at the bar all the time? And he could say, absolutely, that he'd be there at some nebulous time in the future?

Something here wasn't adding up.

"You can just leave the money on the dresser, sweetheart." He was buttoning his shirt, and didn't have so much as a *hint* of a smile when he said it.

But Loreen laughed. Because . . . it had to be a joke.

"Shouldn't that be my line?" She was trying to keep the mood light, but still . . . ew. She didn't like this joke. It wasn't really funny, no matter who said it.

Rod looked at her, confused. "I'm sorry?"

"Oh, nothing, I was just kidding." *Too.*

Right?

He gave a vague smile and gestured with a hand that suddenly seemed a little limp. Something less masculine than it had seemed just a couple of hours before. "Yeah. So, the dresser right over there." He gestured and went into the bathroom. "And tag on a hundred and forty for the champagne."

Oh, God. He wasn't kidding. He was . . . She'd just . . . Oh, God, she'd just hired a male prostitute. How the hell had this happened? She thought back over their conversation, trying to figure out just where the breakdown in communications had occurred.

*Are you looking for company tonight, Loreen?*

What had she said? Oh. *Are you offering?* An innocent question. Flirty. Not really a proposition.

*Yes, as a matter of fact, I am.*

What an *idiot*! How had she not seen this before?

"Loreen?"

She snapped back to attention. "Yes?"

"Is something wrong?"

"No!" She said it too quick. "I was just . . . I just realized we didn't discuss . . ."

He narrowed his eyes at her. Suddenly he didn't look so sexy. "We didn't discuss what, Loreen?"

"Price." It sounded like a question. From a tiny little person. She could barely eke the word out.

His brow relaxed fractionally. "Right. When you didn't ask, I thought you were a regular, and that for some reason I just didn't remember you."

Great. Not only had the whole flattery thing been a game, but he actually thought she seemed like someone who *regularly paid for sex*. From *him*.

The guy actually thought he'd fucked her before—perhaps more than once—and forgotten. And he thought that didn't really matter. Like . . . her feelings wouldn't be hurt?

She felt sick. "No," she said coolly. So much for looking at her like she was a swimsuit model. But it was stupid to be upset with a prostitute for not telling little white lies to be polite. This was all so confusing.

She had to get out of here.

"It's one g." He put Rembrandt Extra Whitening on his toothbrush and started to brush vigorously, presumably to remove all DNA traces of Loreen so he'd be fresh and clean for the next pathetic loser who came along.

"I'm sorry, I don't . . . How much is that?"

He spit a foamy toothpaste mess into the sink, then swished water in his mouth and spit again. Less attractive by the second. "A thousand dollars," he said, taking the hand towel from the chrome rack and blotting his face. "Plus the champagne, like I said."

Her heart leapt into her throat. A *thousand* dollars.

These three hours were going to be *$333 an hour*. She hadn't had a therapeutic massage since Mother's Day six years ago because she couldn't pay the sixty bucks an hour. There was no way she was going to have to pay $333 an hour, times three, for having *sex* with this guy. Good Lord, she'd even gone down on *him*.

He *had* to be kidding.

But this wasn't a guy who was into kidding around.

He was a businessman.

And somehow she had to come up with a thousand bucks *quick*.

# Chapter 2

Abbey Walsh—wife of the sweetest Methodist pastor in Maryland—never dreamed she'd run into anyone she knew in Las Vegas, much less an old boyfriend, with blackmail on his mind, who she'd *thought* was behind bars.

With the band competition over and the children hopefully asleep, the night began peacefully, for her, with a glass of champagne. Bubbly, toasty, with notes of oak and yeast . . . It had been a long time since Abbey had enjoyed a glass of good champagne.

She used to drink it like water. In fact, she used to drink it *instead of* water sometimes. She was young then, and so foolish, though at least she'd had good taste. Jacques Selosse, Charles Heidsieck, Bollinger . . . back then they were her frequent companions. Every once in a rare while, she missed it.

Tonight was one of those nights. After she'd gotten off the elevators with Tiffany and Loreen to go to the bar, the heel of her shoe had wobbled and broken off. With promises to catch up with the others later, she went back up, got a new pair of shoes, resisted the kids' pleas to go back and make the babysitter leave, and went back down to some blissful solitude.

It wasn't a big deal. Abbey was perfectly fine with the idea of having a little alone time. Besides, she knew the others always felt a little stifled around her. It was partly because of the fact that her husband, Brian, was a clergyman, but she suspected it was also partly because she herself was so straight and narrow. Had been for years now.

But tonight some wind had shifted, just for a moment, and she went to the bar and ordered a single glass of their best champagne.

It was every bit as good as she remembered.

She let the bubbles sit on her tongue for a moment, then swallowed, imagining she could feel them go straight to her head and tickle away her troubles. For a moment, anyway.

"Abbey!"

Oh, no. It was Deb Leventer, dragging and practically dangling her daughter, Poppy, into the bar behind her.

"Deb." Abbey set her glass down and looked from Deb to Poppy, who was clutching her hand and looking around with wide—though distinctly *fascinated*—eyes. "What are you doing in here?" What *was* she doing here? Most of the other band parents were staying at more expensive "name" hotels on the strip, several miles from this out-of-the-way hotel and casino.

"Poppy and I were just on our way up to our room to get some shut-eye before we leave tomorrow." Deb arched an eyebrow and looked pointedly at the bar behind Abbey. "Are you *drinking*?"

"Yes." How had she managed to miss the fact that Deb Leventer was staying in the same hotel? "I was just having a glass of wine."

"Oh." Disapproval rose off Deb like a stench. "I see. Well, I won't tell your husband." Abbey supposed that Deb was trying to sound like she was joking, but there was a hard edge to her voice.

"No need to worry about that—he's the one who suggested I come down here and treat myself to a little champagne." It was really hard not to give Deb the snark slapdown she deserved. Instead, Abbey tried to take the high road. "I'd ask you to join me, but I'm sure you're eager to get Poppy up to bed. And out of the casino atmosphere." She couldn't help but add, "Especially since it's so late for a child that age to still be up."

Deb looked simultaneously embarrassed and judgmental. It was quite a feat. "You're right. This isn't the proper environment for children. . . . Where is Parker?"

"In our suite. With a sitter." Abbey cringed inwardly saying the words, knowing that Deb Leventer would perceive this as the height of bad mothering and wouldn't hesitate to tell anyone what she thought.

Abbey didn't particularly care what the woman thought, but she didn't want word getting back to Parker and embarrassing him.

"A sitter! In a Las Vegas hotel! You're braver than I am." Translation: *You're a fool and your child has probably already been sold on the black market by the desperate junkie you hired so you could come down here and get soused.*

Abbey smiled mildly. "She's a delightful older woman. I'm sure the kids are already tucked away asleep." She shook off a mental image of the kids whooping and hollering and swinging on the drapes while the sitter used a skeleton key to open the minibar and take all the little fifteen-dollar bottles of Skyy Vodka.

"Oh." Deb's expression tightened. "Well. Come on, Poppy. We have to get up early tomorrow to fly home. Good night, Abbey." She looked again at the glass in Abbey's hand. "It was . . . nice chatting with you."

Abbey resisted the urge to raise her glass to Deb—that would have been deliciously obnoxious—and instead set it down. "If I don't see you two before you leave, have a nice flight." Broomsticks came to mind.

Deb walked away, tugging Poppy along after her. Abbey watched them go. But her surroundings had lost their luster. Deb's presence, or more specifically, Deb's negativity, had made Abbey's feeling of freedom start to feel like a wet towel.

So she decided to go somewhere else. There was no way she was going to let Deb Leventer spoil her night. She set her glass down and walked purposefully through the lobby and out the front doors into the balmy night air.

All around, the sky was bright with the reflected glow of neon. Abbey couldn't tell if it was overcast or not, but she couldn't see even one star in the sky, because the town itself was so bright.

The sidewalk was more crowded than she would have expected at this hour, but she was glad of it. It was so easy to become anonymous in the sea of milling people. There were a lot of young couples, a fair representation of middle-aged middle-class people, and a surprising number of oddballs.

One craggy-faced older man, with skin the color of seared beef, put a hand on Abbey as she passed, and said, "God blesses the weak *and* the strong."

Abbey was startled by his touch, and could feel the alarm showing in her face as she turned to look at him. "I'm sorry?"

"He watches." The man nodded, to himself, not her, and worked his jaw like a cow chewing its cud. "He protects." He wasn't looking at her anymore, and he started on his way down the sidewalk.

Abbey stood for a moment, watching. There weren't actually a lot of Bible stories that particularly touched her, but there *was* a passage she remembered from childhood about angels in disguise. She couldn't remember exactly what it was—Brian would know—but it said that sometimes the most unlikely people who pop into your life are actually angels in disguise, bearing a message, or comfort, or whatever.

To her knowledge, it had never happened to her, but hope sprang eternal. Maybe the man wasn't just an old crazy person, but an angel telling her something she needed to know.

God blesses the weak and the strong.

He watches.

He protects.

He was, actually, kind of like Santa Claus.

She wanted to believe it. She'd wanted to believe it for as long as she could remember, as long as she'd known the story. But she didn't believe it.

And when she saw the man stop in the distance and speak to another woman, this time one who reached into her purse and handed him money (which he took), she dismissed him as a nut. His words didn't have any significance at all.

She walked on, a little disconcerted. When she turned a corner toward the main strip, thinking it might be a shortcut, the sidewalk was almost bare. This was no place for a woman to walk alone. Just as she was turning to go back, something on the ground caught her eye. A casino chip. She picked it up. It was a ten-dollar chip embossed with the name ALADDIN'S CAVE.

Once again, she found herself with the eerie feeling she was being presented with *A Sign*.

Angels, signs . . . pretty grandiose stuff for a night out in Sin City. The streets were probably littered with casino chips, dropped by stumbling drunks, in addition to the many cards and flyers advertising call girls and strippers. And unlike, say, a penny, which she wouldn't have given a second thought to, casino chips were always stamped with the name. So that wasn't all that strange either.

Still, she'd have to be a cynical fool not to go there.

Just in case some great Fate was waiting for her.

It wasn't hard to find Aladdin's Cave. It was one of the first of many tall, broad, neon-clad buildings on the strip, and not surprisingly, it appeared to be themed after the Disney version of old Arabia.

She went to the roulette table with the ten-dollar chip she'd found and considered her options. Red or black had good odds, but made for a compulsive game, and Abbey didn't want to be here all night playing fifty–fifty. After a few minutes she decided just to bet on her son's birth date, which was January 18.

The croupier called for last bets, then spun the wheel. For a moment all Abbey could think of was Pat Sajak spinning the *Wheel of Fortune* and how boring her life had gotten. But no, her life wasn't boring. It was sinful even to think that, even for a moment.

The ball clicked and bounced and clattered along the spinner until it landed on thirty-one . . . no, it bumped one more time into the next slot.

Eighteen.

She'd won.

She'd *won*.

Boy, it was a long time since she'd felt lucky, and with her single ten-dollar bet earning her $360, she was feeling *really* lucky.

This was more money than Abbey had had in hand for more than ten years. She felt rich. And when a waiter came over and poured her a glass of Bollinger champagne, she probably *looked* rich. And though it wasn't really hers—she'd donate the money to the church, of course— and though she knew it wasn't very pious either, she was enjoying it, just for this one moment.

And what harm did it do? There was no one around who knew her. Yes, Loreen and Tiffany were in town, too, but they weren't right here. Even if they were, they wouldn't judge. The judgmental moms, like Deb Leventer, Nancy Hart, and Suzy Collins, were elsewhere. There was no way they'd venture into the gaming rooms of a casino, Abbey was sure of it.

She smiled slightly at the thought. Twelve years ago she wouldn't have wanted to give the money away. Twelve years ago she wouldn't have wanted to leave Vegas, and she would have stayed in one of the bigger, more ostentatious hotels.

But that was a whole different lifetime. She was on the *right* path now, and if it occasionally led to a low-budget motel or the Big Fresh on Super Sale Tuesday in the name of taking care of her family, she'd gladly do it.

"Bets down," the croupier said.

Abbey returned her attention to the roulette table. The croupier caught her eye, and she shook her head slightly.

Nowadays she knew enough not to push her luck.

She took her glass and got up, knocked aside by a pudgy red-headed woman who had apparently been waiting for a seat. It took about ten minutes to figure out where to cash in her chips, and the route took her past virtually every gaming table. She wasn't tempted, though. With single-minded purpose, she cashed in, put the neat pile of bills in her wallet, and left the casino. She was in the lobby, almost at the entrance, when a voice spoke right behind her.

"Look who it is. Wonders never cease."

She didn't stop. Whoever it was obviously wasn't talking to her. For one thing, it was a man's voice, and the only people she knew who were nearby right now were women and children.

Still, she could have been clued in by the fact that the statement had given her pause.

Two, three steps, then, softly, almost taunting, "Hello-o."

She kept walking.

"Abigail."

Not me.

Someone else.

Heartbeat.

No one calls me Abigail. Not since Dad died. And . . . no, no one calls me Abigail.

The hand on her shoulder stopped her.

"Abigail Generes."

She turned around.

The second or two that followed were surreal. For an instant, while she was turning, she thought she knew whose the voice was, but her memory of the lean, dark-skinned, handsome bad boy from her past didn't quite mesh with the stocky pale-faced man in front of her.

So, mercifully, it was a mistake.

"I'm sorry. . . ." She scrutinized the face. Wait. *Could* it be? Could he have changed that much in just twelve years? Where once there had been the contours of a sharp, square jawline, there was now slightly slack, aging flesh.

"Now, don't tell me you don't remember me," he said, revealing the ghost of a smile that had once left her weak in the knees.

Oh, no . . .

"You must have me confused with someone else." She turned to leave, but he grabbed her arm, making her drop the small clutch bag she had brought with her. Her license, credit cards, and cell phone spilled out and clattered onto the polished floor.

She dropped immediately to pick the stuff up, but so did he, zeroing in on her wallet like a vulture and standing up slowly as he read her license. "Abigail Generes Walsh, fourteen-eleven Lamplighter Lane"—he raised his eyebrows—"and not a bad neighborhood. If you're into minivans." He pulled the cash out and rifled through it before starting to put it in his pocket.

She snatched at it, a cat going for a rat. "I beg your pardon."

"You used to beg for a lot more than that, as I recall."

She was unable to move, unable to do anything but gape at the man before her, with the disconcerting thought that a woman who didn't know him might still think he was attractive.

"I think you have the wrong person," she tried at last.

"Now, honey, it's been a long time, but not so long I don't know that gorgeous bod when I see it." His breath smelled like alcohol. "Believe me, I had a lot of time to think about it while I was in the pen."

Oh, God. It *was* him. Of course, she'd known it from the moment she'd heard his voice. "Damon Zucker."

"That's better." He gave a broad smile, the pirate grin that, when she was twenty years old, had practically made her clothes drop off spontaneously.

Her throat tightened at the memory of his tongue in her mouth, along her body . . . She shuddered.

"I can tell you're thrilled to see me."

"I thought you were in jail."

"Yeah." He gave a mirthless laugh. "Thanks to you."

It felt like cockroaches were running up and down her spine. "It wasn't my fault."

He took a long, thin cigar out of his pocket, bit the end off, and spit it on the floor. "That's, uh, that's not true. When the public defender went to find you, you'd split. Nowhere to be found." He lifted the cigar. "Gimme a light."

"I don't have a light," she said, looking him up and down with disgust.

"Bullshit, you always have a light. Gotta heat the bazooka, am I right?"

She swallowed hard. "I don't do that anymore."

He gave a shout of laughter. "Yeah, and I'm the fuckin' pope." He stopped a woman passing by. "Pardon me, honey, can I borrow a light?" The woman, clearly seeing something in him that was now practically invisible to Abbey, laughed and handed him her cigarette, which he held to his cigar, puffing like a cartoon villain until it was lit. "Thanks, sugar." He gave the cigarette back to her, then turned back to Abbey.

"Charming as ever, I see," Abbey said. "If you hurry, you can catch up to her."

He gave a laugh. "I can catch up to her even if I don't hurry."

She wanted to slap that smug look right off his face. "I see your time in the slammer didn't change you much."

"Not so, Abigail. It taught me not to take no shit from nobody.

Including you. Make that—" He puffed his cigar thoughtfully. "—make that *especially* you. I've been trying to find you, you know. There we were in the same town and it takes a trip to Vegas to find you. We've got business to discuss."

"We don't have *any* business in common."

He took her shoulder and spun her around. "I think we do. And you know damn fucking well what it is."

Something in Abbey cracked. Actually, it might be more accurate to say something *on* Abbey cracked, because the façade she'd been wearing since meeting Brian—polite, mild-mannered, your basic Clark Kent personality—felt like it was crumbling into rubble at her feet. "We've got *no business,* you jackass!"

Damon rose to the occasion immediately. "Look," he snarled. "You *owe* me."

"I don't owe you anything."

Damon's eyes, which used to seem like hot, molten chocolate, were now dull black slits. "You're just lucky I didn't tell the police how involved you were."

Panic coursed through her. What was the statute of limitations on being an accomplice to a felony? "You've got no proof."

He laughed. It was an ugly sound. Cruel. "You wish."

Did he? Could he? Well, of course he could. She wasn't careful in those days, not about anything. There were probably any number of things she could still be arrested for. "You don't scare me."

There was still a smile pasted across his face, like a smudge of pink on a bad painting. "Baby, I spent twelve years in the slammer thinking about you. I know every expression, every movement you have. And the way you're trying to look down on me? The way your hands are moving in and out of fists? The little shake you hope I don't see? You're fucking terrified." He chuckled. "And you should be."

"What do you want, Damon?" But she knew what he was going to say.

And he did. "I want the necklace back."

"I don't have it anymore," Abbey snapped. This was rapidly turning into a nightmare.

Damon snorted a laugh. "Right. You just happened to, what, lose it? *Sell* it?"

"I gave it away."

For just a fraction of a second he looked shocked. Then skeptical. "Like you'd give away a necklace worth eight grand." But there was a question in his voice.

She nodded. "I did." It was true, though she wasn't above lying to scum like Damon in order to get him off her back. "I gave it to the church."

His skepticism exploded into outright disbelief. "You . . . church? Right."

"I did." She didn't want to tell him about Brian. She didn't want him to know anything about her life now. "It seemed like the right thing to do, so I did it."

"Somehow I can't picture it."

Her anger grew disproportionately, and she had a little momentary fantasy about punching him in the face with brass knuckles. "I don't give a damn if you can picture it or not. We're finished here." She turned to walk away.

"Not so fast." He grabbed her arm, hard, probably leaving a red mark behind.

She whirled to face him, shaking his arm off her. "Do *not* touch me," she warned.

He rolled his eyes. "Or what? You'll create a scene and I'll have to contact your husband at one-four-one-one Lamplighter Lane and tell him about your dirty, dirty past?"

Abbey felt the blood drain from her face, and hated the fact that she couldn't control such an obvious giveaway.

He saw it, too. "You used to have a better poker face than that, babe. A little better. Not much."

"You used to be nicer."

He shrugged, a slight movement that somehow suggested sharp anger. "That was before my girl let me down and sent me to jail."

The designation of Abbey as "his girl" sickened her, even if it was true once. She wanted to punch him in his doughy gut. "Like I already said, it's not my fault you went to jail for your crimes."

"Actually, yeah, it is." He nodded and looked off into the distance. He might as well have been chewing a piece of straw and contemplating if it was going to be a rough winter for the crops. "And I think the price for that should be nine thousand. Eight thousand for the necklace you won't give back to me—"

"I don't have it!"

"—and another thousand we'll call interest. Maybe we should make it two. A nice even ten grand."

If she didn't get away from him quickly, his price was going to rise to include her firstborn, and knowing Damon, he'd find a way to exact it, one way or the other. "Tell me where to find you and I'll see what I can come up with." Her voice was hard with anger. "But it should interest you to know, though I doubt it will, that the necklace was valued at five thousand, not eight thousand, and the proceeds went to help HIV-positive children in a foster home in Bethesda."

"Charity begins at home." He shook his head, keeping his gaze leveled on her like a shotgun. "And that ain't my home."

"Five thousand," she said, her voice hard. Somewhere deep in her subconscious she must have known this day was coming. The only way to buy herself enough time to figure out how to deal with it was to pretend to play his game, and to play it hard. "Just tell me where to send a cashier's check."

"Tell you where the police can find me again, maybe on some trumped-up charge you come up with?" He gave a bark of laughter. "I'll contact you. Soon. Just get the money together—*ten grand*—and be ready for me."

# Chapter 3

Tiffany Vanderslice Dreyer had spent enough sleepless nights watching infomercials to know that there were a lot of people out here who spent a *ton* of money on stupid things, particularly expensive clothes, shoes, and beauty products.

She just never thought she'd be one of them.

Her sister, Sandra, was a different story. Sandra spent hundreds of dollars on a single pair of shoes—shoes!—at a time, but on the rare occasion Tiffany would get herself something new, it would be from TJ Maxx or Payless, and even then only when her shoes were totally worn out or she needed a pair for a special occasion.

So the idea that Tiffany might spend her way into trouble was ridiculous.

But, then again, Tiffany had never been much of a drinker either, and tonight, in Vegas, with free drinks and open-all-night shops, bets were off on both counts.

Everything had been just fine until she spotted a clothing shop in the lower level of the hotel, called Finola Pims, named for the British designer. Finola, as Tiffany came to think of her, had classic sensibilities, but with vivid, beautiful fabrics, and a modest-yet-sexy style that spoke to Tiffany.

Everything Tiffany tried on looked amazing on her, even a couple of funky dresses she'd trotted out as a sort of private joke because they were so outrageous, she was sure they'd look silly. But no, they hugged her figure in all the right places while miraculously giving her room to move and bend without showing her privates to everyone within fifty yards. She was tall and blond, with light blue eyes, so she'd gotten her share of attention back when she was dating, but since that time she'd begun to feel like she was in a rut.

Finola Pims lifted her out of that rut.

Within forty-five minutes of walking into the shop, she was sitting in the dressing room with an empty margarita glass and fifteen thousand dollars' worth of once-in-a-lifetime clothes she had to put back.

The pile wasn't so big as one might expect.

But quality cost a lot. And before she put the clothes back, she decided to try on a few shoes. She'd never been a shoe person—that was her sister. In fact, she'd always sort of been an *anti*-shoe person *because* of her sister's weird penchant for them. She couldn't understand how a person could put four-hundred-dollar shoes on their feet and then walk around in them, ruining them with every step. The cost-to-loss analysis on that sucked.

So Tiffany went to Finola's shoe collection, hoping to get herself out of spending mode and back under control.

Now, seriously, Tiffany was *not* planning to love the shoes. In fact, with her long history of shoe disdain, she honestly thought it would shake her out of her shopping spree. If there had been a John Deere dealer in the hotel, it could have served the same purpose, but there wasn't, so she was stuck with the shoe section.

How was she to know she'd love them?

Seriously, how had she gone thirty-six years and never realized that shoes could make your legs look like a movie star's? Especially *these* shoes, which were so blah on the shelf. First there were the pale denim espadrilles with two-inch heels. Easy, right? They were denim—*ew*—with big heels.

It should have been as anti-spending as formaldehyde.

But the pale blue denim enhanced her new Las Vegas poolside tan in a way she could never have imagined, and the height of the heels beautifully emphasized the calf muscles she'd developed carrying two-year-old Andy (currently at his grandparents' house, since Charlie couldn't—or wouldn't—take the time off work) up the stairs almost every night when he fell asleep.

On top of that, the shoes had ankle straps, which she'd expected to look like silly sixth-grade toe-shoe straps, but which instead just added the perfect finishing touch to the shoe, creating a long, tan, shapely leg line that she totally had not expected.

Given all of that, $150—down from $426—truly did seem like a bargain. She'd gone all these years without ever being particularly inspired by shoes, so if these struck her that way, there *had* to be something special about them.

How would she feel if she walked away and didn't buy them?

She could imagine herself going out with Charlie to one of those boring company events three, four, five weeks from now and wishing she had these very shoes, which she could never find again, to set off her outfit and make her a standout.

Not that she could see Charlie agreeing to such a thing. If it were the NFL Channel on cable TV, he might try to find a way to swing it, but it had been established a long time ago that if Tiffany wasn't going to have a "real job" outside of the home, then she wasn't entitled to a whole lot of luxuries.

But, oh, hell, they just looked so damn *great*.

And when was the last time she'd treated herself, or *been* treated, to anything (apart from the numerous margaritas that waiters had been shoving into her hands as long as she was at the slot machines)?

Tiffany *deserved* some new clothes. Yes, she was a leeeetle bit tipsy from all the free drinks the casino had been doling out, so she'd just buy what she was interested in and return the rest tomorrow.

She weeded through the clothes, taking out the more outrageous or event-specific items. (After all, how likely was she to go to the Kentucky Derby in the near future and need this brightly colored sheath dress with the matching large-brim lacquered cotton hat with little rosettes? On second thought, you never know, she decided and put it back in the to-go pile.) In the end she had a total of just five thousand dollars' worth of clothes to choose from.

Okay, yes, five thousand dollars was a lot. But it was for only, what, ten hours on the credit card. There was *no way* it would be longer than that. They were leaving tomorrow afternoon at two, so she would get up early, return the items that she decided weren't absolutely necessary, which would, of course, be most of them, and then she'd explain the charge of six hundred bucks or so to Charlie when she got home.

She'd point out that the last "luxury" she had gotten for herself was the vanilla-flavored Crest toothbrush, and before that it was probably a perm for her 1980s hair, before she even knew him. If he was going to have a problem with that, well, she'd deal with it later.

Meanwhile she was going to have a *blast* trying on all of these things again.

*And* she would save money by going up to the suite and sending the babysitter home. Kate would get a big kick out of helping her decide which things to keep.

All in all, she reasoned in the end, this was going to be a very profitable venture, emotionally if not financially.

And it kept her out of the casino, where the *real* danger was.

✶

An hour later, in the hotel room after dismissing the babysitter, Tiffany had fully realized that the *real* danger was *not* in the casinos but in the Finola Pims shop.

And, now, spread out across her cheap hotel bed.

"I like it all, Mommy!"

Tiffany had hoped Kate would talk her out of some of these clothes, with that trademark child candor that had once made her announce in a Victoria's Secret dressing room that "Mommy's skin" was "spilling over her undies" and "looks gross." It didn't seem like too much to hope she'd make fun of at least a few of these crazily flamboyant pieces and help Tiffany weed them out. But no, Kate seemed to have some of her aunt Sandra's lust for fashion and shoes.

She wasn't going to be any help.

Of course, it was a pretty sad state of affairs when Tiffany was hoping for a nine-year-old to talk her out of extravagant purchases.

Besides, just as it had seemed under the harsh fluorescent glare of the changing-room lights, the clothes looked spectacular on her. It was impossible to decide what was the most flattering, since *all* of it was flattering. So she decided to divide them up according to what was most practical.

"Not the hat, Mommy." Kate snatched it out of the return pile and put it on, preening in the mirror.

"I've got to, honey." Tiffany was sorry to say it. "Put it back. Really."

"Fine." Kate put the hat back in the return pile, looking as petulant about it as Tiffany felt.

"So I don't need the Kentucky Derby outfit," Tiffany said, more to herself than to Kate. "Or the Vegas showgirl outfit." Though she loved that one. Seriously. How did Finola make a leather jumpsuit look so amazing on a real woman? "Or the Audrey Hepburn *Breakfast at Tiffany's* dress. Or tiara."

She looked at her new "keep" pile.

It had gotten pretty small.

"Won't Daddy let you keep the rest?" Kate asked.

"It's not about Daddy, honey. He doesn't tell me I can't get things." Lord, she didn't even want to *think* about what Charlie was going to say. It was important to Tiffany that her daughter didn't grow up feeling like men were in charge of women's lives, even though the reality of their household was that Tiffany sort of *did* defer. It was all out of guilt for staying home and taking care of the children instead of working and contributing to "the household finances," and she knew that was wrong, but she felt it anyway.

"Okay, help me fold these things and put them back into the bag," Tiffany said, moving to the return pile, which was substantial at this point.

Kate came over and helped lift the piles with her thin arms, pushing the clothes into the bags alongside Tiffany.

She was left with just under a thousand dollars' worth of merchandise. And she rationalized it by telling herself that there was no way she'd ever find this same stuff in the D.C. metro area, and if she had to fly back to Las Vegas to look for it, it would end up costing a lot more than it would if she just purchased it now.

And she deserved it.

She was *worth* it. Just like all those L'Oréal models had been telling her from the TV set over and over again for as long as she could remember.

So. With that in mind, Tiffany got the bags full of returns to take back first thing in the morning.

Half an hour after Tiffany had put the children to bed, Abbey came in, looking drained.

"Rough night?" Tiffany asked, smiling.

Abbey looked startled. "Why do you ask?"

"I was just kidding," Tiffany explained quickly. Shoot, she'd of-fended her. "You know, because it's been such a long night with the concert and all."

Abbey nodded and pushed her hair back with a weary sigh. "It's been a long night for sure." She really didn't look well, though.

Tiffany changed the subject. "By the way, have you seen Loreen?"

Abbey shook her head. "Not since we first went down."

"Oh." Hm. "Okay. Do you want to sit down and have some tea or something?" Though the tea bags by the coffeemaker looked like they'd been there for quite some time. "Or wine? The kids are asleep and we could have some actual quiet."

"Thanks for taking care of that," Abbey said. "But if you don't mind, I think I'll just turn in myself now. I'm seriously exhausted."

It looked like more than that. Tiffany wanted to ask her what was wrong, if there was anything she could do to help, but she didn't really know Abbey all that well, and pushing her at this point would probably prove to be more insulting than helpful. Instead she just said, "Sure. Get some rest."

"Good night," Abbey said. "And thanks again for taking care of the kids."

"Sure." Tiffany looked at her watch. It was almost 1 A.M. Not really all that late. And Loreen was a grown woman, but Tiffany couldn't help but wonder if everything was all right. Unlike Abbey, Loreen was one of Tiffany's closest friends, so when another half hour had passed without word from Loreen, Tiffany didn't have a problem calling her up to check on her.

She took out her cell phone and dialed Loreen from the speed dial. It seemed to ring forever before Loreen picked up.

"Hey, I'm just checking up on you," Tiffany said, relieved to hear Loreen's voice. She had gone from simply wondering where Loreen was to being half-sure she'd been dragged off by some seedy gambler in about three seconds. "Are you having fun?"

"Blast," Loreen said shortly.

Was Tiffany getting paranoid? Why did everyone sound like there was something wrong? "Are you okay?"

"Just dandy. But, look, I can't really talk right now. I'll be up in a bit. Would you mind putting Jacob to bed?"

"Already done."

"Thanks. Don't wait up, I'm fine."

"Okay," Tiffany said. She felt like a meddling old aunt, checking up on everyone. "See you in the morning, then."

⁂

"Okay, where is it?" Loreen asked, clipping her cell phone shut.

Rod pointed. "Right over there."

And there it was. A big silver ATM with stickers representing every known bank network. Sort of like an Olympic tribute with all the nations' flags.

Only this wasn't about feats of athleticism and it wasn't about national pride. It was about emptying her bank account so she could pay off a male prostitute, even though it meant she'd have to serve rice and beans for dinner for a month. Or more.

Jacob wouldn't mind. He enjoyed farting.

And he *especially* enjoyed other people farting.

So there it was. She'd done it for Jacob.

"Lorena?" Rod snapped his fingers. "Hey, Lorena. You're passing it."

She turned her attention back to Rod. He'd already forgotten her name and begun calling her by the name of a woman famous for performing a penisectomy on her abusive husband.

Rod was *lucky* she wasn't Lorena Bobbit.

She went to the machine and took out her card. Her hand shook. This was, without a doubt, the most humiliating thing that had ever happened to her. She had foolishly luxuriated in this man's attention, despite the fact that she knew on every level that she wasn't that attractive to men this attractive, and now she was paying the price. She should have expected it. There's a price for everything.

At least for most people.

Her thoughts jumped to Abbey. Gorgeous, perfect, pain-in-the-ass-because-of-it Abbey. God, Loreen hoped she didn't run into her tonight. She couldn't bear to have Abbey look down at her, and possibly figure out what Loreen had accidentally done. Of course, she'd have to read Loreen's mind to figure it out, but maybe Abbey could do that.

She seemed to be able to do everything else.

Loreen vowed to try to be more like Abbey, even though part of her couldn't stand the woman. Abbey was aloof, and too good for the rest of them—like tonight, when she hadn't wanted to come down and have a drink. "I'll stay with the kids," she'd said, like she was the only good mother among them.

Okay, maybe that wasn't fair. Maybe she hadn't been trying to be holier than thou, but it had sort of come off that way anyhow. Especially when she'd completely disappeared, to go off on her own.

"You seem distracted," Rod said, but it wasn't a kind comment. He was prompting her to hurry up and get the cash.

"I was just trying to remember my PIN." Loreen put her card in the ATM slot and entered her PIN—Jacob's birthday, which she'd never forget—and felt a twinge of guilt. No, it was more than a twinge. It twisted around her stomach and heart like a boa constrictor, and made her feel sick.

She pushed WITHDRAWAL.

She bypassed the offered amounts of twenty, forty, sixty, eighty, and even up to two hundred dollars, which she'd *never* taken out at one time but always wished she could. Now, punching in the 1-0-0-0 and 0-0 CENTS, she hoped she'd never see an ATM again.

There was a moment while the machine rattled and blinked, and she felt like she was playing check-card roulette. Would it give her the money or wouldn't it? It was up to fate.

The rattling stopped; a receipt popped out. The screen, and the receipt, said, YOU CANNOT WITHDRAW MORE THAN $500 AT THIS TIME.

"Sorry," she said to Rod, who looked pretty irked. His eyes had turned to little black pieces of coal. "Apparently there's a cash limit."

He sighed heavily. Dramatically. She suddenly wondered if he was actually gay. "There are cash advance windows, you know. You can just get money from your credit card."

"Oh." The embarrassment just wasn't going to end, was it? "Where can I do that?"

He gestured, another flamboyant movement that made her question his sexual preferences. "They're all over the place. There's one right there, behind the blackjack tables."

For the second time in fifteen minutes, she followed his indication to a place that could make her life just a little worse.

When she got to the advance window, the woman there—about thirty or so, with a hard, colorless face—looked behind her and said, "Hey, Rod," before turning her flat gaze back to Loreen. "A thousand?"

Oh, God, she wasn't the first one to do this. The woman knew *exactly* what had happened; she knew *exactly* what a fool Loreen was. How could the embarrassment increase? Loreen had thought she'd reached the bottom, yet here she was, falling further.

At least she had the comfort of knowing that she had, indeed, been charged the going rate. He hadn't found her so awful that he had to charge her extra. That was . . . good.

Plus, she was able to say, "Five hundred, please," and imply that he had, in fact, found her *so* attractive that he'd given her a discount. A mere five hundred bucks for a twenty-minute fuck—yes, it was an awesome fuck, but no wonder! He was a *professional*! And a bottle of champagne and foreplay, to boot.

Oh, wait. *She* had to pay for the champagne. "Make that six hundred and forty, please."

The woman looked at Rod, and Loreen heard him say, "Cash-machine limit."

Asshole.

Loreen dug out her Visa and handed it over. "Can we just get this over with?"

"I'll need to see your license."

Loreen dug through her purse, looking for her license. "I'm not sure I have it," she said, pushing tampons, pennies, and an open lipstick aside in her frenzy to find the license and *end* this.

"No license, no cash."

For a moment, Loreen considered this. If she couldn't pay him, what was he going to do? He couldn't get blood from a stone. Then again, she wasn't a stone, and she most definitely had blood, and in an unsavory town like Las Vegas, the chances of spilling some over a debt seemed greater than usual.

"Come on, Deirdre," Rod said to the woman. "I trust her."

Deirdre snorted. "Sure you do, it's no skin off your nose—"

An expression Loreen had always despised.

"—*you're* the one who benefits from this. Not Loretta or me, huh, Loretta?"

Loreen looked up. "It's L—"

"Lorena," Rod corrected, then frowned and said, "it *is* Lorena, isn't it? Or is it—wait a minute—what's your name?" Apparently as soon as the job was finished, the hard drive that had contained her name for the purposes of romancing her was wiped clean.

She felt like he was shouting it, calling attention to her, though he was probably using a normal voice. "Loreen," she said hurriedly, "it's Loreen. Now, does my thousand bucks at least buy me a little discretion?"

Rod looked surprised. "Sure."

Truth was, she was surprised at herself. Loreen was always so damn polite, no matter what the situation was. When her boss had tried to kiss her at work, she'd given him a peck on the cheek and pretended that she'd misunderstood his intentions. When a guy had rear-ended her in traffic on the beltway, then come out yelling at her for letting her car drift backwards into his, she'd *apologized* (though her insurance money had won the claim from his).

Loreen had good manners. Even in bad times.

Maybe someday she could be proud of that.

At the moment, though, she was a woman who had just spent a thousand dollars in one night, for the first time in her life, and she wanted her money's worth. "I'd appreciate it," she said calmly, "if you could just keep our transaction between us. And, of course, Deirdre here."

Deirdre nodded, as if she were really in on this deal, and—hallelujah!—Loreen found her license. She handed it to Deirdre, horribly conscious of the fact that she was handing a lot of personal information over to a stranger who knew she'd just hired a male prostitute. "Looks okay," she said, handing the license back to Loreen.

What was she supposed to do, thank her?

Deirdre ran the credit card, had Loreen sign a slip that had enough carbon copies to make her imagine them arriving anonymously in her parents' and other relatives' mailboxes, then asked—Rod, by the way, not Loreen—"Hundreds okay?"

"Fine," he said.

"Wait a minute," Loreen said, foolishly up in arms about this one small detail. "Shouldn't you be asking *me*?"

Deirdre looked bemused. "But it's for him, isn't it?"

Loreen shook her head. "As far as you're concerned, it's for *me*. I'm the customer, or the cardholder, or whatever you want to call it, and if you have a question about this transaction, you ask me."

Deirdre was totally unfazed by this. "Are hundreds okay?" she asked, in *exactly* the same tone she'd used to ask Rod that question a moment before.

"No." Where was this coming from? Loreen probably shouldn't be antagonizing a guy who had this kind of information on her, but then again, it wasn't like she was some sort of public figure who had to worry about the story coming out the night before the New Hampshire primaries. She was no one. She'd remain no one, too, so if he wanted to blackmail her, he'd have to get pretty creative to make her really care. "I want ones," she said, nodding definitively.

*"What?"* Rod and Deirdre asked simultaneously, though Rod's cry was far more vigorous.

That was satisfying. "Ones," Loreen said again. "Is that a problem?" she asked, keeping her gaze on Deirdre.

Deirdre shrugged. "No." She opened a drawer and took out stacks of one-dollar bills.

"Come on, Lorena," Rod said, his voice sharp and a little bit shrill. "Loreen, I mean. This is ridiculous. I'll just get in line behind you and change them back to bigger bills."

Loreen turned to him. "Yes, but Deirdre will have to count them out. Both times. Am I right, Deirdre?"

"That's right." Deirdre was counting them out right now, with a deliberation that was probably painful to Rod, who was eager to move on to his next mark.

"Time is money, right, Rod?" Loreen asked him.

He narrowed his eyes at her. "Sometimes it's not worth it."

"Do you want to cancel the transaction?" Loreen asked. "Because I'm fine with that."

"No, I just don't want six hundred and forty ones."

"Do you know what some people would give for six hundred and forty one-dollar bills?"

He dipped his head in acknowledgment. "But you have a choice here, and you can get hundreds. And save paper," he added, like it was a trump card.

"I don't think Deirdre is actually *manufacturing* the money to my specifications, so that argument doesn't hold water."

"Here," Deirdre said, pushing over what must have been twenty-five bundles of ones.

"Oh, my," Loreen said, a small laugh in her voice despite the horror of the situation. That was a lot of bundles. They'd probably be heavy. Lord, she hoped so. "Hold your hands out, Rod. I'll pile them on."

"This is ridiculous," he intoned.

She looked him dead in the eye. "I could not agree more."

"Is it my turn?" he asked Deirdre.

Loreen looked to her for the answer, and Deirdre shook her head. "I was about to take my break . . . but I guess . . ."

It was hard not to smile when Loreen turned back to Rod. "You're in luck."

He shot her a hostile gaze. Something told her she wouldn't be a repeat customer, even if she wanted to be.

Then again, something told her he *knew* she wasn't going to be a repeat customer.

The tan was fake, Loreen decided, watching him step up to the counter.

And no one was that muscular and ripped without spending hours every day in the gym. And frankly that kind of vanity just didn't strike her as all that attractive.

So, good riddance to Rod.

She turned to leave.

"Couple months ago, someone asked for pennies," an older, non-descript woman said as Loreen passed.

Loreen stopped. The woman was wearing a name tag like Deirdre's—one that said WILHELMINA—and was obviously employed by the same cash counter. "What?"

The woman's dull features formed something like sympathy. "Seems like a lot of women don't know Rod has a price. Sometimes they get mad, like you. One got a thousand dollars in pennies. It took ages to get it all, and even then I had to give her two hundred in bills because we didn't have enough."

Pennies. Loreen only wished she'd thought of it. "He seemed nice," she said wistfully, without really even meaning to say it out loud.

"That's his job," Wilhelmina said without inflection.

Loreen looked at her. "Well, I think it stinks."

Wilhelmina's expression softened. "Everybody's got to make a living. But sometimes it ain't fair to everyone else."

Loreen nodded her agreement. "You said it."

Loreen walked away, thinking she had to get back to the hotel, and Jacob, and put the pieces of her self-esteem back together somehow. But she couldn't shake the notion that she was now a thousand dollars poorer than when she'd come to Las Vegas, and she just wasn't able to get by that way.

It was when she was passing the roulette tables that the answer occurred to her. She could earn the money back, bit by small bit, at the roulette table. After all, you could bet on red or black. It was a fifty–fifty chance of winning. Where else in the casino was she going to find those kind of odds?

Nowhere, that's where. She'd majored in statistics in college, and her professor had gone on and on about a statistical strategy on the roulette table called the "triple martingale." She remembered it well—you just bet red or black and doubled your bet every time it was the opposite. Though each go-round was technically a Bernoulli trial, and had equal odds independently, Professor Jellama had contended that there were more mystical, universal laws of mathematics, and roulette was a prime example of how, in fact, the odds build from trial to trial.

It had made sense when he explained it, even though he'd given disclaimers about its scientific veracity in order to keep his job.

But Professor Jellama had been a smart guy, one of her favorite teachers, and she was going to trust him now, when it mattered most.

She went to get chips and discovered she had only fifteen dollars on her, so she went back over to Deirdre's window—now that they'd formed this tenuous bond of sorts—and asked, "Can I get another hundred, or did I reach my limit?"

Deirdre took the card from her. "Until the credit card company says you've reached your limit, you haven't reached your limit." She dragged the card through the magnetic reader and punched in some number. Then she handed Loreen a paper to sign again. "Went through."

Loreen signed, and Deirdre handed over the cash.

"Thanks," Loreen said, meaning it a lot more this time than she had last time.

She meant it just as much the next five times she went, too, each time taking a greater amount to make up for her losses, until eventually she hit the limit on the card and found, from her receipts, that she was down five thousand dollars.

That was counting Rod's fee, of course, but still. Five thousand dollars.

She couldn't afford *one* thousand dollars!

But she also couldn't afford to throw more good money after bad, and, despite four thousand evidences to the contrary, Loreen *did* know when to call it quits. Professor Jellama was an idiot. She hoped he'd been fired for planting such crazy ideas in his students' heads.

What was she going to *do*?

She'd get a night job, that's what. Real estate wasn't all that steady, and until school let out in a month, things were still sluggish, so she'd supplement her income with a steady salary, even if it was at a retail store in the mall. Or maybe waitressing. If she could get a job waitressing at one of the high-end restaurants in Bethesda or Northwest, she could pay this off in no time. It would mean leaving Jacob at home while she worked, though. But Tiffany lived three houses away. Maybe Loreen could get a baby monitor system and put them around the house, and leave the receiver with Tiffany, so she could "babysit" while Loreen went to work.

It wasn't a perfect solution, but it was better than nothing.

And the alternative was nothing.

# Chapter 4

The next morning Tiffany got up before Loreen and Abbey to return the clothes to Finola Pims. When she was about to leave the room with her bags, she noticed Jacob Murphy and Parker Walsh trying to get the window open, while Kate sat nearby watching TV.

"What are you guys doing?" Tiffany asked, knowing the answer wasn't going to be something easy.

Both boys turned to her, faces pale with surprise. "Nothing," one of them said. It didn't matter which one, the truth of *something* was written all over their faces.

"Jacob bet Parker he could hit someone square on the head with a water balloon," Kate said.

"*Kate!*" Jacob objected.

"Are you kidding me?" Tiffany asked. "Where did you even get a balloon?"

"We don't have a balloon," Jacob said.

Parker looked like he'd just eaten something unpleasant.

This made Kate turn away from the TV. "Yes, you do. Don't lie to my mom." She turned back to Tiffany. "The lady that was here last night gave us balloons and chocolates."

Wow. She really should have cleared that with the parents first, Tiffany thought. What if one of the kids was allergic to chocolate? Or latex? "Give me the balloon," she said, holding her hand out.

Both Parker and Jacob produced flat little balloons and handed them over.

"Thank you." Tiffany stuffed them in her bag. "Now, I have to go downstairs for a minute—" She stopped. There was no way she could trust these guys alone while Loreen and Abbey were asleep. God knew what they'd get into next. "And you guys are coming with me."

"Are we going to the casino?" Jacob asked eagerly.

"No. A store."

"Aw, man!"

"Come on." She rustled them up, jotted a note for the others that she had the kids, and headed downstairs to Finola Pims.

It was only three kids, but trying to keep track of them in the chaos of the hotel proved harder than Tiffany had anticipated. The lights and noise seemed to hypnotize them into all sorts of wild behavior.

It was *"Jacob! Kate! Stop playing tag, you're running into people!"*

Or *"Where's Parker?"*

And *"Jacob and Parker, that is not funny. Stop it now!"*

The five minutes down the elevator and out to the storefront seemed to last a lifetime. When they got to the Finola Pims shop, Tiffany rounded the children up outside the store entrance.

"Listen to me," she said in a harsh whisper, bending down before them. "You guys *have* to be *silent* in here, do you understand? Stand like statues, don't make a single *peep*. If you do, I *swear to you*, I will go to the board of education meeting and suggest they abolish summer vacations *completely*." She looked at the blank faces for signs of terror and acquiescence.

"What's *abolish*?" Jacob asked.

"It means they'd *end* it," she said, raising an eyebrow. "School would go year-round with *no* summer vacation." She gave a nod to emphasize her point.

That did it. There was the white-faced fear she'd been looking for: the straight backs, the closed mouths. That was more like it.

"Good." She stood up. "Now, let's go."

They marched into the store like the von Trapp children, in a quiet line, straight to the sales counter. Tiffany waited behind a mature woman who was dripping with jewels so big, she couldn't imagine they were real. Then again, the total of her sale indicated she might actually be able to afford the real thing.

Of course, someone might have said the same thing about Tiffany's purchase.

"Can I help you?" asked the salesgirl, a slip of a thing who looked about nineteen. She glanced at the bags Tiffany was holding and the unmistakable hope of large sales commissions glinted in her eye.

"Yes." Tiffany hefted the bags onto the counter. "I need to return these."

For a moment it looked like the salesgirl, whose name tag announced her as RAYANNE, thought Tiffany was speaking another language.

"They're beautiful," Tiffany hastened to add, in case she had somehow insulted the girl. "But"—she wasn't going to admit she couldn't afford them—"they just don't quite suit me."

"Wow, that's too bad." Rayanne nodded.

Tiffany smiled. "Well, with all the kids"—she gestured—"I figured it would be more merciful to the other shoppers for me to try them on in my room and see what works." She took the receipt out and held it out to the girl, who just looked at it with vague sympathy.

"And they don't fit?" she asked, making no move to take the receipt from Tiffany.

"They're just not quite right for me." Tiffany set the receipt on the counter and pushed it toward Rayanne, like it was a silent bid auction. "So, if you could just . . . do the return."

"I wish I could." She shook her head and let the words plunk down without further explanation.

"Okay, well, can you get someone who can?" Tiffany asked, losing patience. The kids were starting to shuffle their feet and get antsy. She shot them a warning look and mouthed the words *summer vacation*.

"No one can." Rayanne pointed to a sign Tiffany had managed to overlook when making the purchase. It said, in the kind of thin, elaborate script that was harder to notice than to miss: ALL SALES FINAL. NO RETURNS OR EXCHANGES. NO EXCEPTIONS.

"I didn't see that before," Tiffany murmured, as if it would make a difference.

"It's the store policy."

"But . . . why? I mean, Nordstrom doesn't do that."

Rayanne shrugged. "This isn't Nordstrom."

It was undeniable. "Is there a manager I could speak with? Not that I'm saying you're not competent."

"He won't let you return the stuff."

"Why don't you let me speak to him myself?"

Rayanne didn't move. "He won't. People have tried before."

Which led Tiffany to wonder for a moment if they actually removed that sign during a transaction, and put it back when the poor suckers came back to return things. Or maybe it was sort of the Brigadoon of signs, appearing once every so often, and Tiffany was just out of luck this time. "Would you please ask him to come over so I can talk to him?"

"Mom." There was a tugging on the back of her shirt.

"Shhh!" She tossed over her shoulder.

A few moments passed, then another tug. "But *Mom*."

"Kate, honestly, you *have* to just wait a minute, okay?" Tiffany rasped, hoping not to call attention to herself. "I need to talk to one more person, then we'll go back to our hotel room."

"But Mom—"

"Quiet!"

"Jacob *peed in his pants!*"

Tiffany kept her focus straight ahead. Maybe she'd heard wrong. Maybe she'd misunderstood. Surely a nine-year-old hadn't just wet himself in the middle of a high-end store.

She looked back as wincingly as if she were looking at a car wreck. And she was. The front of Jacob's khaki pants was soaking wet, and there was a puddle on the white marble floor of the shop.

Tiffany had to swallow a curse. Several of them, actually.

Jacob shrugged.

Well, at least he wasn't emotionally traumatized by it. Like Tiffany was about to be. "Jacob, what happened?"

"I *really really* had to go."

"Why didn't you tell me?"

This started them all jabbering at once about how *you told us not to talk* and *no summer vacation ever again.*

"I didn't mean . . ." What could she say? More to the point, what could she *do*? There was only one option: to sneak out of the store with the kids and come back before they left for the airport in the morning when someone else could watch the children. "Okay, guys, quick—"

"How may I help you?"

Startled, Tiffany whipped around to see a small man with a pencil-thin mustache who looked like he was doing his best impression of William Powell, only in miniature.

And without the little sparkle of humor in his eye.

"Rayanne said you wished to see a manager."

She glanced uncertainly back at Jacob, then scooted Kate in front of him to, hopefully, block the mess. "Yes, I just had a few returns to make, and Rayanne pointed out that you have a no-return policy." She tried to give a trill of a laugh, like *I'm so rich and silly I didn't even realize it!* "Now, the problem is, I'm going back home this morning, and I was really hoping to get this done right away." She paused, and he continued to look at her in a detached manner. "If you look, you'll see that everything still has the tags on and everything." She lifted the would-be Kentucky Derby hat and pointed out the tag.

"That's good," he said.

"Oh, thank goodness." Tiffany smiled. "I was afraid you were going to stick to your policy, which would be understandable, of course, but—"

"No, no, the hat is good. Exquisite. I'm sure it's quite fetching on you."

"Well . . . not so much. That's why I'm returning it."

"I'm sorry, ma'am, I cannot overturn the store policy." He clasped his hands in front of him and shook his head. "Would that I could."

"You're the manager. I'm sure you can. In fact, I bought them only a few hours ago, so could you just look in the drawer for the receipt and void it out?"

"Well . . ."

"I would be so grateful."

He took a long, deliberate breath. "Perhaps, I could—" He interrupted himself to make a noise like Scooby-Doo encountering a ghost, and clapped his hand to his mouth.

"Mr.—?" Tiffany realized he hadn't introduced himself. "Are you okay?"

He pointed a shaking finger behind her. "Are they with you?"

She closed her eyes for a moment before turning to look behind her and make sure he was referring to the children and not, say, a pack of wild dogs that had gotten into the store.

It was the kids, all right. And Kate had stepped aside, so Jacob was there in all his damp glory.

"They're . . . here." That didn't make sense. She couldn't come up with an answer that would both make sense and make things better, so she tried the truth. "They're not all mine, of course, but I brought them down rather than leaving them alone in the hotel room."

He wasn't listening. "Excuse me." He turned away in horror and clapped his hands in front of his face, walking briskly across the store, calling, "Clean up at register one! Quickly! Spit-spot!"

"Hey, Mary Poppins said that!" one of the kids said.

"Mom, are you finished?"

"I think so," Tiffany said, turning dejectedly to take the kids out. She stepped over the puddle and kept walking, not even bothering to admonish the kids to keep quiet. She had spent five thousand dollars on *clothes* when every penny she and Charlie had was budgeted into carefully constructed categories and needs.

She'd probably just spent a big chunk of Kate's first semester of college on a ridiculous Kentucky Derby outfit she'd never, ever be able to use.

✳

An hour later, Tiffany, Abbey, and Loreen went to the airport with the kids. The kid mood was wild, happy, excited; the adult mood was decidedly morose.

For one thing, Tiffany was wearing the stupid, ostentatious hat she'd bought when, drunk, she'd thought it looked fun. There was no room for it in her suitcase. She'd thought about leaving it behind for the maid, but all she could envision was some tired old cynic of a maid coming in, trying on the crazy $230 hat, then shoving it into the trash bag. Tiffany would rather keep it than that. Even if she had to wear it for gardening.

And take up gardening to wear it.

"I'm hungry, Mom," Kate whined as she trailed behind Tiffany on the way to the gate.

"Me, too!" Jacob chimed in immediately.

"Can we get something to eat?" Parker asked.

"Oh! I want pizza!" Kate started running toward a Sbarro counter.

"Kate, stop!" Tiffany yelled, but Kate didn't even slow. "Katherine Dreyer, you stop *right now*!"

She stopped. She knew what it meant when her parents used her whole name. Unfortunately, Jacob Murphy did not, and he ran smack into her and they both fell onto the hard linoleum.

"My knee!" Kate wailed.

Jacob's face went red. "Sorry," he said guiltily.

"You didn't need to run right on top of me!" Kate snapped back at him.

"Kate." Tiffany went over and leaned down to pull Kate up. "If you can bark at Jacob like that, you can't be too hurt. Let me take a look."

Kate whimpered and pointed to her knee, which was exactly the same pale shade as her other knee.

"She's awright," Jacob groused.

Parker hung back, clearly wanting to remain distanced from any trouble.

"Yup. I think she is," Tiffany said.

"And I think these kids need to eat so they don't whine all the way back to D.C.," Loreen added, behind her. "You know all they serve on airplanes these days is Cheese Nips and pretzels."

"They had a cheese platter on the way over," Tiffany pointed out. "Although it was just American, Swiss, and Whiz."

"I'll take them to get pizza," Abbey volunteered.

"Let's all go," Tiffany said. "I think we could all use a bite."

They went, and they pooled all their remaining cash on pizza, salads, and Cokes before returning to the gate to wait for their plane to board.

Loreen seemed off, Tiffany noticed. She was edgy, pale, and she wasn't making eye contact. It seemed like something was wrong, but Tiffany assumed it was a hangover. That is, until Loreen approached her.

"Can I talk to you a minute?" Loreen asked in an urgent whisper.

"Sure, what's—?"

The look on Loreen's face stopped Tiffany from questioning her further until they were alone, several feet away.

"I made a terrible mistake last night," Loreen said, tears welling in her eyes. "I can't keep it to myself anymore."

*So did I,* Tiffany thought, imagining that in a few minutes both their burdens would be lighter for the sharing. "What is it?" she asked sympathetically.

"It's . . . the PTA credit card. Last night I thought it was mine. I have the same Visa, only my personal one has my middle initial on it, which is how I usually tell them apart. But last night, I guess I wasn't thinking too clearly. . . ." She swatted away her tears impatiently. "Tiffany, I used the PTA card last night."

Oh, that was cute. Typical of honest Loreen, worrying herself half to death because she accidentally made a charge on the wrong card. Of course, there would be paperwork, and that would be a bit of a drag, but it wasn't anything to get too upset over. "It's okay, honey, what's the damage? Forty?" She was being generous. "Fifty?"

"Five thousand," Loreen said without missing a beat.

Which was more than could be said for Tiffany's heart. *Five thousand!* "You're kidding, right?" Only half a second passed before her nerves tightened like guitar strings. "Loreen, tell me you're kidding."

But Loreen only pressed her lips together and shook her head.

*"How?"*

"I got cash advances on the PTA card all night long until I finally hit the limit." Loreen sniffed. "I thought they'd just increased my credit or something. It never even occurred to me that I was using the wrong card, because I hardly ever even take the PTA one out."

"Oh, Loreen . . ." They were in big trouble.

"I know. I'm so sorry! I can't even tell you how sorry I am. Obviously I'll pay it back, somehow. . . ." She went pale. "I don't know how. Five thousand . . . but I will. I *will*. Right away. I'll just get cash advances on my other cards—"

"We'll talk about it later." Tiffany didn't mean to be short with Loreen, but this, on top of her own debt, was just too much to think about before getting into a multiton Tylenol capsule that would somehow have to rise into the sky and take them home.

Desperate and broke, and feeling like her world was closing in around her, Tiffany did something she usually did only in an emergency.

She called the one person she knew who *always* had her shit together, and *always* seemed to know what to do.

She called her sister, Sandra.

# Chapter 5

Sandra Vanderslice regarded the scale under the bathroom sink like it was a sleeping bear. She could continue to tiptoe past it and pretend it wasn't there and couldn't affect her, or she could just wake the damn thing and let it do its worst, thereby stripping it of its power over her.

Except that that wouldn't strip it of its power, because there was always the horrible possibility that after working her ass off— literally—to lose twenty-six pounds last year, then falling off the chuck wagon, she might have gained back more than she'd lost in the first place.

That kind of news would be just too devastating to take. She wasn't sure what she'd do. Probably eat a Twinkie, or four, and wallow in self-loathing. No, she didn't eat a dozen eggs for breakfast or tuck into a shoulder of beef every night for dinner, the way fat people were often portrayed, but emotional eating was a real problem for Sandra, and when she was upset—ironically, it was usually when she was upset about her appearance—she really could down half a dozen snack cakes or eat a pint of ice cream, in minutes flat, all the while feeling horrible about herself.

She hated that she was so wrapped up in her appearance that she couldn't enjoy the real successes in her life—she was a founder of a very promising shoe-importing business, and, thanks to a clever purchase and renovation, she had almost seventy-five thousand dollars' worth of equity in her Washington, D.C., apartment in the trendy Adams Morgan neighborhood. She had so much to be proud of.

But she was thirty-four years old, and she'd never had a real boyfriend. The last guy she'd gone out with, Carl Abramson, had been as sweet as pie, but they'd had only four or five dates before his biotech company transferred him to Omaha.

Sandra wanted a boyfriend, she really did, but she wasn't desperate enough to up and move to Nebraska to try to keep one.

So they'd said good-bye, and apart from the occasional e-mail that eventually petered out to nothing, they hadn't spoken since he'd left, eight months ago.

Before that, there had been Mike Lemmington, a Greek god of a guy she'd gone to high school with (though in high school, he'd been more of a Michelin Man of a guy). They'd spent several happy months going out together before Sandra realized (1) they weren't actually dating, because (2) Mike was gay. (3) Resoundingly so.

She may have been dating him, but he was only hanging out with her. Same Bat-time, same Bat-channel, totally different interpretations of Robin, the Boy Wonder.

Which, like everything else that had ever gone wrong in her life, all led back to the scale. Sandra was good at denying the obvious. And even better at *avoiding* the truth.

This had to stop.

She was lonely.

It was hard even to think of it in such honest, simple terms, but it was true. Sandra spent virtually all her time alone. There were things she enjoyed throughout her days, of course—she liked her work, had a few TV shows she enjoyed, that sort of thing—but there was always the thought in the back of her mind that if she swallowed a forkful of boiled chicken wrong, she might choke and die alone and no one would know until the neighbors called the super about the smell.

And she wanted someone to bitch about Bill O'Reilly with; someone to drape her legs across on leisurely Sundays during the Redskins games. (She wasn't all that into football, but she'd grown up with that being the sound of Sunday afternoons, and there was something comforting about it, and besides, when else could she wear her burgundy and gold Chuck Taylors?) She wanted somebody to remind her that the world wasn't always fair at the end of a hard day but that things would get better; someone who would tell her that he loved her no matter what.

She wanted the kind of best friend you shared your whole life with. She had no illusions that he had to look like Brad Pitt—truth was, if he did, he'd probably be a jerk anyway. She didn't actually care what the guy looked like anymore, as long as he didn't scare small children.

She just wanted him to get her. And to love her for that.

So it wasn't just pure vanity that made her want to lose some weight. It was realism. She knew that men looked at a girl's face and figure first, and even some really nice guys might initially dismiss a girl who was a little too heavy.

Or a lot too heavy, as the case may be.

So what was the choice? To keep indulging in Parmesan artichoke dip and Hamburger Hamlet's Those Potatoes, and a host of other little things that, on the surface, didn't seem that indulgent but which added up to trouble? Or to take the most reasonable—if not easiest—diet approach and limit absolutely everything she loved with the hopes of slimming down and . . . and what?

Not *attracting* her soul mate, because if he was really her soul mate, she wouldn't need some sort of movie star or model figure in order to catch his eye.

But maybe it was reasonable to think that if she lost weight, she might at least stop *repelling* her potential soul mate. Because, honestly, no one was attracted to grossly overweight people. Right or wrong, it communicated a lack of self-care to other people.

She didn't need to be *skinny*, but she needed to be *healthy*.

Sandra pulled the scale out and laid it flat on the cold tile floor, and took off her new white Sigerson Morrison peep-toe medium platforms. (They had cost $368.95 at Zappos.com and were worth every penny, *especially* after she got a French pedicure.) The shoes were fabulous, but she wasn't going to add their weight to hers, though it occurred to her that, depending what the scale said, it might be better if she could blame the shoes for anywhere from one to six pounds.

Then again, if she put on towering heels, really great stilettos, like the Hollywould ones she'd just gotten, could she possibly justify offsetting her weight by adding inches?

It was tempting. And she was ready to vow to wear heels every day for the rest of her life, if that's what it took.

Then again, maybe she needed chunky heels, like they always advised in the Style Network shows about how not to dress fat. *A chunky heel can de-emphasize a chunky ankle.*

Right.

But she knew she had to be honest and face the whole ugly truth.

She stood over the scale for a good minute or two, considering the possibilities. As if one of them was to stay off the scale and thereby not gain an ounce since her last successful weigh-in, so many months ago.

*Do it,* she told herself, like a kid trying to talk herself into diving into a cold pool on a hot July afternoon. *Just do it. Face the truth. Get it over with. You can always join Weight Watchers again. It worked once; it will work again.*

She took a deep breath and stepped onto the scale. The spinner lurched and bounced, and she stepped back quickly.

No. No, no, no. She couldn't do it.

She backed against the wall and slid down, then sat face-to-face with her enemy, the scale.

It was just plain unfair. There were a lot of people who never even had to think about what they ate; they were just naturally slim and gorgeous, no matter what they scarfed down.

Sandra's sister, Tiffany, was one of those people. Where Sandra was short and mousy-haired, with nondescript hazel eyes, Tiffany was tall, blond, and slender, with eyes so insanely blue, they looked like they had to be contacts. In some ways—okay, a lot of ways—it had been absolute hell to grow up in Tiffany's narrow shadow.

*You're Tiffany Vanderslice's sister?*

*Come on, seriously?*

*Is one of you adopted?* Turned out one of them was, though Sandra had only learned *that* last year. Tiffany was adopted and had known it for years, all the while feeling a little bit inadequate compared to Sandra, their parents' *biological* child. It was ironic, since Sandra had felt the same inadequacy in comparison to Tiffany, whom she perceived as "the golden child" to her "black sheep."

Yet it didn't make Sandra feel any differently about Tiffany, or about Sandra's own big fat doughy comparison to her.

To be fair, Tiffany was *not* one of those people who went around proclaiming that they could not gain weight "no matter what I eat!" She was the very definition of *disciplined*. She was the sort of person who could eat *one* Christmas cookie.

She could even resist them altogether, if she feared her waistline was exceeding its twenty-nine-inch limit. (Or whatever, Sandra wasn't actually *sure* what Tiffany's measurements were, only that they were more flattering than her own.)

Tiffany had, all her life, opted for water over Coke, plain milk over chocolate, and she actually *preferred* her salads without any dressing whatsoever.

Sandra was always tempted to point out that it was actually *more* nutritious to eat those greens with a little bit of fat—she'd learned a few things from Weight Watchers—but she was afraid it would sound like sour grapes.

And in a sibling relationship that had always been a little bit strained, Sandra didn't want to add any sour grapes.

Unless they were in the form of wine.

But who was she kidding? Tiffany probably never even had more than a glass with dinner, if any at all. Far be it from Tiffany to lose even one iota of her legendary control.

Which is why it was such a surprise when the phone rang and it was Tiffany, calling from what she described as "the floor of the crappiest, dirtiest part of the dirty, crappy Las Vegas airport."

"Why are you on the floor of the airport?" Sandra asked, immediately alarmed, yet intrigued.

"All the flights are running late because of thunderstorms or something. The place is mobbed." She made an exasperated sound, then said, "But that's not why I called. I need a job. Fast. And I was wondering if you and your shoe people were hiring."

"*What?*" Sandra couldn't process this that fast.

"Your company," Tiffany said. "Are you hiring?"

A year ago, Sandra and some friends had met every Tuesday night to swap shoes in an effort to, if not get rid of their shoe addiction, at least make it cost less. Eventually, in a move that turned their addiction to actual *profit*, they pooled their money to support the work of a brilliant young Italian shoemaker named Phillipe Carfagni. Now their company paid for the manufacture and import of his work, and had gotten it into an impressive number of stores, boutiques, and online shoe sites. But the company was still young and, as such, still struggled to make ends meet with the few employees it had.

"Why?"

"I need a job."

"What? Why do you need a job?" Sandra asked, shocked. "Are you and Charlie splitting up?" Oh! Bad mistake! Tiffany hadn't said a word about leaving Charlie, but Sandra had leapt all over it like *Are you finally leaving the bum?*

Which was how she really felt.

"No!" Tiffany barked. "God, Sandra, can't I just ask you about a job without you leaping to crazy and insulting conclusions?"

"Well . . . yes, it's just . . . you just said you're on the floor of some Las Vegas hotel—"

"Airport."

"—right, airport, and you're obviously in the middle of something more demanding than, say, sitting around doing your nails while watching *The Price Is Right* and deciding you want a new hobby. So . . . seriously, Tiffany, why are you asking about a job *now*?"

"It doesn't matter *why*," Tiffany said, an edge still sharp in her voice. "Maybe I'm just bored waiting for my flight and thought of it. Maybe I'm just trying to make conversation. Maybe—"

"Okay, now I *know* something's up," Sandra said. She'd had more than her share of liars over the phone these past few years, and she could pick them out within seconds. "You should have stopped at the bored-and-waiting-for-your-flight part. I might have bought that."

"Would you buy in-debt-from-buying-too-many-clothes-and-shoes?" Tiffany shot back.

Sandra laughed. "No way. Try again."

"It's the truth," Tiffany said. And this time her voice was different. Serious. Broken.

"What? You got into financial trouble buying *clothes*? And *shoes*?"

"I know it's not like me, but it's the truth. I accidentally spent thousands of dollars on these stupid, impractical designer clothes. Then there was a mix-up with the plane tickets home, so I had to get a first-class seat at the last minute for a nine-year-old who can't be separated from the group, and the whole thing's a mess, and if I don't make a lot of money fast, my marriage is going to be in really serious trouble. So I was wondering if you needed any part-time workers for your company."

Sandra listened to this with disbelief. *Tiffany?* Spent thousands of dollars on *clothes*? It didn't make sense, but the one thing that was obvious was that it didn't *have* to make sense right now. Right now Sandra needed to listen.

She just wished she could do more to help. "The company is really still in its infancy, and I can't hire people unilaterally, and besides, you wouldn't make that much that soon even if we *were* hiring, which we're not. Maybe I could loan you the money, if I tapped into my retirement. How much—?"

"No! You can't do that. I wouldn't let you, so don't even *think* about it. I was just desperate, honestly, and I thought you might have some sort of idea. . . ." Tiffany sniffled. "I don't know."

"I'm sorry," Sandra said, meaning it sincerely. "If there was anything I could do, I'd—wait a minute. You just want work? For money? Fast?"

"Yes." The answer was more of a question, and Sandra could picture Tiffany sitting straighter on her square of linoleum, listening for the potential answer to her problems.

And maybe Sandra had it. "There is *one* thing I can think of, one way to make good money fast. . . . If you're really serious, that is."

"There is?" Hope was clearly rising fast. "What is it? Does it take some special skill or education or something?"

"N-no. Not really. Just a willingness to . . . put yourself out there."

There was a pause. "Sandra, you're starting to make me nervous. What is it?"

"Keep an open mind."

"Sandra—"

"I mean it. I don't want you throwing this back in my face later. It's a perfectly legit way to earn money, and I even did it myself for a while."

"Do *not* tell me you were a prostitute."

Funny how quickly she'd come to that conclusion. "No!"

"Thank God."

Sandra took a short breath then continued. "Have you ever thought about the possibility of being a phone sex operator?"

# Chapter 6

**P**hone sex?" Loreen repeated. She couldn't believe Tiffany was suggesting this! Apart from the irony of Loreen having to turn virtual tricks to pay for the trick *she'd* accidentally become, this was *not* the sort of thing Tiffany Dreyer ever even *talked* about, much less suggested as a PTA fund-raiser.

They were sitting on Loreen Murphy's sofa, trying to sort out the details of the nightmare that remained from their trip to Las Vegas

"Look," Tiffany said with a sigh. "It's not *just* the PTA card that got racked up. I got into a little financial trouble in Vegas myself."

Loreen looked at her. "How little?"

Tiffany swallowed. "Five thousand."

"So we're up to ten thousand," Loreen said, and almost laughed at how ludicrous it was. They needed ten thousand bucks in, like, a month. Fat chance.

Abbey, who had been watching silently—and, Loreen thought, judgmentally—spoke then. "If we're looking to come up with a quick fund-raiser, I could use some cash myself."

For the church, Loreen thought. If Abbey was going to help pay the cost of their sins, she was going to want them to tithe.

Like they could afford *that*.

Tiffany, however, didn't make the same assumption. "Did you lose money *gambling*?" she asked Abbey in disbelief.

Abbey shook her head. "No, it's something else. I . . ." She shook her head. "I shouldn't have brought it up."

"No, no," Tiffany said. "We're putting it all out there. We're going to help each other out of this mess. So how much do you need?"

"Ten thousand."

Tiffany and Loreen exchanged looks. This didn't sound like tithing for the church. Abbey was in some serious trouble of some sort.

"What happened?" Loreen asked.

"It's a long story. It has to do with a charitable donation I made that went wrong." Abbey shook her head. "Not all that interesting."

So in a way Loreen had been right. But who was she to judge? If Abbey would help pay off her mistake, she'd help Abbey pay off hers.

Tiffany took a sip of General Foods International Coffee. "Obviously a bake sale isn't going to cut it." If they were at Tiffany's house, it would have been freshly ground and brewed coffee, but at Loreen's if it wasn't instant, it wasn't happening. "Neither is a car wash."

New panic surged in Loreen's breast. "Please, let's not make the kids do anything to help with this. I just . . . I can't bear the idea."

Good Lord, the *children* working to pay of her *prostitution debt*? It was worse than third-world sweatshops, by far. "I'll sell my kidney first."

How much *did* kidneys get on the black market anyway?

Andy toddled in, stopping in front of Tiffany and raising his arms. "Looks like Kate got tired of babysitting," Tiffany said, lifting the child into her lap and cupping her hand over the soft hair at the crown of his head. "Poor sleepy baby," she said quietly, rocking him gently. "I don't think we have a choice," she said to everyone else.

"We must. How much do you think we could earn doing temporary secretarial work or something?" Abbey asked, tapping the table idly with her fingernails. "Theoretically, two of us could take a job every day, and the other one could take care of the kids."

"I can shift my real estate work schedule around," Loreen said, "in order to take as much solid work as I could get."

Tiffany shook her head. "But that's still just one paycheck at a time. You can't make the kind of money we need working as a temp." She lifted her coffee cup, but didn't take a sip before setting it down again. "I'm telling you, we need to be much more aggressive about this."

"*That* is not the only answer," Abbey said. "If I did it and anyone found out, it could ruin Brian."

It figured, Loreen thought, that of the three people willing to work on this, one had to be married to a pastor. "If I did it and got found out, it could jeopardize my custody case."

"And I risk my marriage by doing it," Tiffany agreed, holding her sleeping child closer. "But I don't have a better answer."

"Me neither," Loreen said.

"I don't either," Abbey added.

Loreen, for her part, was beginning to see the appeal. "Well . . . it's just acting, I guess. Just pretending."

"Exactly!" Tiffany agreed.

Abbey looked dubious.

"Look, my sister can come over to my house on Thursday when Charlie's at his poker game. She'll tell us how to do it. If you want to come, come at seven thirty. If you don't—" She looked pointedly at Abbey, then at Loreen. "—then don't. It's up to you. But I'm going to do it."

★

Abbey spent the next few days worrying over the increasing pile of stresses that was being heaped in front of her.

How could she work as a phone sex operator and still hope to keep her own past from being scrutinized by Brian or his congregation? If they didn't find out about her from her own misstep, she knew Damon well enough to know he was probably ready to take out a full-page ad in the *Washington Post* to expose her if she didn't acquiesce.

Damon, once the stuff of dreams, was now a thing of nightmares. And if Abbey wasn't careful, he would open her Pandora's box for all the world to see.

He could ruin her life *and* Brian's and, worst of all, Parker's.

She should have known this was coming. Someday she was *bound* to run into someone who knew her before she met Brian and changed her life. There were plenty of people within a fifty-mile radius who knew the person she used to be.

The difference was, most of those people didn't care. They wouldn't have found it interesting to try to blackmail her.

It was just pure bad luck that she'd run into Damon.

Did it mean, after more than a decade, her bad luck was returning?

She hated to think that way. Hated it. She didn't want to be superstitious, but how could she not? Fifteen years ago she'd been a wild child, partying every day, every night, ingesting nearly every mood-altering substance she could get her hands on, without regard to her safety or—she would have laughed then to think about it—her soul.

She'd even created a distraction with a hotel maid in New York so that Damon could slip into an elderly woman's room and steal her jewelry, including the necklace he hadn't had time to fence before getting caught.

Then Abbey had died.

And everything she thought she knew turned out to be wrong.

It was a temporary death, of course. On the operating table. So, really, it was just a technicality, but for two entire minutes—she was told later—she had been dead. Yet one miracle, a thing she wouldn't have believed possible, had given her a second chance at life, and she'd made a deal with God. She'd be good. She'd be good no matter what. If only he'd give her a second chance.

Or had he?

Maybe it was just a stay of execution.

If so, was there any harm in disregarding the spiritual implications and helping herself, her family, and her friends by doing a little phone sex?

She scrubbed the kitchen sink, pondering the question, even though she was pretty sure she already knew the answer.

"Mom?"

She was so lost in thought that at first her son's call didn't even register.

The sound of him throwing up, however, did.

She ran to him, stepping gingerly around the vomit on the old Berber carpet. It had probably seen worse. "Honey, what happened? Did you eat something that made you feel sick?"

He shook his little head. "I started to feel yucky after school at soccer practice."

"Why didn't you say something?"

"'Cause." He shrugged. "Everyone'd make fun of me." His eyes widened at the very instant his face turned a blotchy combination of pasty and green. "I think I'm gonna—" He didn't finish his sentence. He didn't have to. He threw up on Abbey, a projectile spew of foamy yellow bile. The mess dripped down over the buckle of her jeans and (she really didn't want to confirm this) inside the waistband.

"Come on, honey, let's get you to the bathroom." She looked at him and thought it looked like he might go again. "Quick." She grasped his arm and rushed him to the powder room, throwing back the door just in time for him to get sick again, this time *near* the toilet but, unfortunately, *on* the plumbing fixtures.

They were hard enough to clean when it was just dirt.

"I'm sorry, Mom." His lip trembled. "I tried to hold it, but I couldn't."

"Shhh." She drew him close, making sure she didn't hold him against the damp patch on the front of her pants. "It's okay. Nothing to be sorry about. When you need to get sick, you need to get sick. It's actually a good thing. You're getting rid of whatever it is that's making you feel so bad."

He nodded, but it looked like he didn't believe her.

"Now, listen. Take off your clothes and put them in a pile here on the floor, okay? I'll clean it up in a few minutes. For now, I'm going to run upstairs and change my clothes and bring you something more comfortable to put on, okay?"

" 'Kay." Slowly he sat down in front of the toilet.

Lord, she felt sorry for him. There was no worse feeling than becoming intimately acquainted with the cold, hard, and usually dirty porcelain of the toilet bowl.

The laundry room was a few steps away, and she hurried in to get a clean towel to wrap around him.

"Here you go." She put the towel around his narrow shoulders and gave him another squeeze. "I'll be right back, okay? Will you be all right if I go for a minute or two?"

He nodded and pulled the terry cloth closer around him.

He looked so small and helpless that she wanted to just gather him into her arms as she had when he was a baby, but doing that would only get them both messier.

"I'll be back before you can count to twenty." She winked at him and ran to her room, taking the stairs two at a time. She pulled off her pants and tossed them, inside out, into the clothes hamper, then took off her top and threw it in with the jeans. "Are you counting?" she called, pulling on her old gray sweats as she sprinted across the hall to his bedroom.

There was a soft reply, probably in the affirmative.

"I'll be right there." She pulled open his pajama drawer, and grabbed the pants from his Batman pj's and an old Thomas the Tank Engine pajama top. It was small; she'd probably only kept it to use as a dust rag, but it looked clean and she didn't want to waste a lot of time looking for a matching set when Parker needed her.

"Here I am!" she sang, arriving breathlessly in the downstairs hall, where Parker was still hunched on the floor in front of the powder room.

He'd gotten sick again, poor thing.

He looked at her like a guilty puppy.

"Okay, let's get you out of those clothes." She was good at this. She'd had experience. Despite the fact that he'd gotten quite sick without a lot of control over *where*, she managed to get him out of his clothes without making him any more soiled. She folded them in on themselves and then helped him into the pajamas, which were way too small on top and big enough to drop off him on the bottom.

She was pretty tired of not having enough money.

"That better?" she asked, touching her knuckle to his cheek.

"Uh-huh."

"Want some ginger ale?"

" 'Kay."

She tossed his clothes at the washer, and went to the kitchen, where she always had at least one small bottle of Schweppes ginger ale on hand for just this kind of emergency. Likewise the red box of graham crackers, which she grabbed along with the soda.

"Here you go." She sat down on the floor with him and twisted the top off the ginger ale. "It's warm, but it works better that way."

He took the bottle she held out to him and took a small sip, then another.

"Think you can choke down a graham cracker?" she asked gently, pushing his hair back from his clammy, cold forehead.

He shook his head.

"That's okay, I'll have them here just in case you change your mind." She set the box down. "Why don't you lie with your head in my lap now. Give your tummy a chance to settle down. If you need the toilet, it's right there."

" 'Kay." He shuffled around and lay down in front of her, his head on her legs.

She put her palm on his clammy forehead—good, no fever—then again her hand along his head over and over again. Ever since he was a baby, that had been the most soothing thing she could do.

"Forty," he murmured.

"What's that?"

"You said you'd be back before I got to twenty. I got to forty."

She gave a small laugh. "In Spanish?"

"No."

"Hm. I should have been more specific. I meant I'd be back before you counted to twenty in Spanish."

"Very funny." His voice was weak, but she took it as a good sign that he was able to joke at all.

She continued to smooth his hair. Eventually, he rolled over onto his side, and his eyes began to blink longer and slower. It wasn't long before he was asleep.

"Sleep it off, little man," she whispered, taking the towel he'd shaken off and folding it into a little pillow to replace her lap when she got up. "You'll feel better when you wake up. I love you. Soooo much."

Some things were more important than her own soul.

She went upstairs and got the laundry out of the machine. There were the remains of dandelions in the washer. At first she'd freaked out, thinking it was some sort of huge spider, but then she realized it was the washed and mushy remains of a dandelion green, undoubtedly "flowers" that Parker had kept in his pocket to give his mother—as he often did—but had forgotten.

She took the greens out of the washer, hesitated a moment, then put them into the small trash can full of dryer lint next to the dryer.

There would be more dandelions. She couldn't afford to keep the tattered green stems of every moment of Parker's childhood, or else she'd end up so surrounded by keepsakes, she wouldn't see what was really happening.

So she chucked the dandelion stems and started a new load of laundry, washed her hands with antibacterial soap, put the graham crackers away, and heated some water for chamomile tea.

Which, on second thought, wasn't nearly strong enough. She ignored the beeping microwave, and the cup of hot water inside it, and took out the bottle of red wine they kept on hand for guests and special occasions.

She'd just finished pouring when the phone rang. She grabbed for it before it rang again and woke Parker, and knocked over her wine in the process.

"Hello?" She cradled the phone on her shoulder and reached for a dishrag to clean up the mess. "Hello?"

*Click.*

She frowned and looked at the phone, as if the receiver itself would give some kind of clue as to who the caller had been. And in most houses it probably would, but Abbey and Brian didn't have caller ID on any of their phones. The hardware was all too old, though the service was probably on the line with the monthly bill they paid.

Immediately she pressed *69. She wasn't completely without modern resources. But not surprisingly, the recorded voice said the last number could not be traced.

He'd blocked it.

She knew, without any shadow of doubt, it had been Damon. He was doing it to rattle her, and it was working.

The phone rang again, in her hand, and she pushed the TALK button immediately. "Hello?"

No response.

"Not man enough to say anything, huh?" she taunted, then worried that it might be one of Brian's parishioners. But whoever it was, they didn't respond, and she held on to the line until she heard the click of him hanging up.

That left little doubt whether the silence was deliberate or merely the confusion of an elderly congregation member.

By the time the phone rang again, she was out of patience. "What do you want?" she demanded impatiently.

Again, there was no response.

"Listen, you evil son of a bitch," she hissed into the phone, one eye on the sleeping child several yards away. "You can call here all you want, but it's not going to get you one thin dime from me, do you understand?"

"*Abbey?* Is that you?"

No.

Oh, no.

It wasn't Damon. It was Tiffany Dreyer. Abbey had just cussed out Tiffany Dreyer *and,* in the process, given up a small corner of the secret she hoped would *never* get out.

"Um . . ." Abbey stalled, wondering if she could hang up the phone and get away with pretending it had been a wrong number.

But she couldn't. Tiffany could just look at the LED readout on her phone and see she'd called the right number. Touch REDIAL once, and she'd have Abbey or the answering machine. Unless, of course, Abbey picked up the phone every time it rang and then hung it up again.

Which was obviously too ridiculous a thing to even consider doing.

She was going to have to face the music. "Tiffany?" she asked, deciding to feel her out to see if she'd really heard everything Abbey had said.

"Who on *earth* did you think it was?" Tiffany asked.

Okay, so she'd heard it all.

"Um . . . I was . . ." Abbey paused. She wasn't good at this. "I thought it might be a crank caller."

"That was a lot of heat for one crank caller," Tiffany said.

"Yes, well, I've gotten several calls already today, and I was just fed up with it."

There was a hesitation before Tiffany asked, "Abbey, is something going on? Do you want to talk?"

"No," Abbey said quickly. "There's nothing going on. Parker's been sick, and I guess my nerves are a bit tight. Even a heavy breather doesn't deserve that kind of lashing out."

"Hm. I don't know about *that*." Tiffany gave a laugh. "Look, I'm actually calling to apologize. I'm really sorry for putting you on the spot about earning money. Of course, I understand why that particular plan isn't really an option for you."

"It's okay." Abbey's heart was still pounding. She took a short breath, trying to dislodge the tension that had gathered in her chest. "I didn't mean to overreact. I'm not a prude, believe it or not. I'm just thinking of Brian's reputation."

"It doesn't matter *why* you don't want to do it, if you don't want to do it. Though, for what it's worth, this really *can* be done with total anonymity," Tiffany said. "I mean, we're all *definitely* taking that seriously. You won't be associated in any way with some sort of scandal—don't worry."

"I'm not worried. You know, we just do what we have to do," Abbey said, thinking how very true it was. "I'd better run now. Parker's sick."

"The puking thing?"

Abbey was surprised, but decided she shouldn't have been. The other mothers at school socialized with each other, so this would be exactly the kind of thing that would come up. "Yes."

"It's going around. Lasts about twenty-four gruesome hours. Tell him I hope he feels better!"

"I will. Thanks." Abbey's other line clicked, and she pushed the TALK button, thinking it might be Brian. "Hello?"

It was no surprise when there was no response. The reason she'd expected it when Tiffany had called was because it was so completely like Damon to play it that way—to make his point, then to make it again, and to basically hammer it into Abbey's psyche until he was absolutely positive he'd gotten to her.

And broken her.

She hung up the phone, looked at it for a minute, then pressed the TALK button again, waiting patiently through the long dial tone and the seemingly endless series of alert beeps until finally there was silence on the line.

Only then did she allow herself the luxury of breathing again.

*We do what we have to do.* And if God wasn't going to help, she was going to do it herself.

# *Chapter* 7

"My name is Sandra Vanderslice, and I am a shoe addict," Sandra said to the puzzled faces of Tiffany and her friend Loreen. "That's how I got into the phone sex business. I had a habit I had no desire to give up, so I had to find a good, solid way to support it. But it doesn't matter *why* you need money; this truly is a good, honest way to earn it."

"Are you still doing it?" Loreen asked.

"Not anymore. I've started a new business with some friends. A shoe-import business. Which reminds me—" She reached for a shopping bag she'd brought and took out a pair of candy apple red Napa-wash-covered wedges, with four-inch heels and, at Sandra's suggestion, rubber inserts at the heel for comfort. "—this is the new Helene shoe. Does either of you wear an eight and a half?"

"I do!" Loreen said excitedly.

Sandra handed them over. "You're in luck. They're too big for me."

"And way too small for me," Tiffany added. She said to Sandra, "Let me know if you get any spare tens, though."

Sandra smiled. "You've got it. Anyway, until I actually got into the shoe business, I had to support my habit doing phone sex. And it was an excellent way to earn money."

"I'm trying to keep an open mind," Loreen said.

Tiffany nodded her agreement.

"The first thing you need to know is that you're *phone actresses,*" Sandra said. "You need to feel as uninhibited as possible by remembering none of your callers will ever find out who you really are."

"And how can we be sure there's no way a clever hacker could trace the call?" Tiffany asked, raising an eyebrow as if this might be something Sandra hadn't thought of before.

It was obvious Tiffany did *not* like being the one who needed help. Traditionally Tiffany was the one with all the answers, the one whose legacy Sandra was supposed to live up to.

This must be quite a comedown for her.

"There's no way that can happen," Sandra answered patiently, enjoying her position of authority, even drawing it out a little. "You log in at a distant network, and your calls are routed through them."

"What network?" Loreen asked. "Where? How do we do that?"

"I made a list." Sandra opened her purse and took out the copies she'd printed for Tiffany and her friend. "I recommend the one on top. They pay the most and can get you started right away. If you do local advertising, you know, like make up your own mini-franchise, they'll give you an even larger percentage."

"So if we do a mini-franchise," Tiffany said, "do we have to claim it that way on our taxes? 'Phone sex'?"

"Well, you *could*," Sandra said, growing a little irritated with Tiffany's tone. "Since it's *legal* and everything. But you can also just call it 'counseling' or something." She reached for one of the snacks Tiffany had set out—had she done these fancy little pigs in blankets as a jab at Sandra?—and popped it into her mouth even though she knew she shouldn't.

"So taxes aren't an issue." Loreen looked relieved.

"Not at all."

"So Abbey could have done this, too," Loreen said to Tiffany.

"I don't think she was worried about the legality," Tiffany said. "It's the *morality*."

"Now, wait a minute." This was one of Sandra's hot buttons. She didn't like to be accused of being immoral because of the phone sex. "Sex is a natural, healthy thing. As long as it's between two consenting adults, I don't think anyone should step in and say it's not *right*—"

"Abbey's husband is a minister," Tiffany interrupted.

"Oh." Sandra felt her face grow warm. "Whole different story, then." Tiffany nodded.

"Not that anyone would have to know she was doing it," Loreen said, a little petulantly.

Tiffany sighed. "Loreen, that's not the point." She looked back at Sandra. "So it's legal, you say."

"Yes. And as far as I'm concerned, it's perfectly moral, too." That sounded sarcastic, so she added, "But I'm not married to a minister."

The doorbell rang, and Tiffany excused herself. She returned a moment later with a surprised expression and a tall dark-haired woman with a light golden tan and amazing bone structure. She looked like a young Sophia Loren. "This is Abbey," she said to Sandra. "Abbey, this is my sister, Sandra Vanderslice."

"Abbey, I thought you weren't coming," Loreen said, looking as surprised as Tiffany.

Abbey shrugged. "There didn't seem to be any reason not to at least hear the details." She glanced at Sandra with an apologetic smile, then said to Tiffany, "I'm sorry I'm late, by the way. The traffic on 28 was barely moving."

"No problem at all," Tiffany said, getting another wineglass from the kitchen. "Do you want some wine? I have red or white."

Abbey appeared to contemplate it for a moment before saying, "White wine would be nice. Thanks very much."

Tiffany had a glass ice bucket with a bottle of white in it. She poured it into a lead crystal glass and handed it over to Abbey.

Sandra looked at Abbey with what she hoped wasn't obvious amazement. The woman was a bombshell. *Definitely* not what you'd picture a clergyman's wife to be. She didn't dress provocatively, but she had the sort of figure that looked sexy no matter what she was wearing. The woman probably could have rocked a nun's habit.

"We were just talking about how we can do this anonymously," Tiffany said to Abbey in what Sandra recognized as her persuasive voice. "Sandra said it's absolutely failsafe."

"Is that right?" Abbey asked.

Sandra sort of liked this. These women were looking at her like she was the Wise One, and that felt . . . pretty good.

"Yes, it is," Sandra said. "It's set up that way to protect phone sex operators—"

"Phone actresses," Loreen interrupted with a smile.

Sandra laughed. "Right. It's set up that way to protect phone ac-tresses and actors—"

"*Men* do this?" Tiffany asked with guileless wonder.

Honest to God, sometimes Sandra couldn't believe how naïve her sister was. After all, they'd grown up in the same *house*. How had mousy little Sandra ended up more worldly than gorgeous—and older—Tiffany?

Two words: Charlie Dreyer. Tiffany had married him right out of college and had been sheltered by the heavy rock of his domination ever since.

"Yes, Tiffany," she said, trying not to sound condescending. "Men do it. For women callers *and* men callers." She leveled her gaze on her sister. "Be prepared for some unusual requests." Things Charlie probably never would have dreamed of doing with his trophy wife.

"Unusual requests?" Tiffany asked. "Like what?"

She didn't want to freak Tiffany out. Why tell her that someone might want her to call him Daddy and hide her "report card" if it might never happen? "Actually, sometimes, maybe more than you might expect, guys who call just want to talk. I used to have a regular caller who used me as his therapist. It probably ended up costing *more* than real therapy, mind you. And it wasn't tax deductible for him, but he'd call once or twice a week anyway."

Tiffany brightened. "That sounds easy."

"It was," Sandra said. "But most of the callers want sex, of course. Don't forget that. And sometimes they want to pretend to be doing it in unusual places. You just have to go with it. And remember *it's no reflection on you*. And as soon as you hang up the phone, the person is gone. They cannot find out and most wouldn't even care to look."

"Well, I don't know about you two, but *I* think this sounds fun," Loreen said with what sounded like great optimism. "So, Sandra, how do we sign up?"

Sandra took a sip of her wine. It was good stuff. Not the cheap stuff she usually got. "If you're going to sub-franchise, which I rec-ommend, you'll have to answer a few questions about your theme, and so on."

"I'll do that," Loreen volunteered.

"Then you'll get a log-in number so you can call a central toll-free line and log in whenever you feel like it. If you've got a spare hour be-tween appointments, or before you have to drive the carpool, you can make some quick cash. You don't usually even talk to anyone there, but if there's a problem, they'll call you back. They're the only ones who know who you are and how to do it."

"How often do they pay?" Abbey asked with a spark of interest in her eyes.

"Weekly. *And* you can get direct deposit. Just open a designated account."

"Do you own stock in the company or something?" Loreen asked with a laugh.

Sandra shook her head, but saw Loreen's point. "Now that you mention it, I probably should. Never hurts to hedge your bets with a sure thing, and phone sex is *always* a sure thing." She was making a good living with her shoe company now, and loving every minute of it, but Sandra had no doubt that if she ever needed quick cash for any reason, she'd go back to phone sex in a heartbeat.

"All right, I'm sold," Loreen announced.

"Me, too," Tiffany agreed. "Absolutely."

"Now for the fun part," Sandra said. "Each of you will also need to come up with alter egos for yourselves."

There was a brief awed silence before Tiffany asked, "Alter egos?"

"Yes, the name you use. And the personality." Sandra was surprised how blank the faces before her remained. "They're not calling you,

Tiffany, or you, Loreen, or you, Abbey, if you decide to do it. You will make up a name, a history for yourself in case it ever comes up in conversation, and you'll also find a picture to put on the Web site to go with your name. Obviously not your high school senior picture. I made an amalgam of bits and pieces of celebrities, using Photoshop."

"You mean we make up characters to be?"

"Exactly." Sandra was relieved that at least one of them got it. "For example, I was Penelope."

"That was the name you made up?" Abbey asked. "Along with a picture and little fake biography? How fun."

"Yup." Sandra was pleased with herself.

But it was short-lived.

"Oh, my God," Tiffany gasped, actually clapping her hand to her mouth. "Sandra, are you serious? You were *always* Penelope." She paused expectantly. "You do remember that, right?"

"What?" Sandra asked. This was not part of her teaching curriculum. "What are you talking about?"

Tiffany laughed, clearly amazed that Sandra didn't remember this tantalizing psychological tidbit. "Every time we played when we were little, you wanted to be Penelope Pitstop and you always wanted me to be one of those horrid thuggish cartoon bad guys."

"Sylvester Sneakly?" Abbey suggested, her face really lighting up for the first time all evening.

"Yes!" Tiffany snapped her fingers and whirled on Sandra. "*Exactly*. I had to be Sylvester Sneakly or Snidely Whiplash."

"Wasn't that *Rocky and Bullwinkle?*" Abbey asked.

"I don't know!" Tiffany was cracking up now. "It didn't matter; I just had to be the bad guy, and she was the beautiful heroine. *Always*. Good Lord, Sandra, do you seriously not remember that?"

She didn't.

Or at least she *hadn't*.

But now it was coming back to her. And she was mortified that everyone was hearing how *she* wanted to be the beautiful heroine while *Tiffany* had to be the ugly bad guy. You didn't have to be a psychologist to figure *that* one out.

"I can't believe it," Sandra said, hoping she hadn't just lost all credibility. "Here I thought Penelope was a totally new invention and . . . wow. Subconscious at work, huh?"

Tiffany raised her eyebrows. "Indeed. I bet a psychologist could have a field day with this."

"Okay, fine, but that's not what we're supposed to be concentrating on right now," Sandra said, only half joking, because she was seriously disconcerted that she'd named her alter ego after her childhood alter ego and hadn't even realized it or all the deeply subconscious implications that went along with it. Wow. In the composite picture she'd made, she'd even given Penelope long blond 1980s Farrah Fawcett hair.

Just like Penelope Pitstop's.

And Tiffany's, at the time.

"Anyway," she finished. "It's evidently a good way to exorcize long-held demons, as well. So frankly, it's all win-win."

"What do you think, Abbey?" Tiffany asked.

Abbey hesitated. Then said, "Do I seem more like a Brandee, with two *e*'s, or a Suzi with an *i*?"

That released the tension in the room—or at least the tension Sandra was feeling—and everyone laughed.

"Brandee, with two *e*'s," Tiffany said. "No doubt."

"Absolutely," Sandra agreed.

"I *love* the idea of having an alias," Loreen said excitedly. "When I was little, I used to tell people my name was Mimi. Don't ask me why—I have no idea. But I think that's who I'll be: Mimi."

"I'm going to be Crystal," Tiffany said definitively. "Because I can't afford diamonds."

"And because you always drank Crystal Light?" Sandra suggested. It was weak, but she lobbed it out there anyway. Plus, it was true.

Tiffany laughed. "Maybe so. It's good to have a deep, dark reason for things."

"We all do, I guess," Sandra said, meaning it more than she could express. "So, with that in mind, let me show you the picture I Photoshopped of Penelope. . . ."

Tiffany got Charlie's laptop, and Sandra showed them Penelope as well as the various chat rooms where they could go to drum up business. She was amazed at the level of enthusiasm the women were demonstrating—even Abbey, who seemed to have more questions about the privacy and profit margin than the technique of phone sex. Interesting.

They talked through two hours and two bottles of wine, plus an entire sheet of the fabulous crescent roll cream cheese veggie squares Loreen had made. Sandra feared she'd been solely responsible for the consumption of at least half of them.

As they were wrapping up for the night, Loreen asked, "So . . . when do we meet again? Next week?"

"Oh! Yes! Can you do that?" Tiffany asked Sandra.

Sandra was surprised. She'd thought this was a one-off thing, but she'd be glad to have something social to do. "Yes, I guess—"

"Good, because I'm sure we're going to have more questions then," Loreen said.

"Probably a lot of them," Tiffany added.

Loreen nodded and looked back to Sandra. "Plus, aren't we going to need some sort of advanced training once we get the basics down?"

"There could be unexpected situations arising," Abbey added with a small smile.

Sandra laughed, though it wasn't clear if the other two got the joke. "You can bet on that."

"No," Loreen said, "no betting. Please. That's how I got into this mess in the first place. Cash advance after cash advance after cash advance." She shuddered visibly.

"And there was my shopping," Tiffany agreed.

Sandra looked at her sister and felt surprise, not for the first time this week. First, she couldn't believe Tiffany had gotten into trouble shopping too much, of all things. But second, it was nothing short of amazing that Tiffany had agreed to this phone sex thing at all, especially when Sandra considered how the conversation had gone when she'd suggested it to her.

That she had now turned it into a sort of Tupperware party among her friends was astonishing.

And really cool. Sandra was enjoying it. She'd really missed having girlfriends to shoot the bull with.

Last year, her Shoe Addicts Anonymous meetings had begun as a way to get out of the house and stop being such a hermit, but they had ended up showing Sandra just how very important it was to have women friends.

When it had turned into a business, selling Phillipe Carfagni's shoe designs, that had been great, but somewhere along the way, the work had taken over the social hours.

Now they rarely had time to get together. Helene was a single mother who really seemed to prefer baby stuff to social stuff; Lorna was doing a lot of traveling to their various accounts to sell the new designs so they could save money by not paying a whole sales team; and Joss had gone and fallen in love with Phillipe and was living in Italy, serving as his inspiration and as the business's Web mistress.

Sometimes Sandra missed the old days so much, she almost wished they'd never started the business. But she'd never admit that out loud.

But now maybe she'd have something to fill that gap. Simply by instructing these women on the secrets of being a phone sex operator, a job she knew inside out (ironically, from the time when she was most agoraphobic and *never* socialized).

"You really make it sound doable, Sandra," Loreen said, sounding hopeful but looking nervous. "I'm willing to try this. But I don't know if I have your confidence. I'm afraid I'll choke when it comes time to perform."

Sandra swallowed the urge to say, *Me? Confident? Get real!* Because she liked the idea so much, she didn't want to disillusion them. Plus, obviously, it would have been counterproductive. Instead she said, truthfully, "Everyone's nervous at first. At least, I was. But as long as you remind yourself that the person on the other end of the line can't see you, you can just"—she shrugged—"ham it up."

Loreen sat back and sipped her wine. "You're going to have to pony up a lot more of your secrets next week," she said, eyeing Sandra like she was holding out. *"The secrets of a shoe addict."* She laughed. "That can be our code. *Phone sex* sounds so tawdry. Though I'm thinking maybe I can use the phone sex tips if I ever start dating again."

"You should *see* Sandra's boyfriends," Tiffany said with what sounded like disbelief that Sandra could score a boyfriend. "At least the one I met a few months ago. Gorgeous."

Sandra didn't correct her. Not yet. She liked—in fact, she was *amazed by*—this perception of her.

"Are you still with him?" Tiffany asked Sandra. "What was his name?"

"I think you mean Mike," Sandra said, trying to think—quickly— how to play this, since she not only wasn't "still with" Mike, but it turned out she never had been. "No, it didn't work out. I'm free as a bird right now."

"So this gorgeous hunk is out there, available?" Loreen joked.

Tiffany's face grew serious, with that expression she always had when she was concocting a plan. "You know, Charlie's brother is in the process of getting a divorce—"

"Oh, good Lord, *Al*?" Sandra said, too quickly. Then, conscious that she might insult Tiffany if she accidentally revealed how much she *loathed* Charlie and his family, she added, "I think 'in the process of getting a divorce' is a danger zone. There's always the possibility of a reconciliation."

Tiffany considered. "I guess I see what you mean."

"Have you tried online dating?" Loreen asked Sandra. "I know a few people who have had really good luck with Match-dot-com."

"Did they meet normal, straight guys?" Sandra asked, cautious about men since Mike.

"Absolutely. A lot of executives and professionals are using online dating to meet people now because they don't have the time or presumably the stomach to go out trolling the bar scene." Loreen shuddered. "I'd rather be single forever."

"So would you do Match-dot-com or something like that?" Sandra asked, intrigued. "Based on what you've seen. Or is it something that's working for other people but you wouldn't do it yourself?"

Loreen looked at her evenly, considering. "If you're asking if I'd recommend it, based on what I've seen, yes. I don't know anyone who's met a George Clooney clone, but would you want to? My friends have met nice, reliable, professional guys with good jobs and health insurance, and occasionally even a sense of humor."

"So you'd do it," Sandra said.

"Yes." Loreen nodded. "Yes, I would. In fact, I might. Soon."

"As long as you're over Robert," Tiffany said. "Like we just said, the divorce process is a danger zone."

Loreen's face went pink. "Robert and I are not getting back together. And anyway, I didn't say I was going to do it tonight. For now, I'm just planning on having sex with strangers."

Sandra noticed that Abbey watched all of this with a serene but amused expression. It was curious how she seemed to be detached from the others, yet not disdainful or disapproving.

At least it didn't seem like she was.

Now Abbey spoke up. "You know, I thought Robert was watching you pretty intently during Field Day last month. He didn't seem as disinterested as you seem to think."

Loreen inhaled sharply. "Really? I didn't even notice. . . ." Unconsciously, it seemed, she raised a hand to her cheek. Then, as if shaking the notion off, she said, "Why are we even talking about this? The divorce is final next month. There's no point."

"Robert *is* a great guy," Tiffany said with conviction. "Believe me, they are few and far between. Are you sure you want to give that up?"

Loreen's expression faltered, slipping into a moment of sadness before returning to normal. "I don't think it's entirely up to me."

"If you have doubts, maybe you should talk to him before it's too late," Sandra said, unable to stop herself from giving what seemed like obvious advice, even though she was the last person in the world to speak with authority on the subject of romance. "Not that I know the situation or anything."

"It's *always* best to do what you can before you *know* it's too late," Abbey agreed. "Just in case there's a chance."

"There's no chance," Loreen said, calmly but firmly. "The relationship is like shredded paper at this point. I don't think we could find all the pieces to put it back together even if we both tried."

"I understand that," Abbey said.

"Well, *I* don't," Tiffany said. "The old pieces didn't work that well anyway. Start with a brand-new clean sheet of paper."

"When you're out of paper, you're out of paper," Loreen said, stretching the metaphor a little too thin. "Am I right, Sandra?"

Sandra pressed her lips together. She didn't believe love was gone until both people felt nothing, but what did she know? She'd never been married; she'd never even had a real long-term relationship. So she could hardly speak with authority to any of this. "So . . . switch to card stock? . . ."

"Ha!" Tiffany clapped her hands. "Perfect! It's stronger anyway!"

"Let's change the subject," Loreen said. "Next week? How about Monday, so we don't have to wait a whole week to get moving on this."

"Good idea," Tiffany agreed.

"Same place, or do you want to come to my house?" Loreen glanced at Abbey. "Or yours?"

"I'm not sure this is the kind of discussion that should take place there," Abbey said with a wan smile.

"Oh." Loreen's face went pink. "Right. Obviously. So what do you think, Tiffany? Monday? My place?"

"Works for me," Tiffany said. "Sandra?"

"You'll have to tell me how to get there, but sure."

"I'll pick you up," Tiffany said. "It's settled."

Sandra didn't object, regardless of the fact that she felt out of her league. It was enough, for now, that they all believed she was some sort of smart, experienced woman who knew the Ways of Men.

They'd learn the truth later, no doubt.

# Chapter 8

Loreen and Abbey's perception of Sandra as some sort of sex goddess continued to flatter Sandra. It was the first time anyone had *ever* thought she might have the edge over Tiffany for *any* reason.

Tiffany still seemed doubtful about Sandra.

And maybe she was right.

Here Abbey and Loreen thought she was this dating machine, with guys sniffing after her because of her amazing sexual knowledge and prowess (obviously not because of her Tiffany-esque looks), and the truth was she hadn't had a date in . . . Lord, she didn't even want to think about how long it had been.

She couldn't let them know what a failure she was with men—that would invalidate everything she was teaching them.

So what she had to do—what she'd been thinking about for a

while anyway—was get a date. Maybe truth would somehow spring from fiction.

So a few nights later, Sandra gathered her nerve, put on her favorite Bruno Magli platforms, with the butter-soft pearlized beige leather uppers, and sat down at the computer and pulled up Match.com. It wasn't her first visit to the site, and most of them—like tonight—took place around midnight, when she should probably know better than to dive into potentially emotional territory.

But if she didn't do it now, she'd probably never work up the nerve to do it in the middle of the day.

Plenty of people did this; there was no shame in it these days. In fact, there was *never* shame in finding your soul mate.

The shame she feared was the shame of being . . . disappointing. The shame of seeing her date's face drop from hopeful expectancy to horror and then, if she was particularly unlucky, pity.

The pity was the worst.

*Stupid girl, did you really think you could fool me once we met? It's one thing to act charming behind the anonymity of your computer screen, but surely you realize I can see you now.*

Sandra stopped that line of thought. It was stupid. Unfair, both to herself and to her prospective dates. No one would be *that* cruel. At least no one she'd communicate with enough to decide she'd like to meet him.

She was the one who was making her weight a problem.

She turned her attention back to Match.com and started to fill out the extensive questionnaire.

*Female.*

*28–34.*

*Nonsmoker.*

*Social drinker.*

*Libra.*

*Go to church occasionally, usually just on holidays.*

When the questionnaire got to "physical build" she had to choose between *slightly overweight but willing to work it off with the right person* and *no answer.* Now, it was theoretically possible to add the Magli heels to her height and come out normal (though on the voluptuous side). The problem, of course, was that after meeting her, anyone might have the idea that *no answer* was more honest than *slightly overweight but willing to work it off with the right person,* because of that *slightly,* and then she'd just have that whole look of disappointment and pity thing to deal with.

So she put the questionnaire on hold and switched over to Zappos.com, the world's greatest shoe site. Last week, Zappos had begun carrying the Carfagni fall line. Seeing the shoes she'd helped bring to the United States in glorious color on Zappos made her heart sing.

This called for a celebration. Every time.

She ordered a pair of Carfagni gilded slides, just to support the team, then switched over to the Manolo Blahnik page. She'd been a fan of the designer since well before *Sex and the City* because, at just over five feet two, Sandra needed serious heels. And heels needed serious comfort.

And that translated to confidence. If there was ever a time she needed confidence, it was now.

So a few clicks later, she had three pairs of shoes and one pair of retro kitten-heel boots on the way to her, via two-day express, and she had bolstered her confidence enough to go back to Match and give her honest answer.

If someone was going to be disappointed in her, then he could go straight to hell. She was going to answer this thing the way she felt, not the way she thought someone else felt.

She took a breath and filled in the form. To hell with it.

*Slightly overweight but willing to work it off with the right person.*

⁎

Brian was at the church, Parker was probably in the school cafeteria eating one of the many variations of pizza that seemed to show up on the menu daily, and Abbey was dappling Parker's white button-down shirt from Easter with a Tide stick in her laundry room when the phone rang.

She'd been waiting for this call even while dreading it, so when it came, it was almost a relief.

"Hey, babe."

"How did you get this number?" she asked Damon, though the point was moot. He'd gotten the number, now he had it, so what else mattered?

He just chuckled. "You're listed, sweetheart. It wasn't hard. Got to be able to get ahold of the preacher if there's a preacher emergency. Hey, is he there? I'd like to have a chat with him."

So he knew who Brian was and probably assumed—rightly so— he was a peaceful man who wasn't going to be a threat to Damon. Unless the situation called for it. "Sorry, he's not here. Would you like to leave a message?"

Damon laughed again. He understood her. She'd give him that: he'd always understood her. "Nah, I think I'll just settle for you. So how's the collection going?"

"Collection?" She knew what he meant.

She was right. "My money. Nine g's. I've decided to give you a break and make it nine g's. You're welcome."

"I don't have it."

"Well, now, you might want to start thinking about *getting* it. Because I'm not kidding around with this. I'll break your fingers one by one if I have to. Oh, and fingers? That's a metaphor."

Oh, crap. This was bad. She knew him well enough to know this was bad. "Metaphor, huh? Where did you learn such a big word?"

"Metaphor," he restated. "Meaning I don't mean I'm going to break your fingers; I'm going to break all the things that matter to you, one by one. Is that big enough for you?"

Something about the way he said it ran fear through her veins. It was one thing for her to stand up to him, especially if it was twelve years ago and she didn't have anyone to feel responsible for besides herself. But it wasn't twelve years ago, it was now, and this son of a bitch was scary.

"Almost big enough," she said, trying to maintain her sardonic tone to keep him from realizing how truly nervous he made her. "As is always the case with you. Still, I get your point."

There was a long silence during which she knew he was digesting her insult and deciding what to do with it. But she also knew *him* well enough to know that he was more interested in recouping supposedly lost money than exacting personal, emotional revenge on someone and risking losing said lost money.

"So where's the money?" Damon asked, getting down to business just as she knew he would.

"Ask the police."

"You didn't call the police." There wasn't even a shade of uncertainty in his voice. "You wouldn't dare."

"No?"

"Mm-mm. From what I gather, you don't want anyone in your little church to know what you used to do. Dealing drugs, sexing for bucks—" He gave a hard laugh. "—blowing cops to get out of charges. Man, you were lucky I kept you around as long as I did."

She swallowed hard. Thank God Parker wasn't here. Thank God no one was here to pick up the phone, or stand nearby asking for Oreos and overhear what Damon was saying.

Would she deny it?

*Could* she deny it? Any of it?

"So I'll ask you again, where's the fucking money?"

"I'm working on it," she demurred. *Play it cool, play it cool, don't let him know he's gotten to you.* "How does that grab you?"

"It grabs me right in the nuts, how do you think it grabs me?" he said. "What, do you have the law involved?"

She gave a snort of fake laughter that she hoped he'd think was real. "You think I want to pay a lawyer to get rid of the likes of you? No thanks. I'm working on coming up with some equitable payment that will get you off my aching back, okay? In the meantime, why don't you give me a number where I can call you when I'm ready?"

"Oh, and you'll just do that, huh? Call me when you have my money?" She could imagine the dark scowl that tightened his features. "No thanks, sweetheart. I'll give you a little more time, and a few more warnings, then I'm going to take something from you that will make up for what you took from me."

His words struck terror in her heart. What kind of warnings? What did he think she had that could "make up for" his "loss"? Damon had never had a proper sense of proportion, so he'd probably end up aiming for her heart, *thinking* it was equivalent.

She had to come up with money for him. Much as she hated the idea, and even though she'd given the necklace away years ago, before she had anything like a family or even a single loved one to protect, now she had to recoup that loss—karmically *taking away* from charity—and give it back.

The very thought made her ill.

But she knew if she showed fear, if she showed any hint of vulnerability at all, Damon would up the ante, and she couldn't afford the ante as it was.

"Damon, you know damn well it's not like I can just go to the ATM and get that kind of money."

"You could give me the necklace."

"I told you I don't have it anymore."

"That's what you said."

"Do you think I'm *lying*?" She clicked her tongue against her teeth and was glad he couldn't see the way her hand shook as she held the phone to her ear. "I thought you knew me better than that."

"I know you better than you think."

Wrong. "Then don't you know that if I had it, I'd give it to you just so I'd never have to see your vile face again?"

"I thought I saw a little spark of desire in your eyes when you saw me. A little of that gleam you used to get before we'd get down and—"

"Shut up."

"Hurts to remember what you lost, huh?"

"Just tell me where to find you when I have the money."

"I told you, I'll come to you. How should I put this? Mmm . . . you'll feel my presence around you all the time. When you're ready, just whistle." He laughed and hung up the phone.

Immediately she dialed *69, just in case he'd slipped up, but he hadn't. Of course he hadn't.

She sank to the floor, holding the phone against her chest, and felt the tears come like a tsunami she was powerless to stop or escape.

She didn't ask herself how her life had come to this. She knew. It had been coming to this for years. How stupid she was to think that just because a few years passed without it catching up with her, she had gotten away with it all scot-free. She'd *thought* she'd turned her life around. *Thought* she'd made up for her past mistakes, or at least made up for *some* of them, but no—here she was right in the thick of it.

It was as if the past twelve years didn't mean a thing.

Brian was an illusion.

Parker was an illusion.

It was the thought of Parker that really got to her. A montage of images raced through her mind—the first ultrasound in which he was declared "normal" despite her past with drugs; the day he was born; the first Christmas; the first day of school; the first lost tooth; and a million days in between—and disappeared into the ether like they'd never happened.

What would happen if Brian found out about her? Would he leave? How could he not? And how could he leave Parker with a woman like her?

Abbey clutched the phone with white knuckles and sobbed until her chest ached. Then she did something she hadn't done in years. Something she'd never thought she'd do again.

She dialed a number she'd tried since high school to forget.

"Hello?" a woman's voice trilled.

"Mom?"

"Becky, where *are* you? I thought you and the kids were coming over to go for a swim!"

Becky had kids now? How could that be when she was just a kid herself? Except that she wasn't. Thirteen years ago, she'd been eleven. Now she was a grown woman.

"It's not Becky, Mom." The silence between her words seemed to echo. "It's Abbey."

The chill that came across the line was nearly palpable. "I told you never to call here again."

The pain was extreme. "Mom, I—"

A heavy sigh. As if they'd just had this conversation five minutes ago and she was fed up with it. "What is it, Abigail? Have you been arrested again? Did one of your *johns* beat you up again?"

Abbey should have felt shocked, but she didn't. These accusations had come before. "I'm not a hooker, Mom; I never—"

"You don't wait ten years and call out of the blue unless you want something. I know your type."

Thirteen years. It had been thirteen. What kind of mother didn't know something like that? And what kind of mother was so hard, so cold, that after thirteen years of silence and uncertainty she didn't have one single soft impulse toward her own child?

"Nothing's wrong, Mom. I have a good life. I'm married, I have a son—" The words caught in her throat. "You have a grandson, Mom. His name is—"

"I have two grandsons. Trent and Kurt, and they're on their way over here now, so I don't have time to argue with you, Abigail. Now if you'll excuse me—"

"Mom, please!" The words came out without thought. Without consideration. Just the primal pleading of a child to her mother, begging for help.

But it was too late for that. Far, *far* too late.

Her mother had already hung up the phone.

Abbey sat still. Motionless. What else could she do, with her life spinning out of control?

Becky had kids: two sons. She'd named one after her and Abbey's father, Kurt.

He would have liked that.

Or he *probably* would have liked it. He died when Abbey was fourteen and Becky was just six, so what did she really know about him, besides the fact that he smelled of Old Spice, always had those round red and white peppermints in his pockets, and was soft-spoken? Like Brian.

And once he'd gone, it was as if Abbey had been left with a mother who more resembled a wicked stepmother from a fairy tale. The more she tried to get her mother's attention, the more her mother hated her. Until they'd finally reached this peak that her mother had apparently never come down from. She hated Abbey. She hated her enough not even to care that she had a grandson through Abbey.

Poor Luella Parker Generes.

She'd never know what her hostility had lost her.

And what it had cost her daughter and her grandson.

# Chapter 9

T his is Mimi," Loreen practiced in a sexy whisper. She was holding her new pay-as-you-go cell phone in her lap, waiting for her first phone sex call. She wasn't quite sure how to approach it. "Hello, there," she said, in a lower voice this time. "I'm Mimi, who are you?" Only she sounded more like Rula Lenska from those old Alberto VO5 commercials. "Mimi here," she tried, with a crisp British accent.

Nope. Decidedly unsexy.

The phone rang in her lap and she was so startled she jumped and it went skidding across the floor.

The ringing stopped.

She scrambled to grab it. "Hello?" Nothing. *"Hello?"* she repeated, more frantically.

A man cleared his throat on the other end of the line. "I—I'm not sure I have the right number."

"You do!" She was too eager. "I mean, this is Mimi," she added, shooting for sexy but hitting psychotic. "What can I do for you? To you? What can I do *to* you?"

Silence.

"Hello? Are you there?"

"Yeah."

"Oh. Good. So what do you want to do?" She sounded like she was setting up a playdate.

"Uh . . . nothing. Thanks." He hung up the phone. And who could blame him?

Jeez, she'd really messed that up.

Hopefully he'd call back.

She waited for a few minutes, phone in hand, but it didn't ring again.

Wearing the new shoes Sandra had given her for inspiration, she tiptoed into Jacob's room, for about the twentieth time, to make sure he was really asleep. He was. Until the phone in her hand rang. She clutched it and ran from the room so it wouldn't wake Jacob up, but in the process she pushed the OFF button and hung up on her second caller.

Why was this so *hard*?

So she wandered back into her own room, hoping the phone would ring again so she could at *least* save her pride and try again.

It did ring again. This time she was ready. Or so she thought.

"This is Mimi," she said, and was actually impressed with her own calm, sexy intonation. "Who's calling?"

"Mom? I've been naughty."

Oh, for Pete's sake. Her shoulders slumped. "I'm sorry, honey, you have the wrong number." She hung up quickly so the poor kid didn't have to incur a big phone bill that he'd later have to explain to his parents.

Then she realized that (1) the caller hadn't sounded like a kid, and (2) every caller got a warning message before the charges started, stating the cost-per-minute and the fact that they needed to be over eighteen. Now, that didn't preclude a younger kid from calling anyway and pretending to be eighteen or older, but it *did* mean that no one could possibly call and sit through all of that and then think he was talking to his mother.

So she'd just lost a *third* caller.

Zero for three.

What was she going to do?

✳

Midnight. Time for Tiffany to be Crystal.

Tiffany crept around the house from room to room, like Santa Claus making sure everyone was asleep before she pulled out her bag of tricks.

In this case, though, her bag of tricks was a crib sheet of dirty talk she'd gotten from Sandra. She called the relay computer and logged in, turning on the virtual neon OPEN FOR BUSINESS sign.

Then she waited in the basement, by the washer and dryer, for calls to come in on her new designated phone. In the meantime she folded laundry, dividing everything neatly into four piles—one for each of them.

When she found a man's bathing suit with huge hibiscus flowers splashed on it in Charlie's things, she hesitated. Why would Charlie have a bathing suit out at this time of year? The community pool didn't open until next week, and his last couple of business trips had been to Cleveland.

Hadn't they?

Was Charlie *lying* to her?

Tiffany pondered this for a few minutes, almost as puzzled by her own lack of feeling as she was by the mystery of the swimsuit. It was possible, of course, that there was a logical explanation for it. Maybe there had been a mix-up at the hotel cleaners; maybe the hotel had even had an indoor pool and Charlie had decided to use it.

But what about when Charlie had called her from Cleveland, supposedly, and she'd thought she heard a steel drum band in the background?

There was only one reason Charlie would lie about being someplace that had a steel drum band, and that was because he was there with someone else.

Still . . . it was hard to imagine. If he was having an affair, wouldn't he be sucking up to her and being nicer than ever? Instead he'd been the same bear around the house that he'd always been.

She folded the bathing suit and put it on top of Charlie's pile, where he couldn't help but see it and know that she'd seen it, too.

It would be interesting to hear what he had to say about that.

In the meantime, she wasn't going to feel quite so guilty about having virtual sex with strangers. If anyone called, that was.

By 12:20, the phone still hadn't rung, and Tiffany was starting to feel like an idiot for sitting in the darkened basement, among the brooms and mops, boxes of Christmas decorations, and the large highly scented boxes of Bounce dryer sheets she'd bought at Costco. At one point, someone had sent her an e-mail with about a hundred things one could do with Bounce sheets—everything from taping them under the kitchen counter to get rid of ants to soaking one in your lasagna pan overnight to loosen the baked-on cheese and sauce.

Rubber banding them to the receiver of your phone in hopes of disguising your voice in case someone you knew called you for sex hadn't been on the list.

But she hoped it worked.

Five minutes of finger-tapping later, there were still no calls, and she was beginning to grow offended that no one liked Crystal. Which was absurd on just so many levels, because Crystal was an amalgam of some of the sexiest women in show business and porn sites today. Tiffany had anticipated more calls than she could keep up with.

She got up and made her way to the spare fridge they kept drinks and overflow items in. There was a box of Franzia wine she'd been keeping for ages because she'd seen on a cooking show that boxed wines were the best to keep on hand for cooking because the packaging really did keep them fresh.

Well, right now, *Tiffany* needed to feel a little fresh. So she rinsed out the lid of the detergent bottle and tapped some wine into it, then returned to her place on a pile of clean folded towels and felt pathetic drinking out of the still-slightly-soapy plastic.

She was so deep in self-pity that when the phone did actually ring, she was so startled she dropped it, knocking the battery out. She scrambled to put it back together, hands shaking with frenzy, but it was too late, the call was lost.

And with it, perhaps the only ego gratification she was going to have all night.

When the phone rang a moment later, she was *still* unprepared, but she made an effort to collect herself and answer, in the most seductive Jessica Rabbit voice she could, "This is Crystal—"

"Tiffany Dreyer?"

*Oh*, shit! Had she accidentally been sitting here holding her regular cell phone instead of the pay-as-you-go one she'd purchased for *Crystal*?

Tiffany put the phone back to her ear. "Yes?"

"Yeah, look, this is Ed at the relay center. It looked like a call was just cut off on your line. Was that on purpose?"

"No, I dropped the phone."

"So you *do* want calls?"

"I'm available for them," Tiffany corrected carefully. She didn't want to put the word out into the universe that she *wanted* calls, exactly. Then again, she didn't want to sound like a petulant brat who was doing this grudgingly.

"Cool," Ed said. "You were specifically requested, so the next time your phone rings, it won't be me."

Tiffany waited just a couple of minutes, flattered that she'd been *requested*, before the phone rang again.

By now, the wine was warming her up a little, so she took a quick breath and flipped the phone open. "Hey . . . this is Crystal. . . ." She turned it up at the end like a question.

"Hey, um . . . Crystal?" It was a husky male voice, not remotely familiar. At least not so far.

"Yes, who's this?" Tiffany cooed.

"This—" He cleared his throat. "—this is Pete, er, Derek. This is *Derek*."

"How are you doing tonight, Derek?" This was easy. So far, anyway.

Particularly since Pete/Derek sounded so much more nervous than she did.

"Good, good." There was the faint sound of him clapping his hands together nervously.

At least, she *thought* it was his hands.

And that it was nervousness.

"Where are you tonight, Derek?" She had her notes from Sandra on hand, but so far she hadn't needed to consult them: (1) call him by the name he wants, even if it's obviously fake, and (2) ask questions to draw him out and use up time *before* getting down to business.

Frankly, she wasn't looking forward to the *getting down to business* part.

"I'm at home."

"Where is home?"

"Kensing . . . uh, Potomac, Maryland." The guy was a terrible liar. It was almost endearing.

"Oooh, I like Potomac. Do you have a nice big house?" Sure. It was probably right down the street from Ted Koppel's place.

"Yeah." He took a shuddering breath she later realized must have been the gathering of his nerve. "And I want to fuck you with it."

Crystal should have gone with this, but Tiffany was so shocked by the change of subject that she said, "I beg your pardon?"

"Huh? Oh. Hey, that's good. So I say I'm from Potomac and you get all hoity-toity like you're from Potomac." He gave an earthy chuckle. "That's good, I like that. Take off your diamonds and jewelry, bitch."

Tiffany was seriously disconcerted by his transition between awkward geek named Peter from Kensington, to Asshole Derek from Potomac, but as long as he was paying the exorbitant fee to talk to her, she was going to try to keep the conversation going.

"All of them?"

"All of them."

The old chain collar they'd used on Rover—yes, Tiffany's family had actually had a dog named Rover, in part because it was so rare—was hanging on the wall opposite her, so she took a few stealthy steps toward it, took it off the hook, and then set it down on the concrete floor, link by link. "There goes my necklace." *Clink clink clink.* "And my bracelet." Then, as an afterthought that felt like brilliance, "Do you want me to take off my nipple ring?"

The idea of having a nipple ring struck Tiffany as so incredibly stupid that it was funny for her to play the role of the kind of girl who would have one. Or more.

Presumably of the expensive variety.

"Is it like Janet Jackson's?"

Tiffany remembered Janet Jackson's Super Bowl wardrobe malfunction, but she couldn't remember the nipple ring. Not that it mattered. She'd never have to prove it. "It's exactly the same," she said, shrugging to herself.

"Can I touch it?"

"Of course." Then, in case that wasn't inviting enough, "I want you to."

"Man," he breathed. "It's cold. Does that cold metal turn you on?"

"Yes." Why not? "Does it turn *you* on?"

There were a couple of grunts and moans, and Tiffany had her answer.

"I gotta go," he said. "Thanks."

He clicked off, apparently unwilling to spend one dime more than necessary once he was finished.

She couldn't blame him, really. You wouldn't pay a housekeeper extra to stick around and talk about the Washington Redskins. Why bother with niceties?

The call had lasted approximately four minutes. It was still more than ten bucks. Way better money than she'd make working retail.

And it had been easy.

When Sandra had first mentioned the idea, Tiffany had had visions of really perverted talk, graphic descriptions, and porn movie sound effects. The whole idea had been pretty daunting.

But this had been no sweat. She could do a hundred of these calls without ever feeling too funny about it.

First Sandra and now Tiffany—was it something that ran in the family? She was adopted, so she and Sandra weren't actually *blood* relatives, but maybe there was some sort of subversive messaging in the old mystery series books they read as kids. Maybe Nancy Drew had a hot life after midnight.

Who knew?

All Tiffany knew was that maybe she'd be able to pay off her Finola Pims debt *and* get herself a little convertible before too long.

⁎

"Put me in a diaper and make it *real tight*."

Abbey, who was on her third call as Brandee, groaned inwardly. Three calls in a row, and all three of them oddballs. Number one had wanted her to bark like a dog to the tune of the national anthem. Number two begged her to speak only pig latin—which she found she was surprisingly good at. Now number three had requested a bare-bottom spanking and then a diaper.

This was *not* the kind of phone sex she was accustomed to.

Well, actually, she wasn't accustomed to *any* phone sex anymore.

But that was changing rapidly. With Brian asleep in bed after a long day, and Parker asleep in bed after a long bath, Abbey had gone outside to the detached garage and was sitting in the car in the dark, taking calls.

There was something almost meditative about it, sitting quietly in the car. And she needed that peace after the day she'd endured. It helped her collect herself. Until the phone rang, that was. Then it was just all carnival.

"How's this?" she asked, reclining the seat and looking out the window at the collection of rakes and shovels Brian had hanging neatly on the wall in order of size and function. "Tight enough?"

Her caller let out a squall that was probably supposed to be his imitation of a baby, but it sounded more like a balloon losing air. "Spank me again. I've been so bad!"

God, she hoped this guy didn't have kids. Given his poor imitation of a baby, and his insufficient understanding of how a diaper works (*tight?* they didn't get that tight without the tape pulling off), she was pretty sure he didn't. In fact, she was prepared to go out on a limb and say the guy was completely unattached.

"Now put me in one of those outfits with the feet," her caller said.

"Pajamas?"

"Yeah, yeah. Footsie pajamas. Made of cotton. With a *really hot* zipper. Like, they just came out of the dryer."

And so it went. She diapered him. She dressed him. She undressed him when the zipper was too hot. She worked on potty-training him. She decided this was the year to take out her raspberry bushes and grow some heirloom tomatoes. (The tomato cages in the corner of the garage reminded her of that—she'd bought them last year but never got around to using them.)

And she accumulated four solid hours' worth of billable minutes.

In the end, it wasn't what she'd call *easy*—she'd never dreamed there were so many whack jobs out there just waiting for the chance to share their depraved fantasies with a stranger.

But it was a good thing there were, because she needed the money.

So she turned off her phone and put it in the glove compartment of her car, figuring this was the perfect place to do business. No one could sneak up on her and surprise her, and if Brian or Parker did head out this way looking for her, she'd see them long before they saw her.

It wasn't exactly an executive's corner office in Manhattan, but it suited her needs just perfectly.

# Chapter 10

So how long have you been a ventriloquist?" Sandra asked Louis Feller (aka McCarthy2 on Match.com) as she steered her Toyota away from Clyde's of Georgetown. She was just filling the silence during the ten to fifteen minutes it would take her to drive him to the Metro at Tenley Circle, but she had already given up hope of good conversation.

The blind date had, so far, lasted an hour and ten minutes but had felt like years. She'd asked herself all night, Was forty-five minutes long enough for her to politely cut out? An hour? At an hour and ten, she'd decided she'd given him plenty of time.

"I'm not a ventriloquist," Arlon said, in Louis's grating falsetto. It was like nails on a chalkboard at this point. "*He's* the one with his hand up my ass."

That was a new twist on what had already been a tedious act. Now Arlon/Louis was getting foul. Nice.

Before tonight, Sandra had not imagined she would ever think about whether the ventriloquist or the dummy was more annoying. Then Louis had spent the entire dinner having Arlon tell Sandra the long and painful story of his life.

Arlon's, not Louis's.

She knew that Arlon had been "born" in Brooklyn twelve years ago, and that he'd traveled to D.C. by train and had gotten lost at the 20016 post office for three weeks until finally someone had found the box under a bunch of mail that was being kept on hold. By the time he was presented to his new owner, his head was loose and Louis had to interview numerous craftsmen before finding someone he trusted to safely repair the doll.

The "surgery" had, apparently, been painful.

His hair hadn't originally been black, but he and Louis decided it would look better in contrast with his light brown molded plastic porkpie hat.

Plus, it covered the occasional imaginary gray hair.

Arlon had an interest in girls with good posture and warm hands. He did not like to vacation near water, though he had a fantasy about "getting it on" in the sand because it reminded him of sawdust. It was an image that was not only disgusting on several levels, but also highly disturbing. Something about the dummy wanting to do that in sawdust—even if it were possible—was uncomfortably akin to a person wanting to do it on piles of human flesh.

Yes, it had been a long night. So long that Sandra was actually contemplating the implications of a ventriloquist dummy wanting to have sex on the beach.

Arlon didn't reveal much about Louis, though Sandra could safely guess Louis had an interest in girls who had an interest in his stupid ventriloquist act.

It was hard to imagine who that would be.

So much for Loreen's grandiose ideas of what Sandra's romantic life must be like.

As they drove on the cracked pavement of the street, Sandra figured she had nothing to lose by goosing Louis for information, if only so she could give a full accounting of this night to the Phone Sex Group later. "Louis, this has been really funny. Especially that thing you did at dinner when you asked the waiter for a glass of water? That was comedy gold." She cringed, remembering, and automatically put a hand to the place on her shirt that was still wet. "But can we put Arlon in the backseat for a while and get to know each other on a more, um, *real* basis?"

Granted, Sandra had not had a lot of—okay, any—boyfriends in her life; nevertheless, she had never anticipated having to ask a date to put his imaginary self in the backseat so she could talk to the real thing.

But her Match.com profile hadn't exactly gotten a lot of visitors, so she was reluctant to dismiss a date out of hand before she was beyond sure things wouldn't work.

Maybe Louis was a great guy whose one glaring fault was that he didn't know when a joke should end.

Maybe that was something he could learn.

Maybe then he'd be perfect for Sandra.

"What are you saying?" Arlon asked, his hinged jaw flapping and clapping. "You don't like me?"

Then again, maybe not.

She glanced at Louis. "Yes, of course I like the puppet. I think you're enormously talented," and until now she'd thought he was kind of cute, with his dark eyes and light, curly hair, "but you've been doing Arlon all night long now and I'd like to get to know Louis."

"The nuns were mean to him in school," Arlon said.

"What?" She couldn't help but look into the puppet's flat, lifeless eyes. Consciously, she shifted her gaze back where it should be, to Louis. "What is he——? What are you talking about? Nuns were mean to you?"

"No, they were fine." Louis tightened his lips into a flat line—much like Arlon's, actually—and looked out the window.

For a moment, Sandra remained hanging between interest in the fact that Louis himself was finally talking, and apprehension at the fact that he was disagreeing with something he'd just said.

"O . . . kay. Well, Arlon just said——" She stopped. She was *not* going to start quoting Arlon and making this into an argument between her, her blind date, and a puppet. "That is, *you* just said the nuns were not so nice to you in school."

"Arlon said that." Louis gave an exasperated sigh. "He's such a fucking liar."

Harsh words for a puppet that he, himself, was animating.

Where had she gone wrong? Was it obvious on his profile that the guy was a whack job? Had she missed it because she was so eager to like him when he wrote? Her last date—no, her last fifteen dates, all of them with Mike Lemmington—had been gay, so she had to give a more than fair shot to anyone else who came along. "Okay, Louis? Seriously, drop the act."

It wasn't bright in the car, but there was enough light to see that he looked sincerely befuddled. "What act?"

Sandra noticed that Arlon's wooden head turned to look at her the same time Louis did.

"The *ventriloquist* act." She was losing patience. Enough was enough. And this was way more than enough. "When you wrote to me on Match, I had the impression you were interested in getting to know me, not just performing for me."

"I didn't write to you."

*"What?"* Now, Sandra had certainly been eager to get a response to her profile, but not so eager that she'd *imagined* he'd written first. Frankly, given his profile answers, he probably wasn't someone she would have picked out and approached herself. "You *did* write to me."

"No, I didn't."

"But . . . yes, you did." Was this all some big crazy misunderstanding? Had he meant to write to someone else, perhaps a mime in Alexandria?

"No, I didn't," he said yet again, with exaggerated patience. "Arlon wrote to you."

*Oh, my God.* "I don't think so."

"You're not my type."

Incredibly, she felt insulted. "I think that's something we can safely agree on, but when I got the note, it clearly said the account was that of Louis F., and you *are* Louis Feller, aren't you?"

Louis nodded. "Of course. But Arlon needed to use my credit card information, obviously. You didn't think he had his own card, did you?"

No. Because expecting a doll to have human qualities was *insane.* "So let me get this straight," she said, a creepy feeling coming over her. She knew where this was headed, but she couldn't stop it. "You're saying you aren't the one that approached me, Arlon is."

"Correct."

"And you just helped him out."

He shot a finger gun in her direction. "Exactly."

"So I'm on a date with—" She hesitated, hideously aware that she was about to hit a new low in dating. "—Arlon?"

Louis nodded again.

Like, of course.

"Got a problem with that?" Arlon snapped.

"Yes, I have a problem with that." Sandra turned the car onto Wisconsin Avenue and accelerated as much as her conscience would allow. She didn't want to hit a person, but she was willing to take her chances with the police in order to get this lunatic out of the car. "I don't date puppets."

"First of all," Arlon screeched, "stop calling me a *puppet*. I have a name."

"Okay, sorry, you're a dummy. Is that better?" Now she was getting sarcastic with her wooden date. Great.

"Both of you calm down," Louis said, sounding oddly like the voice of reason.

The traffic loosened and she drove up the hill out of Georgetown, looking for the comforting sight of the National Cathedral.

"Sorry," Sandra said, without meaning it. "You're right, let's just get to the Metro station and call it a draw. This obviously isn't going to work out."

"You're a bitch," Arlon said.

She was looking at the road, but in her peripheral vision she saw Arlon's head crank to face Louis and—she hated that she knew this— they both nodded.

Sandra's foot went a little heavier on the accelerator.

Louis's voice was next. "Now, that's not entirely fair, Arl."

*Arl.* He had a nickname for his puppet, who, really, *already had* a nickname.

"—she's just ignorant."

Sandra adjusted her grip on the steering wheel and wished she could floor it past all these slowpoke law-abiders who were stopping for red lights and pedestrians.

"I am not *ignorant*," she objected, though, God knew, she should just have kept her mouth shut until they got to the Metro stop. Clearly there was nothing more to say. "I'm *normal. Anyone* would react this way to this situation."

"I'd think you'd be glad to have a date," Arlon said.

She drew the car to a halt at a stoplight and turned a murderous gaze on the dummy. "I beg your pardon?"

"It's not like your profile had a lot of hits." The jaw clapped with every word.

"How dare you—"

"It's true."

The light turned green, and she lurched forward. The Metro stop was within view. Thank God. "I am not so desperate that I am willing to date a *puppet* with an insensitive freak along as chaperone." She didn't care if she got a ticket; it would be worth the price just to get these creeps out of the car.

"You're lucky I gave you a chance," Arlon said as Sandra pulled over to the curb in front of the station.

"Funny, I'm not feeling so lucky about that."

"You should be. Have you had any better offers?"

Pat Sajak and Alex Trebek and a pint of Ben & Jerry's was a far better offer.

But Sandra refused to engage in this argument any longer. She was taking the high road, damn it.

Or at least the high*er* road. The exit for the high road had passed a few miles back.

She put the car in park and hit the button to unlock the doors. "Get out of the car, please."

"Now, come on," Louis began.

"Out!"

Louis rolled his eyes and moved to get out of the car. "Fine. We're going. But you'll be sorry later."

"I'm sorry now."

He stopped. "Then I accept your apology."

"Not that kind of sorry. Go." He started to move toward her, and she held up her hand. *"Go!"*

"No kiss good night?" The exaggerated wooden face came toward her like a specter in the dark.

She pushed him away. "No, jeez, *stop* it!"

"You're fat!" Arlon shrieked, apropos of nothing.

That did it. Of the many sensitive buttons Sandra had, that was the hottest. Without thinking, without even pausing to question the wisdom of it, she balled up her fist and punched Arlon hard, right in his painted bulbous nose.

His head went flying off, slamming against the window and bouncing into the backseat.

Louis looked at Sandra, stunned.

Actually, in that moment, he looked quite a bit like Arlon.

Her heart was pounding. What the hell had just happened? She hadn't meant to break the thing.

Polite to a fault, she started to apologize. "Louis, I didn't mean to—"

"Help! Help!" Incredibly, the voice actually sounded like it was coming from the backseat. It was even muffled. Sandra was slightly impressed, despite herself.

"I'm coming, buddy." Louis dived into the back and retrieved the head, trying to put it back on the severed neck. It was like some sick parody of the Zapruder film. He looked at Sandra with tears in his eyes. "You stupid cunt."

Her guilt dissolved. There were only a few words that got her ire up immediately and completely, and that was one of them. "*That* is verbal assault. Get out of the car before I call the police." She had no idea if she could actually call the police on a date she had gotten herself into, but the threat seemed to work.

He'd probably heard it before.

"I'll send you the bill for this repair," he said, cradling Arlon's body in one hand and his head in the other. "And if you don't pay, I'll sue!"

"Good luck, Gepetto." She jammed her foot onto the accelerator, and the door slammed shut, making the perfect statement. Fortunately there was no oncoming traffic, because in her frenzy she hadn't even looked.

She rounded a corner, and the sidewalk where she'd left Louis fell out of view, and she breathed a sigh of relief. What a nightmare! The entire thing had left her rattled. Her foot shook on the accelerator, and she struggled to keep her focus on the road.

Up until about a year ago, she used to have a standing weekly appointment with Dr. Ratner, a therapist who had helped her with her anxiety and agoraphobia. That last appointment, knowing she was through, had given her a great feeling.

But an experience like this might be enough to drive her straight back to Dr. Ratner's loving armchair.

She was almost home when a dark Volvo swerved in front of her to avoid hitting a drunk who had stumbled into the street. Sandra's reflexes were good, and she got her foot on the brake immediately, but the pedal wouldn't depress. Frantic, she swerved her own car into the oncoming lane—which was mercifully empty—to get around the Volvo.

All she could think was how sad it would be if this was the last night of her life.

Fortunately it was late and the streets were fairly empty, and Sandra pumped at the brake, trying to get it to go down. It was barely budging; she couldn't figure out what was wrong with it. But she knew her time of being able to coast without danger was short, so she put the car in neutral and slowly lifted the emergency brake.

Luckily, that did it, and she was able to pull over safely into a no-parking zone.

It was better than crashing.

She sat for a moment, her hand on her chest, trying to calm down. Could this night get any worse? She was afraid to ask, for fear that fate would give her an answer she didn't want.

Taking a deep breath in, the way she'd been taught in the yoga class she'd attended briefly during her Weight Watchers run, she tried to will herself to calm down. It worked somewhat.

So she reached for the glove compartment and took out the flashlight she kept there for emergencies, aiming the beam toward the brake.

Something was behind it, physically blocking it. Which was potentially good news, as it would mean she could hopefully fix it herself and drive on home. She bent down and reached for the thing, pulling on it with a little difficulty, then, frowning, raised it in front of the flashlight beam to try to figure out what it was.

"Oh, good Lord."

Arlon's hat.

For a long moment she stared at it, turning the molded plastic over in her hands, hating how neatly and ironically it summed up the misery that was her dating life.

Then she lowered the window, tossed the thing out into the street, and drove home.

# *Chapter* 11

Y ou punched a puppet?" Tiffany asked incredulously.

It was Monday night, four days after they first met, and they were sitting in Loreen's modest living room with Abbey while Loreen banged around in the kitchen.

"Yes," Sandra said, "but you're missing the point. Not only did I punch a puppet, but I—" She hesitated, because it was true and it was just too too awful. "I went on a *date* with a puppet. That's even worse."

Loreen was sympathetic, no small feat given the circumstances. "No, you didn't," she said, coming in the room with a big tray of cheeses and crackers. "You went on a date with a guy who turned out to be a wacko. Just because *he* thought you were on a date with a puppet doesn't mean it's true."

"What about that other guy?" Tiffany asked. "Mike?"

"The Adonis?" Loreen supplied.

"Ah, but is he nice?" Abbey asked. "That's the important thing."

"Mike?" Sandra said. "Oh, he's a very nice Adonis." She took a short breath and decided to fess up. "Especially if you're a blond-haired, blue-eyed, Nordic-looking male about six foot two, give or take."

Abbey made a face. "Isn't that always the way?"

"Wait a minute." Tiffany was slow on the uptake with this one. "Are you saying . . . are you saying Mike's . . . *gay*?"

Sandra nodded, amused that the minister's wife was the one who was quickest to understand and accept. "One hundred percent."

"Was he always?" Tiffany asked, and it was difficult to determine if she just didn't know how homosexuality worked or if she had so little faith in Sandra that she believed she could turn an otherwise-hetero male to other men.

"It seems he was," Sandra said, a little crisply. "It's not like I *made* him turn that way."

Tiffany frowned. "I didn't mean that—"

"Did you not know at first?" Loreen asked quickly, then added, "Sorry, I always blurt things out when I shouldn't. But I would just be *so glad* to find out I'm not the only one who can't tell who a man really is until it's too late."

"Well, you're not," Sandra said. "Believe me, you're not. It's a jungle out there. I really envy people who are married, and not just because of the companionship and so on. This dating business stinks. Big time. *Especially* once you're past, say, nineteen."

"I'm past nineteen," Loreen said miserably.

"I'm sorry, I didn't mean to—"

"No, no." Loreen put up a hand. "It's okay. I know it sucks to date.

It sucks to be getting divorced, too. I think dating's even harder after you've been married. I feel like secondhand goods."

"But you haven't really tried, have you?" Abbey asked in a gentle voice, though Sandra was beginning to think there was more to her than just the quiet preacher's wife. "It's not like you *can't* get a date; you just haven't put yourself out there."

"I'm not sure I *should* put myself out there," she said with a laugh. "Too many sharks, and jellyfish, and other things to be avoided in that ocean. Maybe I should be content to have had a marriage and a child. Maybe that's all there is for me, romance-wise."

"I can see where it's tempting to think that," Sandra said. "It's bad enough to be *still* dating after all these years, but to have been married—and brought a child into it—and then *reenter* the dating world . . . Well, that's rough." It absolutely sucked to go out on a date with an abusive puppet, no question, but to run the risk of ending up on a date with a puppet after umpteen years watching *The Tonight Show* in bed with the guy you thought you'd be with forever would be infinitely worse.

"Too rough for me to think about right now." Loreen clapped her hands together, clearly dismissing the subject of her private life and, by the same token, Sandra's, as well. "I have got some questions for you, Ms. Vanderslice."

"What?" Tiffany and Sandra asked simultaneously.

Then Tiffany laughed and said, "Oh, I'm not Ms. Vanderslice anymore. I forgot for a moment."

"Interesting," Sandra said, keeping her eyes on her sister. Then she turned her attention back to Loreen. "What's up?"

"Well, I'm having a really hard time getting the hang of this. I just can't act natural, and I know my callers can tell." She went on to relate the story of the three callers lost in rapid succession in her first attempt.

"I think I got your naughty boy," Abbey said with a shake of the head. "Be *glad* you hung up on him. I spent half an hour diapering and undiapering him."

Everyone listened with rapt attention as Abbey told the whole gruesome story. In fact, all her callers sounded like weirdos, which made Loreen wonder if this was something she'd *ever* be able to get used to.

"So what are you guys calling your operation?" Sandra asked.

"Happy Housewives," Tiffany said, then upon seeing Sandra's look, added, "I thought you'd enjoy that."

"Are you working set hours, or do you have one phone on at all times?" Sandra asked.

"So far we have it set to roll over to the company when we're not logged on so the girls they have on duty get the calls," Loreen said. "But I'm thinking we lose a lot of revenue that way."

"Maybe, but we're not diapering lunatics over breakfast," Tiffany pointed out.

Which was true, Loreen had to concede. But still, the bottom line was bugging her. "If we subcontracted, we'd make a percentage of the calls, instead of giving it all to the relay company."

Sandra nodded. "Totally true. You could advertise on Gregslist for a pittance and have people e-mail you their information and application. I answered an ad two years ago and look at me now." She laughed. "Well, anyway, it worked."

"See, I think that's exactly what we should do," Loreen said. It would be such a relief to know she wasn't just dead weight. If she could set it up so they had employees, then even if she continued to choke when it came time to take the calls, she could at least feel good about the fact that they were making profits from other people's work. "I'll do the administration."

"That could be a lot of work," Abbey said. "Are you sure you don't mind? Because, honestly, I like the idea of hiring out. We'd still get priority when we're logged in, right?"

"You can set it up however you want," Sandra said. "As long as the relay company is getting their cut, they don't care who you want them to send the calls to first."

"So we make the full amount every time we're working," Tiffany said, "then, what, like half when other people are?"

Sandra nodded.

"Isn't that . . . pimping?"

"I prefer the term *madam*," Loreen said, hoping Tiffany wasn't seriously going to draw a moral line at hiring out.

"I like it," Tiffany said slowly. "Abbey? What do you think?"

"Are you kidding? I think it's great."

"All right, Loreen. If you really don't mind—"

Mind? This was the best contribution Loreen could make to the cause. "I'll place the ad tonight."

★

When Tiffany got home, it was nine o'clock, and fortunately, Kate went right to sleep. Andy was keyed up, however, so he took some work.

"Book," he said, pulling *Goodnight Moon* off the shelf.

It seemed like they read it every night, usually more than once. Tiffany never thought she'd get sick of it, but sometimes when she needed just a little alone time, the book felt like an obstacle.

But she wasn't about to tell her son that no, she wouldn't read to him.

So she got into his bed and put her arm out. He climbed under the covers and leaned into the crook of her arm. They'd done it so often now, it felt like puzzle pieces fitting into place.

"Who's going to find the pictures of the little mouse?" she asked. Each color picture had a little mouse hidden in it, and every single time they read it, Andy pointed it out like he'd found it for the first time.

"Me!" He thumped the book with a pudgy hand. "I find the mouse!"

"Okay, baby."

"Me no baby," he said. Charlie used to joke that Andy was like Yoda from *Star Wars,* saying everything backwards.

"No, you're a big boy," Tiffany agreed, then pulled the small, warm body closer in. "But you'll always be my baby. Even when you're bigger and taller than Daddy."

Andy beamed. Clearly the idea of being *even bigger than Daddy* thrilled him, though the truth was Charlie was just under six feet tall, and Tiffany was just two inches shorter than that. Chances that Andy would outgrow Charlie were pretty good.

"Okay, ready?" she asked, opening the book.

"Ready!"

*"In the great green room,"* she read, *"there was a telephone, and a red balloon, and a picture of—"*

"Cow jump over de moon!" Andy cried triumphantly.

"Yes!" She smiled and kissed his downy soft yellow hair. *"And there were three bears. . . ."*

It had taken two *Goodnight Moon*s and a Rolie Polie Olie book to get Andy to simmer down, but finally he'd fallen asleep, and Tiffany had carefully removed herself from the bed, tucked him under the light cotton sheets, and gone back into the darkened, quiet house.

Despite the two sleeping children in their bedrooms, the house felt empty as Tiffany went back to the kitchen to find something to eat. The cheeses Loreen had set out were too loaded with fat to eat more than a piece or two, though Tiffany had been tempted.

Eventually, she settled on an apple and went to sit down on the sofa. With Charlie out of town, and nothing on TV except the depressing news, she turned the TV off and took in the silence. The truth was, she enjoyed the Zen of sitting in silence without anyone tugging at her or asking her for anything.

She used to be afraid to be alone. Actually, all her life she'd been afraid to be alone. It wasn't ghosts or intruders that she feared, but being alone with her own thoughts.

She wasn't afraid anymore.

Now she knew she needed to reflect. She needed to figure things out. Because, for a while now, Tiffany had been thinking maybe . . . she wasn't very happy.

In fact, she was thinking she might be really depressed.

Best not to examine that thought too closely, though. She was afraid if she looked at it, it would become bigger than it already was. Sort of like prodding a snake. Not that snakes got *bigger* if prodded, but they certainly were more dangerous.

Every once in a while she thought about talking to Sandra about it. She knew Sandra had seen a psychologist. And some sort of voodoo acupuncture man who she swore had helped her get over her agoraphobia. Maybe she'd know someone who could help.

But Tiffany didn't want to admit to Sandra that things weren't perfect. For one thing, she could tell Sandra didn't like Charlie, so it stood to reason that if Tiffany said anything at all about being unhappy, Sandra would probably blame it on him and then things would be even *more* awkward—between Sandra and Tiffany, *and* Sandra and Charlie—than they already were.

Nah, Tiffany could handle this on her own.

It was probably just postpartum depression, she reasoned. Andy was two now, but people sometimes had lingering postpartum depression. She needed to exercise more, that was all. A lot of people swore by that as a cure for depression and anxiety.

Half an hour later, she was in her room on the elliptical machine when the phone rang.

She jumped for it, so it wouldn't wake up the children, mopped her brow with a towel, and glanced at the caller ID. UNKNOWN, it said.

It was Charlie.

"Hey, has anyone from work called?" His voice sounded . . . muffled or . . . something.

"No. Aren't you working now?"

"Yeah, yeah. I just mean, if anyone calls, take a message. This trip is building toward a promotion, and there are people there who would be pissed if they knew about it."

"Oh. Okay. So how's it going?"

"What?"

"How is it going?" she enunciated. He was in Cleveland, right? Why was this such a bad connection? For that matter, why did caller ID say UNKNOWN? Why wasn't he using his cell phone?

" 'S aright," he said. "Lots of work. Lots and lots of work. How are the kids?"

Not how are *you*, but she supposed she should be unselfish and be glad he wanted to know about the kids. "Great. The school put the band's third-place trophy, which is totally ostentatious, in the office window, and Kate waves to it every time she passes."

"What trophy is that?"

"From Las Vegas a few weeks ago? . . ."

"Oh, oh, oh, right."

"And Andy wants to ride that Big Wheel thing all the—"

"That's great, but listen, I've got to go. It's a bad connection, and it's getting late. Time for bed."

Tiffany sighed. "I guess I'll tell you about Andy another time, then."

"What?"

There was a strange noise in the background. It sounded like . . . Well, it sounded like steel drums. But that was crazy.

"Never mind," Tiffany said. "Thanks for calling."

"See you in a couple of days."

"I love you," she said a little wistfully. She didn't particularly *feel* it right now, but boy did she want to hear it back. To feel it again, even if only vaguely.

It didn't matter, though, because Charlie had already hung up.

Tiffany hung up the phone and looked around for something to do with herself. She was agitated now. The call had been disconcerting, though she couldn't quite put her finger on the exact reason why. Still, there was what sounded like a steel drum, but didn't every executive hotel lobby across America try to have a manager's reception with cheap wine, Jimmy Buffett and Jack Johnson songs, and overly enthusiastic employees? She would have felt stupid asking Charlie about it, because she *knew* that was what he'd say.

She thought about how Charlie used to be, versus how he was now. Hadn't he been attentive once? Thoughtful?

He used to adorn her with jewelry, but nowadays he wouldn't touch her if she was wearing dish gloves. How had things changed so much, and how had she not noticed it while it was happening?

She hated to think it was because of the kids. That she was too busy dealing with them to notice. Could he resent that? Could he resent *them*?

Could she lessen her devotion to them even if he did?

She pretended to herself that she'd have to think about that, but she knew the answer was no. If she was married to a man who was jealous of her time and attentions as a mother, she'd rather be alone than shortchange them during these short, precious years to accommodate him.

Lonely, in a hollow, echoey way, she went and peeked in on Kate. The light from the hallway cut into the room across Kate's bed, and she shifted. Tiffany withdrew quickly, closing the door as quietly as she could to leave her daughter in the peaceful dark.

Then she went to Andy's room.

It had been hard to get Andy used to having his own room, since he always preferred to snuggle with Tiffany. She didn't mind that, especially since Kate had always been so independent, but Charlie couldn't stand having the children come into their bed, even for half an hour, so she'd broken Andy of the habit through a series of bribes and incentives.

Once in a while, she was ashamed to think, she'd locked the door and pretended not to hear him trying to get in.

That was why she didn't mind reading to Andy as she had tonight, even if it was for the thousandth time.

Now as she looked down at her boy by the light of his Thomas the Tank Engine night-light, his face so soft and cheeks so pink with lingering babyhood, she was overwhelmed with regret for the passing time and how much more she should have been doing with him.

When she'd first found out she was pregnant, after trying for six years, she'd been overjoyed. Suddenly the baby aisle at the grocery store—which had made her feel melancholy before—seemed to sing with the possibility and promise of the future.

It was a promise Tiffany should have kept, but so far she hadn't.

So far she'd spent most of his young life tense and overwhelmed, jumping when Charlie spoke, and putting the best of her energy into quelling her husband's moods instead of into nurturing her children's needs.

If Charlie had been home tonight, he probably would have started calling for her around halfway through the first reading of *Goodnight Moon*.

And she would have gone because that would have been the path of least resistance.

"I'm sorry you don't have the happy family you deserve," she whispered, running her knuckle along his cheek and trying to keep the tears from coming. "Mommy loves you."

Then she sat down on the floor by his bedside and cried.

# Chapter 12

Brian had turned in early, and Abbey couldn't sleep. After tossing and turning in bed for a couple of hours, she finally gave up and went downstairs to have a cup of tea.

She turned on the TV to an old rerun of *The Dick Van Dyke Show*. In it, Laura didn't want Rob to know she'd lied about her age on their marriage license years back. She didn't want him to find out the terrible secret of her past, which was that she was a year younger than her husband believed her to be.

If only Abbey's problems were so simple.

She put a cup of water in the microwave and leaned on the counter, watching the show while the water heated. It was a nice little moment of escape, here in the quiet house, with her boy sleeping soundly, safely upstairs.

The microwave beeped and she dropped a chamomile tea bag into it, and took it over to the sofa with her.

It was a beautiful balmy night and the windows were open. She could hear the crickets outside, mingling with the laugh track of the TV show. It wasn't quite heaven, but it was the most peaceful she'd felt in a long time.

And it stayed that way, through the rest of the show and halfway through *The Brady Bunch*.

Then she smelled smoke.

It wasn't the house. Nothing was on fire. It was cigarette smoke, and the scent was strong.

Someone was standing right outside her open window, smoking a cigarette. And she was pretty sure she knew who it was.

For a long moment, Abbey sat frozen. She'd never felt more vulnerable. If Damon had a gun trained on her, he could get a clear shot right through her head right now. But that wasn't Damon's style. At least it hadn't been more than a decade ago. Who knew how his time in prison had changed him? Who knew how desperate he was to get revenge on Abbey?

No, she was being paranoid. Damon was acting 100 percent true to form, trying to scare her into giving him what he really wanted, what he'd always want more than revenge: money.

She set her cup down with a shaking hand, hoping he couldn't see that. Then she turned the TV and light off so she was in the dark. It took a couple of moments for her eyes to adjust, but when they did, she stood up and walked to the window and looked out.

"Hello?" she called softly, on the off chance it was just a neighbor and not Damon at all.

But there was no answer, just the pale orange glow of a cigarette being tossed through the air into her backyard.

She felt sick. The son of a bitch was trying to gaslight her, to make her so paranoid that she spent her whole life in fear that he was there. Well, she wasn't going to do it. She wasn't going to live like that.

"Next time I'll call the police!" she shouted.

The only answer was the sound of someone whistling as they retreated into the distance.

It was the theme to *The Brady Bunch*.

✳

Loreen, who was now in Mimi mode, finished with a late appointment on Wednesday, picked Jacob up from his friend Austin's, took him home for a quick crap dinner of frozen pizza, then let him watch TV while she went to Gregslist.biz to place the ad for Happy Housewives employees.

*Phone actresses needed. Excellent phone voice and manner necessary. Must be uninhibited. Experience with telephone counseling helpful. Discretion required. Contact Happyhousewives .com for more details or click here.*

"Mom?"

Loreen jumped. "Shit!" She'd forgotten Jacob was up. She'd been concentrating so hard on the ad that she hadn't even heard him come in.

"I heard that!"

She grimaced and shut down the computer page she was working on. "I know. I shouldn't have said that. You startled me."

"So I can say that if I'm startled."

She leveled a look on her son. "I didn't *mean* to say it. And anyway, no, you can't."

Jacob shrugged. "You shouldn't either."

"I know. I shouldn't. I'm sorry."

"Dad called."

"He did?" She looked at the clock. It was a little after ten. "When?"

"Just now. Didn't you hear the phone?"

She really *was* out of it. "No, I didn't. Is everything okay?"

"Guess so. He just told me to tell you to call him."

"Okay."

"Can I watch TV some more?"

"No."

"Come on, *please?*"

"It's way past your bedtime."

"But there's no school tomorrow!"

"There isn't?" Loreen clicked on the calendar on her computer. Professional Day for teachers, no school. "Oh, yeah. Well, then, I guess you can. For half an hour. No more than that, you understand?"

"All right, all right." Jacob was only nine, but he'd already perfected the art of male glumness.

Loreen tried to keep from laughing as he schlumped off, looking for all the world like a miniature version of his father. It gave her a strange combination of pride and melancholy to see that.

Then she took a minute to steel herself to call Robert—these days she never knew if a conversation with him was going to be tense because of their new separation or comfortable because they both remembered what it felt like to be in love with each other.

She tried not to think about that too much, because it only hurt. There was no redeeming value to the sadness at all.

"I was wondering if you'd mind if I got Jacob tonight," Robert said, and again Loreen marveled at how sad it was that they had to talk to each other in this formal way. Would she ever get used to it?

"I don't know," she said. "It's pretty late."

"But there's no school tomorrow, right?"

Jeez, Jacob had *just* reminded her of that! "Right, but like I said, it's late. Why do you want to get him tonight?"

"There's a meteor shower. With all the rain this afternoon, I didn't think it was going to clear up, but it has, and I'd really like to take him up to Little Bennett Park to see it."

"That sounds great," Loreen said, wishing she was, at least occasionally, the one who came up with this sort of thing. How could she refuse? "Of course I don't mind."

They hung up and Loreen went upstairs to tell Jacob to pack his things. He was thrilled to be going on an adventure like this in the middle of the night.

Thank goodness Robert was always on top of this stuff. If anyone was the June Cleaver in their fractured family, it was him. He found the Halloween events—like the Sea Witch Festival in Rehoboth Beach last year; he took Jacob to the Christmas concerts and light displays, like at the Mormon Temple in Kensington.

Yes, Loreen kept Jacob clean, fed, and healthy, but there were many occasions on which she thought she could, and should, do better. In her lower moods, usually right before her period, Loreen worried that she'd failed her son since becoming a single mother, because now she wasn't always able to be the mom who took him strawberry picking, pumpkin carving, Christmas caroling, and so on.

But she was so harried all the time, what with her real estate business—such as it was—and her PTA work that she rarely had a spare moment to do something purely recreational.

Even if it was for her child.

But that had to change, she decided.

After tonight, that was. Tonight wasn't going to win her any Mother of the Year awards. While Robert was taking Jacob out to do wholesome educational activities, she'd be home performing phone sex for money in order to pay off her male prostitute and gambling debt.

Though, actually, if this phone sex thing worked out the way Tiffany thought it might, maybe Loreen *would* be able to relax enough to do those things with her son that now seemed like such luxuries. This was no justification, the Happy Housewives business was a means to an end, and as long as no one got hurt, what was the harm?

Robert picked Jacob up twenty minutes after they spoke, and Loreen watched them both walk off into the night, and into Robert's dark sports car, with a sense of loss and longing she couldn't quite understand.

Why was she so melancholy lately? Everything made her feel like crying. Life was one big long-distance phone commercial, with one maudlin moment after another.

Good thing she had enough to keep her busy tonight.

Loreen spent the next two and a half hours carefully piecing new images together out of movie stars and models, careful not to use enough of any one person to make them recognizable and therefore actionable. She wanted to have a good stable of characters in Happy Housewives, even if there weren't really that many of them yet. There would be, she hoped. The sooner their overflow and off-duty calls stopped going to the relay company for *them* to make the money, the better.

She wasn't sure how many guys would be calling during any given time period, but Sandra had cautioned them that the callers were likely to comprise everyone from the family man who was calling from the broom closet at 2 A.M. to the slacker who was sitting in front of *Wheel of Fortune* and paying for his calls with his unemployment check.

But she had to be glad for all of them, because each of them was helping pay off her debt.

Yes, it was a little unorthodox. And no, she'd never been the type to talk dirty in—or out of—bed, so this wasn't exactly going to come naturally to her. She was actually a little bit afraid that she'd freak out in the middle of a call and hang up, getting a bad reputation for the Happy Housewives and screwing things up for everyone.

But . . . could she do it?

Suddenly she missed Robert.

She missed the family life she would have had with Jacob and Robert. Maybe *they* would have been home watching TV together, or playing Uno. Maybe she and Robert would have read Jacob a story, tucked him in, and gone downstairs to have a glass of wine and relax together. Maybe she would have the peace and security she was suddenly lacking.

But that wasn't true. Things hadn't worked out with Robert. She couldn't give him what he needed. She was alone again. A single mother.

And she was taking steps now—great, determined steps—to be the very best mother she could be.

✳

Something was going on with Tiffany Dreyer, Abbey Walsh, and Loreen Murphy, Deb Leventer just knew it.

First off, there had been a peculiar absence of crowing after the band competition, even though Tuckerman had come in third. If Deb had been PTA president—as she *should* have been—she would have made absolutely sure there was a big celebration, maybe a banner, and *certainly* a trophy case put up in the entrance hall. Yes, that would have cost some money, but it was the first time Poppy—that is, the school students—had ever won anything, and it deserved recognition.

She noticed it now as she walked into the school. She'd been called in because Poppy wasn't feeling well. There, by the door, was the perfect space for a trophy shelf, but instead they had that big construction paper chart of "character kids," otherwise known as kids who never won anything legitimately and needed to have a pat on the head. A lighted cabinet would be *perfect* there, and if they wanted something more than the band trophy, there was no reason Poppy couldn't lend them her T-ball participation trophies. At least until they got something else.

After all, she *was* a student in the school.

The PTA should already have thought of all this, set up incentives like this for the kids. But no. The current PTA officers always seemed busy chatting away on their phones instead of paying attention to *school matters*. As a matter of fact, she'd noticed all three of them, at various times, blabbing on their cell phones in line to pick up the kids. Whom were they talking to? Each other?

Deb was positive they were plotting next year's election coup. In fact, they were probably cheating, because it was the only explanation Deb could come up with for her baffling loss in the last election.

What Deb wouldn't give to listen in on one of *those* conversations. There was Loreen Murphy now, Deb noticed. What was she doing in the school office? Her bratty son had undoubtedly gotten into some sort of trouble. Again.

"Mrs. Leventer," Sally Tader, the school secretary, called as Deb walked past.

"Hello, Sally. No time to talk, I've got to go get Poppy from the health room."

"Poppy's not in the health room. She's in the principal's office," Sally said, indicating Deb should come in and wait in the chair next to Loreen Murphy.

This made no sense. "Why is she in Dr. Steckman's office?" Deb asked. She cast a sly glance at Loreen. "Did someone do something to her?"

The buzzer on Sally's desk went off, and she said, "Dr. Steckman can explain all of that to you. Go right in." She looked at Loreen with, it seemed to Deb, some sympathy. "Dr. Steckman will explain everything."

Obviously that brute Jacob Murphy had done something to Deb's Poppy, and she would say it right now, she was not afraid to take legal action if that's what was called for.

They went into Dr. Steckman's office, where Poppy and Jacob were already sitting, hands folded in their laps, looking shamed, while the principal ushered the parents in.

Jacob had a black eye.

Good. Poppy had defended herself. Deb was glad to see it.

"Jacob, what happened?" Loreen ran to her son and cupped his face with her hands. "Good Lord, that looks awful! Does it hurt?"

He cast a hostile look at Poppy, then said, "No."

"It seems that Poppy tried to kiss Jacob during recess," Dr. Steckman began, and gave a chuckle like this was perfectly normal. "And from what I understand, Jacob didn't want that, and things got a little ugly, as you can see."

Jacob's face turned beet red.

"He attacked her?" Deb asked incredulously.

Dr. Steckman and Loreen looked back at her like they didn't understand what she was asking.

"*Jacob* is the one with the black eye," Loreen said sharply.

"Only because Poppy got a good shot in defending herself," Deb said. "Isn't that right, Pops?" She really hoped it was right. Because none of this was stacking up in a way that made sense to her. Particularly the fact that Poppy wasn't standing up for herself.

"He was being a jerk," Poppy said.

"I was not!" Jacob growled back. "You just wouldn't leave me *alone*. I *hate* that! Just leave me alone."

Deb had a hard time not rolling her eyes. "Clearly this boy is very hostile toward my daughter," she pointed out to Dr. Steckman.

"Deb Leventer, you are trying to incriminate my son over something he didn't do," Loreen snapped, a bit wild-eyed. "I am so sick of the way you do this!" She turned her attention back to Dr. Steckman. "Is there anything else we need to discuss here, or can I take my son home?"

"I think we've covered everything."

"Good." Loreen huffed up and told her son to come with her.

Deb watched them go, and then turned back to Dr. Steckman. "There's one to keep an eye on," she said, putting her arm around her daughter, as if that gesture could protect her from all the Jacob Murphys the world would throw at her. "I expect you'll be doing that."

Dr. Steckman, surprisingly, didn't look all that sympathetic. "We'll keep an eye on *both* children," she said, then turned her attention to Poppy. "And I don't want you to take any more potshots at anyone, young lady, do I have your word?"

Poppy hung her head. "Yes."

"Yes, ma'am," Deb corrected automatically, even while she herself was already mentally composing a letter to the superintendent of schools to complain about Dr. Steckman's incompetence.

Imagine! Blaming a little girl for just trying to defend herself! What kind of message was this woman sending?

As she bundled Poppy up and huffed from the office, she thought about how different Dr. Steckman's attitude might have been if *Deb* were the PTA president, as she should have been, instead of Tiffany Dreyer.

*Then* maybe both Deb *and* Poppy would get the respect they deserved.

✳

Tiffany was doing the dishes after dinner when Charlie came in holding a piece of paper.

"What the hell is this?" he demanded.

"I don't know." She fished Charlie's dirty napkin out of his milk glass. She hated how he did that.

"It's a receipt," he said, and her blood ran cold. "For a store in Las Vegas called—" He looked at it. "—Fiona Pims." He looked at her expectantly.

Now was not the time to tell him it was *Finola* not *Fiona*. Unfortunately, she didn't know what this *was* the time for, since she was blank on what to say. "I don't know," she said. "What about it?"

"It's for five thousand dollars," Charlie said, not letting up an inch on his indignation. *"Five thousand dollars."*

"Okay, someone spent five thousand dollars at a store in Las Vegas." She put a plate in the dishwasher and hoped the shaking of her hands wasn't so noticeable to him as it was to her. "So what?"

Charlie just looked at her. "Tiffany, don't embarrass us both by lying. This is your credit card number at the bottom of the receipt."

Tiffany felt her face grow hot. He'd caught her lying, he knew what she'd done, *and* he'd been going through her purse. Though she didn't really have a *best defense* at the moment, Tiffany decided nevertheless to try the only offense available to her. "Why were you going through my purse?"

"I wasn't *going through your purse*. I was looking for a pen. And don't evade the point. You spent five grand on clothes." He shook his head. "This is exactly why I separated our finances."

"Why you what?" She stopped midrinse and set down the plate. "What do you mean?" She turned off the water.

"I took my name off of this credit card, and took your name off of mine. Don't use the Bank of America card anymore, by the way."

This was unthinkable. "You've been shuffling our names around on our finances without telling me?"

He shrugged. "It was just a business maneuver," he said evasively, "for my expense accounts and whatnot. But now I see it was very fortunate."

Tiffany was not buying the "business move" nonsense at all. "The company provides the credit card for your expense account."

Charlie gave her a hard look. "Are you questioning my business?"

"No, I—"

"Let's stick to the point. This is a huge debt, and I resent the idea that it might come out of the income I work hard for. I think it's time you got a part-time job."

She was dumbstruck. "You do."

He nodded. "Yes, I do."

"In between taking care of the kids, keeping the house clean, making dinners, and handling everything from your dry cleaning to cooking for you and your buddies, you think I should get a job." It didn't matter that she already had one. He didn't know about it, and she wasn't about to let him find out. Their relationship was winding up toward something ugly, she suspected, and she didn't want to give him any ammunition against her.

He nodded, and an outsider might have thought he looked patient. She knew he looked condescending. "I think it's best. Also, I've opened another bank account and need you to sign off on me leaving the joint account we've been sharing."

*"What?"*

"We'll still pay the bills from that account," he said, as if reassuring her. "Nothing will change. I just want to shift our liabilities." He smiled, but it didn't seem even remotely warm. "Don't worry, as far as the running of the house goes, nothing will change." As he turned to go, he added, "Like I said, it's just business."

Yeah. Monkey business. Charlie was positioning himself to leave her, Tiffany realized with great clarity. And he thought she was too stupid to understand that. He thought he could baffle her with talk of expense accounts and liabilities.

Her whole body shook with anger and pain that bounced around inside her without an outlet. This was surreal. And yet, at the same time, it felt inevitable. Somewhere inside she'd known her marriage wasn't right. She wasn't sure what hurt more: the fact that the man she'd spent so many years with, and had two children with, wanted to leave her and apparently was willing to leave her high and dry; or the fact that after all this time, he clearly didn't know her at all.

She sat down at the kitchen table, tapped her fingers for a minute, then stood up again. Where should she go? What should she do? She needed a drink. First things first.

She opened the freezer and took out the frosty blue bottle of Skyy Vodka. Then she took out a glass and poured some vodka in. The first sip she took burned down her throat and into the pit of her stomach. Good. Maybe it would burn all traces of Charlie out of her.

The second sip went down easier.

The third made her pick up the phone and dial a number she knew by heart even though she rarely called it.

"Hi, it's me. Can you . . . um . . . can you come over? I'm having sort of an emergency. No, no, everyone's okay, it's just—" Sudden tears filled her eyes, and her voice faltered. "I need to talk."

# Chapter 13

S o," Sandra said, after having a shot of vodka at Tiffany's insistence, and nibbling at the cheese and crackers Tiffany had set out. "You've told me about Kate hating her ballet class, Andy wanting a bike, your neighbor killing her azaleas with too much Miracle-Gro. . . ." She looked at her sister, frowning. "Is this really what you needed to talk about?"

Tiffany sliced off a big chunk of Brie—highly unlike her—and popped it into her mouth. "Mmmn." She shrugged, then swallowed. "It's just been a while since we got caught up."

"Okay." Sandra wasn't buying it. "So what's really going on?"

"What do you mean?"

"Is Mom or Dad sick or something?" Though that didn't make sense. They probably would have told Sandra first, knowing she could handle it better than Tiffany. "Just tell me straight."

"Mom and Dad are fine," Tiffany said, then looked uncertain. "Why, do *you* know something?"

"Tiffany!" Sandra said, exasperated. "You called me up, sounding like the world was about to end, asked me to come over right away, and so far you've had three shots of vodka, more fat than I've ever seen you consume in one sitting, and you've told me absolutely nothing of import. *What* is going *on?*"

"Charlie's having an affair."

Sandra opened her mouth to speak, then clapped it shut. Had Tiffany really just said that? "Are you sure?"

Tiffany nodded solemnly. "And he's a jerk." Tears filled her eyes and rolled down her cheeks, fast and furious. "I'm not sure which is worse."

"They certainly go hand in hand." Sandra shook her head. "Did you talk to Mom?"

"No!" Tiffany looked stricken. "You can't tell her. Promise me."

"Sure, okay, I promise. I just thought, you know, she might have a suggestion."

"Mom would tell Daddy, and Daddy would *kill* Charlie first and ask questions later."

"True." Sandra wasn't sure what to do. Tiffany had entrusted her with the most important news of her life, but she was totally unprepared to deal with it. This might be the first time anyone had ever fully counted on Sandra. She had to do the right thing. Even if the right thing was to first make sure that asshole Charlie wasn't getting blamed for something he didn't do. "Now back up. Tell me everything that led up to this. That way we can figure out what to do next."

So Tiffany talked. She told Sandra about the call from Cleveland, which sounded a lot more like a call from the islands, she told her about the late nights and the scant explanations for them, and she told her about his wanting to divide their accounts.

"That definitely sounds like he's up to *something*," Sandra said when Tiffany finished.

"I know," Tiffany agreed. She sounded thoughtful now, not miserable like she had at first. "He is. I think I knew it even before he gave me all the evidence."

"So what do you want to do next?" Sandra asked carefully. This marked the first time in her life she didn't envy Tiffany's life over her own. Not that she ever coveted a life with Charlie—far from it—but it had looked, from the outside, like Tiffany was blissfully happy and secure.

Sandra should have looked a little deeper.

"I'm not sure." Tiffany sighed. "I know I can't stay with him. I'm just not sure how to proceed. You always hear stories about women who get totally screwed in divorces, and I don't want that to be me."

"So cover your financial bases first," Sandra said. "Buy your credit report online and make sure he hasn't put your name on anything that can get you into trouble. Real estate, credit cards you don't know about, and so on."

Tiffany looked grateful. "Good idea."

"And get your name off of anything you can that has both your names on it."

Tiffany nodded. "Except the house. That could be tricky."

"If it gets tricky, you hire a lawyer."

Tiffany took a long breath. "I don't want to let him know I know anything until I've got all my ducks in a row."

"Good thinking."

"It's going to be hard. I'm afraid he'll see it all over my face."

Sandra shook her head. "You've had some practice acting lately," she said with a smile. "Just . . . act."

The garage door sounded then, and Tiffany said, "He's home!" Then, in a very casual voice she said, "You know, I love those shoes you're wearing."

"Funny you should mention that," Sandra said. "Where's my bag?" She reached for her oversize hobo bag and produced a pair of simple black satin ballet pumps, with leather soles and comfort pads at the heel and toe. "*These* are for you. You always say you can't wear heels without towering over Charlie, so I thought these were perfect for you. They're the Carfagni Bowen models. Size ten."

Tiffany took the shoes. "Wow, they're so cool. Like something Audrey Hepburn would wear." She kicked off her shoes and slipped the new ones on.

Sandra nodded. "They'll go with just about everything, too."

Tiffany took a few steps. "Comfy."

"I'll get you hooked yet." Sandra smiled.

"Hooked on what?" a gruff voice asked.

Sandra noticed Tiffany stiffen.

"Hey, Charlie," she said drily, before she even turned around. "How are you doing?"

"Excellent," he said. "Excellent."

Tiffany looked . . . It was hard to say just what that expression was. It was like every negative feeling she could have rose into her face and she was trying to cover it up. "What are you doing here? I thought you were working late."

"Game's on tonight. A few of the guys are coming over to watch. Make some of those little hamburger things you do, okay? Gliders?"

Andy, who had been playing quietly with his blocks, got up and toddled over to Charlie, saying, "Dada!"

Charlie gave him a dismissive brush on the head. "Hey, bud."

"Sliders," Tiffany said, reaching for the child. "I can't, Charlie. I'm having people over, too."

He barely glanced at Sandra. "It's just your sister."

Lord, Sandra wanted to slap that smug, condescending look right off his face.

But she and Tiffany were raised to be polite.

Hence, Tiffany's response, "No, I'm having other people over, too. Maybe I could order a pizza or something for you and the guys." Andy played with Tiffany's hair, pulling and tugging, but she continued to talk to Charlie and work in the kitchen *and* hold the child without missing a beat.

Did Charlie know he was married to a superwoman? Or did he just take that for granted?

"Gah." He waved the notion away as if Tiffany had suggested she could just sneeze on toast for him instead. "Come on, babe. Those burgers don't take long. And since when do you have people over anyway?"

Tiffany's glance flitted toward Sandra, who immediately took the cue to give them some privacy. "You know, Tif, we could just go to my place so Charlie can crank the game."

"Now *that's* thinking." Charlie pointed at Sandra like she was the model wife. "You and your girls can clear on out of here after you make the burgers."

"If you two will excuse me a moment, I'm going to get some fresh air." Sandra took Andy from Tiffany's arms, gave her sister a *give him hell* look, and carried the boy away, thinking about how Charlie's bullshit wasn't about burgers at all, but about power.

She hated to see Tiffany bow to it.

Leaving Tiffany's and Charlie's rising voices behind her, she stepped outside and let Andy down. "See if you can find Aunt Sandra a dandelion," she told him. "Can you find one? A little yellow flower?"

"Dandlon!" Andy ran off into the yard, looking for weeds in the dusky light.

Sandra, watching him, opened her phone. She had Loreen's number but not Abbey's, so she called Loreen.

"Are you on your way to Tiffany's?"

"I'm about three blocks away," Loreen said. "Why?"

"Charlie showed up and he's being . . ." She swallowed a bunch of expletives. "Difficult."

Andy ran over to her and handed her a dandelion, then said, "I get more!"

Loreen hesitated, then said, "Difficult. That's code for Charlie's being an asshole, right?"

Sandra nearly bit her tongue. There was a fine line between betraying family and trying to help by talking to Tiffany's closest friend. "You've seen him like this before?"

Loreen gave a dry, humorless laugh. "Like, every time I see him at all. He treats Tiffany like dirt. I don't know why she puts up with it."

Neither did Sandra.

In high school, Tiffany had been the belle of every ball. She'd had many, *many* wealthy, attractive guys after her. And it had continued on through college. Sons of senators and pro football players, who had gone on to be senators and pro football players themselves—all of them had vied for her attentions.

How she'd ended up with domineering Charlie, Sandra couldn't figure out.

"I don't either." She gave a heavy sigh. "And I hate it."

"Me, too."

"So we need to go someplace else tonight. We can go to my apartment, but that's in Adams Morgan, and I know you've got Jacob with you and he needs some sleep. Would you rather we go to your place?"

"Sure. Absolutely. I don't mind either way. Did you talk to Abbey?"

Andy returned, breathlessly, with another dandelion.

"No, I don't have her number. I was hoping you could—" Sandra stopped as a light-colored sedan pulled up in front of the house. "Never mind, I think she's here. Look, I'll send her your way, and Tiffany and I will be along soon, okay?"

"Great," Loreen said firmly. "See you in a few."

Sandra flipped her phone shut and walked over to Abbey's car, keeping an eye on Andy the whole time.

Abbey rolled the window down as she approached, like she was already ready for trouble.

"What's wrong?" Abbey asked.

"Tiffany's husband came home unexpectedly."

"And he doesn't want a bunch of women in the house, right?" Abbey laughed.

"You've met him."

"Yes, but more than that, I've met his type. Time and again. So is the meeting off or are we going someplace else?"

"Loreen's."

"Yay!" a child cried from Abbey's backseat. "Jacob has *the coolest* Transformers."

Abbey glanced toward the backseat and then gave Sandra a smile. "Hard to argue with that. Is Loreen already there?"

"Probably, by now."

"Okay." Abbey put her car in gear. "Get Tiffany out, and we'll see you over there."

Sandra watched her drive away and took a moment to appreciate the fact that both Abbey and Loreen had been quick to understand and quick to change plans without a lot of awkward explanation.

Sandra got Andy, and went back in the house to tell Tiffany their plans had changed and they were going to Loreen's.

She found her at the stove, frying up little square hamburgers. On the counter there was a platter of sliced buns, with a bowl of chopped onions, a bowl of relish, and bottles of ketchup, mustard, and mayo.

Just like Charlie wanted it, Sandra had no doubt.

"And the burger wars have a winner," Sandra said, sitting down on a stool beside the counter.

"It's easier than arguing," Tiffany said. But her face had lost some of its glow. She looked stressed.

And, for the first time, Sandra noticed she looked older.

"You don't have to do this, you know," Sandra said. "You can stop right now and we can leave and order a pizza on the way out. That might send a powerful signal."

Tiffany flipped the burgers on the skillet. "This will just take a few more minutes."

"Why are you so cowed by him?" Sandra asked quietly.

"I'm not." Tiffany met Sandra's eyes. "It's just easier than arguing."

"Why?"

"Because if I argue, there's always some sort of retribution, and I'm not in the mood for that today."

A cold chill ran through Sandra. "Like what kind of retribution?"

"Stony silences, being short with the kids. Just big, impossible-toignore unpleasantness. You know, it doesn't matter how big your house is, the strongest mood *always* wins. And if I piss him off"— she peeled the plastic off American cheese slices—"it's going to put him in a pretty crappy mood." She finished with the cheese and looked back at Sandra. "And I just don't want to deal with it."

"I get that." It was clear that Tiffany knew she was dealing with a jerk. Sandra decided there was no point in hammering her about the injustice of it now. "Is there anything I can do to help?"

"No." Tiffany smiled, then picked up Andy, who had come to tug on her shirt. She picked him up, gave him a kiss on the cheek, and said to Sandra, "But it means a lot that you would ask."

✷

Two days later, despite the fact that she was half-ready to spend the rest of her life alone on the couch eating Ben & Jerry's, Sandra had another blind date. One she'd screened as carefully as possible for any signs of bossiness or domination, like Charlie. It was hard to tell from an online profile, but she was at least aware of it from the word *go*.

From what she could tell, Zach was a normal beta male, more sensitive than bossy.

As she drove to the restaurant, Sandra wondered if it was a bad idea to keep meeting blind dates for dinner when she was so self-conscious about her weight. Maybe it would be better to wait a few months, until she'd slimmed down some, and *then* set about the task of presenting herself to the small world of available men in D.C.

At the moment, the very fact of meeting in a restaurant put her in the position of feeling defensive and embarrassed.

The auricular therapy bar in her ear—an acupuncture needle that was supposed to stay in and keep her from overeating—wasn't doing a lick of good, and the problem with the homeopathic appetite-suppressant tablets, apart from the fact that they didn't do squat, was that they sort of tasted good.

Dieting was making her nuts, but it wasn't making her thin.

But if she *was* going to date, what were the alternative meeting places? A bowling alley? The carousel at Glen Echo Park? The mini-mart at Tenley Circle, in front of the processed cheese food or the motor oil?

Restaurants just made sense. They were neutral, public, and everywhere.

Besides, if a guy was going to judge her that way, she was better off without him, right? Which meant she was, indeed, better off without the scores and scores of boys and men who—all her life—had overlooked her because of her appearance.

The ones who didn't dismiss her because of her appearance wanted to be her buddy.

It was getting old. It was getting really, really old.

And Sandra wasn't getting any younger herself.

So she went to Sephora at Montgomery Mall before the date, hoping to get some miracle cream or eyeliner or *something* that would make her miraculously beautiful. Or at least reasonably attractive, since she didn't seem to be making at least that modest goal.

"Are you finding everything all right?" an impossibly thin black-clad girl of about nineteen asked her when she was wandering the Stila aisle, marveling at the names and descriptions of the products.

"Actually," she said, "I haven't really found anything yet. I'm looking for . . . something great. Something that maybe won one of those *Allure* awards. Is there a product here that's a real desert island keeper?"

By this time another employee had walked up on the conversation and seemed as interested in the challenge as the first.

"What about Bad Gal Lash?" Number two (whose name tag identified her as Belinda) said to number one (whose name tag labeled her Estelle).

"I don't need more mascara," Sandra said. "I've got my Maybelline Great Lash, and no one can tell me there's something better. No, what I'm wondering about is some miracle concealer or foundation or something."

"Have you tried Smashbox Photo Finish?" Estelle asked. "It's just a primer for foundation or blush, but it fills in fine lines and large pores." She narrowed her eyes and looked more closely at Sandra's skin. "You should try it."

Physical scrutiny was, of course, Sandra's kryptonite. "Do you have any samples?"

These seemed to be the magic words for Estelle. She said, "Go to one of the seats in the back. I'll be right there," and set out looking for every miracle product in the place to sell to this poor sucker.

And this poor sucker was so ready for a makeover that she was willing to be late for her date on the promise that she might make a positive impact upon meeting him.

An hour later, she had to admit, she *did* feel . . . well, if not *stunning* at least attractive. Estelle and Belinda had gone to work on her, lining this, highlighting that, until Sandra barely recognized herself in the little hand mirror they provided.

She liked it that way.

Of course, she left the store with more than two hundred dollars' worth of new products, which she might or might not be able to use effectively at home. If she kept spending like this, she was going to have to go back to being a phone sex operator herself, just to supplement her income.

She drove up Wisconsin Avenue, looking for the address her date had given her for "a cool little pizza joint in Bethesda." She liked a guy who wasn't afraid to suggest pizza for a first date instead of something ostentatious and pretentious, so she was able to work up some optimism for New2This, aka Zach Roisin. Additionally, he had no interest in puppetry, stage magic, or any other performance art. Sandra had felt him out on that first thing. Subtly, she hoped.

Either that, or he was thinking of her as "the puppet hater."

Which, come to think of it, might not be a bad user name for her on Match.com. Then she wouldn't *have* to ask the puppet questions, it would just be obvious for puppeteers to stay away.

She couldn't believe she was thinking about this.

Lorna Rafferty, her friend and business partner and the original shoe addict, called when she was sitting at a stoplight.

After a few minutes' chat about a boutique chain in California that was going to carry the Carfagni fall line, Lorna asked where Sandra was on her way to.

Sandra told her about the online dating and her reluctance to give it another try after the Puppetmaster, but told her she was heading for a pizza place now. "If they can afford a lease in Bethesda, the food's probably decent at least," she said.

"True," Lorna agreed. "What's the name of it?"

"Actually, believe it or not, he didn't say. Or if he did, I don't remember. But I have the address, and it's an Italian place, so I should be good."

"Do you want me to call you in half an hour or so to give you an out if the date sucks?" Lorna asked.

Sandra thought about it for a second before saying, "No, with my luck, he'd hear what you say and know I was faking. Or that I'd set up the call in advance. Either way, I don't think it's a good idea."

"Okay, but I'm on call if you need me. I'm just sitting here overlooking San Francisco Bay, drinking a mojito."

"Show-off!"

"You could have come with me. I'm hitting New Mexico and Arizona in a couple of weeks. Come then."

It sounded tempting. If Sandra didn't hate flying so much. "Maybe."

Lorna laughed. "I know what that *maybe* means. Come on, it'll be fun. Get the acupuncturist to put a fear-of-flying bar thingy in your ear."

Sandra wasn't sure if it was a good thing or a bad thing that her friend knew her so well. "I'll think about it." She pulled up to a light. "I'm in the neighborhood now, so I'd better start paying attention. Wish me luck."

"Good luck! And, listen, in all seriousness, give the guy a chance. They can't *all* be freaks."

"God, I hope not." She hung up the phone and looked at the clock on her dashboard. She was ten minutes early. That should give her enough time to park. As luck would have it, she found a space right outside a camera shop on the same block, so she pulled in, did one last check of her makeup, and got out of the car.

She walked along the block, looking for the restaurant. There was a strip mall, anchored by a Chuck E. Cheese on one end and a TCBY on the other, but none of the shopfronts had addresses. It seemed she really should have gotten the name of the place after all. What had she been *thinking*?

She walked the length of the mall once; then, when nothing

jumped out at her as being remotely Italian, she walked it again. Yogurt, office supplies, a frame shop, CVS, a toy store, Chuck E. Cheese. No Italian restaurant.

She was flummoxed.

"Sandra?"

Hearing her name, she turned around to find a short—well, her height—guy with wispy blond hair and a mouth full of braces. That, in itself, wasn't a problem, but he was so thin, she guessed he probably had to shop in the boys' department, so she felt huge next to him.

"Y . . . es?"

"Zach Roisin." He held out his hand.

"Oh. Nice to meet you, too, Zach." She shook his hand.

"It's *Zach*, actually," he corrected, pronouncing it *Sock*.

"Okay. Sock."

"Zach."

She was already tired of this. "Zsock," she tried again, and was relieved that his face softened with apparent approval.

Their hands fell apart, and Zach said, "So?"

"So . . ." What? "I'm sorry if I'm late." *Was* she late? "But I didn't write down the name of the restaurant. Actually, it's a good thing you happened along, because I don't know what I would have done. Am I on the wrong block?"

"Nope." He made a grand gesture toward the Chuck E. Cheese.

She nodded, waiting for him to elaborate. Then it hit her. "That? Chuck E. Cheese? That's the *little pizza joint*?"

"You got it!" He looked thrilled with himself. "Usually when I tell people I want to meet here, they think they're not interested, so I've begun just calling it a pizza place. Because they do have the most fantastic pizza in the world."

Wait a minute, what happened to "New2this"? He'd actually met so many people here that he had a system for lying in order to *lure* them here? "I've never had it," she said honestly.

"Get ready." He ushered her toward the door. "Oh, by the way, did you bring change?"

"Change? Money? No. I have credit cards. Why?"

"For the games. But most of them take tokens, so you can get those with your credit cards. Don't worry."

Oh, yeah. *That* would alleviate the worry.

He opened the door and she was immediately struck by the amount of noise. Kids screamed, laughed, and cried over loud music. There appeared to be an animatronic rat spotlighted on a stage, dancing and singing, though no one seemed to be paying much attention.

"Isn't it great?" Zach asked enthusiastically.

"It's—" What was the word? "—big." But there *was*, undeniably, a festive air about the place. It was different—that was for sure. And, let's face it, she wasn't particularly in the mood for another quiet, awkward, blind date dinner.

Besides, it was nice that Zach was willing to share his inner child with her on a first date. He was just going to let it all hang out, right up front. That made sense. She appreciated that.

"Get some tokens," he said eagerly. "We'll play foosball." He jingled his pockets, which were evidently full of tokens already. "I'll save the table. Meet me there."

"Wait, shouldn't we just use the tokens you have?"

"These are *my* tokens," he said, then gave a quick smile. "And they're worth collecting, Sandy, because pretty soon this place is going to switch to rechargeable cards, like Butch and Blaster's did, and these are going to be worth something."

"Who are Butch and Blaster?"

He frowned for a moment. "You've never been to Butch and Blaster's? The restaurant arcade where the fun has just begun?"

No. But she could tell from the slogan that she didn't want to go. "Oh," she said, as if she'd just misheard. "Butch and Blaster's! The . . . the *place*."

"Yeah." He nodded. "Hurry up and get the tokens before someone else gets our table."

"Okay." She watched him go for a moment. She was willing to be open-minded about his choice of venues, but it *did* seem a little weird that he had a bunch of tokens that he wasn't willing to share. That he would, in fact, rather stand guard over a table while she fumbled with the token machine, just so he could keep his tokens to himself.

Sandra's phone rang while she was struggling to get the token machine to accept her card. She expected it to be Lorna, but it was Tiffany.

"I need another word for *cock*," she said without preamble.

"I'm sorry?" The coins rattled into the dispenser, and Sandra gathered them, holding the phone between her shoulder and her ear.

"What was that?"

"Nothing. Just a change machine. What were you saying?"

"I'm sick of all those *Penthouse Letters* sort of euphemisms for body parts," Tiffany said. "There's got to be something . . . more artistic."

"Well, you can work around them."

"How?"

"You know, say things like 'You're getting me hot' and 'I'm so wet' and—" She stopped. Good God, she was in a Chuck E. Cheese. She couldn't say that kind of thing here! "You get the idea."

"It's really very complicated work."

"You can do it."

The lights went down and a voice blasted from speakers that must have been hidden every three feet in the walls, "Liiive from our fabulous showroom. Here he is, the *master of fun,* Chuck E. Cheese!"

"Sandra?" Tiffany asked.

Sandra's face burned. "I've got to go."

"Where *are* you?"

"I'm on a date."

"But *where?* I could have sworn I heard—"

She was interrupted by an invisible band winding up with a very loud variation on "When the Saints Come Marching In."

Tiffany gasped. "When Chuck E.'s band comes marching in! Oh, honey, are you on a date at Chuck E. Cheese?"

Sandra's humiliation settled on her shoulders like a heavy wet shawl. "Do *not* tell *anyone.*"

"I will try my hardest not to." Tiffany was laughing. "But I want to hear all about it later."

Sandra rolled her eyes and hung up the phone. She did *not* need Tiffany putting a weird spin on her date with a guy who was just—she reminded herself of what was becoming her new mantra—fun-loving enough to reveal his inner child on a first date.

Unfortunately, it turned out Zach's inner child was a competitive brat in need of some serious discipline. The fact that Sandra was not good at this sort of game only made things worse, and it turned out that Zach didn't have a lot of patience for people who couldn't keep up with him on the foosball table.

When the stage show started up again, and strobe lights began flashing, things only got worse.

"Just *hit* the ball back toward my goal!" Zach shouted. She preferred to think he was trying to be heard over the din of noise than that he might actually be *ticked off* that she didn't have any points.

"I'm trying!" She laughed.

He did not.

"It's easy," he said. "You just hit them with your players' legs. Like this." He spun one of his poles and, sure enough, the ball went flying toward her goal.

She tried to rush over and maneuver one of the players to block it, but she was too slow.

She wasn't sure, but she thought she heard Zach give an exasperated *Sheeesh!*

"Maybe we should take a break and get something to eat," she suggested, already planning to eat without regard to Weight Watchers. She'd worry about that later.

"The game's not over yet." Zach leapt back, knocking the ball around. "Get back to your station!"

She tried, she really did, but she wasn't quick enough.

And then, with a loud *"Like this!"* Zach whipped his pole around and sent the ball flying right off the table and into Sandra's cheekbone.

"Aaah!" She raised her hand to her cheek, which was already pulsating, sending blood north to form what would undoubtedly be a big, ugly, black-and-blue bruise.

"Well, that's not supposed to happen," Zach said, as if the table had come to life and deliberately attacked her itself. "Why didn't you duck?"

"Why didn't I—?"

"You should have ducked. I mean, I can see you're too heavy for, like, a game of touch football or tennis or something, but you'd think you could have at least gotten out of the way."

Too *heavy*? Was Peter Pan here actually insulting her weight?

That was it.

"Thanks for the game, Zach, I really enjoyed it, but I think I'm going to go home. And put ice on my cheek."

"I guess you should do that," he agreed. "Can I have your tokens?"

"I'm sorry?"

"The tokens you just bought. Since you're not going to use them, can I have them?"

She reached into her purse and started to get out the five dollars' worth of tokens she purchased, then stopped. "Look for them on eBay," she said, then turned and left without looking back.

Mostly because it hurt too much to move her aching head.

# Chapter
# 14

It was shortly after noon, Loreen had shown two houses that morning, and her client had been seriously interested in one of them. Things were looking up.

So it was with great optimism that she logged on and decided to take a call or two before Jacob got home. She was going to turn this around and get good at it, like Tiffany and Abbey seemed to be.

It didn't take long for the phone to ring.

"Hello?" That was a mistake. She modulated her voice and added, "This is Mimi. Who's calling?"

"Hey, Mimi, this is Caveman, calling for some fire."

"C-caveman?" No way, that was nuts. Two seconds in, and she'd already made another embarrassing mistake. "I'm sorry, I must have misheard you."

"*Caveman*," he repeated. "What is this, did I call my fifth-grade math teacher?"

"Were you . . . did you *want* to talk to your fifth-grade math teacher? Is that your fantasy?"

This wasn't going well.

"You're joking, right?"

Um. Sure. "Whatever you want. Caveman."

"Aw, man. This blows." He hung up the phone with a dramatic clatter.

She'd failed *again*.

And it should have been a no-brainer.

Loreen considered it with skepticism. What if it was Caveman again, calling to yell at her? Then again, if it was, he'd be paying handsomely for the privilege, and listening to that would probably be easier than listening to the sexual fantasies of someone who called himself Caveman.

The phone kept ringing.

Finally, she grabbed it. "This is Mimi. . . ." She took a chance. "Caveman?"

There was silence.

"Hello? Caveman? Are you there?"

"Mom?"

She dropped the phone and uttered a word she would have grounded Jacob for saying. "What are you doing here?" she asked, knowing her voice was too sharp and her face was as red as a Halloween mask.

"It's a half day." He put his Spider-Man backpack down. "Who are you calling Caveman?"

"It . . . ah . . ." She had no answer. She had not one damn answer that could make sense to *anyone*, much less a child. Except . . . wait a minute, this *was* a child she was talking to. "It was GEICO," she said, referencing the car-insurance company that featured cavemen characters that never failed to crack Jacob up.

His face broke into a wide grin. "Cool!"

Loreen cleared her throat. "Get washed up and go downstairs. I'll make you a snack."

"Jack Bryson's coming over," Jacob said. "We're gonna practice pitching."

"Great!" She meant it. She was utterly unprepared to have Jacob home, and she needed some time to recover from the shock of him showing up, and the horror of what he *could* have overheard if she'd been any better at her job.

Her poor performance was almost equally disturbing. As she dialed the number to log off of Happy Housewives, it occurred to her that she really wasn't pulling her considerable weight in this endeavor. Every call required instant sexual banter, and while obviously she should be ready to do that, she wasn't. She needed something equivalent to a musician's fake book, a list of lines she could use as springboards for conversation.

She needed to call Sandra.

✳

"I need to lose weight," Sandra told Dr. Kelvin Lee. "Fast. So can you do acupuncture *and* auricular therapy?"

Dr. Lee looked at her in that patient, unflappable way he always looked at her. She wasn't sure if he was just used to her or if *all* his clients were this neurotic. Probably most people saw an acupuncturist for physical pain more than for mental and emotional needs.

Still, last year he'd worked wonders in getting rid of her anxiety and agoraphobia, so she'd begun to think he was a miracle worker.

She just couldn't believe she hadn't thought of asking him about weight loss before.

"Certainly," he said, ushering her into room 4, which was the one without a window. She liked room 2 better. "But first, some arnica root would be helpful in healing that bruise."

She raised a hand to her cheek. Apparently her cover-up hadn't worked so well as she'd hoped. Now Dr. Lee probably thought she was in some sort of abusive relationship. "I got hit in the face by a ball in an arcade the other day," she explained. "It actually looks a lot better now than it did at first. So about the weight-loss auricular therapy? . . ."

He nodded. "And we have some very effective homeopathic remedies, as well."

"I'll try anything," she said. "Everything." And who, upon being insulted by a puppet *and* an overgrown, overcompetitive man-child, wouldn't?

"Very well, then. Lie down."

She climbed onto the table, and Dr. Lee walked to the end by her head and started manipulating her earlobes, looking for the spot for the needle.

Sandra knew the ropes at this point.

"Can you put, maybe, a larger needle in or something?" she asked. At this point she was willing to look like a Zulu tribeswoman if it meant she got to be skinny, too. "Is there a way to make it work faster?"

"Sandra, you know it is not possible. The art of acupuncture is based upon stimulating your body's existing responses. It's not a 'more is better' proposition."

"It never hurts to ask." She jumped slightly as he put the needle in her earlobe.

Dr. Lee just shook his head and chuckled. "No, it doesn't hurt to ask. But my answer will remain the same."

"I'm afraid my question will, too," Sandra said. "Ouch! It hurts! It didn't hurt last time."

"It is a new meridian. This one perhaps needs more work." Dr. Lee looked at her, and even though she'd never seen even one shade of judgment in his eyes, she felt embarrassed.

"My weight has certainly been a problem longer than my anxiety," she said, half expecting him to say something reassuring.

Instead, he simply nodded. "That could be why. Now, turn over and I will complete the acupuncture."

Recently, Sandra had become less self-conscious about lying on the table in her underwear while the man put acupuncture needles in her. She rolled over onto her stomach and closed her eyes as he inserted the barely perceptible needles into her pressure points.

"Relax for fifteen minutes and I will be back." Dr. Lee turned down the lights and turned up the PA to the gentle lull of James Galway's flute lilting over Debussy.

It really was relaxing, odd as that seemed.

Until her cell phone started ringing.

Now, Sandra wasn't normally one to panic, so the first time it rang, her initial thought was that she'd just call whoever it was back. When the person hung up and called right back, she felt mild irritation that the caller couldn't just take a hint and leave a message.

But the third time it rang, Sandra's nerves tightened. Maybe it was an emergency. Had someone been hurt? Or . . . worse? It had been six years since anyone she knew had died, and oddly enough, it had occurred to her a couple of weeks ago that, God forbid, something bad might be about due.

Gingerly, she pushed herself up from the table, careful about the needles sticking out of her like a half-bald porcupine.

The phone was in her purse, which, unfortunately was deep. This was unfortunate because she had needles in the back of her hand, so she couldn't just dig into the depths of the leather bag to find it.

Very carefully, she pulled the flaps open and reached for the light of her ringing phone.

"Hello?" she asked urgently.

"Sandra? It's Loreen."

"Oh." This was surprising. "Loreen. Is everything okay?"

"Yes. I mean . . . well, yes. But I need some advice. About . . . you know . . ."

"Yes? . . ."

"I need some ideas of what to say. How to get a conversation started." She hesitated. "And keep it going."

"Oh. Well, it's not so hard. You just sort of feel the guy out to see what he needs. You know, *Why are you calling me tonight, Bart?* That sort of thing." Sandra started to sit down and remembered the acupuncture needles just in time.

"What if he asks what *I* want to do."

"Then you say something along the lines of *whatever you want to do, big guy, I just want to make you happy*."

There was a knock at the door and the nurse poked her head in. "Is everything okay in here?"

"Yes. Fine. I just had a call."

The nurse bowed out, but Sandra wondered how much of the conversation she'd heard.

"Look, I'm at the doctor's now," Sandra said, lowering her voice. "Do you want me to stop by on my way home?"

"I don't want to trouble you—"

"It's no problem."

"*Seriously?* Because I'd really appreciate it."

"Sure." Sandra turned to look at the clock. "It'll be about forty-five minutes."

"I'll be here. Thanks!"

"No problem at all." Sandra hung up the phone and went back to the table. She liked Loreen. It would be fun to stop by and help her out. Certainly a lot more fun than sitting home alone watching *Wheel of Fortune* and wondering if she should go on another blind date.

She arrived at Loreen's house just under an hour later. Loreen was ready with cups of instant coffee and a plate full of Girl Scout cookies. Thin Mints.

This was really going to put Sandra's acupuncture to the test.

Loreen told the story of her debacle, beginning with her call from Caveman and ending with a lot of self-punishment about how badly she'd "failed." By the time she was finished, Sandra was feeling guilty for getting her into this business in the first place.

"But I really want to do this," Loreen said with absolute sincerity. "I really do. I'm not a prude. I'm just a bad improvisational actress."

"Okay," Sandra said, pushing back from the plate of cookies and leaning against the sofa back. "So the guy said *light my fire,* right? You could say something like *Okay, baby, because I'm really burning for you.*"

"Ooh, that's good." Loreen looked impressed. "But what if he just lobbed me another one-liner, trying to get *me* to start the juicy stuff?"

"Then you just—" Sandra made a swooshing tennis-type motion.

"—hit it right back over to him. Say something like *I like your voice, you're getting me hot . . . tell me what makes* you *hot.* Guys eat that stuff up."

"Yeah?"

Sandra nodded. "Get him interested, make him feel like he's turning you on, but keep sending it back to him so you can mirror whatever it is he wants."

"Brilliant."

Sandra laughed. "It works. *And* it keeps them on the phone longer. Even though your talk with Caveman didn't pan out, you got *something* out of it just in the time it took him to tell you it blew."

Loreen nodded. "This is good stuff, Sandra. And I swear it would work for dating, too. Guys love to talk about themselves. What better way to turn them on than to make them think you're turned on by every little thing they have to say?"

Sandra thought about that. "You might have a point. Actually, a good point. Of course, the first thing I'd need to do is get a decent date. So far that hasn't happened."

"Not even one?"

"Not one." Sandra reached for the Thin Mints. She hated thinking about her miserable dates. Chocolate would help.

Chocolate *always* helped.

Chocolate and shoes. They'd never let her down.

# Chapter
# 15

Abbey was cleaning up the dishes after dinner Saturday night when she heard Brian at the door, talking to someone.

Pulling a dishrag down to dry her hands, she went to the door and was shocked to see Damon standing in her foyer.

"Honey," Brian said when he saw her. "Come here. I want you to meet one of our new parishioners. This is Lloyd. Lloyd, this is my wife, Abbey."

*Lloyd?*

"Nice to meet you," Abbey said through clenched teeth.

"Hey, Abbey." He put out a large, meaty hand. "Nice to meet you, too. I was just dropping off some clothes for the church charity drive. My wife sent these over for ya." He held up a stuffed kitchen trash bag with God knew what in it.

"How nice," Abbey said, taking the bag. *Go away!* her mind screamed. *Go away, go away, go away!*

"Lloyd's new to the area," Brian said.

"Sort of new," Damon corrected. He was looking at Abbey with open amusement now. "I haven't really been to church in a while, but I'm thinking it's time to wear sheep's clothing again."

His message was loud and clear.

"Excuse me a minute," Brian said, giving Abbey a look she recognized as *Nice guy, huh?* "Lloyd, I'll get you the schedule and the information about Bible groups."

"What the hell are you doing here?" Abbey rasped when Brian was gone.

"Fine language for a preacher's wife."

"I mean it!"

"I told you I'd be around. Here I am."

"Just delivering clothes for the poor, huh?" She held up the bag. "Does anything in here explode?"

"You better hope not."

"I want you out of my home."

"Now that's not very Christian of you. What if I came here for help? Do you do counseling, Mrs. Walsh?" He took a step toward Abbey and raked his gaze across her so brazenly, she suddenly felt nude. "I understand sometimes pastors' wives do that."

Abbey took a step back. "Stay away from me."

Brian returned at that moment. "Here's the worship schedule, and some other programs we have. Do you have any kids, Lloyd?"

"No, sir." Damon shook his head as if he really regretted that. "But I'm hoping to maybe adopt an older child." His eyes met Abbey's. "I always wanted a son."

My God, was he threatening *Parker*? Would Damon sink *that* low? Of course he would.

"Thank you so much for your donation," she said, walking behind him and opening the front door for him to leave. "I don't have any donation receipts here, but if you want to give me your address, we can send one from the church office." She looked at him pointedly.

He got it. And lobbed it right back. "No, that's all right. It's enough just to give. That feels good."

"We appreciate it," Brian said, oblivious.

"I'm sure you do." Damon kept his eyes fastened on Abbey. "I'm sure you do."

As soon as he'd gone, she went straight up to Parker's room, with the bag still in hand. She opened the door and peeked in, just to make sure Parker was still safely in bed. He was.

So she took the bag into her room and opened it to see what was inside it. She was prepared for anything. Small dead animals, old photos of her in a compromising position—she braced herself for the worst.

But all she found was a handful of clothes with Wal-Mart tags on them, undoubtedly stolen on the way over here.

He'd gone to a lot of trouble to make sure she knew he knew where to find her and how to identify her husband. That visit had been a warning; she had no doubt about that.

She just wished she had the money to heed it.

✳

Charlie was asleep. He'd gotten in late this evening from yet another business trip, and, after throwing dinner down his gullet, he'd gone straight to bed. She'd put Andy down about an hour before that, and Kate went about an hour later, leaving Tiffany at 8 P.M. with the downstairs to herself.

She celebrated by taking a bottle of chardonnay downstairs with her to "work." She poured the wine into the cap from the Tide bottle.

After folding some laundry—there was always laundry—she logged on and got a call almost instantly.

"My name's Mick," the gravel-voiced caller told her as soon as she introduced herself.

"Hi, Mick."

"You know, like Mick Jagger," he went on. "I know a lot of guys lie about who they are, but I don't see the point unless you're ashamed."

"Me neither, Mick." It was, of course, Crystal talking. "There's nothing to be ashamed of here."

"I'm glad we agree. Now, what kind of panties are you wearing?"

"I'm not wearing any." She feigned a giggle. "I hope you don't mind."

"Hell no." He let out a long sigh. "That just means we can get down to business faster. I want you to touch yourself."

"I have been ever since I first heard your voice," she lied, then wondered where that audacity had come from.

Clearly, it pleased him. "Touch yourself," he said.

She wasn't used to the bluntness, but she'd seen enough late-night shows on Cinemax to be prepared for what this would inevitably entail.

"Ahhhhh." She tried to sound like she was enjoying herself, but it had come out more like a yawn. "Oh, Mick."

"Feels good?"

"So good."

He proceeded to issue instructions to her: touch this, touch that, suck this, lick that. It wasn't her thing, but then again, she didn't really have to do it. It was just a virtual game of Simon Says.

So she groaned and giggled and did all the appropriate things. "It feels *so* good," she said, then remembered something else Sandra had told her. Make sure he feels it's personal. "I'm pretending it's you touching me."

He seemed to like that. "Keep going, baby." His voice was growing rougher. "Now take your hand and put it back on your pussy."

*Simon says masturbate.*

"Ooooh," Tiffany said. Then she got up and quietly refilled the Tide cap with wine. It no longer mattered that the wine was cheap and tasted too sweet. It beat the heck out of what this guy *wanted* her to be tasting.

He moaned. "I love the way you sound when you start breathing heavy."

Oh! Heavy breathing! She'd forgotten to maintain that. That was one of the basics, Sandra had said.

So she started. "You . . . are . . . amazing." She added a squeal, hoping it would lend sincerity to her statement.

It seemed to work. "Oh, yeah."

She could hear him working on himself in the background.

The wine must be getting to her, because this was sort of starting to turn her on.

"Spread your legs," he uttered. "I want to see your dripping love juices."

*Love juices?* Hm. That put the brakes on the turn-on.

"I'm putting my dick in your pussy now," he said.

"Oh, you're so big." Men loved to hear that stuff, didn't they? All of them. No matter how patently untrue it sometimes was.

"I'm running my tongue down your neck."

"Ahhhhh." Tiffany was losing track. Wasn't some of this stuff physically impossible to do simultaneously?

"What's in your refrigerator?" he asked suddenly.

"What's in . . . what? My *refrigerator*?" Where was *this* headed? Would he want a postcoital snack? That *would* be consistent with the whole Happy Housewives theme.

As a matter of fact, food and eating were very sensual things. Maybe that would be Tiffany's—well, *Crystal's*—hallmark. She'd describe food in wonderful, sensual detail. She'd be the Nigella Lawson of phone sex. She could even—

"What do you have that you can use as a dick? Cucumbers? Two or three carrots?" His voice deepened. "Let's see how many you can fit in there."

Tiffany was prepared to do a lot of things, and *say* a lot of things. She was aware of the fact that it wasn't always going to be fun. But she just couldn't picture herself sitting in the basement with a capful of wine by her side, saying *I got another carrot in and boy does that feel awesome.*

"I have a zucchini," she said quickly, then added, on a hunch, "it's really big, though. I'm not sure it will fit."

"Do it," he said immediately. "But first put a rubber on it."

She almost laughed. "I have black, red, or green," she said instead, enjoying the image of a dressed-up zucchini. "What do you want me to use?"

"Black. Put on the black one."

She crinkled the dry cleaner's paper on one of Charlie's suits.

"Lay back and spread your legs," he said. "I'm going to fuck you with that cucumber."

"Oh, baby." No point in correcting him and telling him it was a zucchini. But why did so many people get those two things mixed up? They were *totally* different things.

"I'm going to fuck you hard," Mick was saying.

Tiffany moaned and tried to calculate how much this call had earned her so far. It seemed like she'd been on the phone forever.

"Oh, baby, I'm going to make you come over and over again," Mick panted.

"Take your time," Tiffany said, making her voice coo. "We've got all night. *All night long.*"

Which seemed easy until Mick suggested he was going to put the cucumber where normally it would come *out*.

The image was so unexpected that Tiffany's response was immediate. "Ew!"

"What?"

Oh no, she'd broken the spell. "Ooooh," she said, trying to include a little of the *ew* sound, so he'd think she'd been into it the whole time. "Do it." No zucchini bisque for her in the near future.

"Yeah, baby."

Then, just as she felt she was hitting her stride, Tiffany heard footsteps overhead. Heavy footsteps.

Charlie had woken up.

And he was probably looking for her.

So she ratcheted up the dirty talk, whispering the filthiest, most provocative things she could think of, impatiently waiting through Mick's labored moans and groans until finally, thank God, he finished.

"Oh man, Crystal, you are fucking incredible," he said, breathless. "I've never heard a woman talk like that. I'm going to request you next time."

"I can't wait," she whispered. The door to the basement opened.

"Tiffany?" Charlie called.

*Shit! Shit shit shit!* "Call me back," she said to Mick quickly. "Soon." Then she flipped the phone closed.

What else could she do? It wasn't like she could just put her hand up to tell Charlie to wait while she finished the guy off.

It was bad policy to end a call quickly; she knew that. But it was probably a whole lot worse to have the caller hear your husband calling for you.

Unless, of course, that was the fantasy.

Tiffany shook off the thought. She couldn't figure all of this out right now. She just needed to appease Charlie.

"I'm here," she called, then downed the rest of her wine and put the cap back on the Tide bottle.

Oh God. Oh God, she couldn't let him find out what she'd been doing.

"What're you doing down here?" Charlie asked, sounding irritable. "I'm trying to sleep."

What was she doing? She was enjoying herself with another man, more than she'd ever enjoyed herself with Charlie, and the other man wasn't even actually there.

So she decided the best defense would be a low-key offense. "What does my being down here have to do with you trying to sleep?" she asked, kicking the dryer door shut to sound like she was doing laundry.

"I didn't know where you were," he said, as if that were the same as not having a blanket or, perhaps, oxygen.

"Well, I'm here."

"I think you should come up."

"I have more to do here," she said. "Then I'll be up. Just go on to bed."

"What *things* are you doing?"

Would he never let up? "I had some things in the dryer and I wanted to fold them so I wouldn't have to iron in the morning, that's all." No, that wouldn't take long enough. "And I have to soak some things in bleach."

Her guilt was immense. It wasn't like she was having an affair down in the basement of their house, and there was no way he'd suspect she was doing phone sex, but she still felt a tremor of fear that he'd find out and go ballistic.

She turned on the washer, dumped in some bleach, and dropped in a pillowcase that was folded on top of the dryer.

Never in her life had she preferred work of any sort to relaxing in bed. It was probably a bad sign that she preferred it now.

# *Chapter* 16

So who did you get last night?" Loreen asked Abbey. Abbey's stories were becoming legendary for their unrelenting freakishness.

Loreen and Abbey were standing with Tiffany outside the school on the sidewalk by the bus lane, waiting for the kids to get out. They had about ten minutes before the bell rang.

"Well, there was Carl, who wanted to pretend we were on a tropical island *being watched by hungry cannibals.* And there was also Boo—yes, *Boo*—who wanted me to dunk his head in the toilet." Abbey raised an eyebrow. "Not what *I'd* call a turn-on."

Tiffany shook her head. "I just can't believe it. You get all the freaks."

"You mean you get normal guys?"

Tiffany nodded. "As normal as a guy can be if he's willing to pay that much per minute for phone sex, yeah."

Abbey considered. "Maybe it's something about the picture I put together for Mimi. Maybe *she's* a freak magnet, not me."

"You just keep telling yourself that," Tiffany said with a smile.

"I will." Abbey sighed. "Every time I pull on my Wonder Woman costume."

"Ix-nay," Tiffany said suddenly, as Deb Leventer approached. "Change the subject." She raised her voice. "In retrospect, it really was one of the most memorable trips ever."

"Hello, ladies," Deb said, oozing condescension even in those two small words. "What are we gabbing away about so secretively?"

"The trip to Vegas," Loreen said, sounding casual. "It was a great time, wasn't it?"

Deb looked doubtful. "Hm. When I last saw some of you there, it looked like you might be heading toward some mighty headaches." She gave a spiky laugh. "I'm writing to the school band association to suggest that Las Vegas was a terrible choice for the competition. Next year they should choose a more wholesome place."

"The kids seemed to have a good time," Tiffany said. She was pretty good. Her face didn't betray anything of the trouble the adults had gotten into.

"They'd have just as good a time in Salt Lake City," Deb snapped. "Or, my goodness, Washington, D.C. Think of all the history right around the corner from us."

"Vegas has a lot of history," Loreen said, knowing Deb would *never* agree. "Frank Sinatra, Dean Martin, Bugsy—what was his last name? Warren Beatty played him in that movie where he met Annette Bening."

Deb ignored her. "Excuse me, I think I see Hannah Brooks over there."

Loreen was glad they'd gotten off so easy. The less time they spent talking to Deb, the less likely it was that she'd figure out something was up with the PTA funds. And, given the fact that Deb was a letter-writer and a complainer, it was best that she never, ever find out what had happened or what Loreen, Tiffany, and Abbey were doing about it.

Later on, Loreen dropped Jacob off at Robert's work, because the office was moving and Robert had decided it was a good opportunity to "hire" Jacob to help, thereby instilling some good work ethics in him at an early age.

It was also good for her son's ego to feel like his dad needed him to help with the manly work of moving heavy stuff.

Loreen, on the other hand, went home to do the womanly work of hauling out the trash, cleaning up about fifty gallons of soapy water from where the washer had overflowed (a sock she didn't even recognize had blocked the laundry tub drain), and heating up a low-fat dinner that tasted more like the waxy cardboard it was wrapped in than the lasagna it was supposed to be.

She had some work to do on a few of her real estate listings, but the market had gone depressingly flat, so she was finished by six thirty and reminded of how tight money was.

She considered the time. Robert was taking Jacob out to dinner after work. They wouldn't be back until about eight. That gave her an hour and a half to log in to Happy Housewives.

The phone rang almost immediately.

"This is Mimi," she said, in her best Marilyn Monroe imitation. Which, actually, wasn't very good, but it was, at least, consistent. "Who are you?"

There was a long pause, then, "Call me Dawg."

"Dog?"

"Daw-g."

"Dawg," she tried, then, in a moment of whimsy, "can you howl for me?"

"Not that kind of dog," he snapped in a voice less deeply masculine than what he'd initially been going for.

"What do you want to do, *Dawg*?" she asked. She'd learned, at least, not to get wound up in stupid details that didn't matter. "Are you horny?"

"Obviously. That's why I called."

She wondered how he'd like it if she just called him Jackass. "What do you want to do about that?" she cooed instead.

"What the hell do you think I want to do?" he asked, apparently content to spend an exorbitant sum of money just to argue. "Turn me on."

"How about if I slip my red panties off, Dawg?" she asked. "Do you want to see me?"

"You know it." It was a sad thing that the only thing that made this guy less of a jerk was for her to stop thinking and just turn herself into his sex object.

Then again, that's what she was getting paid for.

"Now, I'm taking off my red bra," she said slowly. "Could you unbuckle it for me?"

"Rip it off," he growled. "I'll rip it off."

"Do it!"

Apparently he did. At least, she assumed that's what that spitty slashing sound was supposed to be.

Then there was another sound. One she wasn't expecting.

Robert and Jacob coming into the house!

*Why* did her family keep showing up when they weren't supposed to? Admittedly, she should have known about Jacob's half day, but she was absolutely sure Robert had said they'd be out for at least another hour.

"Go down on me," Dawg barked "Do it now! Take my dick in your mouth."

Oh, good Lord, whether they were supposed to be here or not, Jacob and Robert were plodding up the stairs. She heard Robert tell Jacob to go get something from his room; then Robert knocked on the door.

"Take my dick," her caller repeated.

"You've got it," she said, trying to soften her voice but still sound businesslike so Robert wouldn't hear and figure out what was happening. "Mmmm."

Robert knocked again, louder. "Loreen?"

This was a mess. It wasn't possible for her to get far enough from the door that her caller couldn't hear, and there was no way she wanted anyone to know her real name.

So, with no alternative, she opened the door to Robert and held up her index finger. *Business,* she reminded herself. *Sound professional.* "That's one hell of an asset you've got." She cupped her hand over the phone and whispered to Robert, "Business call. I'll be right down."

"Suck my meat," Dawg said.

She turned on the light and said to him, a little too loud, "It's prime. Prime plus." God, she could *not* let Robert find out what she was doing. If he did, he might think she was an unfit mother, and she might find herself in a custody battle for Jacob and—

"Yeah," Dawg groaned. "And don't be afraid to use your teeth. I can take it."

"Okay," she said.

Robert looked at her a little oddly, then nodded and turned to retreat down the hall.

"Next I want you to suck my toes," Dawg said.

"What?" It was so unexpected, she couldn't help her startled reaction.

Robert stopped and turned back.

"Oh, sure," she said into the phone, waving Robert off with a smile, like she'd just seen a spider or something. "There's definitely interest," she improvised, knowing Robert could still hear her if he was listening. "Getting lower. And lower." She watched as Robert rounded the corner and went down the stairs; then she closed the door and sat on the edge of the bed, heart pounding. "I just can't get enough of you," she said into the phone, but she knew it didn't sound like she meant it at all.

Fortunately for her, she'd been convincing enough up to that point that Dawg was past caring. Within five minutes, the call was over and Loreen was able to straighten herself up enough to go down and face Jacob and Robert.

"I got *twenty dollars*, Mom!" Jacob held up a crisp twenty-dollar bill. "Dad's secretary said I was the strongest guy there!"

"I bet you were." Loreen went over and ruffled his hair with her freshly washed hand. "Sorry about that," she said to Robert. "One of my clients needs me to hold his hand through all the financial stuff. I've explained it over and over, but he just doesn't seem to get it."

"I'm sure he got it this time," Robert said, quirking a smile that made her wonder how much he'd heard.

"Jacob," she said, keeping her eyes fastened on Robert's. "Go get your jammies on, okay?"

"Do I *have* to?"

"Yes!" Robert and Loreen said simultaneously.

"It's a school night," Loreen added.

Jacob rolled his eyes dramatically, and said, *"Okay."* His eyes lit up. "Do I get ice cream?"

"You already had dessert at the restaurant," Robert said. "Now go. Get your jams on."

Jacob slumped out of the room dramatically. When he was gone, Loreen breathed a sigh of relief.

For a moment.

"So," Robert said, leaning back against the sofa and steepling his hands in front of him. "What were you up to when we got home?"

"I told you." She swallowed and licked her dry lips. "I was on a business call."

"Then I'm afraid to ask what your business is."

She felt her face go red hot. "What do you mean?"

Robert lowered his chin and looked at her in that way she recognized to mean *cut the bullshit*.

"How much did you hear?" she asked, deflating. She already knew the answer: enough to humiliate her.

"It's none of my business," Robert said. "I shouldn't have listened—"

"You listened?"

This time Robert blushed. "I can't lie to you, Lor. I couldn't turn away. At first I thought it wasn't you," he went on. "We never . . . you know, we never talked that way to each other."

Maybe they should have. "I know," she agreed.

"So . . ."

She could tell he wanted to ask if she had another man. And she wanted to reassure him on that point. Not that she owed him fidelity or anything anymore, but it would be a little hard for her if she knew he was sleeping with someone—and maybe he was, who knew?—so her instinct was to tell him that wasn't the case.

But was it better for her to say she was a phone sex operator?

What would be harder for him to take?

She looked into his pale blue eyes. They always had that puppy-dog quality, just as Jacob's did, so that shouldn't have suckered her, but there was a deeper hurt in them that made her decide she had to tell him the truth.

"It's not what you think," she started.

He lifted an eyebrow. "It's not?"

She winced. "Oh, Robert, this is not easy to explain."

"You don't owe me an explanation."

"I know. But you want one, don't you?"

He gave a laugh. "More than you can imagine."

She swallowed. "Okay. So what happened is this. You know how we took the kids to Las Vegas for the band thing, right?"

He nodded.

"Well, some of us did a little gambling. A little too much gambling. Actually . . . it was a *lot* too much gambling. And I was the most foolish of everyone."

Robert looked skeptical. "*You* gambled?"

"You have no idea." She shuddered, remembering the night. "I was like a different person."

"I can't even imagine you doing that." He didn't say it in a judgmental way. He just sounded . . . interested. "Looks like I'm learning a lot of things about you I never knew."

She gave a dry laugh. "Just be glad you got the good stuff and I saved the bad stuff for *after* our separation."

"Why do you do that?"

"Do what?"

"Denigrate yourself. There's nothing wrong with gambling. There's nothing wrong with losing at it either," he added before she could say it.

She leveled her eyes on him. "Even when you do it with the PTA's money?" she challenged.

He cocked his head. "You lost me."

"I was drinking," she began, then held up a hand. "Yes, I was drunk. I'm telling you, it was a strange weekend. Anyway, I got confused in the casino and accidentally got cash advances on the PTA credit card instead of my own."

Robert gave a shout of laughter. "Not good."

"Well, they *are* from the same bank." She hesitated. There was no point in trying to defend herself. "No, it was stupid. Anyway, I racked up thousands of dollars' worth of debt on the PTA card. Because I'm the treasurer, you know." She smiled. The irony . . . it was all too ridiculous.

"I don't want to butt in, but where are you going to get the money to pay it off? The real estate market isn't exactly hot." He laughed. "Despite your call earlier."

She clicked her tongue against her teeth and drew a breath in. "Funny you should mention that, because that's what I'm doing to supplement my income."

"Getting a boyfriend?" He looked confused.

"No." She shook her head and held his gaze. "Phone sex." Then, to be absolutely clear, "I'm a phone sex operator. Lonely men call 900-HOUSEWIVES and I tell them whatever they want to hear for however many minutes they can afford. Or, rather, *Mimi* does."

"Mimi?"

She nodded. "My stage name."

The shock on his face was complete. "You're . . . Are you pulling my leg?"

"No. But I could. In fact, for two ninety-five a minute, I could pull just about anything you want me to."

"You're kidding, right?"

She shook her head. "I wish I were."

"You're having phone sex with strangers for money."

"That's about the size of it."

He stood up and paced the floor in front of her. "When we were married, you didn't have the time or energy to hold my hand. Now you're jacking off strangers over the phone?"

"I don't *want* to," she said, looking down. "It's just the only way to pay back the debt quickly."

"So if I'd *paid* you—"

"Don't go there," she interrupted. "That is *not* what this is like."

"Do you know how long I waited for you to be with me again? After Jacob was born, I understood it would take a while, but not *years*. If you had come to me at any point, if you had *tried* to put the intimacy back into our relationship, we might not be where we are. But all you did was rebuff me, and now . . ." He threw his hands in the air. "I can't believe this."

Loreen saw, for the first time since they'd separated, that Robert wasn't being *critical* of her time with Jacob, he was *missing* her time with *him*.

How had she been so blind to that?

"It wasn't that I didn't *want* to . . . be with you." Funny how hard it was to find the words when she wasn't on the phone. "Back then, especially, with Jacob so young, it was just hard to find the right time."

He looked doubtful.

And maybe, in a way, he was right.

"I didn't feel good about myself," she said plainly.

Robert looked startled. "What? What are you talking about?"

"After having Jacob." She gestured toward her hip and stomach area. "I was never able to get my old shape back. I didn't—I *don't*—feel like myself."

"But you *are* yourself. Did you think I was judging you?"

She thought about that for a moment. "Maybe. I don't know. Maybe I was judging myself so much that I couldn't imagine you weren't. Especially since you were seeing all the changes so"—she shrugged—"intimately." Tears reached her eyes. She was embarrassed to say all of this out loud, and embarrassed that it was true. Her brief time with Rod, aside from the part where she got the bill, had felt "safe" because she knew she'd never see him again. She wouldn't have to face him in the morning and wonder if he was thinking about how doughy her butt was compared to someone else's.

Robert looked uncomprehending. "But I loved you. And any changes in your body, not that they were nearly as significant as you think, were because you carried and delivered our son. Your body is beautiful and strong and perfect just like it is."

The tears ran down her cheeks, and she sniffled unseductively. "That's nice of you to say—"

He grasped her arms. "Loreen, I *mean* it."

She swallowed. "Even if you do, that doesn't make me less self-conscious." It would have been easy to say, *Then why didn't you just go on a diet?* But Robert knew better.

"So you do it over the phone and you look however you want to."

She thought about it a moment, then nodded. "Not that it's been any great turn-on." The conversation was making her uncomfortable. "It's late, Robert. I need to get to bed."

He looked at his watch. "It's seven thirty."

"You're kidding." It felt like midnight. "I must be coming down with something."

Robert looked concerned. "Could be stress."

She gave a dry laugh. "That's for sure."

"Want me to stay and put Jacob to bed?"

She did. But she couldn't. "I'll do it," she said. "But thanks."

He came to her and bent to kiss her cheek. He smelled of the same aftershave he always had. And soap. Robert always smelled clean.

He left, and Loreen went back to the sofa to sit down for a minute and rest.

She woke hours later. The room was dark, she was disoriented, and the only light in the house seemed to come from Jacob's room, along with the very loud and *extremely* annoying sounds of *LEGO Star Wars II* on the PlayStation.

Loreen went upstairs and pushed Jacob's door open. She shielded her eyes from the light. "What time is it?" she asked.

Jacob glanced at her then turned back to his game and shrugged. "Is Dad still here?"

"Dad left." Loreen's eyes fell on the clock. "Two hours ago. It's ten, Jacob, what are you doing up still?"

He shrugged. "No one put me to bed."

"Well, you're ten years old. Can't you put yourself to bed when it gets late?"

"I just figured you'd come up like usual."

"Okay, I'm up now. Turn the game off, get your teeth brushed, and get yourself in bed."

"But—"

"*Now!*" It was way too late to argue about it.

Jacob put the game on hold, didn't turn off the TV, and stalked off to the bathroom, where Loreen suspected he held the electric toothbrush up toward the door for a minute or two in the ON position before coming back out.

"Okay?" he asked, splaying his arms sarcastically.

He was at least three years too young for that kind of sarcasm. She hadn't even attempted it until she was thirteen, and it had taken another three years to truly perfect it.

"Bed," she commanded. "Right this minute."

"Just lemme finish this game!"

"Jacob Henry Murphy, you have been up *hours* past your bedtime. Do you really think you should beg to stay up even longer to play a video game?"

Put that way, he seemed to get it. He hung his head. "No. I guess not."

"Sleep. Got it?"

"I got it."

"Good." Loreen headed for her bedroom, knowing she'd have to get up in a few minutes to check and make sure Jacob hadn't turned the game on again.

Fortunately the nap had done her good, and she had some energy to do a little administrative work she needed to catch up on. They now had five outside workers—or "actresses"—on the roster, and when she went to the site to check their statistics, she saw they were logging a lot of hours.

She went to the spreadsheet she'd created and made note of what they were owed. Loreen had arranged to pay weekly, on Fridays, via a PayPal account she'd created just for that purpose.

Taking calls was hard, but it was amazing how easy it was to be a virtual madam to *other* phone actresses.

And how lucrative.

She switched screens and checked the Gregslist listing. She *had* been planning to take it down, to keep the operation small, but she decided that she could handle a staff of maybe five more workers. The money was certainly persuasive.

She'd keep the ad up.

And she'd be a madam for just a *little* bit longer. After all, it was the best contribution she could make to the group.

# *Chapter* 17

Abbey had done a lot of soul searching in the weeks since they'd gotten back from Las Vegas, but she couldn't decide if she thought running into Damon was a coincidence or punishment for her long-past sins.

Not that it mattered. In the end, the result was the same: She had to pay him his money or run the risk of having him expose her past. Getting indignant at the injustice of it wasn't going to chance the facts, and all her fantasies about telling Damon to go to hell were just that: fantasies.

If he went to hell, he'd made it clear he was taking her with him.

Fortunately, Loreen had just told them all that the business was going even better than they'd thought. They'd done some advertising with their limited funds, and by advertising to students in the local college newspapers, Loreen had managed to add more part-time operators to the coffers. Still, they paid their employees half the earnings, so it was still more lucrative for Loreen, Abbey, and Tiffany to do their own work.

In fact, that was what she was doing this evening since Brian said he wouldn't be home until eight. It was now seven fifteen, Abbey had given Parker a healthy dinner and plunked him down in front of the TV, and then she had come upstairs to the master bedroom, where she could close the door to the hall *and* the door to the bedroom.

With that double layer of protection and a quiet voice that would hopefully be read as sultry, she was set.

And she was in the middle of her third call of the night when the house phone rang. How could she have forgotten to turn the ringer off in her room?

"Hey, is that a phone ringing?" her caller asked, obviously drawn out of the matador moment he'd been having.

"Well, of course, honey," Abbey said, thinking fast as she ran downstairs to the basement where he wouldn't be able to hear the phone anymore. "I'm a real person at a real house and someone's calling. You didn't want to talk to some impersonal operator in a big room somewhere, did you?"

Her ploy worked. "No. I like that. You're at home?"

"Yes, I am."

"Where do you live?"

"Near the University of Maryland's Baltimore campus," she lied quickly.

"Oooh, are you a student?" He sounded like he wanted the answer to be yes.

So it was. "Yes," she said. "But please don't tell anyone I told you so. We're supposed to be older than that."

"That's okay, baby." He was into this. No surprise there. "You don't have to be a housewife at home cooking me a pot roast. As long as you know what to do with a hot dog, we'll get along just fine."

The phone rang again; she could hear the distant trill upstairs.

Abbey paused. Maybe it was an emergency.

If it was, though, it was for Brian, and she couldn't help, except to take a message, and the machine was already doing that.

"I do just fine with hot dogs," she said, and finished the call while she organized the winter clothes in the storage room.

When the call was over, she had clocked an impressive thirty-five minutes. Usually the guys didn't last that long. They were either too excited to keep it up, or too cheap to let it last that long. Now and then she'd heard the telltale beep of the call being taped and she knew her caller would be replaying it later instead of calling back.

What could she do? She wasn't going to reprimand guys for being frugal. After all, this was supposed to be Happy Housewives not Mean Mommies.

Speaking of which, she hadn't checked on Parker in more than half an hour. It was probably time to unglue him from the *Star Wars* video game Brian had just gotten him and put him to bed, where his agitated brain wave activity would probably keep him up for hours.

"Why'd the phone keep ringing?" he asked, making the red guy on screen crash a sword into the brown guy.

"I don't know. I couldn't get to it. I was straightening up downstairs. I'll check the messages." She took the game controller from his hand and turned off the TV. "You go get ready for bed."

"I'm not tired! It's only eight thirty!"

Eight thirty. She looked at the clock with an odd knot in her stomach. But why? What was wrong with eight thirty?

"The rule is," she said, though she'd said it a hundred times already, "that you're supposed to start getting ready for bed and winding down between eight fifteen and eight thirty. You need to be *in* bed, *in* the dark by nine. By my calculations, the timing should work out just about right."

"But—"

"Oh, honestly, Parker, do you have to argue about *everything*? Just get ready for bed, would you?" She went to the kitchen, took a grape from the fruit bowl on the counter, popped it into her mouth, and called the voice mail center.

"This is Shady Grove Adventist Hospital, could you please call us back at 301-279-32 . . ."

Abbey swallowed the half-chewed grape and jotted the number down with a shaking hand.

Oh, God.

She called the number back.

*"ER."*

Abbey tripped over her words. "I'm calling for—I need—patient services,"

"Name, please."

"My name is Abbey Walsh." She didn't want to say the next part, didn't want to somehow make it true in between giving her name and his. "My husband is Brian Walsh. He was supposed to be home half an hour ago and he's not home yet, so I hope everything's okay." She was rambling, her voice growing higher and higher, like a helium balloon. "But he's not home yet." She dropped her head in her free hand and waited for the woman on the other end of the line to speak.

"One moment, please."

The subsequent wait seemed interminable. There was no hold

music. Presumably they didn't want next-of-kin to have to listen to "Love Will Keep Us Together" while waiting to find out if their loved ones were alive or dead.

"Mrs. Walsh?" It was a man's voice.

"Yes?" She didn't know whose voice she was using. It certainly didn't sound like hers.

"Mrs. Walsh, this is Dr. Fram. I'm your husband's attending physician."

"My husband's attending physician?" She gripped the phone hard enough to squeeze juice out of it. "Why? What's happened? I don't know what's going on."

"Okay, calm down—"

"Tell me what's going on!" She'd ignored the phone calls from the hospital because she was doing phone sex with some creepy stranger, while her husband was in the hospital, maybe dying.

Maybe dead.

"Your husband was in a car accident—"

She leaned against the wall behind her and slid down. "Oh, God." *Damon.* She should have known he wasn't going to give her a break.

"—He was brought in at eight ten. We need to do surgery, Mrs. Walsh, do you understand? We need your permission to do the surgery."

"What kind of surgery?" Not that she was qualified to give an educated yes or no either way.

"He has internal bleeding. His spleen is ruptured. We need to remove it as soon as possible."

She'd have to be a fool, or a Scientologist, to say no to any surgery an ER doctor deemed necessary. "Do it."

"Can you come in, Mrs. Walsh?"

She batted tears from her eyes and cheeks. "Yes, of course. Do you need my signature?"

"Yes, but there isn't time. I'm going to have to go with your oral consent."

She nodded convulsively.

"Mrs. Walsh?"

"Do it," she said again, trying to swallow the hard lump in her throat. "Do whatever you need to do. I'll be right there." She didn't wait for an answer, or a rebuttal. Maybe she should have, but she was running on pure adrenaline and perhaps flawed instinct now.

"Parker!" She ran into the bathroom, where he was brushing his teeth in micro-motion. Other nights she would have corrected him.

Tonight, she took the toothbrush out of his hand and tossed it onto the counter.

"We have an emergency," she said, then tried to soften it. "I have something I have to do very quickly, so you're going over to Mrs. Dreyer's house, okay?" She hadn't asked Tiffany's permission yet, of course. That potentially faulty instinct she was applying told her to take Parker to Tiffany's and ask questions later.

She bundled him up, grabbing clothes for tomorrow, just in case, and his Game Boy to keep his mind off the fact that his mother and father were missing in action, and got into the car.

It was deep twilight, the most beautiful time of a summer day, Abbey thought. Or at least she *usually* thought. At the moment, she wished it were dark, to cover everything—all the things around her that held memories—she could see only the ten feet in front of her headlights.

She had to get to Brian.

Tiffany lived only a few blocks away, and the drive had lasted only minutes, but to Abbey it felt like hours. When she finally got to the house, she jerked the car to a halt in the driveway.

The lights were on inside, making a beacon of light in the lowering cloak of dusk.

Abbey knocked on the door, a staccato punctuation to the still twilight.

Tiffany answered, and her expression went from blank curiosity to grave concern in a split second.

For the first time since she'd gotten the call, Abbey felt her strength buckle. "There's an emergency." Her voice faltered. "The hospital called." She whispered it. "Brian had an accident."

Tiffany didn't need more explanation. She stepped back, opening the door as she did so, effectively ushering Parker in. "Hey, Parker. Can you stay awhile?"

"What's going on?" Parker asked. He'd been asking it over and over since Abbey had put him in the car.

"I . . ." Abbey's chest tightened. There was nothing to say. What on earth could she say that would be the truth? That she was scared witless? That his father was hurt and might not live through the night? Might not, in fact, live long enough for Abbey to get there?

That would hardly make Parker feel better.

Tiffany must have seen the panic on her face, because she said, smoothly and easily, "Your mom asked if you could come over while she ran some errands. I've been wondering where you two were."

Parker looked to Abbey for confirmation.

"You stay here and play with Kate, all right?" She flashed a grateful look at Tiffany, who, with the slightest of nods, made Abbey feel like everything was going to be all right.

"I'll come back as soon as I can."

"I'll wait," Tiffany said quietly. "Take your time. No matter how long."

Tears burned in Abbey's eyes. She'd never had a friend like this in her life. Even when she was way younger, and had friends she'd go out with and party with every weekend, she'd never in her life had the kind of friend who would wait for her through the night without even knowing why or how long.

But she needed it tonight. "Thank you," she mouthed, then kissed Parker on top of the head and said, "You be good for Mrs. Dreyer, all right? Because she'll tell me if you're bad."

"I'll be good," Parker assured her. Then asked Tiffany, "Where's Kate?"

At this moment, Abbey really could have used the comfort of his small embrace, but she wasn't about to exact it from him and make him panic about what was really going on.

Why should he worry before everyone was *sure* there was something to worry about?

With Tiffany's reassurance that she would put the kids to bed and plan to keep Parker until she heard otherwise, Abbey drove to the hospital. Though it was really about a fifteen-minute drive, it seemed like hours, and every time she approached a red light, her leg shook so much that she almost couldn't depress the brake.

When she finally got to the traffic light from Shady Grove Road into the hospital driveway, the light seemed to stay red forever. There was no traffic coming for at least the quarter mile or so Abbey could see in the distance.

Finally, heedless of the law, she gunned the engine and blew right through the light.

To hell with anyone who tried to stop her.

But no one did, and she parked in a daze and hurried into the emergency room.

"I g-got a call," she stammered, laying her clammy palms on the cold desktop. "My husband is here. Is this the right place to check in?"

Probably not. The elderly gentleman sitting there looked very kind but utterly clueless.

"What's your husband's name?" he asked, pushing his half glasses up the bridge of his nose.

"Brian Walsh." She tapped her fingers on the countertop, faster, faster, faster.

The man clicked something onto the keyboard and looked at the screen in front of him. "One moment." The man looked at her with sympathetic, watery blue eyes. "I need to call someone."

"Call someone?" she repeated, her voice sailing into near hysteria. "What do you mean you need to *call someone*? Is he dead? Are you not allowed to tell me he's dead?"

"Um." He pushed his glasses up again, only this time it was with a hand that shook. "I'm just a volunteer."

The beige cardigan should have told her that. People who worked in an atmosphere as stressful as this full-time didn't have the optimism to wear something like a beige Mr. Rogers sweater.

She waited for what seemed like hours, trying to keep from throwing up, while he picked up the phone and spoke in lowered tones for a moment. She caught the words *Brian Walsh* and *wife* and *very upset.*

Then he replaced the receiver and said to Abbey, "Mrs. Duncan will be right with you."

Abbey swallowed a sarcastic retort about how quickly Mrs. Duncan might move, because the poor man didn't deserve it. No one here did.

She was just lashing out because it was the only thing she could do, apart from cry.

And she couldn't afford to do that right now, because if she started, she knew she wouldn't be able to stop.

Another eternity passed before a dark-haired woman in a trim, tailored blue suit came around the corner. "Mrs. Walsh?"

Abbey nodded, mute.

The woman extended her hand. "I'm Ida Duncan, the patient services representative here. If you'll follow me, we can speak privately in my office."

Abbey followed. She was numb. Were they going to some sort of soundproof office where Ida could deliver the bad news?

What would Abbey tell Parker? How was she going to explain he didn't have a father anymore? How was she going to raise him without a father?

And what if Damon showed up again?

She'd kill him, that's what. She'd already fallen off the pious wagon. No matter how hard she tried, apparently it wasn't good enough for God, so she wasn't doing him any favors anymore.

*Vengeance is the Lord's* her ass.

She should have known this was going to happen. Damn it, damn it, damn it, it was all her fault. She knew how ruthless Damon could be. Had she imagined a decade in prison had *softened* him? Of course not. And now she'd dragged Brian into her own swirling black karma, and now he was the one paying the price. And Parker.

And yes, she was, too. But it wasn't fair that there should be other casualties.

All because of some stupid stolen necklace some jerk had asked her to hold on to a thousand years ago.

A jerk she never thought she'd see again.

"Mrs. Walsh?"

Abbey only half heard her name, then realized Ida Duncan was talking to her. "Yes. I'm sorry."

"Your husband is in surgery."

Surgery. They wouldn't operate on a dead man.

There was hope.

"How serious is it?"

Ida glanced at what appeared to be notes on Brian's case, on her computer. "We won't know anything until the doctors come out."

Abbey slumped in her chair and raised a trembling hand to push her hair back out of her face. "Do you know what happened? I mean, I know there was an accident, but I don't know where, I don't know how, I don't know anything."

"Mr. Walsh was in a single-car accident on Glen Road. No one else was involved."

Glen Road. Abbey hated that winding, hilly road with all its blind hairpin turns.

"The police are trying to piece together what happened, but it appears that he lost control of his car while rounding a curve."

"But he's a careful driver," Abbey said, more to herself than to Ida Duncan.

Yet it was Ida Duncan who answered. "Accidents happen sometimes, even to the most careful driver."

No they didn't. Not to Brian.

He was just caught in the crossfire of her war with God.

"You can wait in the waiting room now," Ida said, standing up.

Once again, Abbey followed the slight woman through the sterile halls of the hospital, until they got to a waiting room with uncomfortable-looking wooden chairs and several TVs with a fuzzy picture of CNN playing with the volume down low.

A young couple sat, looking worried, on one side of the room, so Abbey took a seat on the other side so all of them could have privacy in their anguish.

"Can I get you anything?" Ida asked. "Coffee or tea maybe?"

Abbey shook her head. "Thank you."

Ida looked like she wanted to say something else, but she just smiled and gave a single nod. "The doctors should be out soon."

∗

It was 2 A.M. when Abbey, after hours of waiting, half watching CNN, and drinking cup after cup of bad coffee, finally left the hospital, assured that Brian was in stable condition post-surgery.

He'd had a ruptured spleen and a punctured lung, in addition to several cracked ribs and broken teeth. The doctor had told her that, although Brian looked a mess, his chances for a full recovery were excellent.

She'd been allowed to see him, though only for a moment, because he was recovering in the intensive care unit.

At first, she hadn't even recognized the swollen, purple-bruised face as her husband's.

"Sorry . . . I'm . . . I'm late." His voice was labored, and he gave a feeble smile.

That was when Abbey lost it. The waiting room experience had been very much like her ritual on an airplane, concentrating all her will to make everything come out okay. She hadn't exactly felt *strong*, but she'd been stoic.

Now that was over.

She clasped his hands in hers and bowed her head. "Don't try to talk."

"'S okay."

"No, it's not. You have to save all your energy to get well."

"Just wanted . . . some . . . time off."

She gave a laugh through her tears. "Haven't you ever heard of the Caribbean?"

"Too . . . obvious."

"Oh, Brian." She closed her eyes against a new onslaught of tears and felt them drip off her lashes.

"Go home," he said, and raised a hand to try to stroke her hair. But the IV made it cumbersome and he was weak, so he dropped it back down. "Sleep."

"I don't want to leave you," she said.

"I'm going . . . sleep." He looked at her through lids at half-mast. "Go."

"I don't—"

"Go." His voice was weak but commanding. "I . . . mean it. Go. Parker."

She knew him well enough to know he meant it. And that she wouldn't do him any good hovering over him all night.

"I'll be back first thing in the morning," she told him. "Before you even wake up."

"Don't . . . dare wake . . . me up." His blinks were becoming longer and longer.

She knew he needed to sleep.

"Good night," she whispered, and bent to kiss his swollen cheek as lightly as she could. "I love you."

She meant it more than she could possibly express.

# Chapter 18

Tiffany was wide awake.

Fortunately, Parker had knocked off hours ago. After staying up an hour and a half past Kate's bedtime, running around like zoo animals—much to Charlie's disapproval—Kate and Parker had finally conked out on the bunk beds in her room. For once, Tiffany didn't care if Kate was up too late. Some things were more important than a regimented bedtime schedule.

"How long is that kid going to be here?" Charlie wanted to know. He'd just spent the evening in his "den," a fairly soundproof room in the upstairs loft, complete with a fifty-inch high-definition TV, a stereo that cost more than some cars, and a couple of recliners. It wasn't like it had been a hardship for him to go up there.

"He'll be here until his mother comes back," she said crisply. "Maybe longer than that. His father was in an accident."

"Oh." She hoped that would shut him up. But no. "Don't they have family around somewhere?"

Ever since their conversation about finances, Tiffany had begun to see Charlie in a new light. Or maybe it was the same light, but it *felt* new. Something inside her had wilted, but with the newfound freedom she was discovering with her work, she realized that she didn't *need* to stay in a marriage that made her feel so awful all the time. She was able to make it on her own, if she needed to.

And she was really beginning to think she needed to.

"They have *friends,* Charlie. *Me.* And I'm going to take care of that boy, and help his mother, until they don't need me to anymore."

"Okay, okay." He raised his hands in surrender, but the gesture was far too little and way too late. "You don't have to bite my head off. I was only asking."

"No, you weren't. You were *telling.* You were telling me that this emergency of someone else's was interrupting life in your little world and you don't like it. Not only do you not like it, but you blame *me.* And I think that really stinks, Charlie, I really do."

He rolled his eyes and let out an impatient puff of air. "I only asked one little question. Give me a break, would you?"

She looked at the man she'd married more than a decade before and realized, with sickening clarity, that she didn't really know him at all.

More important, she didn't really *like* him.

"By the way," she said, surprised at how detached she felt, "when I was doing laundry the other day I came across a bathing suit in your stuff. What was that all about?"

"I don't know what you're talking about."

"Of course you do. It was right on top of the pile of laundry I took upstairs."

He shrugged. "No clue."

She hadn't been prepared for complete denial. Lies, yes. Pretend befuddlement, sure. But pretending the suit didn't even exist at all?

She didn't know what to say to that.

"Stop trying to obscure the point," Charlie said, clearly coming out on the offense now. "A man has a right to privacy in his own home."

"Apparently he thinks he has a right to it in his marriage, too."

"What the hell is *that* supposed to mean?"

"Separate bank accounts, separate credit cards, separate lives, Charlie."

"I told you that was for business."

She thought about answering, but why? There was no winning this argument. She didn't even want the prize.

"Leave me alone," she said.

"Gladly." He walked off, the years and pounds weighing what was once a lanky gait into what was now an angry one.

She watched him go and it occurred to her that she wouldn't mind one bit if he just kept right on walking.

Something inside her was changing, and it wasn't just tonight, or the mysterious bathing suit, or the accident, or Charlie's remarkable lack of hospitality.

It was everything.

A year ago, she wouldn't have thought going broke and becoming a phone sex operator would be *good* for her, but to her surprise she found herself worrying less about every little thing. Just realizing how unpredictable life could be, and how things seemed to work out even in unexpected ways, was strangely reassuring.

And freeing.

So at this moment, when she'd normally be envisioning all kinds of terrible outcomes for Brian Walsh, she was actually pretty sure Abbey was going to come back and say he was going to be okay.

While she waited for that, Tiffany watched all the late-night interview shows, even the ones she normally couldn't stand. Finally, at 1:45 A.M. she decided to make a cosmopolitan. Actually, she decided to make a pitcher, just in case Abbey needed one when—and if—she returned tonight.

Fifteen minutes later, Abbey's headlights illuminated the front window, and Tiffany went outside to meet her.

"Is Brian okay?"

Abbey sniffled. It sounded like maybe she'd been doing a lot of that. "It looks like it."

Tiffany's shoulders relaxed for the first time all night. "Oh, thank God. I was so worried."

"I'm sorry," Abbey said immediately. "I should have called and given you an update earlier." She frowned as if that were an important detail. "I don't know why I didn't think of that."

"Maybe because your husband was in the hospital." Tiffany put her arm around Abbey. "Come on in. Would you like a drink?" She didn't care that Abbey was the pastor's wife; she was her friend, and she was going to offer her a drink without worrying about right or wrong.

"I would love a drink," Abbey said, giving a weak smile. "Make it a double."

"Cosmopolitan okay?"

"Moonshine would be okay at this point. Listerine. Anything."

Tiffany slipped her arm through Abbey's—a gesture she'd never done before—and said, "Come on, then. You've had a hell of a night. It's time to relax a little, if you can."

It took some time before Abbey's cool façade broke. Tiffany had taken her to the back sunroom, where they could have complete privacy, and had poured out three cosmos before Abbey finally said something meaningful instead of just polite.

"It's my fault."

"What?" Tiffany wasn't prepared for this. Abbey was always so strong, so cool.

"I'm sorry." Abbey waved a hand weakly, then put her hands over her eyes.

"Abbey." Tiffany didn't know what to do. Pour more cosmo? Offer coffee? Ask her to say more? Distract her so she didn't get too upset? "Don't blame yourself."

"It's *my* fault," Abbey insisted, almost angrily. "It's my fault." She leveled her gaze on Tiffany with an unmistakable challenge in her eyes. "This is all about me."

"What do you mean?" Tiffany asked.

Abbey closed her eyes. "I can't."

"You can talk to me. Abbey, it's clear you need to get something off your chest."

Abbey shook her head, wordless.

Tiffany put a hand on Abbey's. "You can talk to me." She meant it. She had never seen someone in so much pain as Abbey was, and she wanted to do anything she could to help. And at the moment, it looked like Abbey needed to let something out or burst.

"Can I?" Abbey looked up at her with reddened eyes. Her pupils were small, giving her an almost hostile look.

But Tiffany stood her ground. "Yes."

"And you think you could just listen and keep it to yourself?" Abbey challenged, like a child who was angling for one answer but fearing another.

Tiffany nodded. "Yes."

And then Abbey broke down.

She could not remember a time in her life when she had cried so much or so hard. Sobs came out in silent heaves, her tears hot and seemingly endless.

Later, she'd probably be embarrassed. But right now it felt like if she didn't let it out, she'd explode.

"I married Brian for the wrong reason," she said through ragged breaths. "He deserves better."

"What do you mean?" Tiffany soothed. "Why did you marry him?"

Abbey took one long, slow breath. Then another. Feeble attempts to quell the hysteria bubbling beneath her surface.

She had to get it out.

She had to tell the truth.

Finally.

"I married him to save myself."

"Save yourself?" Tiffany looked puzzled. "Save yourself from what?"

Abbey swallowed. Hard. "Eternal damnation."

✳

Three thirty in the morning, and Loreen couldn't sleep. She'd been tired all day, barely able to keep her eyes open, so why she woke up suddenly in the middle of the night was a mystery.

After tossing and turning from 3:01 A.M. until 3:30, she logged on as Mimi and waited for the phone to ring.

It didn't take long. She wasn't sure why that surprised her, but almost immediately she had a call from a guy who sounded *almost* young enough to be calling on his parents' dime while they were out of town.

Another ten minutes passed in the darkened room, and the phone rang again.

"This is Mimi," she said, trying out a new Mimi voice. This was more of a Betty Boop thing.

"Mimi?"

"Yes."

"This is Anonymous."

After weeks of doing this, she was prepared for just about anything. "Hey, Anonymous. What can I do for you?"

"I tried to call you earlier, but you weren't working."

"You can talk to anyone at Happy Housewives," she said. The Betty Boop voice had been a mistake, though. This was going to be very hard to keep up. "We're all glad to talk to you."

"Nope." His voice was starting to sound familiar. "They tried to pass me off onto someone else, but I wanted to talk to *you*."

She went with it, despite the disconcerting feeling she might know him. "Okay, Anonymous, what do you want to talk about?"

"My wife."

Wait a minute.

Loreen shifted in bed. "Your wife?"

"That's right."

It was Robert.

"Maybe you should call your wife on her own phone instead of paying three bucks a minute to talk to her," Loreen said.

"No, no. This will do."

She dropped Mimi's sexy inflection altogether. "Not if you have a kid going to college in a few years."

"I can afford it," Robert said. "It's for a good cause. I understand some happy housewives got into a little bit of trouble in Vegas."

Loreen smiled to herself. "Okay, then, Anon, what's up?"

."Well, like I said, I want to talk about my wife. That is, my soon-to-be ex-wife."

That *ex*. It always bugged her. It sounded so . . . hostile. "What about her?"

"Well—" He expelled a sigh. "—she probably wouldn't believe it if I told her, so I thought I might run it by you first. Maybe you can advise me."

"What is it?" Was he going to tell her he'd met someone? That he was getting married? Was he so afraid she'd freak out that he wanted to pay the PTA for her time, to mollify her?

She braced herself for his answer, trying to steel her heart against breaking, even though they were about to be divorced and she wasn't really supposed to feel *any* of this kind of stuff anymore.

"Well . . . my soon-to-be ex-wife—I'll call her Lor . . . etta."

"As in Lynn?"

"Exactly. She *loves* country music."

Loreen rolled her eyes. She *hated* country music. "What about Loretta, the country music queen?"

He clicked his tongue against his teeth. "Thing is, I think I'm still in love with her."

Loreen's stomach clutched. "*What?*"

"I know, I almost can't believe it myself."

"Is it . . . true?"

She could picture him nodding. "I'm afraid it is."

"Wow. So. What would you want *Loretta* to do with that information?"

"I'd want her to consider it for what it is: the truth. See, I told her I thought she was a control freak and that she was concentrating too much on our son and not enough on me, but I learned recently there was more behind it."

Loreen swallowed. "And how did that make you feel?"

"Like a jerk for not wondering what was going on with her sooner. Instead I got pissy about how it was affecting me." He sighed. "We probably should have gone to counseling."

Tears welled in Loreen's eyes. "She probably should have taken care of you more," she acknowledged. "If she had, maybe you'd still be married."

"We *are* still married," Robert said.

"Technicality."

"It doesn't have to be." He took a long breath. "I love her. I want to grow old with her."

She gave a laugh because it felt better than crying. "Women don't like to think about growing old."

"But, if we're lucky, we all do it. And I want to do it with my best friend. And that's what she is. She's the best friend I ever had."

She swallowed, but her throat was so tight, it hurt. "There's a lot to be said for marrying your best friend."

Robert hesitated. A costly hesitation, considering how much he was paying per minute. "So what do you think about divorcing your best friend?"

She took a breath. "I don't really like it, but I think sometimes if two people initiate something like that, maybe their initial reasons are sound."

"Okay, but think about this." Diplomatic Robert was here. "What if you're wrong?"

There was no Diplomatic Loreen. Just Reactive Loreen. "I don't want to make a mistake because I fall for the passion of the moment."

"*This* is not a passionate moment. This is an *honest* moment." Robert gave an exasperated sigh. "We're facing the possibility of pissing our whole lives away, each of us alone, because we're afraid to get hurt again."

Loreen shook her head in the dark, unable to take on such a huge possibility.

"I can't do this right now, Robert."

"Anonymous."

"Robert."

"Okay, Loretta."

She had to laugh.

"When *can* you do this?" he asked. "We need to talk about this. That is, unless you know beyond any shadow of a doubt that your answer is no." He waited a second. "Is that the case?"

She shook her head, but the lump in her throat prevented her from speaking.

"Loreen, I hear fabric rustling. Does that mean you're nodding or shaking your head?"

"Shaking my head," she said. "We'll talk about this later."

"You promise?"

She swallowed. "Yes."

"Okay, then. We'll talk soon, Loreen. Very soon."

She hung up the phone and held it to her chest, considering the possibilities. *Could* she get back together with Robert? Was that what she really wanted?

God knew she thought about him often enough. She'd loved being married to him. In fact, until the end, when they'd butted heads repeatedly over the issue of her detachment from the marriage, she'd loved just about everything about being with him. She even loved to go grocery shopping with him.

And, actually, she missed going grocery shopping with him.

She missed a lot about him.

Plus, there was the whole physical contact thing. Once upon a time, they were great together in bed, and she hadn't been with anyone—except Rod, and Lord knew she was trying not to think about *him*—since they'd split up.

It wasn't just the sex either. It was the casual intimacy of draping her legs over him while they sat on the couch watching TV together. It was lying in bed next to him while they read before kissing good night and turning off the lights.

It was that spatial intimacy that you just couldn't have with someone you weren't romantically intimate with.

She missed that.

She missed *him*.

But was she setting herself—and Jacob, there was no leaving Jacob out of the consideration—up for disappointment if they tried again and found out it didn't work?

She closed her eyes against the possibility. It was all too much to think about so late at night. She just wished she could somehow relax and get back to sleep.

She needed what her late-night callers got: a nice warm cup of orgasm.

The phone rang.

Damn it. She should have turned it off. She wasn't focused.

It rang again.

She tried to collect herself. She had to answer. Everyone knew she was the reason they needed so much money.

That got her. She opened the phone. "This is Mimi."

"Mimi, this is Anonymous."

She laughed. God, she was glad it was him. "Anonymous! Long time!"

"Too long."

"So what can I do for you?"

"Actually," he said, lowering his voice, "it's what I can do for you."

She frowned. He wasn't going to press her on the getting-back-together thing, was he? Robert ought to know her well enough to know that wouldn't go well.

"And what is that?" she asked him cautiously.

"Well, you do this service for guys all the time, but has anyone bothered to reciprocate?"

Interesting. "No," she said. "As a matter of fact, no one has done that."

"Exactly what I thought. So tonight I don't want you to do a thing. Don't lift a finger—" He paused. "—unless you want to." He laughed. It was a nice sound.

Actually, a sexy sound.

Was she really going to fall for this?

"I don't, huh?"

"Mm-mm. What are you wearing? No, wait—don't tell me. This time of year, it's probably either the Eeyore nightshirt or that pink and green thing with the buttons that you got at Target about a hundred years ago."

"Wrong." She gave Eeyore, holding a cup of coffee on the shirt she was, in fact, wearing, a silent apology for denying him. "I'm wearing a black satin teddy with garters and fishnets. You know, my usual work clothes."

"I'm unhooking those garters now. And pulling the stocking off your right leg." He hesitated. "And now your left leg. And I'm running my hands back up, slowly across your thighs. Both hands, both thighs. You're not wearing panties. . . ."

"No," she whispered.

"Good. Why waste time? I want to taste you. It's been too long, and I want to taste you now."

She sucked a breath in.

"Can you feel it? Can you remember?"

"I can." Her voice wavered.

"Me, too, baby." That voice. She loved his voice. "Remember what I'd do with my hand about now?"

She closed her eyes and imagined it. "Yes." She was going for it. She needed this.

She'd needed this for a long time.

# *Chapter* 19

Sandra walked in to find Tiffany frying hash browns.

It was galling that someone as thin as Tiffany could have *hash browns* for breakfast, while Sandra's body just seemed to prosper and expand on one small Slim-Fast shake.

"Hey," Tiffany said when she saw Sandra. "I hope you're hungry."

"I am *now*." Sandra sat on one of the barstools in front of the counter. "I brought you more shoes," she said in a singsong voice. "The brand-new, just-unveiled Lorna from Phillipe Carfagni." She plunked down a pair of round-toe platform pumps in deep mahogany kidskin leather, with an arch like the rolling hills of Italy, where they were made. She absolutely adored them, and figured Tiffany would, too, maybe especially since they'd make her tower over Charlie. "Aren't they fabulous?"

Tiffany set the spatula down. "They're gorgeous. I can't wait to try them on." She picked one up, examined the heel, and gave Sandra a knowing look. "I really like them."

"Good. Now don't make me stay and eat whatever it is you're making."

"*Papas fritas,*" Tiffany said, putting the shoe down and picking up the spatula again. Then, in what Sandra always joked was her *menu voice,* she added, "A nest of hash-brown potatoes, topped with a poached egg, hot chili sauce, sour cream, and Jack cheese." She raised an eyebrow and returned to her normal voice. "And you *have* to stay."

Sandra wanted to. Boy, did she want to. "I don't think that's on Weight Watchers."

"Oh, come on, you can't worry about that all the time." Tiffany set a cup in front of Sandra without asking, and filled it with coffee. Then she went to the fridge and got out the half-and-half, just like Sandra liked it.

Tiffany was the perfect hostess.

"Well, I do." Sandra took a sip of the perfect, creamy coffee. "So is that Abbey's car outside?"

"Yes." Tiffany set her spatula down and looked at Sandra. "Everything's okay now, but her husband was in a car accident last night, so she brought her son over here while she went to the hospital." Tiffany shuddered. "It was really scary there for a while."

"How awful. Is *Abbey* okay?"

Tiffany shrugged. "Seems to be." Tiffany picked up the spatula again and gestured at Sandra with it. "And I'm sure she'll be glad to see you, so you *can't* leave."

"Okay, fine. So Brian's really going to be okay?" Sandra confirmed. "They're sure?"

Tiffany nodded. "And, actually, in some perverse way I think the experience was good for Abbey."

"*Good* for her?"

"Yeah, we had a really nice talk last night when she got back. She opened up about some things that have been bothering her for a long time, and I think she feels better now."

Sandra didn't ask what kind of things Abbey had opened up about. She knew Tiffany would never break a confidence. This had always been convenient for Sandra when it was *her* secret Tiffany was keeping, but infuriating at all other times, when Tiffany appeared to have the goods on someone and wouldn't tell who. Or what.

Tiffany looked up and behind Sandra. "Speak of the—" She stopped herself. "Hi, Abbey. How are you feeling this morning?"

Sandra turned. "I heard it was rough going there for a while."

"It was," Abbey said, running her hands up and down her arms as if to warm up. "But I think everything's going to be all right now. And actually, that was the best I've slept in a long time. Go figure, huh?"

"Sometimes when your life is turned upside down, you find out *that's* right-side up," Sandra said. "If that makes any sense."

"It does." Tiffany looked at her thoughtfully. "It actually makes a lot of sense." She added a pat of butter to the pan.

Charlie came into the kitchen then. "Baby's crying," he said to Tiffany, taking out a cup and pouring coffee into it.

Tiffany gaped at him. "Why didn't you get him?"

"I didn't know what you wanted to do."

"I want you to get him."

"I'm on my way out to play golf."

"I'll get Andy," Sandra said quickly, obviously trying to defuse a situation that no one—especially Abbey—needed to witness right now.

"Thanks. Just put him in the den to play with the other kids, okay?" Tiffany took a travel mug out and poured Charlie's cup of coffee into it, then handed it to him. "You wouldn't want to be late."

He gave her a quick look, then turned his attention to Abbey. "Was it your husband in the accident?"

"Yes," she said. "It was."

"You better get pictures of the car," he said, grabbing a piece of bread as he passed the counter. "Insurance companies always wait too long for that."

"Oh." Abbey frowned. "Okay. Thanks."

He nodded. "I'll be late," he said to Tiffany.

She raised a hand dismissively. "No problem."

He left just as Sandra came back into the room.

"I'm sure now that Charlie's having an affair," Tiffany said, looking after where he'd just left.

"Oh, Tiffany—" Sandra said.

Tiffany was almost surprised by her own words. "I'm sorry. I don't know why I brought that up. It's not nearly as important as Brian's health and well-being right now."

"Brian's going to be fine," Abbey said in a soft voice. "I'd welcome the distraction. Tell us about Charlie."

"Well, for one thing," Tiffany said, "he separated all of our bank accounts a couple of weeks ago. And for another, he just went to play golf without taking his clubs." She gestured to the corner by the laundry room, where his golf clubs had been since last Saturday.

"You need to hire a detective," Sandra said.

"I agree," Abbey said. "You need evidence *now*. Apparently he thinks you're not on to him, so it shouldn't be hard."

"I know someone," Sandra said, taking out her cell phone.

"You know a private detective?" Tiffany asked.

"A friend of mine dealt with him last year," she said. "He's got a soft spot for nice women getting dogged by their husbands. I'm going to get his number and we're going to hire him *today*."

※

Later that afternoon, after private investigator Gerald Parks had been hired and sent after Tiffany's cheating husband, Abbey went to the impound lot where Brian's car had been towed. Tiffany and Sandra had offered to come with her, but she'd refused, afraid of her own reaction. Instead she asked them to keep Parker so she could go take pictures, as Charlie had suggested.

And she *would* take pictures. She might as well, in case they did need them for the insurance company, but that wasn't the real reason she was going. She was going because she had to see for herself, somehow satisfy herself that this had been an ordinary case of losing control of the car instead of the much more sinister possibility that Damon was involved.

How she was going to prove that to herself she had no idea. But she was going to begin by examining the back of the car for any scratches, dents, or any other sign that Brian was hit from behind.

She stopped at the office, and a scruffy guy with a two-day beard looked the car up on a list and told her where to find it.

She drove through the lot, noticing windshield after windshield with a head-smash on it. Why didn't people wear their seat belts? The evidence was so conclusive that—

Her thoughts stopped. So did her heart, for a moment. There was Brian's car. Or, rather, what was left of Brian's car. It looked like a cheap toy accordion. When Abbey saw where they'd cut Brian from the driver's seat, the metal torn and impossibly thin-looking, she broke down into sobs.

How close had she come to losing him?

What on earth would she have done without him?

She couldn't even bear to think about it, yet, looking at the car, she could think of little else.

But she had to. She'd come to see if this was Damon's work, and that was the one task she had to complete. She examined the bumper, the license plate, the taillights, the wheel hubs, everything on the back of the car, but it was as shiny as if it were new. So she moved to the side of the car. The passenger side was also in fair condition, but she checked it out first, since the driver's side was the one that had hit the tree, and it stood to reason he'd done it because he was avoiding something on the passenger side.

But there was nothing of note there either.

So she moved to the driver's side. She'd been dreading that because of the bloodstained air bag and seat, and when she saw them, she had to fight back the despair. Yes, it was a terrible accident, and yes, she might have lost Brian, but she *hadn't,* and she needed to concentrate on that.

She tore her eyes away from the bloody mess that was the driver's seat and scanned the side of the car.

It was so small that at first she didn't see it. But there, between two folds of metal that had been the driver's door, she saw, scratched firmly in the paint, the clue she'd been looking for.

*10K.*

The very amount Damon insisted Abbey owed him.

He *was* behind this.

She wasn't surprised, of course. This was what she'd suspected. It was the reason she'd come, and yet seeing it like this, part of her just couldn't believe it was true. Before Vegas she hadn't given Damon a thought in years. Now, suddenly, he was casting a shadow across her entire life. Whereas for years he'd seemed not to exist at all, now he had the power to change—to *ruin*—her life.

She needed to stop him.

She was going to call the private investigator, Gerald Parks, herself. She wanted—no, she *needed*—to find Damon Zucker before he found her again.

★

"These are called Michelle, and I brought a pair for each of you. Just promise you'll wear them everywhere and tell everyone they're Carfagnis." She smiled and handed out boxes of the Michelle, metallic pink pointed-toe slippers with brushed leather soles. "You won't believe how comfortable they are."

"I will," Loreen said. "I've worn those Helenes almost constantly. I never knew how different really *good* shoes could feel from the discount store crap I've been wearing."

"I know it." Sandra nodded knowingly. "It's a lesson we all learn sooner or later. If we're lucky."

"I've certainly learned it," Tiffany said. "Honestly, I used to think you were just some sort of freak with all your shoes, but when I put on those high heels you gave me, I swear I felt like I was walking in seven-league boots. They made me feel *powerful*."

"You *are* powerful," Sandra said. "But I'm glad you like the shoes."

It was weird, Sandra thought at the next get-together, how much the phone sex business had changed Tiffany. Or maybe it was just the independence, the making money—good money—and finding out she didn't have to be completely reliant upon Charlie in order to support her children. Tiffany was like a whole new person.

Although damned if she didn't seem to be enjoying it. It was like she was undergoing her own little private sexual revolution.

Whatever it was, Tiffany had grown more relaxed, more fun. She let the kids play without checking on them obsessively, and Sandra had even seen her put a piece of cheese or two in her mouth when they met at Loreen's, where the food was always fabulous and fattening.

It was nice to have her sister back. Or to have her sister for the first time. It was hard to say which it was. And it was nice to have Abbey and Loreen, too.

"So when's the next date?" Tiffany asked Sandra. "I'm thinking the third one is bound to be the charm."

"Once I would have agreed with that," Sandra said. "But given the first two, my confidence on this one is seriously wavering."

"Not everyone is a weirdo," Loreen said.

"I'm not so sure," Abbey said. Then she smiled. "But the odds of you meeting another one without anyone even remotely normal in between do seem slim."

"God, I hope you're right." Sandra was still tired of being alone. She still wanted a companion, someone to enjoy the little things in life with. But she was tired of humiliation, too.

"What's his name?" Tiffany asked.

"DLadd," Sandra said, trying to look at the positives. "Not PuppetMaster, not FunkyChicken, nothing weird. Just DLadd, for Doug Ladd."

"What does he do?" Loreen asked.

"Architect."

"Sounds normal," Tiffany offered. "Where are you going."

"We're meeting at Normandie Farm for Irish coffee." Even if the date was a bust, she loved the restaurant and hadn't been there for years.

"Oh, I'd forgotten about that place." Tiffany sighed. "Mom and Daddy took us there when we graduated from high school."

"I know. I was hoping our history with it would be lucky." Sandra thought. "Though I'm not sure I need luck. We have so many interests in common."

"Like what?" Loreen asked.

"Let's see . . . a lingering attachment to the band the Pixies, a preference for cats over dogs." What else was there? "He lives in McLean Gardens, like three miles from me. He's not into puppets and he's not into arcades. I asked." She smiled. "And from the picture, he looks really cute."

"I have a good feeling about this," Loreen said. "Seriously. And every once in a while my feelings turn out to be premonitions. Every once in a long while, that is. But still."

Sandra nodded. "I sort of do, too. I screwed up the courage to tell him the truth about my struggle with weight, and he wanted to meet me anyway. That's good, right?"

"You should be able to expect that from a decent guy," Tiffany said dourly.

"Yeah, but decent guys don't always *act* all that decent at first." Loreen turned her attention back to Sandra and nodded. "I think it's a very good sign."

"Especially since he might be imagining someone with a *much* more obvious weight problem than you have," Abbey added. "I bet he'll be bowled over by how cute you are."

"From your lips to God's ears," Sandra said.

"Don't count on *that*." Abbey gave a laugh. "But let us know how it turns out."

Sandra still held to her theory that it was better to be the first one there, and this time it worked out. She sat down in the lounge of Normandie Farm, pleased to see that the lighting was quite dim, and listened to the gentle strumming of the musician's guitar in the other room.

Doug came in at eight on the dot, and the hostess showed him to the small table where Sandra was sitting.

"Sandra?"

She'd been so lost in her thoughts that she hadn't realized he was coming. Startled, she looked up into one of the best-looking faces she'd ever seen in her life. He wasn't just *cute*; he was *gorgeous*.

So, reason told her, he had to be the manager or something coming to tell her that her date had called to cancel.

"Y-yes?"

He smiled, and the face only got better. Tanned skin, light eyes, sandy hair. "I'm Doug Ladd."

He was Doug Ladd.

And she was speechless.

"Can I . . . sit down?" he asked, looking a little disconcerted by her silence.

"Oh! Of course! I'm sorry, I—" She what? There was no reasonable end to that sentence. "Please, have a seat."

He sat down and motioned for the rapt hostess to wait a moment. "Do you want an Irish coffee?" he asked Sandra.

"Sure." She nodded. "Yes."

"Two," he said to the hostess. "Could you tell our waitress?"

"Uh-huh." The hostess nodded and peeled her gaze off Doug, looked questioningly at Sandra for a moment, then went on her way.

"Sorry, I just hate starting to talk and then being interrupted two minutes later to place an order," Doug said when the hostess was gone.

"I do, too," Sandra said, and she was impressed that he'd thought of that. It made life easier for everyone.

Three Irish coffees later, Doug still hadn't made a false step, and Sandra, who had switched to decaf after the first one, found herself really relaxing into the groove of their conversation.

This was easy.

*Too* easy.

And something told her she knew the reason why. "So, Doug, I know you like the Pixies, but what else do you like to listen to?"

"All kinds of things. Just about everything, in fact. Everything from country to show tunes, I guess."

"Show tunes?"

"Sure."

"So, like, Judy Garland?"

"Okay." He paused. "In her younger years."

Hm. "What about Christina Aguilera? Are you a big Christina Aguilera fan?"

"She's got a good voice," he said, looking at Sandra curiously. "I guess. But she's not my favorite."

"What do you think of Rupert Everett?"

"What?"

"Never mind."

"Are you a—" He looked a bit lost. "—big music fan?"

"Sort of." She nodded.

"Have you ever been to the open mike at the Outta the Way Cafe in Derwood? The guy gets some seriously good musicians in there."

"Open mike? Is that like a drag show?"

He looked puzzled. "No. It's just regular music. Good, free entertainment." He set his drink down. "I'm sorry, I feel like you're trying to get at something, but I don't know what."

"Me? No, I'm not trying to get at anything." She tried to smile and brush it off, but this just wasn't feeling right. "I've just never been to an open mike before. Wasn't sure what it was."

"So what do you like to do?"

"I used to go to the Nine Thirty Club when I was younger, but I haven't been for ages. Lately, I don't know. I haven't really gone out and done much of anything interesting." She took a sip of her drink and lobbed the ball back into his court. "So how long have you been dating on Match?"

He splayed his arms. "You're my first."

"Really?" She set her glass down. "I can't believe that."

He shrugged. "I was in a relationship for a long time, and when that ended, I really dug into my work and forgot to socialize."

"Architecture."

He nodded. "That's right."

"Have you done anything I might have seen?"

"Probably not. I mostly do home interiors now. Remodeling, additions, that sort of thing."

"Like decorating?"

He smiled. "There's a certain art to it, yes."

Oh, boy. It was as she suspected. The pieces were falling into place now.

Sandra looked at the gorgeous, educated, successful man sitting before her and couldn't think of two reasons he'd want anything to do with her.

She could think of only one.

He was looking for a "beard," a woman to take out now and then to prove he wasn't gay.

Which he totally was.

"I guess you really need to be in touch with your feminine side for that."

He frowned. "I . . . suppose." There was an awkward silence. "Sandra, why are you asking me all these questions all of a sudden?" he asked, shifting uncomfortably in his seat. "I've never in my life felt like my work or musical tastes were cause for an indictment."

Sandra heaved a long sigh. "I think we both know what this is all about."

"We do?"

"Of course." She nodded, trying to be kind. "I've been here before. You're gay and you don't want anyone to know, so you want some girl to hang around now and then and make it to the events where you really need to appear straight."

He drew back. "What?"

"It's okay, Doug. I get it. The thing is, I just don't want to be that girl, you know?"

"That's funny, because I don't want to be that guy."

She nodded. "I understand, but I wish you'd just be yourself and say to hell with the rest of the world, but if you're looking for a cover-up, it's not me." She reached into her purse and took out a twenty, which she thought would more than cover her portion. "I'm sorry," she said, setting it down on the table.

"Are you serious?" Doug asked, looking truly astonished, though she couldn't say why.

"It's been a long night," she explained. "Actually, sort of a long month. I'm not going to do this, but I certainly wish you luck. You're a great guy."

Doug, who had stood up and made a move to barricade her exit, sat down and let her go. "Thanks, Sandra. Right back at ya. Have a good night."

"Thanks," she said, but she didn't even mean that. Mostly she was so disappointed with the way things had turned out, she could cry. She'd gone into this with a bad feeling, and every minute she'd spent there made her feel even worse.

Every one of these stupid, useless, and occasionally insulting dates felt like it pushed her that much further away from the companion—and the family—she'd always assumed she'd have someday.

And the hell of it was, she still wanted it.

She wanted children. Christmas mornings, Easter egg hunts, Halloween costumes that smelled like rubber cement and fell apart halfway through Halloween night.

In other words, just a *normal* life. And that wasn't a sketchy normal; it was normal by *most* people's standards.

Just not most of the people she had found to date on Match.com.

It was too bad Doug wasn't straight. And she wasn't a model. Because between the two of those things, they could have had a lot of fun together.

# Chapter 20

Y ou accused him of being gay," Tiffany repeated incredulously.
"Oh, my God, Sandra, tell me you did *not* really do that."

"I know, it seems so dumb now, in retrospect." Sandra covered her face with her hands and groaned. "I'm *such* an *idiot.*"

Abbey looked at Tiffany, then Loreen, sensing that they were all fighting the urge to agree.

Tiffany was the only one who did, though. "No kidding. The poor guy."

"Did he do *anything* to make you think that?" Abbey asked.

"Yes." Sandra met her eyes. "He had the unmitigated gall to be good-looking and act interested in me."

"Then the fool was just asking for it." Loreen laughed and leaned over with an arm around Sandra. "Come on, honey. It was a mistake—that's all. Coming from a deep, weird insecurity inside of you that he couldn't possibly understand."

"Maybe Mike Lemmington could explain it to him," Tiffany suggested.

"Mike would end up making a pass at him." Sandra sniffed, then straightened her back. "No, this was a lesson hard-learned, but an important one. I have to have more confidence. After I stop beating myself up over this colossally stupid mistake, that is."

"You could call him," Abbey suggested. "At least apologize."

"I should," Sandra agreed. "But I can't. I just can't. I can't ever face him again, even over the phone. I'm just going to stop dating. That will be my sort of universal apology to the guy."

"You can't stop dating," Loreen said.

"No, I can't *keep* dating," Sandra corrected. "*That's* where the trouble comes from. I'm just a loser."

"You've just had a run of bad luck," Abbey said. "It happens to all of us, believe me. You don't lose unless you quit."

"That's true," Tiffany said, nodding enthusiastically. "Seriously."

"I don't need a pep talk," Sandra said. "I need a nun's habit."

"Bullshit," Loreen said. "You need a good date. Try one more time. I guarantee you things are going to go better if you just give it one more shot."

Sandra looked at her skeptically. "Are you psychic?"

"Sure," Loreen said. "If that's what it takes to make you believe me, because I'm *right*."

"I agree," Abbey said.

"Me, too," Tiffany added. "So now you *have* to try again."

Sandra gave a laugh. "Because the committee has decided so?"

Tiffany nodded. "Yes."

Abbey felt sorry for Sandra. She knew she was lucky never to have had this particular brand of insecurity with men, and she'd certainly never had such comically bad luck on dates, but— A movement outside the window caught her eye.

Someone was by her car. A man.

Damon.

"Fine," Sandra said. "I'll do it, but frankly it's only to prove you guys wrong so you'll leave me alone about this."

"I can live with that," Tiffany said.

Abbey's heart raced as she kept her eyes fastened to the window and tried to decide what to do.

"Me, too," Loreen said. "Abbey?"

"Um," Abbey faltered. "Right. Me, too . . . I think I left my phone in my car—could you guys excuse me for a minute?" She didn't wait for an answer, but just hurried out, calling over her shoulder, "I'll be right back."

She flew out into the hot midday sun, looking for Damon, ready to kill him with her bare hands if necessary. She'd had enough of this waiting and wondering, enough worrying; at this point, she'd take an assault charge over the artfully silent stalking he was doing.

"Damon!" she yelled viciously. "Where are you? I saw you. I know you're here!"

Her words fell dully in the silent, sunny block.

"Da*mon*!"

Nothing.

Then she noticed a mark on the side of the car: *10K.*

Again.

She had to end this, once and for all.

Somehow.

She went back inside and was relieved to find everyone right where she'd left them. Apparently they hadn't heard or witnessed her momentary lapse in judgment.

"Did you get it?" Tiffany asked.

"What?"

"The phone. Because I thought I heard your purse ringing while you were outside, but I'm not sure."

"Oh. That would explain why I didn't find it." Abbey gave a false laugh and rummaged through her purse until she produced the phone. "There it is. Go figure." She glanced at the caller ID. "Just the dentist's office. So what did I miss?"

"Actually," Loreen said with a smile, "I was just about to say that this month we made enough money to pay off nearly three quarters of the debt. Can you believe it?"

Sandra clapped her hands. "Wow, you girls have been busy. I'm so proud of you!"

"It's thanks to you," Abbey said. She wondered how long it would take her to earn enough money to pay Damon off if she kept working at it. "If you hadn't come up with the idea and told us how to do it, I don't know *what* we would have done."

"I suspect I'd be in jail right now." Loreen's face grew serious. "I can't thank you enough." As she spoke, her eyes grew bright with tears. "*Any* of you."

"It hasn't really been as bad as I expected," Tiffany said. "And this"—she gestured at all of them—"us getting together every week has been great."

"What are we going to do when we've paid everything off?" Loreen asked. "We'll need to find a new excuse to meet."

"Hm." Sandra looked thoughtful. "How do you all feel about shoes? . . ."

✳

The money was rolling in. Loreen checked the number two and three times because she just couldn't believe how profitable this business was. And it wasn't just Loreen, Abbey, and Tiffany who were benefiting from the success of the Happy Housewives venture. They'd decided from the beginning that they were also going to take a percentage of their earnings and use it for PTA programs.

They were already making plans to pay for Nick Nicholas, a nationally renowned kids' educator known as the Math Magician, to come and do a workshop for the Tuckerman kids.

Normally that kind of special program was the sole domain of the wealthier private schools, but the Tuckerman Elementary PTA was suddenly feeling pretty optimistic about its finances.

Not everyone shared that optimism, however. Deb Leventer and her group of friends were beginning to question the motives and means of the current PTA heads. Deb was bitter that she'd lost the vote for president, so every time there was an opportunity for her to cast doubt on Tiffany's competence, Deb was right there doing it.

"Where is the money coming from?"

"Wouldn't it be more prudent to save it, in case of an emergency?" What PTA emergency Deb thought they needed to save for was a mystery. It was hard to imagine Deb envisioning something like, say, one of the officers using the school funds to pay for a male prostitute.

And there was no way on earth Deb had any inkling of what was going on, because if she did, she would have blown Loreen, and her reputation, sky high a long time ago.

"We've got a little more than a thousand to go," Loreen told Tiffany over beer and pizza that evening, after balancing the books.

They were just at Bambinos Pizza, a few blocks from the school, where the kids had stayed late to rehearse for their fifth-grade graduation ceremony.

"A thousand?" Tiffany set her Heineken down and looked at Loreen with amazement. "That's *it*?"

"Yup. Can you believe it?"

"I almost can't," Tiffany admitted. "It seems too easy."

"I'm not sure I'd say it was easy," Loreen said.

"No?"

She shook her head. "I don't know that I've had one successful call yet. I know I haven't had any repeat business."

"But you are the one who did the piles and piles of paperwork to get us into business for ourselves."

Loreen shrugged.

"Then you advertised and got those part-timers working for us, just like Sandra used to do for Touch of Class. Putting the sign up in the drama department at Montgomery College? Brilliant move. That's worth even more!"

"I hope you mean that."

"I do."

Loreen raised her beer to her lips, but the taste was repellent, and she put it down right away.

Tiffany noticed. "What's wrong?"

Loreen rolled her eyes. "Just my stupid hormonal problem. I've got all these mock pregnancy symptoms."

"Ugh. Really?"

"Yeah." Loreen picked up a thin slice of pizza. "It's like my body chemistry is changing, and suddenly my premenstrual symptoms are like early pregnancy."

"Lucky you! All that *and* your period, too!"

Loreen took another bite and nodded. "It's due any second now." She hesitated. Seemed like she'd been thinking her period would start "any minute now" for a long time.

Oh, well, that's how it was lately. Her cycle was less predictable. Suddenly it was like she was in seventh grade again, never knowing when Aunt Flo was going to show up unexpectedly and embarrass her to death with some public appearance.

"I tell you," Tiffany was saying, "I'm thinking about taking my pills for three months at a time nonstop so I don't get it so often. They say you can do that now, you know." She sipped her beer. "I seem to get it at the worst time every single month. Last month it was while we were in Vegas, and this month it was over Memorial Day weekend when, of course, Kate wanted to spend the entire weekend at the pool."

Last weekend was Memorial Day. So Tiffany had gotten a period *twice* since Vegas, and Loreen hadn't had it since . . . when was it? Before Las Vegas. Like, *well* before Las Vegas. A couple of weeks.

"What's wrong?" Tiffany asked.

Loreen put her pizza down. She was losing her appetite. "I think I missed a month."

"What do you mean?"

"My period. I think I missed an entire month, and with everything that's going on, I didn't realize it."

"Are you worried? I mean, it's not like you're pregnant or anything."

Loreen didn't answer.

She just sat there, feeling her skin prickle all over.

"Loreen." Tiffany looked concerned now. "What's the matter? You look like a ghost."

"What if I *am* pregnant?"

"You said you hadn't done anything since you and Robert split up." She lowered her voice to a whisper. "So how could you possibly be *pregnant*?"

"Oh, God." Loreen pushed the plate of pizza away from her. Then she took her napkin and twisted it in her lap. "You don't want to know. I don't want to tell you."

"What? Is it something to do with Robert?"

Robert. No. This was feeling worse by the second. She swallowed, but her mouth was as dry as cotton. "Yes. Well, we've been talking about getting back together, but nothing's for sure." If her hunch was right, he wasn't going to be too eager to resume relations now.

"Loreen Murphy, I cannot believe you've been holding out on me!" Tiffany raised her beer bottle in a mock toast. "I had no idea you guys were getting back together. And had *been back together*. Wow, can you imagine if you *are* pregnant, after everything you two went through? It would be like kismet."

"It would be something, all right."

"So why don't you look happier?" Tiffany's smile was broad. "It's fate!"

"I've got to get out of here," Loreen said. She felt a surge of adrenaline run through her veins like ice water. "I've got to get a test. I have to know."

"Okay, okay, calm down. Look, you go next door to CVS and get a test. I'll pay up here and meet you at the car."

Loreen nodded convulsively. She couldn't speak.

Walking through the aisles of the drugstore was like something from a dream. Or, rather, a *bad* dream.

A hideous nightmare.

The fluorescent lights overhead were a little too bright, lending a disturbing hypnotic quality to the five minutes she spent finding the pregnancy tests (next to the condoms, all of which she eyed with skepticism now), paying, and wandering into an oncoming car in the parking lot.

The car stopped before hitting her, and she was almost sorry.

Tiffany saw the whole thing and came running. "Look, Loreen, you're scaring the bejeezus out of me. One minute we're having a perfectly nice little meal—then, within the span of two minutes, all the blood leaves your face and you're a walking zombie now, carrying a pregnancy test in a plastic bag. *Why* has this got you so freaked out?"

"Because something tells me I *am* pregnant."

"Okay. But is that really so bad? You've been there before." They stopped in front of Tiffany's minivan. "You used to want this so bad, remember? And you *know* you won't be on your own. You know you'd have Robert, and you'd have me, and Abbey, and Sandra."

Loreen closed her eyes against the horror of it and said, "But . . . Robert wouldn't be the dad."

There was silence and Loreen opened her eyes to see Tiffany looking at her, stunned.

"Are you *serious*?"

Loreen nodded miserably. "Unfortunately."

"Then who would?" Tiffany asked. It was clear she was trying not to look shocked, but she looked like she'd just swallowed a bug. "You didn't tell me you'd met someone."

"Oh, I met someone. Let's get in." Loreen opened the passenger door and got into the car.

Tiffany did the same. "Okay, who? And *where*? And how on earth did I miss all of this?"

Loreen took a long breath and said, "Suffice it to say that I'm afraid what happens in Vegas doesn't necessarily *stay* in Vegas."

"Huh?"

Loreen shook her head. "I don't want to be mysterious about this, but can we just run back to your place so I can do the test before I go insane? I can't concentrate until I know what's going on." She tried to keep her voice from wavering, but the fear was clutching her esophagus.

"Of course." Tiffany turned the key in the ignition and left it at that.

Loreen knew the curiosity had to be killing Tiffany, but she just couldn't tell her the whole ugly truth unless she knew she had to. If she didn't, well, she'd just make something up.

They got to Tiffany's house within about seven minutes, and as Loreen approached the front door, the smell of Bounce, coming from the dryer duct under the front window, nearly knocked her over.

Normally she *adored* the smell of Bounce.

This didn't bode well.

"Why don't you go on up to the bathroom in my room?" Tiffany suggested. "I'll make some herbal tea. Does that sound good?"

"Do you have something like ginger ale?"

"Always." Tiffany nodded. "You never know when someone's going to puke. I'll pour a glass."

Loreen went upstairs into the large master bathroom and took the pregnancy test sticks out of their wrappers. Then she sat down on the toilet with them both and had the stray thought that she wished she had a separate soaking tub, too.

She also wished she had a stable marriage, and home, and her period.

But when she peed on the sticks—both of them—things didn't really become more clear.

"What did it say?" Tiffany asked, taking the glass of ginger ale to Loreen. Her expression changed when she got closer. "Positive?"

Loreen shook her head.

Tiffany set the glass down and pulled Loreen into a strong, comforting hug. "Oh, honey. That's what you wanted, isn't it?"

"Yes." Loreen sniffed. "Of course it is, but some part of me . . ." She shook her head. She couldn't finish.

"I know," Tiffany soothed. "There's something really incredible about getting that positive result. Knowing, all in that moment, that there are two of you, not one. It's a rush, even if you don't know what to do next." Tiffany guided her to a seat on the couch in the great room and sat down next to her, taking her hand. "Do you want to talk about what led up to this?"

Loreen looked at Tiffany, so earnest, so nonjudgmental, and the whole story spilled out of her. Meeting Rod, the way she'd felt when he'd paid special attention to her, how incredible it was to throw caution to the wind and have a one-night stand for the first time in her life, and how completely, utterly humiliating it was when he'd given her a bill at the end of it.

"That's how it happened," Loreen said. She was cried out. Her voice was now just a thin blade of shame. "I got all those cash advances on what I *thought* was my card in a pathetic, unstoppable attempt to come out of it even."

"I totally understand that," Tiffany said, to Loreen's surprise.

Loreen gave a humorless laugh. "Come on. You're way too perfect for that."

"I am *not* perfect," Tiffany said. "Far, *far* from it. And I absolutely see how this happened. You weren't just trying to even out your finances, you were trying to even out your self-esteem. Give yourself something to feel okay about at the end of an evening that had made you feel terrible about yourself."

Loreen closed her eyes against a fresh onslaught of tears, but it didn't do any good. They seeped through her lashes and burned down her cheeks anyway. "That's it." She nodded and put her hands up to her face.

Tiffany took her hands and held them in hers, looking straight into Loreen's eyes. "As crazy as it is, it could have happened to *anyone*. The weirdness wasn't *yours*; it was *his*. You're a normal woman who assumed the guy she was talking to in a bar was a normal man."

"But I told him to tell the other women he was taken. That was, like, code for *turn off the red light for now*, in retrospect."

"Well—" Tiffany gave a laugh. "—it *was* a poor choice of wording."

Loreen joined in the laughter. "You know, I might even have come close to joking, *How much do you charge?*"

Tiffany laughed harder. "Oh, no, *did* you say that?"

"I might have—I don't remember anymore!" Loreen's laughter was bubbling into hysteria.

Now tears were streaming from Tiffany's eyes. "Oh, my God, and he would have said a thousand dollars . . . and you . . ." She was having trouble catching her breath. ". . . would no doubt have said—"

"You're hired!" they both said at the same time, and dissolved into fits of giggles.

"It could have been me," Tiffany assured her, sobering at last. "I mean, if I weren't married."

"Do you really think so?" Loreen wanted to believe it. "Tell me the truth."

"I am! Look, if I'd been with you, I wouldn't have thought one thing about the exchange. You would have gone off with him, and I would have thought *go for it*."

"You wouldn't have said that at the cash-advance window, though."

"*Only* because I was too busy buying thousands of dollars' worth of impractical clothes I couldn't return later." She cocked her head and looked earnestly into Loreen's eyes. "Honestly, I don't know who Deb Leventer would judge more harshly in this situation, you or me."

"Me," Loreen said definitively. "What if I'd been pregnant by some ho boy in Vegas that I'd never see again? Imagine the possibilities for complications. Health background, the child's right to know his biological history . . . It would have been a mess. But now, finding out I'm not . . ." Loreen's voice broke. "It's almost worse."

Tiffany nodded. "I understand. It would have been a baby."

"No, it's not that." Tears flowed; Loreen barely had enough Kleenex to stanch them.

Tiffany looked surprised. "No?"

Loreen shook her head. "The hormonal fluctuations, the sore boobs, the late period . . . This probably means I'm already going into . . ." The tears came harder. "*Menopause!*"

✳

Now that Loreen had decided that time was marching on and that this must be perimenopause and she was a whisper away from death, she decided it was time for her to stop keeping secrets like a child. Things had been getting better with Robert; she hoped they were headed toward a reconciliation. Now that she was staring down the barrel of old maidness, she decided that she was going to come clean, lay her cards on the table, so to speak, and let the chips fall where they may.

So Loreen told Robert the truth, albeit the bare bones. Met a guy, thought he was cute, knew nothing would come of it, had been drinking champagne and feeling lonely, went back to his hotel room with him, and one thing led to another. . . .

Robert went silent.

And stayed like that for a long, long time.

"Please say something," Loreen said. "Tell me I'm stupid, tell me you never want to see me again, tell me everything's off and I'm on my own with this, but please don't just look at me like that."

"I don't know what to say," Robert managed at last. His voice was that of someone who had been clocked in the head with a baseball bat and was dazed.

"Say *something*."

He flattened his lips into a tight line, and appeared to think for a moment before shaking his head. "I'm sorry, Loreen. I've got nothing other than the fact that our *marriage* split up because you didn't have time for anything but Jacob, and now I have to understand how somehow you managed to leave him with a stranger in a Las Vegas hotel room so you could have sex with a stranger."

She winced, over and over, at his words. But she couldn't argue with any of them.

"In fact—" He stood up and shoved his hands into the front pockets of his jeans. "—I think I'm going to just go. I need to think."

"I'll get Jacob from the Dreyers' house," Loreen said.

Tiffany had taken Jacob so that Loreen and Robert could have this talk, though the plan had originally been that Robert would pick him up.

Robert looked grateful to be relieved of that duty. Or at least as grateful as he could, given that most of his facial expression was still devoted to shock and horror.

He left, and Loreen waited until his car had disappeared down the street before she allowed herself a good, long cry.

So she was going to have to give up the idea of getting back together with Robert, and she hadn't even realized that she'd allowed herself to think it was going to happen. And she had to accept that it was the natural consequence of what she'd done.

There was a price for everything, and in this case it was even more than five thousand dollars.

# Chapter 21

This is Crystal."

"Spread your thighs," Tiffany's caller said without preamble. "I'm gonna finger-bang your pussy."

"Do it," she said, turning off the lights in her bedroom and leaning back on the bed to relax. Charlie was gone again, and—again—she didn't mind it. Particularly since the private investigator, Gerald Parks, was following him. "Do it hard, baby."

"Call me by my name," he growled. "You should know it by now. This is Mick."

"Mick." She let the word roll off her tongue like warm caramel. "It's nice to hear from you again, Mick." She had a regular! This was his third call. This was a very good sign that she was a success.

"I want to pull your panties off with my teeth and bite your clit until you scream with ecstasy."

It didn't sound all that ecstasy inducing to her, but Tiffany was surprised to feel a little tingle anyway. "I'm waiting for you," she said. "I've been waiting all day for you."

"How many fingers can you handle?"

How on earth was she supposed to answer that? "Try me," seemed like the most diplomatic response she could come up with. "I love your hands. Your long, strong fingers." She found herself picturing Jude Law. He probably had nice hands.

She was a hands girl.

The call went on for perhaps fifteen minutes, during which time Tiffany got more and more into it. She lost track of the fact that she was getting paid, and dived straight into the thrill of it.

Mick, if that truly was his real name, was unlike any man she would ever be attracted to in real life. He was blunt, his attitude toward women was Edwardian, but something about the anonymity turned Tiffany on.

So much so, in fact, that she didn't hear Kate until she was right outside the door. "Mommy? Are you talking to Daddy?"

Tiffany scrambled off the bed and pulled her rumpled clothes together. The back of her hair was a rat's nest from moving against the pillow, but she couldn't fix that, finish the call, *and* distract Kate all at the same time.

"Mick! I have to go. My husband is here!"

"You little sneak," he said, sounding delighted to be "banging" another man's wife, even if it was imaginary. She'd been pretty sure he'd feel that way.

"Call me again? . . ."

"You know it."

She clipped the phone shut just as Kate tried the locked doorknob.

"Mommy, why is the door locked?"

"Is it?" Tiffany tried to sound surprised, but guilt and annoyance at the interruption mingled in her voice. Why was it that the kids always popped out of bed at the worst possible time? Tiffany reached for the door and opened it, unlocking it at the same time in one smooth move. "It wasn't locked."

"Yes, it was," Kate insisted.

"No, it was just jammed. Now, why are you out of bed?"

Kate shrugged her narrow shoulders. "I couldn't sleep."

"No?" Tiffany ran her hand through her daughter's long, soft hair. "Why not? Did you have a bad dream?"

Kate shook her head. "I had a fight with Poppy Leventer and Lucy Titus today. They said you weren't really the PTA president."

Tiffany rolled her eyes. "That's just nonsense."

"They said if you were a good PTA president, you'd put the band's big trophy in a trophy case."

"Hmm. Think about that. What's better for all the kids in the school? Seeing your trophy in a big, expensive case every time they walk in, or taking part in fun learning activities, like when you had the Spanish breakfast?"

"I loved the breakfast!"

"And I love the trophy, but it isn't something *all* the students got to take part in, so I think it's better to concentrate PTA funds on things that everyone can enjoy. Don't you think so?"

Kate nodded solemnly. "Yes. I do."

Tiffany smiled at her daughter's maturity. "That makes me proud of you."

"I'm proud of you, too, Mommy." Kate wrapped her arms around Tiffany and squeezed. "You're the best PTA president there could ever be. Way better than that mean old witch Mrs. Leventer." She then made a *p-tuey* sound that Tiffany totally agreed with.

But this was not the time to indulge that kind of pettiness. "Be respectful of your elders," Tiffany reminded her daughter. Then added silently, *even when they don't deserve it.*

✳

The talk with Tiffany the night of Brian's accident had done Abbey an unbelievable amount of good. Once she'd finally told her story to another human being, she felt better, and she'd felt a lightness in her step for days now.

Of course, it was better still that Tiffany had *not* thought Abbey was the monster that Abbey had felt herself to be.

But, truly, the best of it was that after she spilled all the squalid details, she felt the proverbial weight had been lifted from her chest.

So she sat on it for a few days, knowing she had to come up with just the right plan to deflect Damon. Ultimately she realized there was only one way to confront Damon, and that was to take away any power from the one thing he was holding over her head: telling Brian.

So she had to take that power away from him. It was a chance she was taking, because she was only going to confront him the one time, and if he didn't accept what she had to say, she was going to have to call the police and get involved in a trial and everything.

But at this point, she'd decided that she had no choice. She couldn't live under his threats any longer.

"He's blackmailing you for ten thousand dollars?" Tiffany asked when Abbey finally opened up to her. She'd decided she ought to, just in case things went wrong and someone needed to know who the culprit was. "Then he'll leave you alone?"

Abbey had nodded, pretty sure Damon was simple enough for that to be the truth. "It's what he says. And I think he's done enough rudimentary Googling to know I'm not Miss Gotrocks or anything. He's not going to be able to squeeze millions out of me."

"But you gave this necklace to charity."

Abbey nodded again. "It's how Brian and I met. He'd come to the hospital when I had the accident and given me his card, so when I needed a charity to give the necklace to, he was the first one I thought of. He thought it was too valuable for me to give away. At the time, I think he figured it was a personal vendetta against some man, rather than, well, you know. Penance."

Tiffany had nodded right away, looking as if she really, truly *did* understand. Like it was normal. "I don't like the idea of you giving him the money, though," she said.

"But it's *his* lot," Abbey had argued. "In a way, he's right, he gave it to me to hold on to for him, and I didn't. That sort of makes me responsible. Doesn't it?"

"Unless you're FDIC insured, I don't think so."

Abbey's inclination was to agree with that, yet something in her said she owed a debt.

When she told Tiffany that, they'd come up with a solution that felt right to Abbey.

The first thing she needed to do was find Damon. Once that was over with, she'd tell her bigger truth to Brian.

So she contacted Gerald Parks, as everyone had suggested, and Parks had been able to locate Damon in less than an hour just by checking his parole records.

Damon was living in Bethesda, Maryland, his old stomping grounds. *Her* old stomping grounds, too. For some reason she'd expected he was a full-time Las Vegas resident, trying to rip people off there, but as it turned out, it had been just a sheer lack of luck that she'd run into him when she did.

He lived within twenty miles of her.

Well, fine. She'd been to hell and back—or at least purgatory—and she flat-out refused to let Damon ruin the rest of her life, blackmailing her over some stupid necklace that wasn't even worth significant blackmail money when you came right down to it. Seriously, ten thousand? That was nothing in Damon's circles.

Abbey asked Tiffany to get Parker after school; then she drove to the address Gerald had given her. It was a crummy old apartment building off Arlington Road, a line of residences that looked more like an old abandoned hotel than anything else.

She gathered her courage and went straight up to his door and knocked, fully expecting that he wouldn't be there.

So when he was, she was momentarily stunned.

So was he.

"Got my money?" he asked as soon as he recovered from the apparent surprise of seeing her. If he was curious about how she'd found him—and he had to be—he resisted the urge to ask.

Abbey lifted her chin and her left brow. "Eight thousand dollars," she said, holding an envelope out to him.

"I said ten—even nine. Never eight."

"Repeatedly. But I decided you weren't worth the interest." She shook the envelope at him. "Take it or leave it."

He took it. "This is awfully thin," he said. "I hope it's a cashier's check."

She said nothing, but stood there watching as he tore open the envelope, took out the contents, and looked puzzled.

"What the fuck is this?" he demanded.

"What does it say?"

He shot her a hostile look and read, *"A donation has been made in your name to the Arthritis Foundation."*

Abbey nodded. "Eight thousand dollars. Exactly what you said the necklace was worth. Nothing more, nothing less."

"You gave my fucking money to a fucking charity?"

She was unfazed by his anger. "I did. I figured with all the bones you'd broken, the Arthritis Foundation made sense."

"This better be a joke."

"Oh, no, Damon, it's no joke." She slid the words at him like an arrow, swooshing out of its sheath. She wasn't afraid of anything he could do to her now. He had no power over her. "I gave the necklace to charity years ago, but when you came back to demand remuneration—" She saw his baffled look. "—in other words, *payback*, you did manage to make me nervous for a few weeks."

"You should be."

She gave a small shrug. "I'll give you that: I was. So I figured, the necklace was your responsibility *in a way*, so *in a way* it was right that you got credit for it. That's the result in your hands." She didn't tell him it was only $5,000 that she'd donated, but that was all she'd been offered for the necklace in the first place, all those years back. Under those circumstances, it didn't matter what something was worth retail; it only mattered what the black market would bear.

Damon's features gathered into a dark storm of fury. "You're going to be sorry."

"I don't think so." Abbey was blasé. "You can't do a thing to me. As a matter of fact, you're *lucky* I donated that money in your name, because it might be your only shot at not being perceived as a completely evil person for your entire life."

He gave a fake, hard spike of a laugh. "I wonder if your husband will think so."

Never mind that it didn't make sense. Abbey got what he was saying, and responded with a laugh of her own. "My husband couldn't care less about you. And this great truth you think you can tell him about me? This truth that's going to change everything and ruin my life because of the damn necklace you stole?" She shook her head. "He already knows it all. You can't touch me."

Strictly speaking, it wasn't true. Brian didn't know the truth yet. It made more sense for her to take care of the problem that was Damon before talking to him, so she could lay it *all* on the table at once. But Damon didn't need to know that. It wasn't as if he could get to Brian before she could, and turn him against her.

"I've got a receipt," she went on. "So, no matter how you decide to approach this—if you're stupid enough to approach this again at all—there will be no indication that I ever had the necklace and that, in fact, I made this donation in cash."

"But you *did* have the necklace."

"Prove it."

His face grew blotchy and pale as he blustered, "But you *did*."

"And you're going to what? Call the police and tell them I won't give you your stolen necklace back?"

The blotches left his face, leaving only paleness. "You know goddamn well I can't do that."

She nodded. "In fact, if you contact the police with *any* of this, you're liable to get your butt thrown back in the slammer for another ten years. Maybe more. I don't think they ever got you on that particular grand theft, did they? And yet"—she shook her head—"I can prove you took it. And on top of that, blackmail is a federal offense. I'm not sure your parole officer, William Minor, would be pleased to hear what you've been up to."

"You're a fucking bitch."

She was so glad to hear it because it meant Damon definitely knew he was powerless, and now he'd slink off into the darkness like one of those huge D.C. rats.

It was over. At least as far as Damon was concerned.

Now she had only to tell the truth to Brian. Regardless of how that turned out—and she hoped to heaven it turned out well—it was the last great hurdle for Abbey. The last thing that kept her past from fully reconciling with her present and future.

✳

Timing was everything.

Unfortunately, Abbey didn't have the luxury of waiting for the optimal timing. Whatever that would have been. So it was the first night that Brian came home from the hospital, after she had put Parker in bed, that she had the talk with him that she'd been needing to have for a decade now.

"How are you feeling?" The edge of the bed squeaked as she sat down next to him.

"Not too bad, actually," Brian said. "Like I'm getting over a monster of a flu."

"Do you need anything?"

He reached for her. "Just you."

She smiled, but pulled back gently. "I need to talk to you for a few minutes—are you up to it?"

It didn't take a hammer over the head for Brian to realize his wife had something serious on her mind. "What's wrong?" He looked worried.

A man who was married to a woman who looked like Abbey was always vaguely worried.

"It's about me," she said quickly, trying to assuage the fear she saw in his eyes. "My past. I need to tell you about it, and I know it's not a good time, but circumstances have come up that don't allow for me to wait for a good time."

Brian gave a patient nod. "I'm listening, honey. Tell me whatever you want to. I'll love you anyway, you know." He gave a small smile.

Something inside Abbey tore. She wanted so much to spend her life with this man. She knew that now. It hadn't begun that way, but over the past month she'd come to know, more and more each day, how very lucky she was to have him.

All she could do was hope it wasn't too late and understand that it might be.

"I love you, too," she said up front. "Honestly. With all my heart. You and Parker mean everything to me, and the fact that I have to tell you some sort of ugly ancient history doesn't affect that at all."

"You're not leaving." He said it as a statement, but it was a question.

"No." She closed her eyes and shook her head. "Not unless you want me to."

"Never."

It was time to just spit it out. "I didn't marry you because I loved you, Brian," she said, shocked at the honesty of her own words. "I married you because I was scared. Terrified."

He looked surprised. "You married me because . . . you were scared? Of what?"

"I was scared I was damned." She meant every word of it literally, but it sounded like a stupid joke when she said it out loud. "When I was younger, before I met you, I wasn't exactly living what you'd call an exemplary life. I messed with drugs, alcohol, men—" She took a ragged breath. "—you name it. God—your God, *any* God—was never, ever part of my equation. In fact, I think the real truth is that I looked down on people like us."

He nodded. "You weren't alone. What changed your mind?"

This was hard. She didn't want to say it. "I was responsible for my best friend's death." She hesitated for a moment, before adding, "And my own."

There was silence. He didn't ask what she meant, just waited for her to go on when she could.

So she did. "A few months before I met you, I was a mess. A real mess. Like no one you'd ever want your child to hang out with, much less end up like. I experimented with everything, absolutely no regard for what it was or what it could do to me."

"Why?" He looked genuinely curious. Not judgmental, just curious. "Your childhood wasn't so bad, was it?"

"No." She shook her head and closed her eyes against the image of her parents' stricken expressions the first time she was arrested at school for marijuana possession. "I put my parents through hell, and I have absolutely no excuse for it. I can't fix it now." They were perfectly fine parents. Not particularly affectionate, maybe. But they kept their children clothed and fed and made sure they were educated, at least through high school. They'd certainly never done anything to provoke rebellion in her.

"Fix it? I thought your parents were dead."

Abbey shook her head. "My dad died years back, but my mother is still alive."

Brian looked surprised. "You didn't tell me."

"No. I . . . it's too complicated. Too ugly."

"Surely it's not too late," Brian said, and she could tell from his tone that he thought—as anyone might—that her mother would welcome her back into the family no matter what had happened in the past.

She shook her head. "My mother pretends I don't exist. I tried to talk to her once, recently actually, but she'd moved on. She made it absolutely clear that I don't exist to her."

"That's unthinkable."

Abbey shrugged. "I can't really blame her. I was selfish. Hedonistic. Reckless, even, because I remember thinking I didn't care if I lived or died. I was all about the moment. Until the moment came that I wrapped my best friend's Honda around a parked BMW on M Street." Abbey met Brian's eyes with sincere sorrow. "She died at the scene. I suspect part of her parents did, too, they were so close." The pain that had thrummed dully in Abbey's chest for all these years hammered hard, threatening to punch a hole in her chest.

"I'm sure it wasn't your fault," Brian began.

"Oh, it was completely my fault." She took his hands and looked into his eyes. "Make no mistake on that, it was my fault. I'd had at least a bottle of champagne to myself, in addition to three or four lines of coke. Yes," she said, in answer to an expression she expected but he did not make, "I was using cocaine too."

"You're not the only one who's done that."

"I was the only one doing it in the car that night. It was absolutely my fault. I didn't even know Paulina was dead when the ambulance came. I was *still* out of it. I remember bits and pieces of the ambulance ride, but the next thing I remember is waking up in Washington Hospital Center two days later and they told me I'd died on the operating table." She gave a humorless laugh. "They told me how *lucky* I was to be alive."

"You were."

Abbey looked into his eyes and waited a moment before saying, "Don't you want to ask me?"

"Ask you what?"

"What I saw. *Who* I saw." She tried to keep the bitterness from her voice. "Which childhood pets came gamboling over the expanse of green meadow to greet me? *Everyone* wants to know that stuff."

"Okay," Brian said slowly. "So tell me. What and who did you see?"

"Nothing." She met his eyes. "Absolutely nothing. No loved ones, no light, no meadow, no angels, no goddamn dogs." She stopped herself and said, "I'm sorry."

"Please don't apologize to me at a time like this."

"I have to, Brian, don't you see? I didn't see heaven, because I wasn't going to heaven. *Everyone* has stories about the white light and the feeling of peace. You never, ever hear anyone say they died on the operating table, or in an accident, or whatever, and came back with no memories at all. No demons, no angels, nothing whatsoever to indicate I rated any sort of afterlife." Tears were burning her eyes now. "Just blackness. Just . . . nothing."

"So what?" Brian asked. "Maybe that just meant it wasn't your time. Or it happened and you didn't remember."

"Or maybe it meant I was damned for all time. And maybe when I met the pastor of the local church, I could save myself by attaching myself to him, marrying him, having his child. . . ." She was crying now, although the last thing in the world she wanted was Brian's pity. "Maybe I compounded a lifetime of sins by making a calculated effort to take the easy way out by marrying a man of God."

She tried to catch her breath. "Maybe that, more than anything else, damned me."

Brian looked at her for a long time, though she could not tell what was behind his expression. It was almost as if he were examining some new specimen of dolphin or something, looking at her with curiosity but without feeling.

Then he said, "If that's the case, I'm damned, too."

She looked at him incredulously. "Why?"

"Because when I met you, I wanted to save you."

"You want to save everyone." She didn't understand his implication.

"I wanted to save *you*," Brian said. "And I don't think it was part of my job."

She looked at him.

"I've had a secret or two of my own," Brian went on. "I know about your accident. I was in the hospital for other reasons that night and they were looking for a priest but no one could be found, so I guess I was better than nothing. They told me what had happened and called me to your bedside to pray for you. They didn't think you'd make it. But as soon as I saw you, I knew you would." He gave a labored sigh. "I should have mentioned this a long time ago, but, you must know, it never really came up. It would have held so much weight if I'd brought it up out of the blue, like you were lying to me—"

"I *was*!"

"No, you weren't. I know who you are. I knew who you were when we got married. What you did two months ago or two decades ago wasn't relevant."

She frowned. "And yet—"

"And yet." He said it definitively. As if nothing else mattered.

But it did. "So my life before—"

"Didn't matter," Brian pronounced. "*Doesn't* matter. I'm glad to hear anything you want to tell me, but I don't want you to tell me anything out of guilt or out of a misguided belief that you have to fess up and do some sort of penance before I can accept you." He put his arm up around her shoulder and drew her closer. "I accept you, I *love* you, no matter what."

"Even if I married you as a sort of buoy for my soul?"

He laughed, then winced, as he was still in some pain. "I would have taken you under whatever circumstances I could get you. But I'm not stupid, Abigail. I know we have a great marriage. So I don't care *how* it began."

He was right. They did have a great marriage. Even in the beginning, it had been a good marriage. It wasn't as if she'd made some huge sacrifice to be with him in order to save herself. Granted, she hadn't married for love, but she also hadn't married while plugging her nose and swallowing her distaste.

Brian was cute, smart, kind, and he loved her. It had been easy to marry him.

And it had been easy to fall in love with him.

Which was why she had to make sure he knew the whole truth now. So she told him about Damon, about meeting him in Las Vegas, where he tried to blackmail her, telling her she owed him money, and how she had had to join a phone sex operator business—she didn't say whose—in order to pay him off.

When she was finished, Brian was—she almost couldn't believe it—laughing.

She wasn't sure what to make of his laughter, so she refrained from joining in.

"That's incredible," Brian said. "Really great." He splayed his arms, then drew her in again. "My hat's off to you. Not many people would have the nerve to do that."

"You think so?" She was so encouraged by his words, she almost couldn't believe it. "Really?"

He laughed again, really sincerely. "Yes. Come on, Abbey, you know I'm not one to get pious over things."

"Well, no, not when they involve something other than your wife."

"I love my wife," he said sharply. "Make no mistake. I'm not so stupid that I could live with someone for eleven years and not know who they are." He looked so deeply into her eyes, she felt like he could see her spleen. "I know who you are," he said, in a commanding voice. "I should have said something a long time ago. If this mess is anyone's fault, it's mine."

"No, Brian." It just wasn't true. "No."

"You know what?" he asked. "I don't care whose fault it is. I'm married to the most beautiful, wonderful woman in the world, and I'm happy with her." He eyed her. "Are you happy with me?"

She considered a moment, before answering with the same words she would have said automatically. "Yes. Happier than I ever dreamed I could be."

"Then forget the past. Forget the business with dying on the operating table. You know, in my business we like to preach that that is significant, but the scientific truth is that it's *only* a trick of the mind. So forget it. You weren't dead. You came back. You have no idea what it's like to *really* die." He cupped her face in her hands and spoke emphatically. "But I'm positive that when you eventually do, around the age of a hundred and twenty, I hope, you'll see all the lights, loved ones, and pets you want to. Though honestly, I'm not even sure that's how it goes. It's hard to take the word of a living person on what it's like to die."

"So it doesn't matter to you that I lived that way, that I hung out with Damon, and that I ended up having to do phone sex to pay Damon off for a debt?" She was challenging him, putting things in the worst possible light so he'd have almost no choice but to dump her.

*Almost* no choice.

"No." Brian looked thoughtful for a moment, then shook his head for the second time. "No, it really doesn't. I can't get worked up over that." He cocked his head and lowered his chin. "I'm not interrupting some big, significant confession, am I? You've told me the worst? There aren't a bunch of bodies buried in our basement?"

She laughed finally. "No, I've told you the worst. No skeletons in the crevices of our house anymore. Unless they're yours."

"Mine? But you know I'm practically a saint." There was humor in his eyes, and in his voice, despite the fact that both were marred from the accident.

She clung to the joke, not the bruises. "Not if I blackmail you about some of the things you've told me tonight."

"See? There's the resourceful woman I've come to know and love."

They spent the next hour sitting there on that bed, joking and laughing and talking about things that neither ever thought the other would understand. At the end of it, Abbey felt as light as a cloud, floating over the conversation without one worry to weigh her down.

Finally—*finally*—the weight was lifted.

Until Brian, toward the end of the evening, made one final request.

"I'm thinking," he said, "that maybe you should stop the phone sex business now."

"Well, I'd already figured that. It's not exactly something I thought you'd approve of."

"It's not that I don't approve." He gave a sly smile. "The truth is, I just want you all to myself."

# Chapter 22

L oreen had just gotten Jacob to sleep on Thursday night, after about twenty unnecessary post-bedtime stall tactics, ranging from *"one little glass of water"* to *"I can't find my LEGO Darth Vader."* She was sitting on the sofa, watching some depressing recap of the days' events on MSNBC, when there was a light knock at the door.

She looked at the clock. It was 10:15. Ever cautious, she grabbed the portable phone from between the sofa cushions—she already had 911 programmed in, just in case—and went to the front door to look through the peephole.

It was Robert.

She opened the door with a sigh of relief. "What, your cell phone doesn't work? You could have warned me you were coming—you scared me to death."

"I tried to call. The phone's off the hook."

She looked at it. Sure enough, the TALK button was lit. She must have sat on it. "Come on in," she said, tossing the phone aside. "Can I get you something?"

"No, thanks. Actually, I have something for you." He held up a cardboard tube, like the kind he (and Mike Brady, she happened to know) used to store and carry plans around.

"Did you get a new contract?" She sat down on the sofa and watched him as he came and sat down next to her.

"Well, it's a new project, but it's not a new contract. I just hope the client likes it."

"So you want me to look it over first?"

"Exactly." He brushed some magazines aside on the coffee table and took some large sheets of paper out of the tube. "Now, here's the main house." He spread the paper out.

Loreen looked. Then did a double take, assessing the rooms. "Hey, that's *this* house."

He gave a quick nod, his face growing a little pink in the cheeks. "It is for now. But I was thinking maybe we could expand this closet—" He pointed to a linen closet that never contained more than a bottle of Tylenol and a small pile of washcloths she didn't know what else to do with. "—and bump it out to make a proper office for you." He laid a transparent sheet over it, as she'd seen him do a thousand times before, but this time it was *her* house. "You always said the one in the basement was too cold and dark."

"It is." She hated going down there. "I love this, but—"

"Good, because . . . I had another idea, as well." He carefully pulled another transparent sheet from the tube and laid it over the existing plans.

This one showed the back of the bedroom pulled out, with the addition of a three-sided fireplace—Loreen had always wanted one—and a sitting room.

"It's fantastic," she breathed. "My dream house, but . . . why? I can't afford this, and I can't let you help. Unless . . ." Her voice trailed off. She dared not say what she was thinking: that it would all be worth it, in fact it would all be *perfect,* if he'd just come back home.

So when he said it, she wasn't prepared.

"Funny you should mention that, because I was thinking that maybe if there was someone else living here with you, they could, you know, kick in on the bills. Maybe someone who already has an interest in you and Jacob?"

She was hopeful, but not certain. "Do you know someone like that?"

"I have someone in mind."

"Is he just looking for a place to stay for a while or, maybe, a family for a lifetime?"

"The family." He nodded. "Absolutely. Forever."

Loreen pressed her lips together. "You're talking about you, right? Moving here? I don't want any misunderstandings."

He moved closer and reached for her hand. "Yes, I'm talking about me. Moving here. Being a family with you and Jacob again. I love you." He was looking tearful now.

"I love you, too," she said, feeling her eyes burn.

"I just can't walk away from you." He looked uncertain for a moment. "Unless you want me to. I—" He faltered. "Loreen, I don't want to push myself on you. I just want to be with you again."

She wanted to believe it. She wanted to dive straight in and believe every word without question. But she was old enough, experienced enough, and just plan cynical enough to ask questions first. "Are you sure you're not going to change your mind later? I'm still me, you know."

"I thank God for that. You are all that I want."

"I want this to be true," she said, a lame attempt to stop herself from crying *Yes!* at the top of her lungs.

"You know me," Robert said simply. "I think you know you can believe in me."

She did. "I do." She swallowed over the lump in her throat. Nothing was going to dislodge it except a good, hard cry. So she said, "I do," again, and gave in to the emotion of finally, *finally* coming home.

✴

That was it; Sandra was finished dating. And when Tiffany, Loreen, and Abbey got a load of *this* night, they couldn't possibly tell her to keep trying.

She'd take up a hobby, maybe sewing or crocheting or something. Get a bunch more cats. She'd be like Mrs. Exstorm, the weird old lady on the corner of Candlelight Lane and Old Coach Road, when she and Tiffany were growing up. Everyone was afraid of Mrs. Exstorm. There were stories that she was a witch who grabbed children and ate them for dinner, and that her cats were her familiars, who crept out to peer in the windows of the children late at night, scoping out victims.

The parents had said no, she was just a lonely old woman whose health wasn't what it used to be. Sandra and Tiffany's mom swore it was because of the millions of cats in the house. It wasn't a healthy atmosphere for *any* of them.

"It's hard to breathe with all that cat hair and dander flying around," Sandra's mom had said. "It's a wonder any of them are still alive."

So Sandra would be sure to keep her cat acquisition to no more than five or six.

Kids would still talk, parents would still pity, but at least she wouldn't die of cat hair asphyxiation.

She'd made this decision after a particularly humiliating night in which she went to Galaxy Zed to meet Kenny, aka Pullmyfinger on Match.com. Yes, she realized she was now scraping the bottom of the barrel if she was willing to give a shot to a guy with a handle like Pullmyfinger, but when she'd first read it, she hadn't realized what it said. She thought it was just another nonsense screen name.

But it wasn't a deal killer in any event—he seemed nice, he didn't smoke, and he shared a few interests with Sandra.

It was worth a shot, as the girls had kept telling her.

But as it turned out, it had *not* been worth it. She'd gone into the restaurant, a bit nervously, and stopped at the hostess. "Hi, I'm Sandra Vanderslice and I'm supposed to be meeting a Kenny . . . something"— she was embarrassed that she didn't know his last name—"here. Has anyone come in asking for me?"

"Um, not exactly," the hostess said, "but *that* guy's been sitting there alone for a while." She pointed at a nice-looking, if ordinary, man who was sitting alone, looking around uncertainly.

"Thanks." Sandra approached him with similar uncertainty. "Excuse me," she said. "Are you—?"

"Yes, yes, I am." He'd looked relieved. "I thought you weren't going to show. Or that you had, and you'd left because you didn't like the way I looked." He'd laughed at that horrible possibility.

How they made it through twenty minutes of pleasant conversation without ever actually addressing each other by name, Sandra couldn't later say. At the time she'd thought he was a really nice guy and, while maybe not her dream man, certainly someone she could see dating for a while. In any event, it gave her hope that not everyone out there was a wacko.

That's what she'd thought at the time.

Later, of course, all she could think about was that startling moment when he'd looked at her and asked, "So let's get down to it. How long have you been into pony play?"

"Pony play?" Had she heard him right? "You mean, like betting on horses?"

He'd frowned. "I'm sorry . . . betting?" He'd smiled, and it was a nice smile. "I don't get it, is that a euphemism? I'm . . . sort of new to all this."

Now she was really confused, and embarrassed because this didn't seem like that complicated a conversation. Was there something in his profile that she'd missed? Or something in *her* profile that made it sound like she was into horseback riding or something? "Look, I'm really sorry, but I'm lost. What do you mean by *pony play*?"

He drew back like she'd slapped him. "Wait a minute, aren't you Flicka from Ponyplayers-dot-com?"

"Flicka?"

"Manny?" A woman with long, wavy auburn hair came rushing over to the table. "Are you Manny?"

"Yes."

Sandra looked at him. "You're not Kenny?"

"Who's Kenny?" Flicka asked. Then she held out her hand to Sandra. "Sorry, forgot my manners. I'm Flicka."

"Sandra," Sandra said in a voice that sounded like she wasn't even sure of her own name. This was starting to sound like "who's on first."

"*Sandra?*" Manny asked. "I thought you were Flicka."

"Well." Sandra gestured haplessly. "*That's* Flicka."

"Yeah, I'm Flicka."

"Apparently we got our signals crossed," Sandra said, pinpointing at least the tip of the obvious iceberg.

Flicka looked from Sandra to Manny. "You didn't tell me you were bringing anyone. Not that I mind or anything, but does she have a stud?"

"A *stud?*" Sandra repeated.

Manny had begun to look distinctly uncomfortable. "Wait a minute." He held up both hands. "I think this is a misunderstanding. Are you here to meet an Internet date?" he asked Sandra.

"Yes. Kenny. Pullmyfinger?" Even as she said it, she was realizing that Kenny had nothing to do with this. "From Match-dot-com?"

Manny nodded. "I'm here to meet Flicka from Ponyplayers-dot-com. That's who I thought you were. Obviously you thought *I* was this Kenny guy from Match-dot-com."

"And you're not?" She didn't know why she said it. Clearly he was not.

"No." He shook his head and looked at her like she was stupid.

Indeed, she was beginning to feel stupid. "So all this time, I was thinking you were Kenny, and you were thinking—"

"You were Flicka." He pointed a finger gun at her and clicked his tongue against his teeth as he pulled the trigger.

"But *I'm* Flicka." Flicka looked confused now. "Are you or are you not Man o' War?"

Manny's face colored, and he cleared his throat. "Er, let's go to our table, okay?" He put his hand on the small of Flicka's back to usher her the hell away from Sandra and gave a single nod. "It was nice to meet you. I hope you enjoy your date."

"Thanks. Sorry." Sandra watched him go, feeling utterly humiliated.

She looked at her watch. If Kenny was coming, he was either twenty minutes late or standing in the vestibule thinking *she* was.

The hostess tapped her as she passed. "Um, are you Sandra?"

Sandra turned to face her. "Yes." It was the same hostess she'd told her name to twenty minutes ago.

"Yeah, some guy came by? And I told him where you were sitting? And he asked me to tell you he had an emergency and wasn't going to be able to make it tonight after all." She nodded and looked painfully sympathetic.

Everyone knew what that meant.

"Oh. Okay, well, thanks for the message."

And Sandra had left, dejected. Quite apart from the whole bizarre experience with Flicka and Manny, her *real* date had come in, taken one look at her, and bolted, leaving the dim-witted hostess to break the news to her.

And that was it.

No more dating.

And no more contentions from friends that she should keep dating.

The next evening she told Tiffany, Loreen, and Abbey the story in Tiffany's gleaming kitchen, a place that made it seem like Nothing Bad Ever Happened.

"Ew, I don't know what's worse." Loreen shuddered. "The fact that this jackass ditched you or the fact that you almost went out with a pony player."

"What the hell *is* a pony player?" Tiffany asked.

"I don't know!" Sandra was still baffled by this apparent secret code between her nondate and *his* date. "Maybe it's some subculture of people that everyone on earth knows about except me and you."

"Everyone who watches *Real Sex* on HBO." Loreen took a sip of coffee. "Honestly, I'm surprised you never had a pony player call. I had one last week." She set the coffee mug down. "Creeped me out."

That did it. Sandra's curiosity was piqued. "Okay, I'm out of the loop. I'm a bad phone sex operator, and a worse date. I don't watch HBO. What *is* it?"

"It's a premium cable channel," Tiffany said, *clearly* holding back a smile.

"Tiffany!"

"Okay, okay."

Loreen said, "It's these people who are into pony play, like to dress up as horses—you know, with bridles, martingales, saddles, even synthetic tails—and have sex like that. Like horses."

"Oh, my God. Like those clown people?" Sandra took a steadying sip of wine. She'd seen *Real Sex* once, and the people had dressed up as clowns—something Sandra found personally terrifying—and had indiscriminate sex with each other.

It had freaked her out.

"Exactly." Tiffany poured herself some wine. Just half a glass. She filled it the rest of the way with seltzer. That was the kind of restraint she'd always had. "I saw that one, too."

"So this guy . . ." Sandra thought back. He'd seemed so normal. So nice. So *normal*.

You just never knew.

"Total fruitcake," Tiffany said with a nod.

"We shouldn't have advised you to get back on the horse so fast," Abbey said, suppressing a smile.

"Funny," Sandra said. "Very funny. Can we talk about something else?" She looked around. "Anyone?"

Loreen sighed. "I've got something to say. And if you're faint of heart, stop me now, because it ain't pretty." She moved her uncertain glance from Sandra to Tiffany.

"I got you started as phone sex operators," Sandra said, reaching for one of the Thin Mint cookies Kate had sold during the Girl Scout fund-raiser. She knew once she started she couldn't stop, but she couldn't stop herself from starting. After what she'd been through, she *deserved* Thin Mints. "Is it uglier than that?"

"Hey," Tiffany said. "You saved our butts. Don't joke about *that*."

Sandra looked at her sister. "That's the nicest thing you've ever said about me."

"Oh, I say lots of nice things about you," Tiffany said. "Just not to your face. Don't want you to get bigheaded."

"I've been on a date with a puppet," Sandra said. "And a gay man, and a pony player. I don't think I'm in any danger of becoming bigheaded. Oh, my God, did I tell you I ran into Louis at the grocery store?"

Loreen gasped. "Louis the Puppetmaster?"

"Exactly." Sandra nodded. "It was terrifying. I went over to, I don't know, apologize. Make nice. Whatever. But he was standing there with his fist balled up, like he was going to punch me. So the whole time he was telling me Arlon was *in the hospital,* he was clenching and unclenching his fist."

"I hope you got out of there fast," Abbey said.

"I did," Sandra said. "But not before catching a glimpse of his fist." She pressed her lips together and told them. "He had a face painted on it. You know, like kids do in elementary school? Where the thumb is the lower lip and you can make it talk?"

Loreen, Abbey, and Tiffany shrieked with laughter.

"I guess he was desperate for *something* while Arlon was gone. I'm certainly glad the fist didn't talk to me. Sooo," she said, wrapping up her social life in one neat finish, "that's what my dating life's been like this year. You can try, but it's hard to beat."

"I had a one-night stand with a hottie in Las Vegas," Loreen said flatly. "Afterwards he wanted a thousand bucks for his services when I was just glad the drinks were free."

Sandra took a moment, looked at Loreen to determine if she was serious.

Loreen nodded. "It's true."

"You win," Sandra said.

"A male prostitute?" Abbey repeated incredulously. "*That's* how all this started?"

Loreen stiffened visibly. "Yes. And I totally understand if you never want to talk to me again, because I drew you into this mess, which I know is sinful, and didn't fully disclose the reason to any of you."

Abbey laughed. "Loreen, I don't think it's sinful. I'm just so glad to hear you had such a good reason."

"Good reason?" Loreen echoed dumbly.

"Well, it's one thing to rack up a bunch of gambling debt because you're bored. It's a whole different thing to rack it up because you're panicked."

"You thought I lost all that money just because I was bored?" Loreen asked. Her expression softened. "And you still risked everything to help pay it off?"

Abbey's face took on a slight pink hue. "I wouldn't say I *risked everything*, but you were in trouble. It didn't really matter all that much why."

Tears filled Loreen's eyes. "I don't deserve friends like you guys, I really don't."

Tiffany put an arm around her. "Yeah, well, you're stuck with us anyway."

"Really stuck," Sandra added with a laugh. "Since I'm not dating anymore."

"Actually . . . speaking of dating and not wanting to ever date again, Robert came by last night," Loreen said. "I don't think we'll be getting divorced."

Tiffany was clearly delighted. "You're *not*?"

"Well." Loreen reached for the bowl of fruit and took a banana, peeling it deliberately as she spoke. "We were talking about getting back together, so I told him about my night in Vegas." She bit the banana and went on, while chewing, "When I told him about *that*, he freaked out."

"Naturally," Tiffany said. "But he got over it."

"Um-hm." Loreen swallowed. "Go figure."

"Look, you made a mistake," Tiffany said. "Big deal. We all do sometimes. Frankly, I'd be disappointed if Robert couldn't get over it."

They pondered that for a moment.

Then Sandra's phone rang. She took it out and looked at the caller ID, as was her habit. Just in case it was something urgent.

It was Doug, her date from Normandie Farm.

That was weird.

"Answer it," Tiffany barked when Sandra announced the caller. "Find out what he wants!"

Sandra opened the phone. "Hello?" She held up a finger and walked a few steps away.

"Sandra?"

"Yes?"

"Doug Ladd. We met a few weeks ago?"

Like she could possibly forget. "Hi, Doug." She made a puzzled face at the others. "How are you?"

"Good, thanks. Listen . . . do you have a minute?"

"Sure."

He let out a short sigh. "I realize you might just not be interested in seeing me again, and if that's the case, it's fine. Just tell me. But I really thought we had something going when we met, and then . . . I'm not sure what happened. It turned weird."

Of course it had turned weird. She'd asked him if he was gay. "I'm really sorry about that," she said. "All I can say is that I've been burned before . . . well, actually, I've had a series of bad dates, one more bizarre than the last, so . . ." She shrugged, even though he couldn't see her. "I'm gun-shy."

"I think I understand," Doug said. "I got that you weren't the most confident person in the room."

"No, that would have been you." She laughed.

He laughed, too. "Far from it. Anyway, look, I've had some bad dates, too, and I just find I keep thinking about you. I'd like to see you again."

Her jaw dropped. "Why?"

"I'm sorry?"

"Seriously, Doug, I'd love to, but why would *you* want to see *me* again? You're a great-looking guy. You've got everything going for you. Why would you want to go out with *me*?"

"Why *wouldn't* I?" He sounded genuinely puzzled.

Did she have to *say* it? "I'm not exactly Cindy Crawford."

Tiffany made an exasperated sound, and Sandra shot her a silencing look.

"So what?" Doug asked. "Neither am I."

She laughed again, but didn't point out that she'd stopped just short of asking him if he was. "Okay, but you're practically George Clooney. Why would you want to go out with a fat girl?"

All three of them—Tiffany, Loreen, and Abbey—made noises of objection. Sandra held up her hand and *shhh*'d them as she left the room for more privacy.

She found a spot in Kate's room and sat down.

"Fat?" Doug was saying. "Give yourself a break, Sandra. You're just . . . you're like a luxury model of these vain skeletons I've been meeting. You're real. You have an appetite for life, for food, for drink. I'm good with that."

Hope seized her, and she immediately squelched it. It was a habit from a long time back.

"You're not just, like, a fetishist, are you?" Because she'd met one too many of *those* this month.

"Jesus, Sandra, you act like you're a circus freak or something. Give it a rest. I really liked the woman I met at Normandie Farm. I want to see her again. Is that really so surprising?"

She could have gone on arguing, but the lack of confidence would be far more unattractive than any of the things she was worried about, and besides, Doug seemed really sincere.

Both when she met him and now.

She was *not* going to blow this for herself by being insecure.

"No," she said firmly. "It's not weird at all. So. Where are we going?"

# Chapter 23

Charlie was in a foul mood.

And Tiffany did not want to deal with it. Gerald Parks had called and said he had the evidence she was looking for, so she wanted to go get it, and have it in hand before potentially having another explosive conversation with Charlie.

Charlie made her feel bad. About herself, about their life, for their kids. Charlie was cranky grumpy, unhappy, domineering, and about a hundred other unpleasant adjectives.

Over the past several months he'd gone away on business more than ever before, and Tiffany had realized that she not only enjoyed the time when he was gone, but she dreaded his return. The news that he might be having an affair, in fact that the private investigator had pictures she could use against him, would have been devastating a year ago, yet today it was welcome. Cause for celebration, even.

This was not a subtle clue that something was wrong in the marriage; it was a big neon sign.

Tiffany had already asked Loreen for help in figuring out her budget, so she could take care of the kids on her own. The presumption was that, if she and Charlie divorced, she'd get child support at least, but Tiffany didn't want to count on that. She wanted to be sure she had enough to do everything by herself.

Unfortunately she hadn't yet had that conversation, or the one with Gerald Parks, when Charlie came in, practically breathing fire.

"I need to use your bank account," he said—without preamble and without greeting his children—when he came into the kitchen.

"I'm sorry?"

"There's been a . . . a problem. Identity theft. My bank account has been cleaned out."

There was more to the story. She'd been with him long enough to know that. *"Identity theft?"* she repeated.

He nodded. "It happens all the time. I'm . . . working on it. Meanwhile, I need to tap into the family account."

"Wait a minute," Tiffany said. "There's *your* account and the *family* account?"

"Yeah." He nodded.

"What about me?"

"What about you?"

"Where's my account?"

"Where's your income?"

*In my account,* she wanted to say, but she wasn't going to tip her hand. The fact that she had a private account to pay off the PTA debt, and so on, didn't mean he could just separate their marital finances the way he had. "I don't think a court would see that as relevant."

Charlie's stance was belligerent immediately. "So now you want to take this to court?"

She straightened her back. "I'm not against it."

He frowned at her, then turned to Andy. "Go see your sister upstairs," he told him.

"What are you doing?" Tiffany demanded.

"We need to talk. Alone." Charlie took Andy out of his seat and shooed him toward the hallway.

Tiffany took Andy to the stairs and called up to Kate to come get him, which she did.

Then Tiffany went back to the kitchen and asked, "What in the world did you have to do that for?"

"You two are in cahoots, aren't you?"

"What?"

"You're working together. You and Marcia."

"Marcia who?" Tiffany said. Then it dawned on her. "Marcia your secretary?"

"Like you don't know."

"Charlie, I *don't* know. What are you talking about?"

"I'm talking about Marcia threatening to tell you about us, then the next thing I know my accounts are cleaned out."

Marcia! Tiffany never would have suspected she'd do something like this! "I don't know what you're talking about," she said. "Are you having an *affair* with *Marcia*?"

"Like you don't know. You weren't behind that guy following me with a camera?" His hesitation lasted only a fraction of a second before it started to crackle with uncertainty.

"*Marcia?*" Tiffany demanded again.

Charlie went pale. "You didn't know?"

Tiffany shifted her weight and stared him down. "What scares you more, the idea that I did know or the idea that I didn't?"

"Stop playing games," Charlie snapped. "Were you involved in cleaning out my accounts?"

"No," Tiffany said icily. "Was your mistress?"

Charlie's voice was tight. "I didn't say—"

"Yes, you did," Tiffany answered quickly. "You said your mistress cleaned out your accounts."

He paused again, then ran his hand through his hair and took a step toward Tiffany. "Oh, baby," he said, reaching for her and pulling her into a stiff embrace. "I've made such a mess of things. Can you ever forgive me?"

"For having an affair and losing all your money to her?" Tiffany asked. "Yes. Yes, I can forgive you."

Charlie tightened his grip on her. "Oh, thank God."

"But I can't take you back."

His grip tightened more still. Then he pulled back. "What?"

"I can't take you back," Tiffany repeated. "You've betrayed me too much." She decided to go with the vague because it seemed clear now that he had betrayed her more than once.

"You were so wrapped up in the kids," he said, but it sounded like he'd practiced it before. Like he was ready for this conversation.

But even if that weren't the case, his contention was so laughably untrue that she couldn't take it seriously. "So you slept with your secretary."

"She was *there*," he said. "She was *responsive* to my needs."

"She *took your money*," Tiffany added. "How did she do it? With your social security number?"

He nodded. "We had a joint account," he said. "For business, but apparently she wanted to use it for more."

"You had a joint account with your *mistress* but not with your *wife*." Tiffany shook her head. "Unbelievable."

"I'm sorry." It might have been the first time in their marriage that he'd ever apologized.

"I bet you are. It sounds like you've got your hands full, what with fixing your banking errors and moving out of here."

"Moving out?"

Tiffany nodded. "Maybe Marcia will take you in."

"But—"

"Or not. I don't know. But all I know is that I'm not going to take the brunt of your miserable temper anymore. If you've got a mistress, let *her* deal with it. And if you don't, get one. I'm sure it won't take long."

"But the money—"

"Will be sorted out in court. It's not my fault you were stupid enough to be taken by your girlfriend. You'll still owe child support and alimony. And heaven knows your job pays well enough to cover it."

"But you're my wife!"

"You should have remembered that a *long* time ago," Tiffany said heatedly; then, after waiting a moment for a response that didn't come, she walked away.

And, actually, she felt good about it.

Because, in reflection, it wasn't about what Charlie was doing or not doing . . . at least not entirely. The main problem with their marriage was how he made her feel. How *bad* he made her feel almost all the time. So she already knew that ending it was inevitable.

That he had given her such a maddening—and convenient—out was just a bonus. But she was going anyway.

And now she was gone.

# Chapter 24

Tiffany pushed the grocery cart through Giant Food, talking on her new Bluetooth earpiece. She'd gotten it so she could multi-task while working, but she'd found it was a miraculous little thing for driving, shopping, whatever, and now that she was single, it was even more of a bonus because she had a lot less to think about and worry about since Charlie wasn't at the house anymore, hovering, ready to criticize her at any given moment.

Tiffany loved being wireless.

She also loved shopping for just herself and the kids. No more big old steaks. No more ten-pound bags of potatoes.

"So everything's paid off?" she asked Loreen as she walked through the cereal aisle and opened a box of Cheerios for Andy, who was in the petri dish of a seat.

"Everything. Plus we have an extra hundred and fifty-eight in the coffers for programs." Loreen sighed. "All we need is another four hundred and fifty."

"Bingo the Clown is six hundred bucks?" Tiffany cried, then hushed herself. "You can't be serious." She handed Andy some Cheerios to munch.

"No, it's not for Bingo. I thought we decided to go with Merle the Spelling Wizard."

"Oh, that's right." Tiffany stopped in front of the coffee. She loved the General Foods International Coffees, but they were getting so expensive. "Still, six hundred bucks . . ."

"That's with a discount," Loreen told her.

"Ouch." Tiffany tossed a can of Café Français into her cart. She'd work a little longer and pay off the $4.75. "I hear he's worth it, though."

"Oh, totally. I saw him at an Urbana Elementary function once. I can still spell *acquiesce*, thank you very much."

"How apt." Andy threw a Cheerio and hit her hair. *"Stop it!"* she hissed at him.

"What?" Loreen asked.

"Let's do it. If we keep the business going, there's no reason we can't pony up personal donations. You know, they're probably even tax deductible."

Tiffany stopped to get some unsalted almonds from the bulk section. "I like it. The Happy Housewives have been good to us," she agreed.

Tiffany thought about it for a moment. Initially this was supposed to be just to pay off the PTA stuff, but they'd gone to a lot of trouble to come up with the name, form the business, put together a Web site, and piece together models, to say nothing of the ten employees they now had. She hated the idea of just demolishing it all. "Let's do it," she said. "Get the best programs we can. No one needs to know how we paid for them."

"Okay." Loreen sounded a little giddy. "Does it say something bad about me that I don't want to give it up?"

"If it does, it says the same thing about me," Tiffany said, then lowered her voice. "Who would have thought professional phone sex—no, make that phone *acting*—could be so much fun?" Her phone started to beep. "Hey, my battery's dying, I've got to run."

"See you tomorrow night?"

"Absolutely. Bye." Tiffany snapped her phone shut and cursed the stupid battery. Perhaps from the amount of use it had been getting, the charge seemed to be going quicker and quicker. Sometimes it felt like she got only fifteen minutes' use out of it. It was a huge drag to be tethered to the electrical outlet by the dryer during her calls.

She stopped and dug a spare battery out of her purse and clipped it in. Now that she was a single parent, she had to be available to the school at all times, in case of emergency.

She turned the phone on again, then pushed the cart around the corner and almost ran smack into Deb Leventer.

This was one of the consequences of living in a development with only one grocery store within ten miles.

"Deb!"

"I thought I heard your voice," Deb said, tipping her frosted head to the side. "And here you are."

"Here I am," Tiffany agreed, and Andy threw another Cheerio.

Deb would undoubtedly consider that bad breeding.

"I hear we have Merle the Spelling Wizard coming to give a

presentation," Deb said, tipping her newly frosted head. "How on *earth* did you swing that?"

"Just good fortune, I suppose." Tiffany wheeled her cart toward checkout four, where Mary—who Tiffany had long thought was the fastest cashier there—was working. "Will you be bringing Poppy?"

Deb shrugged. "I'm not sure. Frankly, Merle's act is a little old at this point. I was hoping we might get the Pluto Group to come talk about the solar system."

"Why don't you mention that at the next PTA meeting?" Tiffany suggested. "We'll see what we can do."

Deb raised an overly dark eyebrow. "I'll just bet you will."

A large, very hairy man rounded the corner holding a family-size bag of chips. "I've been carrying this all over the place, looking for you." He dropped the bag into the cart. Then he looked at Tiffany. "Oh, hey. Did I interrupt something?"

"No, we were just discussing PTA business," Deb said. "This is Tiffany Dreyer," she added, with a distinct *the one I told you about* tone. "She's in charge of the programs."

"Mick." He held out a hairy hand. "Like Mick Jagger."

Tiffany's breath caught in her throat. Did every guy named Mick say that? In that same particular way? Or was this, in fact, her regular caller?

The one who was so proud of using his own name.

Her eye fell on a bag full of zucchini in their basket.

Tiffany knew her face was turning pink, and she was barely able to hide the laughter that threatened.

Deb Leventer, high and mighty, was married to a regular Happy Housewives patron!

"Where's Poppy?" Deb asked her husband.

"I thought she was with you."

"No, she was with *you*. *Find her!*"

"That little sneak," Mick said. "She's probably in the cookie aisle." Without another glance back, he went off, looking at the signs at the end of the aisles.

*Little sneak,* huh?

Mick was *Mick* all right.

This was incredible.

What a stroke of luck.

"Excuse me," Deb said. "But I have lots to do."

"Well, it was good to see you, Deb," Tiffany said, meaning it more than she ever could have before. "And I just loved meeting your husband."

Deb just looked impatient. With a toss of her new hair she said, "Ta ta," and started to wheel her organic-food-filled cart away, but the wheels caught on the wheels of Tiffany's cart, and tipped it over. Tiffany grabbed Andy from the seat just in time, but food, soda cans, and the contents of Tiffany's purse spilled across the floor.

"Oh, no!" Looking genuinely embarrassed, Deb bent down to try to pick the items up, along with Tiffany. "I didn't mean to do that," she said a bit defensively.

"I know." Tiffany shifted Andy onto one hip, then grabbed her prescription bottles with the other hand and plopped them back into her purse.

The confusion was multiplied when the bag boy showed up and started putting the food into Deb's cart instead of Tiffany's, which got a rise out of Deb.

Finally, with each cart sorted out and everything but a few dimes and pennies Tiffany didn't feel like chasing down in place, Tiffany went through the checkout line and took her bags, and her boy, out to the car.

She had a new bounce in her step and she knew it.

"Mommy happy?" Andy asked.

"Yes, Mommy is very happy. Are you happy?"

He nodded. "I happy."

"If you're happy and you know it, clap your hands," she said in a singsong voice, and Andy picked up the tune.

She joined in, but all she could think about was getting home and finding some privacy so she could call and tell Loreen what had just happened.

✳

The ringing phone was driving Deb crazy. She'd left the grocery store, dropped Mick off at the mechanic's to pick up his car, then gone on to the post office and Target, and everywhere she went, she heard that obnoxious song.

"Mom, what's that song?"

"I don't know," Deb said as they pushed a cart through the girls' department. "But you hear it, too?"

"It's coming from your purse."

Deb bent down to put her ear closer to her purse. Sure enough, that's where the noise was coming from. What the heck was that? She reached in and fished out her cell phone. At least, she *thought* it was her cell phone. But now that she looked at it, it didn't have the crack in the screen from when she'd thrown it at Mick last week after he forgot her birthday.

And, of course, it didn't have her ring.

She fished in her purse some more and produced the cracked phone. So where had the extra one come from?

Then she remembered. When Tiffany Dreyer had run into her cart, everything had spilled. She must have grabbed Tiffany's phone, thinking it was her own.

"I want the Bratz pajamas," Poppy said, grabbing things off the racks and throwing them into the cart. "And that jean skirt."

"That's too short," Deb told her, still holding on to the phone. She looked down at it and noticed she'd pressed a button and it was dialing. She pushed END quickly.

"It is not!" As usual, Poppy went from zero to ten in less than one second. "All the other girls get to wear them. You're so mean!"

"I don't care," Deb started, but then the phone rang again.

Tiffany's phone. The caller ID said UNKNOWN. Ooh! A mystery caller!

The curiosity was too much for Deb to resist.

"Go try the skirt on," she told Poppy. "Take that shirt, too," she said, pointing to a pop princess shirt she objected to on every level but which she knew Poppy would want to try.

Sure enough, Poppy skipped off to the dressing room happy as can be.

With only a fraction of a second's hesitation, Deb opened the phone. "Hello?"

"It's Ed from the relay center," a voice said. "I got a call from your phone. Are you logging in?"

"Can I have the skirt in black, too?" Poppy called from the dressing room.

"Yes," Deb said to Poppy, but it was the man on the phone who answered.

"You got it," he said.

She hung up, shaking her head. Whatever.

The phone rang again, almost immediately. Probably Ed from the relay center again.

"Hello?"

"I was afraid you weren't working and they were going to send me back to the relay for another girl."

Deb frowned. "What?"

"I've been waiting all day to talk to you."

"Okay . . ." She'd never been good at imitating voices, so Deb figured her best bet was to say as little as possible.

"Unzip me."

"What?"

"Unzip me. You know, with your teeth. I want you to suck my cock before it bursts."

Deb gasped so loudly that two women turned to look at her.

She clipped the phone shut, her face burning.

That had to be a wrong number. Deb had met Charlie Dreyer. There was no way a good, dignified man like that would stoop to talking to his wife like that.

She kept the phone in her hand and walked to the waiting area for the dressing rooms to sit down. This was seriously disturbing.

She wished Tiffany had gotten the call instead of her.

The phone rang again. Deb looked and, again, the caller ID said UNKNOWN. Was it possible that the call really *was* intended for Tiffany?

"Hello?"

"Crystal—"

"No—"

"—I've been thinking about you all day. Gimme some sweetness."

"Who is this?"

There was a hesitation. "Is this Crystal?"

"No."

"Which one are you?"

"Deb." As soon as she'd said it, she regretted it. She never should have given her real name out. Now Tiffany would find out she'd answered her phone! Oh well, she could get away with that by telling the truth, that she thought the phone was hers after the confusion when Tiffany rammed her cart into Deb's. It certainly wasn't Deb's fault!

She wouldn't mention the fact that she'd answered the phone even after she knew it wasn't hers, however.

"Deb," he said. "I haven't seen you on the site. What do you look like?"

"What site are you looking at?" she asked.

"The Happy Housewives site," he said. "Listen, I don't want to pay two ninety-nine a minute for this shit. Are you going to get me off or not?"

"Um, that would be *not*," Deb said crisply.

He hung up.

Okay, that was two sexually explicit calls in ten minutes. One could have been a crank call or a wrong number or some other coincidence, but two?

She had to get to this Happy Housewives Web site.

"Poppy, we have to go."

"But I haven't finished trying everything on!"

"I don't care, put it in the cart. If things don't fit, we'll return them later."

Deb drove home as fast as the speed limit would allow, ignoring the ringing phone, even though she was *dying* to know who was calling now.

Once home, she went into Mick's den to use his computer. She didn't want to use the one in the kitchen, in case Poppy came in and saw something sexually explicit.

The desktop came up, and she clicked on Internet Explorer. But before she was finished typing *happyhousewives.com,* Internet Explorer automatically finished it for her.

And took her to a site for phone sex, promised by women who could cook, clean, and caress at your leisure. There were thumbnail photos of Crystal, Mimi, Brandee, Sophia, Lulu, and a host of other cosmetically enhanced bimbos. None of them were Tiffany.

That was strange.

Then again, if Tiffany was involved in phone sex for money, she probably wouldn't be stupid enough to use her real name or put her real picture on the Web site.

Deb scrolled around, looking for any information that could lead her to Tiffany's connection. All she could find was a counter at the bottom of the home page that listed how many hits there had been since a date that was about a week after they'd returned from Las Vegas.

Which was about the time Tiffany and Loreen had seemed to get so secretive and weird.

This was so exciting!

And Deb knew *exactly* how to use this to her advantage.

She wasted no time. She looked up Tiffany's home phone number and called it, waiting with bated breath for her to answer.

"Hello?"

"Tiffany, it's Deb Leventer."

"Hi, Deb. Look, I'm in the middle of something, so I can't really talk right now—"

"Oh, I think you want to hear what I have to say."

"I beg your pardon?"

"The jig is up, Tiffany. I know what you've been doing. And unless you and your entire board resign from the PTA right away, I'm going to tell the rest of the world."

There was a short, tense silence. "I don't know what you're talking about," Tiffany said in a voice that betrayed she knew *exactly* what Deb was talking about.

But that was okay. Deb didn't mind elaborating. "I'm talking about the fact that you are a phone sex operator. A *whore* if you want to get right down to it. And I do *not* think that's the kind of person we need as a PTA president."

Tiffany let out a long breath. "I don't know what you're talking about."

"Yes, you do. Funny thing happened today. I accidentally picked up your phone at the grocery store because it looks like mine."

She could hear Tiffany scrambling, probably rummaging through her purse, on the other end of the line. "You took my phone?"

"Mmm-hmmm." Deb was enjoying this. "And Ed from the relay center called. You know Ed, don't you?"

The answering silence told her that yes, Tiffany certainly did know Ed.

Deb gave a carefree laugh. "Well, the next thing I know, all sorts of calls were coming through. *Unsavory* calls."

"You were answering my phone?"

Deb sighed. "I couldn't resist. I know it was wrong, but not nearly as wrong as what you've been doing. Wouldn't you agree? Tiffany?"

"What do you want, Deb?"

"Funny you should ask. I want you and all your friends off of the PTA board. And you have until tomorrow at noon to resign formally or I'm going public."

✳

Deb was so pleased with herself. She kept replaying the conversation in her head over and over, imagining the look of horror that must have crossed Tiffany's face when she realized she'd failed to put this one over on Deb.

It was delicious.

When Tiffany's phone rang again, she had the feeling things were about to get even *more* delicious.

She looked at it. What to do? She could put Tiffany out of business. But then there would be no evidence to take to the school board. Surely the county didn't want a phone sex operator in charge of the PTA!

So it was best for Deb not to answer it.

But the curiosity proved too much.

"Hello?"

"It's Mick. I've got to be fast because I'm in the men's room at the car dealership. Blow me quick, lots of teeth."

*"Mick?"*

Stunned silence. Then, "Deb?"

"Yes, Deb." She glanced at the phone. Was it *hers* and not Tiffany's? "What the heck are you talking about?"

"I—I must have dialed the wrong number."

"And who exactly were you trying to call?"

"Suzannah." Suzannah was Mick's secretary. "She's handling a time-sensitive deal for me."

"And you were calling her from the men's room?"

"Yeah, look, uh, I've got to go. Talk to you later." He hung up before she could object.

What the heck was going on? She looked at the phone. It wasn't hers. There was no crack, and . . . and no way around it. The phone was Tiffany's.

*Mick* had just called *Tiffany's* sex phone.

Mick probably thought the phone lines had crossed and dialed from his phone book—their cell phones did that with some frequency—but Deb knew the sad truth. He'd been calling Tiffany for sexual gratification.

It just didn't seem possible.

Maybe it was a mistake. Or a onetime thing.

She went into the history cache of Mick's computer to see how often he'd been to the Happy Housewives Web site.

Apparently he'd been there a lot. A *lot*. Suddenly Deb felt unclean sitting at his desk. He'd ruined everything for her, all in the quest of his own stupid, hedonistic pleasure. Deb was devastated. This should have been one of the best moments of her life, finally getting the goods on her worst enemy.

Tiffany Dreyer was a phone sex operator.

But Mick was one of her clients.

# Chapter 25

"What's the emergency?" Loreen asked, coming into Tiffany's house without bothering to knock first. "Are the kids all right?"

"They're upstairs watching a movie, armed with popcorn, Ho Hos, and everything else I could think of to keep them from wanting to come down," Tiffany said. "I don't want them to hear a word of what's going on."

"Well, what *is* going on?"

Sandra was there, looking anxious from her vantage point on the sofa. "I don't know," she said when Loreen looked at her. "She won't tell me."

Tiffany was pale. "I don't mean to be mysterious." She used a corkscrew on a large bottle of Mondavi wine and carried it and four glasses over to the coffee table. "We just have a huge problem and I'd rather tell you all at once."

There was a knock at the door, and Tiffany looked up from pouring the wine and called for Abbey to come in.

Once they were all seated, practically holding hands as they looked nervously at Tiffany, she told them the bad news.

"Deb Leventer knows."

There was a thick silence before Loreen asked, "What, exactly, does she know?"

"She knows enough." Tiffany swallowed hard. "She has my phone. She talked to Ed."

"Oh, no." Sandra shook her head.

"Yes." Tiffany shook a shaky breath. "And she called this afternoon and demanded that we all resign from the PTA by tomorrow at noon or she's pretty much going to call a press conference."

Abbey gasped. "She can't."

"But you know she will," Loreen said sharply. This was sickening. "Unless we can somehow stop her."

"Short of hitting her with a bus, I don't think that's possible," Abbey said, her usually gentle voice tinged with anger. "Though I'm not advocating hitting her with a bus, no matter how tempting that might be at the moment."

"It's all my fault." Tiffany put her hands over her face. "I was so stupid, walking around the grocery store, talking about it right out loud even though the place is just full of people from the neighborhood and school." She sniffed and looked up, red-eyed. "Never mind Deb, you guys must want to kill *me*."

"Hang on, she figured the whole thing out from the conversation you and I had?" Loreen asked dubiously. Maybe there was hope.

It was short-lived. Tiffany shook her head. "No, but we dropped our stuff, and everything in my purse went flying, and she picked up my phone and took it with her. Then I guess she started getting calls."

"How is that even possible?" Sandra asked. "You were logged in while you were in the grocery store talking to Loreen?"

Tiffany's face grew an even deeper shade of red. "No, but for some reason Ed called and logged me on. Or logged Deb on. Or"—tears flowed—"all of us. I am so, so sorry."

"What a mess," Sandra said, pouring more wine into Tiffany's glass.

"Brian will be ruined," Abbey said in a tremulous voice. "If Deb comes out with this, he'll never live it down."

"She doesn't know you're involved," Tiffany told Abbey quickly. "Or you, Loreen. For all she knows, I'm working for some company on my own. She'll never know about you two."

"But you're *not* on your own," Loreen said, reaching for Tiffany's hand. She couldn't let Tiffany take the fall for this alone. "We're in this together."

Tiffany gave a small half smile. "If she's going to expose me, it's not going to make me feel any better for her to expose you, too." She drank the wine Sandra had just refilled. "The crazy thing is I left there on such a high because I thought I had the goods on her, but she trumped me. She trumped me big-time."

Sandra refilled Tiffany's glass again, then topped everyone else's off, too.

Tiffany looked up abruptly, frowning. "Wait a minute."

"What is it?" Abbey asked hopefully.

Loreen held her breath.

Sandra leaned forward in her seat, as if Tiffany were about to whisper something.

"I'm so stupid!" Tiffany cried.

"Please stop beating yourself up over this," Loreen said, though she was half-ready to agree. That wouldn't have been fair. This was a mistake any of them could have made, especially when someone as devious as Deb Leventer was involved. It wasn't Tiffany's fault.

"No, no." Tiffany wiped her eyes. "You don't understand. I *do* have the goods on her."

"Better than what she's got on us?" Abbey asked.

Tiffany nodded. "I think so. See, Deb's husband is *Mick*."

"I don't get it," Abbey said.

But Sandra did. "*Like Mick Jagger* Mick?"

Tiffany nodded.

Sandra explained to Loreen and Abbey, "He's one of Tiffany's regulars."

"Can you prove it?" Abbey asked eagerly.

The mood in the room shifted, and suddenly there was an air of excitement all around.

"If you could get the phone records, you could prove it," Loreen said. "But, of course, you can't. It's not a legal case."

"It could be," Abbey said thoughtfully.

"How?" Tiffany and Loreen both asked at once.

"Blackmail is against the law," Abbey said. "Believe me, I happen to know this. If Deb blackmails us, we can call the police, and then *everything* will come out in the wash. She's not taking us down without coming down with us."

"You guys are diabolical," Sandra said approvingly. "I like it."

"It's not *us*," Tiffany said. "It's *me*. If you keep talking about jumping off this cliff with me, you're just going to make me feel worse."

"*No one's* jumping off of any cliff," Loreen said. "You've got to call Deb. Right away. Until she agrees to back off, we still have a problem and you need to stop her before she starts telling her friends."

"If she hasn't already," Abbey added, then looked skeptical. "She probably has. She and Kathy Titus are like clucking little hens in the coop."

"I'm calling her now," Tiffany said. She got up and retrieved the house phone from the counter, and the phone tree list for Mrs. Rosen's class from the side of the fridge, and dialed Deb's number on speaker.

Deb answered on the first ring. "Hello?"

"Deb, it's Tiffany Dreyer."

"Oh." The response was flat. "What do *you* want?" It wasn't the triumphant tone of someone who had just brought her opponent to her knees.

Loreen, Abbey, and Tiffany exchanged curious glances.

"As you might expect, Deb, I'm calling about the threat you made against me earlier."

Deb sniffled and Loreen could imagine her straightening her back, readying herself for a fight. "It wasn't a threat, it's just my intention. Someone has to do the right thing."

Abbey rolled her eyes.

"There are different degrees of right and wrong," Tiffany pointed out. "Just like there are differences between legal and illegal. Now, having phone sex is legal."

"Maybe so, but it's not moral." Deb's voice was shrill. "And you know darn well that if the PTA body finds out you're doing this immoral activity, they'll call for your head."

"Is blackmail moral?"

Two beats passed.

"What are you talking about?" Deb asked.

"Threatening to expose me if I don't resign from the PTA and convince the other officers to do the same. That's blackmail. And it's not only immoral, it's *illegal*."

There was a long pause. Then Deb asked, tentatively, "Am I on speaker phone?"

"Yes," Tiffany answered cheerfully. "Yes, you are. I wanted my lawyer to hear everything we said."

"Lawyer?"

"Yes. So, as I was saying, it's *illegal* to blackmail someone, while, according to you, it's *immoral* to have phone sex. Presumably you're talking about both participants, am I right?"

"What are you getting at?" Deb snapped.

"If you don't drop your threats, I'm going to have to call the police, and if the police get involved, they will undoubtedly subpoena all of our phone records." Tiffany looked up and shrugged.

Sandra gave her the thumbs-up.

"Do you know what they'll find on those phone records, Deb?" Tiffany went on.

Loreen listened intently for the answer. Her heart was pounding so furiously that she could barely hear over it.

"No," Deb said. "And I don't want to."

"Oh, but I think you do. Because I have a regular caller. His name is Mick. You know, like Mick Jagger?"

Deb didn't answer.

Which was strange, actually, because that should have riled her.

"Are you there, Deb?"

"There are a lot of men named Mick," Deb said after another telling moment of hesitation.

"How many of them live in your house and use your husband's cell phone?" Tiffany asked.

Deb hung up.

Tiffany frowned and looked around the room. "What do you suppose that means?"

"I think it means there's only one guy in her house named Mick who uses her husband's cell phone," Sandra said with disgust. "And she knows it."

Abbey looked thoughtful. "Yes, but I don't like it. If she panics, she might spill the story without thinking about it first."

"I don't think so," Loreen said. "Once she heard her husband's name, she clammed up. She believed you, at least somewhat. I think the first thing she'd do is check with him."

"But why would he tell her the truth?" Tiffany asked.

Loreen gave her a look. "Would *you* lie to that woman's face? She'd reach in and rip your organs out if she thought you were being dishonest."

"And I'll bet Mick values his organs," Abbey said.

"I can tell you he does," Tiffany agreed with a laugh. "Some much more than others."

"Our pal Gerald Parks has done some good work for us lately," Loreen said. "Do you think he could get the phone records for us?"

"He might be able to," Sandra said. "But they wouldn't do any good. If you wanted to show them to this Deb person and she didn't want to believe it, she'd probably just think they were forged."

"Which would be easy to do," Abbey agreed.

Tiffany sighed. "I wish I knew what was going on. Who has the upper hand right now?"

The phone rang.

Tiffany looked at the caller ID. "It's Deb."

"Put it on speaker again," Loreen whispered. "Let's all find out who has the upper hand."

Tiffany did. "Deb."

"I've decided to spare the PTA the pain of finding out what sort of woman they have running the programs," Deb said without preamble.

Tiffany's eyes widened. "What are you saying?"

Deb let out a hiss of breath. "I'll keep your secret. Not because I believe any of that nonsense about my husband, you understand."

"Of course not."

"But if the truth about you came out, it would only hurt the children, and, well, that is my main concern."

"That's big of you, Deb," Tiffany said, rolling her eyes. "I'm concerned about the children myself."

"So . . . you wouldn't want the truth to come out either." Deb sounded uncertain. "Right?"

"Right," Tiffany said. It was clear they both knew what they were talking about and they agreed they could both lose equally. "Why, if the client list became public, just think how many community members might be implicated. As a matter of fact, Deb, even you participated in this."

"I did not!"

"You did. When you answered my phone."

Deb made an exasperated sound. "You could never prove that."

"Are you sure?" Tiffany asked. "Are you absolutely sure?"

"This conversation is over," Deb said. "I don't ever want to hear anything about it again. Do I make myself clear?"

"Oh, yes." Tiffany smiled. Finally, she knew beyond the shadow of any doubt, everything was going to be all right. "Crystal."

# Epilogue

## Six Months Later

Girls' night!" Tiffany opened Kate's door. "Andy's asleep, the pizza's in the oven, and *Anne of Green Gables* is in the DVD player waiting for us."

"Yay!" Kate came running toward Tiffany in her pink flannel nightgown and threw her arms around her mother. "I *love* girls' night! Is Aunt Sandra coming?"

"Of course! She switched her plans with Doug to tomorrow night just so she could be here with us—isn't that nice?"

"I *love* Aunt Sandra!"

"Me, too!"

They went downstairs and Tiffany checked on the pizza. It was almost ready. The salad was in the fridge, along with sparkling soda for Kate and champagne for Tiffany and Sandra.

Tonight was a celebration.

"Hello?" Sandra tapped on the door as she opened it. "Anyone here?"

"Aunt Sandra!" Kate went running to her. "Did you bring the ice cream?"

Sandra held up a Safeway bag. "Mint chocolate chip. Thank goodness you and I don't like the same flavors, kid." She smiled and handed the bag to Kate.

"Can I have some now?" Kate asked Tiffany. "I *promise* I'll eat all my dinner."

"Nope. Put it in the freezer."

Reluctantly, Kate carried the bag to the kitchen, where she shrieked with delight upon seeing the silver foil Jiffy Pop popcorn package Tiffany had gotten for them to eat during the movie. It was a junk food extravaganza tonight.

Freedom was really suiting Tiffany.

Sandra, on the other hand . . . "Let's see it," Tiffany said excitedly.

"Hmm? See what?"

Tiffany flashed her a playful look. "Don't play games with me, sister, let me see the ring."

Sandra laughed and held out her left hand. The emerald-cut diamond sparkled madly between two straight sapphires, all set on a gleaming platinum band. Doug Ladd had excellent taste, both in women *and* engagement rings.

"Gorgeous!" Tiffany breathed. It truly was exquisite. "Are you happy?"

Sandra looked liked she could burst. "Yes!"

"*So* happy?" It was a game they used to play in childhood, only back then it used to be *so sorry* more often than anything else.

"*So* happy. I just . . . I can't even believe it!"

"I can." Tiffany gave her sister a hug and held on for just a moment longer than usual. "I'm so thrilled for you. Really. He's just the greatest guy."

"I know! But let me tell you about his friend, Ron—"

"No way." Tiffany held up a hand. "Not yet. For the first time in my life I'm sleeping in the middle of the bed; I'm making what I want for dinner when I want to make it; I'm in sole possession of the TV clicker. . . . Don't mess this up for me." She laughed. "I've never been a single girl before. To tell you the truth, I'm *really* liking it. So back to *you*. When are we going shopping for your dress?"

"Anytime," Sandra said. "I've already got the shoes picked out, of course."

"You're going to match the dress to the shoes?" Tiffany asked in disbelief. "You're not going to pick the dress first?"

Sandra shook her head. "Good Lord, no. A dress is easy to find, but when you find the perfect shoes, you have to grab them. And *these*"—she took a page from a catalog out of her purse and handed it to Tiffany—"are the perfect shoes for my wedding."

"The Sandra," Tiffany read, then looked at her sister. "Oh, my gosh, he named a style after you?"

Sandra beamed and nodded. "Read on."

"Pointed-toe pump, in a white pearlized kidskin upper, with stiletto heel and cut-out side quarters." She looked at the picture and commented, "They're so sexy, they're almost indecent!"

"I know!"

"Well, *this* is cause for celebration as much as anything else." Tiffany led Sandra to the kitchen and took the bottle of champagne out of the fridge, along with two flutes from the cabinet. "What an honor." She tore the foil off the bottle.

"It's amazing," Sandra said. "So what about you? How's the real estate business going? Is Loreen a good teacher?"

"The best." She pulled the cork off the bottle and poured the bubbly liquid into the glasses. "I think she was really glad to lighten her load by handing it over to me." Tiffany handed Sandra a glass. "To the blushing bride and inspiration for the hottest shoes this season."

"And to her sister, the uncontested president of the *blue ribbon award–winning* Tuckerman Elementary PTA."

"Hear hear."

They clinked glasses.

✶

"Close your eyes," Brian told Abbey. "I've got a big surprise for you."

"You're not going to *believe* it," Parker added excitedly.

"Don't give it away, bud," Brian said, then to Abbey: "Seriously, close your eyes."

"You don't need to give me anything," she said. "It's enough that I have you two."

"That's nice, sweetheart, and I know it's true, but you don't have to be a saint *all* the time." He gave her a nudge. "Every woman likes a little something special now and then, so close your eyes."

"Fine." She laughed and closed her eyes. "They're closed."

"Sure you can't see?" Parker asked, and she felt a tiny breeze on her face and knew he was fanning his hand in front of her eyes.

"I can't see a thing."

"Put your hands out," Brian instructed.

She did.

"Here you go." He set a long slender box in her hands. "You can open them now."

She opened her eyes, and sure enough, the box was of the kind jewelry came in. She couldn't help that her heart did a little leap.

Then she panicked. Quickly, unexpectedly, with the certainty of a premonition, she panicked, knowing that inside the box was the necklace she'd sold so long ago to give money to the church. The necklace Damon had almost killed Brian in order to get.

Brian had tracked it down. He'd probably saved his pennies for years to buy it back for her, thinking it was a long-lost token.

"You remember when we first met," Brian said, as she listened, frozen. "You had a very special piece of jewelry that you sold in order to donate money to the church."

"Yes." Her mouth was dry. The sound that came from her throat was barely more than a croak with a vowel in the middle.

"Well, I've felt bad about that for a long time," Brian went on.

*Stop,* she thought desperately. *Please stop. Please please please don't go on, don't make me open this box.*

"—because a woman like you, as beautiful as you are, deserves something beautiful for herself." He nodded toward the box. "So . . . go ahead. Open it."

There was no way she could get out of this. No way to just say *no thanks* and set it aside. *Thanks for the thought, that's what really counts.* No, she had to open the box, see the necklace, and then . . . what?

She'd given up the phone sex. Once the bills were paid and a nice little nest egg was established for the PTA programs fund, there had been no reason to continue it. She was just a *real* happy housewife now.

But if she opened this box, how would that change?

"I'll help," Parker said, pushing his sticky hands in the middle of things to open the little box.

Inside, on the black velvet, was a thin gold necklace with three little solitaire diamonds on it.

It was not *the* necklace.

"I know it's not the same as the one you gave up," Brian said, echoing her grateful thoughts with an unnecessary apology in his voice. "But it's always bothered me that you didn't have something to replace it. So I found this at a jeweler in the mall. Each of the diamonds represents one of us. You, Parker, and me. And, if we're ever blessed with another addition, we can add another diamond. Although I hope it won't be too soon, because my wallet is still smoking." He was kidding, of course. She knew he wanted another baby more than anything, and that money would never be a consideration for him.

He was just trying to put her at ease because he knew that *she* knew this was a rare extravagance.

"Brian Walsh, you are the most thoughtful man in the world," she said, holding back tears.

"What about me?" Parker wanted to know.

"You, too!" She pulled them both into a hug. "I love you guys more than you'll ever know," she said.

"We love you, too, Mom."

"Yes." Brian caught her eye. "More than you'll ever know."

✳

"This is Mimi." Loreen lay back against her sateen sheets and switched off the light.

"What are you wearing?" the gruff male voice asked.

"I'm wearing a burgundy lace teddy with a black garter, fishnet stockings, and a pair of kitten-heel Carfagni mules in black leather." She really was. And the shoes were outrageously comfortable, too.

"I want to take it all off of you. Piece by piece."

"Oh, I want you to." She sighed. "Believe me, I want you to."

"Then I want to kiss you all over your body. Every square inch."

She considered. "That could take a while."

"We've got all weekend. I plan to have my way with you, over and over and over again. Beginning right now."

"And then?"

"Then we do it again."

She laughed. "And then?"

"Then I make you breakfast in bed. Strawberries, pancakes, coffee with cream—"

"*Now* you're talking my language."

"I know how to get to you."

"Then, for heaven's sake, Robert, hang up the phone and get up here." She smiled. "I want you *now*."

"Two minutes." There was the distinct sound of utensils being put into the dishwasher. "I'll be right there."

"I'll be waiting," she said, thinking there was no bigger turn-on than a man who arranged for his parents to take the kids for the weekend so he could do every little thing for his wife for two days in celebration of her birthday. "Oh, and Robert?"

"Yeah, babe?"

"I love you."

There was a clattering in answer.

"Robert?" She frowned. "Hello?"

"I love you, too." He was coming in the door, pulling off his shirt as he walked toward her. "The dishes can wait. But this—" He got on the bed and pulled her close against his bare chest. "—can't. I'm not wasting one more second of my time with you, ever again."

Turn the page for a sneak peek at
Beth Harbison's new novel

# Hope
## *in a*
# Jar

AVAILABLE JULY 2009

# One

*I can bring home the bacon, fry it up in a pan,*
*and never never never let you forget you're a man . . .*
—ad for Enjoli perfume by Charles of the Ritz

The only thing worse than finding out your boyfriend is cheating on you with a beautiful woman is finding out he's cheating with an average woman.

Allie Denty learned this the hard way, when she got off work early and walked into her bedroom to find what appeared to be a seal flopping under the covers of her previously made bed.

It was hard to say who became aware of whom first, or who was more surprised. At almost the moment Allie entered her bedroom, a woman she'd never seen before popped her head up from under Allie's 450-thread-count Martha Stewart sheets and screamed like a banshee.

"But—" Allie began in shock, as if they'd been in the middle of a conversation.

She didn't have time to finish the thought, whatever it might have been, because the woman leaped off the bed, stumbling to pull the sheet around herself, only to reveal Kevin, whose hands were bound over his head with his Jerry Garcia necktie.

The tie Allie had given him for Christmas last year, even though it cost more than all the other ones at Macy's.

Every muscle in Allie's body clenched and she looked in alarm from the banshee to the boyfriend she'd so foolishly—and so *completely*—trusted.

"What the—" Allie tried again. "Kevin! *What* is going *on*?"

The woman had stopped screaming, but her breath continued to sputter out in ragged gasps.

"Allie," Kevin said, but it sounded like he was trying on someone else's voice. He cleared his throat and tried again. "Allie, this isn't . . ."—it was clear halfway through his sentence that he knew how lame it was—"what it looks like."

"It looks like you're fucking some other woman in my bed," Allie said. To hell with manners. She'd just discovered that she was less attractive to her boyfriend than a woman who, now that she got a better look, could have played the *before* in an ad for just about any diet, exercise, or lifestyle cosmetic ad in *The National Enquirer*. Her light brown hair was lank and shapeless; her eyes were the same dull shade as her hair; her mouth a thin pink line, too small in a somewhat doughy face.

And her butt—which Allie unfortunately got a good look at— was even more cottage-cheesy than Allie's.

Granted, she had a perfect, straight nose. But was that what Kevin was attracted to? A model-perfect nose on an otherwise completely unremarkable face?

"Well," Kevin said, struggling out of his bindings. "It's complicated . . ."

Allie didn't remember what came after that. Not a denial exactly. How could he deny it? Good Lord, the condom was still hanging off his shrunken skipper. Wasn't what it looked like? It was *exactly* what it looked like.

Nothing complicated about it.

"I should go," the woman said, hastily pulling her clothes on.

"You think?" Allie gaped at her. Then a horrible realization came over her. "Wait a minute, aren't you the one who brought those paper samples to the office last month?"

"Your order will be ready on the seventh!" the woman said defensively. "There was a delay with the printer for the watermark."

This was surreal. The unremarkable woman who had sold them Kevin's new letterhead at a deeply discounted price, the woman who had asked to use the restroom and who had then—Allie couldn't help noticeing—taken a very long time and emerged with a bit of toilet paper stuck to her shoe, was now in bed with Kevin and marking the end of Allie's past two years.

"Allie, we can work this out." Free of the necktie, Kevin got out of bed, just like Allie had seen him get out of bed naked a million times before. Only there wasn't usually another woman in the room.

Fortunately, Paper Girl didn't wait around; she just thundered from the room and a moment later the front door slammed.

Fine.

One gone, one to go.

"Really, Kevin? The discount paper vendor? Seriously?"

"She didn't know about you," Kevin said in defense of the one person whose emotional stake in this was the smallest.

"What, did she forget I was the one who placed the order with her a few weeks ago? When she got here, did she miss the pictures of *us* all over the place? My stuff in the bathroom? Is she *blind*? She shouldn't have been here, Kevin"—her voice shook with anger—"but more than that, *you* shouldn't have *brought* her here—"

"I know."

"—so now *you* get out."

He was maddeningly calm. "Let's talk about this—"

"Get *out*," Allie said, and her voice grew stronger as she said it. *"Get out!"* She picked up his jeans from the floor, his underwear, his stupid *Star Wars* T-shirt. "Get the fuck *out*!" She hurled his clothes at him and pushed him out of the bedroom toward the door.

"But—"

"You can get your stuff out of here later. Or I'll send it. Just"—she shoved him toward the front door—"get"—she picked up his damn Hanes 32 briefs and threw them into the hall, hoping modesty would make him go after them like a dog—"*out*!" She slammed the door and turned around.

Immediately she heard a noise in the hall.

A woman's voice.

Oh, God, she'd been waiting for him. Coconspirators, keeping secrets from Allie, comparing notes, hooking arms and leaving together. It was disgusting to contemplate.

For a long moment Allie stood there, listening to the murmuring voices through the door, fearing she might hear a giggle or an outright laugh. But all she heard was talking, then shuffling footsteps, the ding of the elevator's arrival, and then . . . nothing.

Nothing except for the low moan that rose in her own throat, a moan that slowly rose to an explosion of sobs. She hadn't seen this coming. That had always sounded so stupid when it was other people saying it, but it was the honest-to-God truth. She'd never dreamed

Kevin would be anything less than faithful to her, just like she was—unquestioningly—to him.

Come on, it wasn't like he was some sort of hot-stuff hunk with movie-star looks. He was an average Joe. An average Kevin. With a high IQ and a decent personality. Every once in a while he'd made her laugh. Well, chuckle anyway.

For two years—two long, ignorant years—Allie had given up the dream of finding a soul mate because she believed Kevin was so good for her. They'd just moved into her apartment together, and were looking for a new place. A bigger place they could buy together.

She'd thought they were on the path to a pretty good life partnership.

Instead, he was sleeping with another woman when he thought Allie wasn't going to be home.

Who *was* he?

If he wasn't who she'd thought he was, who *was* he?

And what had happened to the guy she thought she knew? Did he just . . . not exist? Could she have been that wrong?

"Allie!" Kevin's voice was faint outside the window but it still startled her. "Allie, please!"

She stood motionless, like an animal frozen with indecision. Cross the road or run back in the woods?

"Can you at least throw me my wallet and my keys?"

Her eyes fell on the bedside table. There they were. Just like every night. Evidently that was his bedtime ritual, no matter what he was going to spend his time doing in bed.

And no matter with whom.

She considered throwing them in the incinerator. That would certainly create a moment of great satisfaction.

Revenge was always tempting. However, it was seldom satisfying and almost always had some stupid ramification you didn't think of. In this case, she'd probably have to endure an hour and a half of him sitting out there, waiting for AAA to come open his door, or for Lexus to cut him a new key and bring it to him, and then there would be calls from his credit card holders, and—she didn't want to deal with it.

She grabbed the wallet and keys and went to the living room, where there was a tiny balcony.

He was standing in the grass below.

"You want these?" She held them up.

"Yes, Allie. Please."

"Then take them." She hurled the wallet, and enjoyed the solid *thump* when it hit him in the forehead. That was one good thing about having had an older brother growing up—she didn't throw like a girl. "And don't forget your keys." She raised them in her hand.

"Not in the face!" he shrieked.

Even in her anger, the pool of betrayal and hurt feelings, she wished he would be a little more of a man about it.

What would the neighbors think?

She dropped the keys over the railing instead of hurling them. There. Let him climb through the azaleas to find them. He was no longer her problem.

She went back to the bedroom, stripped the sheets off the bed, stuffed them into the washing machine, set the water to hot, and dumped in half a box of soap. After a moment's hesitation she added several cups of bleach.

Then she went to the bathroom to wash her hands. She spent a long time at it, scrubbing as if she could wash the last hour away, to make it so it had never happened.

Finally she gave up and stood in front of the mirror, gazing into her own confused face. What had just happened? Where had she gone wrong? And when?

The woman gazing back looked like she'd given up a long time ago. Her hair was dry, and where once it had been a silky light blond, now it was brassy from home coloring. Her cheeks looked soft . . . no, doughy. The lines by her eyes, which didn't bother her most days, looked, today, like they were carved in with the sharp edge of a putty knife.

Worse, by far, the optimism that she'd always taken for granted in her soul had gone to sleep somewhere along the way—maybe a long time ago, now that she thought about it. There was nothing happy in her eyes. She looked defeated.

She *felt* defeated.

She was defeated.

Allie sank to the floor, her body suspended not by bones but by deep, heaving sobs. She couldn't believe this was happening. Had happened. Had probably been happening for a long time and she just hadn't noticed.

Stupid.

Stupid stupid stupid.

She hated Kevin.

But when it came right down to it, she knew this was her fault. It wasn't the other woman she couldn't compare to—it was herself. Where had *Allie* gone?

Somewhere she'd let go of her dreams and, at the same time, she'd let go of her hopes. She'd settled for a life of tedious temp jobs and a rented apartment and a man she didn't really love, a man who clearly didn't *deserve* her trust.

Allie had settled for all of that.

And for that she hated herself most of all.

✳

"Noah, it's me. Again. I'm sorry to be a pain, but I just . . ." Allie swallowed, trying to keep her voice from wavering. She didn't want to sound pathetically needy.

Though, given the fact that this was the third message she was leaving on his cell phone—and the fact that he would see she'd called about a dozen more times without leaving messages—she was already in the first-class section of the Pathetically Needy Train.

". . . just wanted to talk to you," she ended lamely.

Where *was* he anyway? Noah was a workaholic—she could *always* get ahold of him because he was always at his architectural drafting board, either at home or the office, working.

Then again, he had mentioned he was seeing someone "newish," so maybe he was out with her, whoever *she* was.

Allie disliked her already.

The poor girl didn't stand a chance. And Allie was feeling just uncharitable enough to hope that Noah would dump her soon so Allie could have him to herself again.

Not "have him" have him, of course. There wasn't anything romantic going on. Never had been. They'd been friends since eighth grade, as soon as it was no longer taboo for boys and girls to talk to each other without making dramatic gag noises.

Not that it would be hard to fall for a guy like Noah. Allie and her friends used to joke that he looked like Matt Dillon's better-looking brother back when Matt Dillon was a current reference (and not long after Allie's room had been plastered with magazine cutouts of Matt

Dillon). At six feet, he was a comfortable four inches taller than Allie, and he was broad enough that she felt feminine next to him (as opposed to Kyle Carpenter—from the summer after college—who, at five foot nine, had made her feel like an Amazon).

But despite the fact that he looked like her teenage crush and was the *perfect* height for her, Allie never even hinted at having a Thing with Noah because she didn't want to lose their friendship.

Really.

He was her best friend and the only person she could call in the middle of the night with a question about, say, *Green Acres* and get an answer that was (1) correct and (2) didn't involve expletives about calling in the middle of the night with a question about *Green Acres*.

That wasn't the kind of friendship a person should risk.

So instead Allie had dated a series of guys who weren't *quite* right for her: from Luke Dashnaw, who quit his job as an investment banker to become a clown ten months into their relationship; to Stu Barker, who was a Buddhist and spent one day every week in complete silence, meditating and fasting; to Kevin, who had sex with the paper salesgirl in Allie's bed when Allie wasn't home.

Allie was beginning to wonder if she'd be better off by herself.

She was also beginning to worry that soon she wouldn't have much choice. Despite very frequent and *very* concerted efforts to the contrary, she knew she wasn't as pretty as she had once been. Her thirty-eight-year-old face was starting to sag a little; the years of indulgence had puffed out her chin and hips; the summers at Tally-Ho pool in Potomac, languishing under the sun with only a thin film of baby oil between her skin and the UVA and UVB and UV-Whatever-They-Discovered-Next rays, had etched lines into her face that wouldn't otherwise have been there.

Thinking about it now, Allie felt her spirits dip even lower.

There was only one thing she could do to feel better. It would cost her, of course, but sometimes you couldn't put a price tag on mental health.

Or, actually, you could, and if you considered that it was $150 per hour and maybe once a week, a little shopping trip was nothing.

So she went to Sephora.

It was like taking a short trip to paradise; a place where everything was pretty, everything smelled good, everything was tempting, and all of it promised to ease life's little problems.

Immediately upon walking into the overlit, glistening black-white-and-red that was her personal heaven, Allie felt better.

Not that she came here that often. To the contrary, she usually settled for the drugstore brands, but every once in a while she just couldn't resist going.

Now was one of those times.

Because not only had she just ended a relationship—one of the top three reasons to go straight to Sephora—but she had her twentieth class reunion coming up. Come to think of it, that had to be in the top three, too. In fact, she'd stand her ground in saying *either* of those were a better reason to splurge than a wedding.

Anyway, here she was.

"Can I help you find something?" a girl who was *almost* half her age *and* half her size asked Allie.

"Yes." Allie was prepared. She had a wallet full of credit cards. "Show me all of your favorite things."

The girl looked confused. "What exactly are you looking for? Like, mascara, or"—she looked Allie over—"microdermabrasion?"

Under any other circumstances, Allie might have been insulted, but she'd been as low as she could go this week, self-esteemwise, so she was willing to admit she needed help.

"I want to know about anything you have that will make me look better," she said. "Show it all to me."

The girl was like an obedient dog, tentatively moving toward the hamburger that had been dropped on the kitchen floor. "Are you sure?"

"Yes. Absolutely."

"Cool. Because we just got this moisturizer that everyone is saying gets rid of fine lines in, like, days. . . ."

For the next hour, Allie followed the waif through the store, trying mascaras, foundations, creams, lotions, perfumes, even tooth whiteners. There was Dior, Lancôme, Fresh, Urban Decay, bareMinerals, LORAC, and a hundred other brands Allie wouldn't normally have even considered because their prices were so high.

She wasn't able to get it all—a hundred and twenty-five bucks for an ounce of skin potion was still too much, no matter how desperately unhappy she was—but she got enough to make for a very satisfying walk back to the car and drive home.

She'd realized, as she'd shopped, that her anguish wasn't really all about Kevin. In fact, very little of it probably had to do with Kevin. Every time she tried to fit him into the puzzle piece of her heart that felt missing, he didn't quite fit.

Yes, he'd cheated on her, he'd betrayed her, he'd made her feel like a loser and a fool, but maybe she understood why. At least a little bit.

She and Kevin had a very *companionable* relationship. They went on nice dates together, liked the same restaurants and the same wine. But at night when they came home, more often than not Kevin would stay in the living room, watching the Biography Channel or

Discovery or something while Allie went into the bedroom and watched *Sex and the City,* or *Six Feet Under,* or *Big Brother.* Something that Kevin would regard as far too lowbrow for his tastes.

And while they *did* have sex regularly, it was just that: It was just *regular* and, frankly, it was just *sex.*

There were no fireworks.

There weren't even pathetic little sparklers.

The *New York Times* bestseller
that's a perfect fit

Four very different
(but equally shoe-
obsessed) women
meet Tuesday nights
to trade shoes and,
in the process, form
friendships that
will help them
each triumph over
everything life
throws their way.

"I would happily recommend *Shoe Addicts Anonymous* to anyone who loves shoes...or to smart, funny, realistic women."
—JENNIFER WEINER, AUTHOR OF
*IN HER SHOES* AND *THE GUY NOT TAKEN*

A NOVEL

shoe addicts
Anonymous

"I read it addictively (ignored my children, forgot to eat) in one sitting."
—VALERIE FRANKEL, AUTHOR OF
*HEX AND THE SINGLE GIRL* AND *I TAKE THIS MAN*

beth harbison

"Chick lit with heart and sole."
*–People magazine*

Visit www.stmartins.com/BethHarbison and sign up
to receive a FREE short story from Beth Harbison.

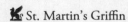 St. Martin's Griffin